NIGHT AND SILENCE

Aline Templeton

Hodder & Stoughton

Copyright © 1999 Aline Templeton

First published in Great Britain in 1999
by Hodder and Stoughton
A division of Hodder Headline PLC

British Library Cataloguing in Publication Data
A CIP catalogue record for this title is available
from the British Library

ISBN 0 340 75056 1

Typeset by
Phoenix Typesetting, Ilkley, West Yorkshire
Printed and bound in Great Britain by
Mackays of Chatham, Plc, Chatham, Kent

Hodder and Stoughton
A division of Hodder Headline PLC
338 Euston Road
London NW1 3BH

For *LIZZIE* and *MICHAEL*,
friends as well as family,
with my love.

SESSION ONE

Thursday 23 July

Session One

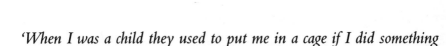

'When I was a child they used to put me in a cage if I did something wrong. Is that what you want me to talk about? That sort of thing?'

'Talk about anything you want to talk about.'

'Oh, there's nothing I want to talk about. There isn't any point, is there? It's not going to make any difference.'

'What had you done the first time they did it?'

'I bit my stepmother. I can still see the mark I made. Two nice, neat half-moons – dark blue and angry red, they were, with blood all swelling up where I'd broken the skin. It tasted disgusting, her skin; sweet and faintly sticky.

'She had smooth, soft pudgy hands. When She fondled me or my brother – only if my father was watching, of course – they stank, stank of insincerity and cheap hand cream. Rose perfume. To this day the smell of rose perfume turns my stomach.'

'Why did you bite her?'

'She had leaned across the Sunday lunch table to chuck my chin, laughing after one of her silly remarks. "Come on," She said, "smile, just for once." I hated her; She was always my enemy, and quick as a thought I slashed at her with my teeth. Like an animal.

'Only animals raised by my father didn't bite. He trained all his gun dogs by love and patience, and they had mouths like velvet. Even the ferrets with their steel trap jaws never closed them on his hands. He gentled them into tameness, and he was proud of that. He wasn't soft, though – don't get me wrong. His gentleness was as powerful as some men's cruelty.

'So he was mortified as well as angry. As She screamed he jumped up. His face was crimson, but my brother's had gone white, his eyes and mouth three round 'O's of shock.

'She started sobbing, of course, always the drama queen. Her tears made streaky white runnels in her make-up, and the mascara that always clogged her eyelashes began dissolving into sooty panda patches round her eyes. I wanted to laugh.

'He went to her and helped her out of the chair, his arm round her, protecting her, I suppose. She was ungainly in late pregnancy, and She stumbled a little. Deliberately, probably. That would have been typical of her.

'As my father steadied her he glared at me. He had warm blue eyes, you know, with crinkles of good humour at the corner – kind eyes. But they were savage now. I'd never seen him look like that before.

'"We have been patient, and more than patient." That was what he said, and he said it terribly. Then, "Enough is enough."

'When they drove off to the hospital in his old battered Land-Rover, the stones spurted up from the gravel at the side of the cottage as he turned it too fast.'

'How did you feel then about what you had done?'

'I didn't care. I was glad, I think. Yes, I was glad I had hurt her, because She had taken my father away from me.

'I said to my brother, "Stand with me. Stand together and we can drive her away. She'll find somebody else, just the way Mum did."

'He nodded at me solemnly, as if he agreed, then put his thumb in his mouth. Well, he was only five, after all, four years younger than me.

'He had missed Mum, of course. I hadn't. She was a wicked woman, my mother. There were – men, men who came when Dad was away doing a shoot, when she would send us to play in the woods and lock the door. She hit me for telling Dad that. Then she just left us. I didn't care. I'd taught myself not to care, but I had to try to teach my brother. If you don't care, they can't hurt you. Most people are a lot more than nine years old by the time they work that out, aren't they?'

'How did your father manage after she left?'

'Oh, it was good, it was good. We were close, just the three of us. A team. We didn't need anyone else. We managed somehow, the food and the cleaning and the laundry and we laughed a lot, though my brother cried sometimes at bedtime. I didn't like him to cry; "You've got me," I used to say to him in the darkness of our bedroom. "No matter what happens you've always got me and I've always got you."

'"Forever and ever and ever?" he would say, and I would say, "Forever and ever and ever," and he would stop crying and go to sleep.

'Then She came.'

'Who was she?'

'She was working in the pub he went to on a Saturday night. Oh, not that he was a drinking man, my father, but I suppose it was a bit of company for him. She got her claws into him, and then he married her and ruined everything. She would look after us, be our mother now, he said. But we had him; what did we need a mother for? Anyway, we still had the chores to do, because She wanted to keep her fat little white paws soft and paint the nails glossy and red as if they'd been dipped in fresh blood.

'She hated me, and She complained to my father all the time about what I did, or didn't do. He talked to me — or at least, he said words to me, but I couldn't talk back and reach him, with her in the way. She circled round me, killing my laughter, killing my comfort. Trying to kill my soul.'

'Why did you feel so threatened by her?'

'Oh, don't be stupid! If you can't see why I felt threatened, there really isn't the smallest point in talking to you. Anyway, I've had enough. I don't want to talk any more.'

Friday 10 July

Chapter One

'Now, ladies.' The woman who stood in front of the relentlessly swagged drapes and layered nets of her lounge bay window might be little more than five feet tall and upholstered in electric-blue double jersey as snugly as one of her overstuffed armchairs, but she wore her lilac-rinsed cap of tightly-permed curls like a military helmet. There could be little doubt that her 'Now ladies' equated to the 'dear friends' more famously exhorted before a more celebrated battle.

Tessa found herself sitting up instinctively straighter in her chair — a white rickety one with a cane seat pressed into service from the bathroom — then glanced about the packed room feeling foolish. The other women nearby, the ones astute enough to have annexed one of the components of the drawing-room suite or a Parker-Knoll brought in from the family den, seemed unmoved, having no doubt been subjected to Dorothy's Agincourt address before. It was Dorothy's custom to 'throw the house open to My Ladies', as she termed it, for the final meeting to put the last touches to the plans for the Friends of the Hospital coffee morning and summer fair tomorrow.

'A dozen scones,' she was saying now, 'and a dozen cakes from each of you. And ladies, I want *really nice* cakes. Everyone always says that the Friends' coffee morning is something quite special, and we don't want to lose our reputation, do we? And apart from that,' her voice sank to a suitably hushed tone, 'we mustn't forget it's for the sick that we're doing this, so nothing but the best will do. *Really nice* cakes, remember! And Marjorie, I'll be relying on you to mastermind the coffee, of course—'

How, Tessa found herself wondering insubordinately, were the sick to benefit from Really Nice cakes, as opposed to ordinary ones, consumed by the healthy and prosperous Stetford ladies who would patronise the hospital coffee morning largely because the price charged for the coffee, the scone and the Really Nice cake was hopelessly unrealistic, undercutting every tea room in the town by approximately fifty per cent. And then of course there was the additional benefit of the stalls, where by a bit of judicious waiting they could snap up bargains at the end once the price had been reduced, and still go home in a warm, self-satisfied glow because they had done their bit for charity.

Oh dear. She was trying hard to conform, but she couldn't help her rebellious thoughts, could she? She sighed unconsciously, earning herself a sharp look from Mrs Superintendent Barker, sitting next to her as her sponsor for Dorothy's very select Friends of the Hospital committee. There were, Tessa had been given to understand, women who would kill for the privilege of sitting on a creaky bathroom chair, breathing the air scented by Dorothy's orange spice potpourri while admiring the coal-effect gas fire, the awesome architecture of the silk floral arrangements and the collection of Lladro figures above the Adams-style fireplace with its inset Wedgwood-style plaques.

Mindful of David's career, Tessa smiled at Mona Barker, humiliatingly aware that she was raising her upper lip a little too far in an ingratiating gesture any passing chimp would instantly recognise. Not that a chimp was likely to pass through Dorothy's lounge, more was the pity. She would have more in common with one of the upper primates than she had with the women packed in here like very superior sardines (the chocolate kind in blue tinfoil you can buy in Paris, perhaps), unassailable in their designer knitwear two-pieces, with their expensively-coiffed heads and the layers of gold chains whose brilliant brassiness proclaimed as vulgarly as a car bumper sticker, 'I've been to the gold souk at Dubai.'

For David's sake, Tessa had made a real effort. She had pulled back her heavy fall of straight brown hair into a black velvet scrunchy for the occasion, and put on her favourite raspberry crushed-velvet pants with a silk shirt made up from one of her own screen prints. She had put on the delicate silver ear spirals her friend Marnie Evans had made for her birthday, and the necklet she had bought to match them with the birthday cheque from her mother.

She had presented herself for David's approval when he had appeared unexpectedly for five minutes at lunch time, as he had been doing more often recently, on his way up to a police station in one of the Welsh valleys on the outlying edge of their patch.

'You're an inspector,' she said. 'Inspect me. Will I do?' Laughing, she performed an exaggerated twirl.

David turned from his rapid assembling of a cheese and pickle sandwich to look at her, a tall, coltish girl with a creamy skin and glowing brown eyes. He still couldn't quite believe that after all the messiness and misery of his divorce, and all the loneliness which had followed it, that this embodiment of warmth and vitality was really his.

'Delectable,' he said huskily, then added on a lighter note, 'You did say it was all old biddies on this committee, and not any hunky young men?'

'I think it's a coven,' she said solemnly. 'But Mona Barker made it clear she was paying me an enormous and probably unmerited compliment in asking me to go along, and I realised that if I wasn't suitably grateful or didn't come up to scratch you'd find you'd been demoted to one of the Welsh valleys yourself, on the instant.'

'It's very kind of her, I suppose.' He caught her sceptical look, and grinned sheepishly. 'You'll knock them sideways anyway, my love. Have fun.' With his sandwich in his hand, he snatched a kiss on the way back to the car.

As Mona greeted Tessa on her arrival, however, her hesitation and the slight freezing of her smile were both eloquent, as was her manner of introducing her to their hostess.

'This is Tessa Cordiner, Dorothy. You remember I told you, George's new inspector's wife. She's very *artistic*, you know.'

And Dorothy, eying her equally doubtfully, had echoed, 'Ah, artistic! I see.'

Now, as Tessa sipped tepid dark brown tea out of a wide cup with a rose-infested pattern, and balanced a finger of Paterson's shortbread in the saucer (Dorothy's Ladies clearly did not warrant Really Nice cakes), she fielded the inevitable questions expecting the answer yes about whether she was enjoying Shropshire after London.

She had only lately realised what a handicap it was to be by nature incorrigibly truthful. After a bad experience at the supper party the Barkers had so kindly given to 'let you meet everyone' (everyone over the age of forty, that was), she had taken time to jot down phrases which were polite without being untruthful; she deployed some of them now.

'So lovely to breathe fresh air instead of petrol fumes.' 'It's certainly a change to have trees instead of traffic jams.' 'It's all so *green*, isn't it!'

Those always went down well. 'It's so peaceful, after London,' had been a distinct failure though; she had tried that one on Mona, who had bridled and said, 'Good gracious, there's never a moment's peace in Stetford! I can't remember when George and I last had an evening in together. Once you've been here a little longer, my dear, you'll realise that people in small towns are always far busier than you ever would be in a city.'

Dorothy, who was moving round the room dispensing graciousness and stewed tea, paused to ask Tessa kindly how she had enjoyed her first meeting.

Taken by surprise, Tessa choked on a crumb of shortbread and had to take a gulp of tea to wash it down. Relentlessly refilling her cup, Dorothy smiled reassuringly at this evidence of becoming shyness.

'Now don't worry too much about the cakes, dear. Being an artist, I expect that's not really your forte! So just for this year, why don't you do extra scones instead, just till you're more into our ways, you know. It won't matter; I always do an extra dozen or two of my butter-cream angel cakes anyway.'

Tessa was lost for words, and Mona hastened into the breach, with the air of Nanny covering up for the gaucherie of her charge. 'You're always so good, Dorothy. Perhaps Tessa could find a few of her little pictures for the craft stall instead. That would go down very well, I'm sure.'

Mercifully at that moment a woman with a face like a disgruntled Pekingese claimed their attention and they did not see the crimson tide of rage which Tessa felt must be visibly darkening her complexion. That was it. Enough! Finish!

She couldn't trust herself even to produce the formulaic 'thank-you-for-having-me-I've-had-a-lovely-time'. Setting down her cup, she slipped between the oblivious groups of chattering women and escaped to her car.

It was an ancient Morris Minor, acquired ten years ago with the unexpected windfall of her first major commission. She had sprayed it sea-green and painted sunflowers on the doors; it was called Boris after one of her art teachers who had also been of uncertain temper.

'Don't dump me in it now, for heaven's sake,' she muttered as she turned the key in the ignition, but Boris responded with commendable docility and she was able to make a swift getaway down Dorothy's tarmac drive.

A few of her 'little pictures' for the craft stall! Which did Mona mean, one of the witty, accomplished London scenes which Roddy Anselm had been flogging in his St James Street gallery for £700 a throw, or one of the abstract oils in Mediterranean colours inspired by their honeymoon in Provence, going for more than twice that? She could just see her 'little pictures' priced at a fiver each and sold off at £2.50 at the end because none of the Philistines in this cultural black hole would know how to appreciate them.

In a red haze of fury she flashed through the traffic lights – fortunately at green – then realised that the speed she was doing, in her highly-noticeable car, was hardly appropriate for the wife of Stetford's newest detective inspector. And she had been well warned that, as a member of a policeman's family, even her most trivial accident would involve a report to the Crown Prosecution Service.

She slowed to a more decorous thirty-five. At least she had the benefit of inside information on that one; Sergeant Stan Gittins, Traffic, had told her that if they went round picking people up at that speed the system would collapse from over-load.

As she headed out of the little English market town, skirting the common which rose behind it and over the Welsh border into the hills beyond, it started to rain. What a surprise. Her spirits plummeted like a stone dropped into a deep, dank well as her indignant rage faded and she remembered what she was going back to. She changed down and floored the accelerator to force the protesting Boris up the long slow rise.

It was just so sad, after their high hopes, that things should have gone so badly wrong. It had seemed such an idyllic place when first they saw it on a blustery, sunny Saturday morning in early March, when the unfurling leaves in the arching tunnel of trees leading to Llanfeddin seemed impossibly green and fresh, after the greyness and grime of London.

Tessa had been enraptured. 'Oh David, do *look*!' she kept saying. 'Those hills – you'd think they'd been sketched in green pastel, and then smudged with somebody's thumb! And the sheep – how can they possibly be so white? Do you suppose there's someone at the Welsh Tourist Board whose job it is to go round and give them all a shampoo and blow-dry before the tourist season? And the lambs – I just don't believe in them at all. They're so impossibly cute, I reckon they're actually virtual lambs they've had designed specially.'

David took his eyes off the narrow twisting valley road to smile at her enthusiasm. It was wonderful to hear that note back in her voice after the days of house-hunting in the respectable streets of Stetford, when she had got quieter and quieter.

'All these houses,' she had said bleakly at last, coming away from a particularly oppressive example, 'have smug, boring personalities. They all say to you, "Don't be different. Don't be adventurous. Don't think. Just do as everyone else does, and even if you don't want to, we'll see to it that you do."' She shuddered. 'I could almost feel the sticky cobwebs snatching at my face.'

David had been anxious, very anxious. For Tessa, pretty, talented and sweet-natured with a loving family and a multitude of friends, the sun had always shone. His own experience had been very different, and sometimes the nine years between them seemed like a lifetime.

His responsibility for her happiness weighed heavily. It reminded him of how he had felt about a very beautiful, shiny toy car he had been given, unusually, one Christmas, and how painful it had been when he had marred its precious perfection with the first mark on the paintwork. And in choosing to come to an environment as different from familiar London as it was possible to be, they were, so to speak, risking the paintwork on their glossy new marriage.

He tried to tell himself that after all, it was only once his car had collected the inevitable dents and scratches that he'd been able to enjoy playing with it, but even so it was a relief to think that this pretty valley would be a congenial setting for his Tess.

The little grey stone house they had come to view faced south above the valley, with a steep terraced garden in front and a green hill rising behind with a tiny stream spilling down over its own miniature waterfall. There was a luxuriant climbing rose trained up over the trellis porch, and a yellow jasmine bush was in flower by the front door; they had made their mind up almost before they had stepped over the threshold and the discovery of a glassed extension at the back giving good north light clinched it.

'I'll put my easel here, in the middle. The old armchair can go in the corner by the window and you can sit and watch me and tell me when I've put paint on my nose. Then I'll have shelves all along the back wall for my stuff, and I'll turn over a new leaf and keep it all really tidy and organised—'

'Oh, I see, you're fantasising, are you? I thought you were actually making plans—'

He dodged outside into the back garden to avoid her vengeance, and then they stood together under a huge old apple tree looking up at the steep hillside behind, with a couple of little copses of trees. The only sounds were the crisp tearing of the lush grass by a couple of sheep grazing nearby, and the bubbling chuckle of the stream bouncing down its stony course.

Tessa's hair blew about her face in a sudden gust of wind and she flung her arms wide to the heavens, taking a deep, satisfied breath.

'Isn't it wonderful?' she cried. 'You can feel free here, with nothing but the hills and the sky and peace and privacy, with no nosy neighbours to watch what you're doing and cluck about it. I could probably sit out here and paint stark naked, if I wanted to.'

'I shouldn't, if I were you. Those sheep are giving you very old-fashioned looks as it is.'

They were; they had stopped browsing to stare, their jaws still rotating busily in unison.

'They look as if they're in a class doing exercises to ward off a double chin,' Tessa said, and laughing, they went back inside.

He could almost convince himself, with hindsight, that he had felt the chill of foreboding as they went back into the dimness of the house itself. He had certainly said, a little doubtfully, as he noticed the grudging deep-set windows and meagre rooms; 'You don't think it's going to be a bit dark and depressing?'

Tessa didn't want to hear. 'I think it's mainly because we've just come in from the sunshine. And think how lovely and cosy it will be in the winter with the curtains drawn and the lamps lit and a log fire,' she said blithely. 'And during the day, of course, I'll be working in the studio, so it won't matter.'

'A patio,' she had said, waving her hand largely as they locked the front door and stood on the narrow plateau outside. 'We can lay a patio here. South-facing – it should be perfect.'

David had agreed. He would have agreed if she had said she wanted to dismantle the house stone by stone and build a Gothic folly instead. They'd never got round to making the patio, though. It hardly seemed worth it for the three days in the past three months when it hadn't been either too cold or too wet.

On the way back, David had driven more slowly so that they could take stock of the hamlet of Llanfeddin itself, about half a mile from the house.

'Oh, a church,' Tessa exclaimed happily. It was a very small church with a huddle of gravestones in a plot beside it, all very plain and stark. 'I've often felt bad in London about never going—'

'Er – chapel,' David pointed out. 'Welsh Presbyterian. I don't think it would be quite your scene.'

Tessa was briefly deflated, but the appearance of a pub and a useful shop restored her to high spirits, and as she saw a woman turn from locking the door of the shop for Saturday early closing she smiled and raised a hand in greeting.

The woman did not smile back. She was short and over-weight, with a pale round face and deep-set black eyes, like pieces of coal set in the featureless face of a snowman, and her expression as she watched them out of sight was sullen, almost malevolent.

'Good gracious!' Tessa said blankly, then, determined not to allow anything to spoil her mood, looked at her hand comically. 'I didn't by any chance accidentally put up two fingers when I waved, did I?'

'It certainly looked as if you might have.' It was trivial, of course, but the little episode made David feel uncomfortable. George Barker, his Super, had raised his eyebrows when he had mentioned where they were househunting. 'They're a bit funny, up the valleys,' he had said, and George was a sound man.

Still, if it made Tessa happy—

She was pointing again. 'Look at that old stone! It looks very interesting—'

He pulled the car into the side. They were a little outside the village now, and in the bank was set a carved grey stone, weath-ered and green with lichen. They walked over, and bent to study it.

It was a primitive face, carved so that it stood proud of the surface. The features were worn but unmistakable; a man's face, distorted and leering, the eyes sly and the gap-toothed mouth twisted in an ugly lecherous grin.

Tessa gasped and drew back, disconcerted. 'That's – that's horrible!'

'Nice little chap, isn't he?' David said lightly. 'I'd pick that one up on sus if I saw him just walking down the road. Never mind, whoever modelled for it must have been dead for a few hundred years by now. Come on, we'd better get going.'

His eye caught a piece of litter wedged among the stones in the ditch below and with a policeman's instinct bent to pick it up. As Tessa crossed to the car ahead of him he glanced down at what he was holding, and had to suppress a gasp himself.

It was a crude pencil sketch, drawn almost as a child might draw, but there was nothing childlike about its content. And the man involved in the perverted act it showed had, like the carving, a leering, distorted face. Almost as if it had been left in tribute.

He crumpled it up and thrust it in his pocket. He shuddered as he got into the car.

Tessa glanced at him. 'Are you all right?'

If only he had said, 'It's this place. There's something about it that I don't like.' But he hadn't. It seemed foolish: a surly woman, a dark house, the pathetic scribble of some inadequate youth – and they had to live somewhere. And if Tessa liked it . . .

'That's quite a cold wind,' was all he had said, as he started the car and drove away to set in hand the making of the biggest mistake of their lives.

Tessa sighed as she turned off into the valley road, under the depressing arch of dripping trees, past the grotesque, ancient carved stone which always made her shiver. In her fancy it marked a boundary where safe, if stifling, provincial life gave way to something altogether older and darker.

She came to the doctor's house, where his wife was out in the rain, working in their beautiful garden. They had met the Webbs at the Barkers' party, but unfortunately she hadn't been terribly forthcoming. Well, she'd been drunk, actually, not to put too fine a point on it. She didn't look up from her weeding as Tessa drove past.

That was when she remembered the milk, and swore.

Milk, Tessa had discovered since she came to live in the country, didn't grow in bottles on the doorstep. Somehow she couldn't get her mind round this simple fact, which provoked a cereal crisis at breakfast every other day.

It was simple enough when she was passing the Llanfeddin Stores to pop in and get a couple of pints. And it would be childish and cowardly to turn round and drive the eight miles to and from Stetford, just to avoid five minutes of being treated like one of the lower forms of invertebrate life. Sticks and stones, she reminded herself grimly, and gritting her teeth she turned into the little car park.

There were two cars and a dog parked there already. The dog, tied to a railing, was a young springer spaniel, brown and white, and as she came towards him he stood up, ears pricked and mouth wide in an engaging grin, feathery tail swinging hopefully. Tessa bent to stroke him.

He was well-mannered but enthusiastic, the wag rate increasing as he snuffled at her hands. It was quite a novelty to find someone in the valley who was pleased to see her. With a final pat she straightened up and went inside.

The Llanfeddin Stores was a big, gloomy barn of a place, with windows that were never quite clean, cracked vinyl on the floor and a permanent miasma of dust and tired vegetables which assailed anyone opening the door.

To the left was the post office counter, presided over by the owner, Glynis Rees. She was a squat, dark woman in her forties with small, deep-set eyes and a short nose which gave her somehow the look of an ill-natured pig. She had little fat feet, too, which like a pig's trotters didn't look quite big enough to support the bulk they carried. She was proud of them, and still crammed them into the pointed, high-heeled styles of her youth, which were so old-fashioned that they had been back in vogue three times in the years she had been wearing them. She had a gift for unpleasantness, nurtured over the years as carefully as a gardener tends a prize marrow.

Her husband Dafydd, a soft, good-natured lump of a man, had faded out of existence some ten years before. He was in the graveyard by the chapel under a headstone inscribed, in Welsh, 'Rest in peace', which state would, it was widely held, be something of a novelty for the poor man after fifteen years of being married to Glynis.

Bronwen, her daughter, who theoretically did the cleaning and manned the checkout in the grocery section, was another frustration. A round-faced, loose-bodied girl with her father's yielding nature, she would never, as the saying went, give anyone a sore heart. The resultant pregnancies and the demands of her miscellany of offspring provided the perfect excuse for her erratic hours and haphazard approach to her work.

The back of the shop was given over to 'Welsh crafts by local craftsmen', as a standing notice-board outside proudly proclaimed. This was the responsibility of Hannah Guest, Glynis's sister, returned to her native valley after a failed marriage to a Shropshire farmer. Like Glynis, she was short, dark and poisonous, but she was slim and slight and her manner was as silky as a tarantula's fur.

Glynis always described the craft shop as being there 'to draw in the tourists', as if once over the threshold they would then be seized with an irrepressible urge to purchase quantities of extra stamps or a dozen limp lettuces. It was unfortunate that on a good day in high summer this passing trade might amount to three people, most of them seeking directions back to the main road.

The board outside had, however, drawn in Tessa when first she arrived in Llanfeddin, charmed by the notion of some local artistic community. She nodded politely to the unsmiling woman she had seen locking up the shop the first day they visited, then made her way past the post office counter and through between the shelves of groceries to the back of the shop.

It was so dark that at first Tessa didn't notice the other woman, who rose from a chair in the corner to come forward with an ingratiating smile.

Artistic presentation could never be said to be Hannah's forte. The merchandise, rather than being displayed, seemed to have been parked randomly on grubby shelving round the walls or crammed on to one of two trestle tables. The stock itself wasn't appealing either: lamps chipped out of grey stone and topped with hand-sewn plastic 'parchment' shades adorned with anaemic dried flowers; chunky pottery with unbalanced handles in various shades of sludge; some amateurish daubs representing the Welsh hills; a flock of woolly sheep with bound pipe-cleaner horns; a stack of scratchy rugs in muddy colours, hand-woven from the wool of Jacob's sheep, as the label proudly explained.

The glass box holding the exquisite silver jewellery, however, shone as the one creative good deed in the naughty world surrounding it. The pieces had been displayed – by their creator, presumably – on black velvet, airy, elegant twists and scrolls linked delicately into necklets and bracelets, earrings and brooches.

'These are lovely,' Tessa said, appreciation intensified by relief at having found something she could honestly admire.

'Beautiful, isn't it.' The Welsh lilt was very pronounced. 'Marnie Evans, she does them – lives just ten minutes up the valley there. Talented girl. That's her cards, look.'

A stack of boldly-designed cards lay on top of the case; the woman handed one to Tessa surveying her the while, emanating a curiosity so powerful that she could almost smell it.

'Visitor, then, are you?'

There was a certain pride in Tessa's smile. 'No, we live here, just along the road. I hope I'm well on my way to becoming a native.'

The other woman gave a tinkling laugh, though somehow the sound was not altogether friendly. 'Hardly that! You know what they say around here – "Calls himself a Valley man and I remember when his grandfather moved here." But I know who you are now. You must be Mrs Cordiner.'

Amused, even charmed, Tessa laughed. 'That's right, I'm Tessa. I'm very impressed by your intelligence system. I'm going to have to behave myself, aren't I?'

She simpered. 'Not much you can do around here without everyone knowing about it. I'm Mrs Guest.'

They exchanged the little, awkward nods people give when shaking hands seems inappropriately formal.

'You're a bit of an artist, so they tell me,' Mrs Guest went on. 'Well, bring in one or two of your things and we'll see if they would sell. Might do each other a bit of good, isn't it?' When she smiled this time, two little dimples showed by the side of her mouth.

Taken completely by surprise, Tessa could only stammer, 'Er – well, actually, I have an arrangement with this man in London—'

The smiling mouth suddenly went small and hard. 'Oh, London, is it?' She pronounced it 'Lundun', giving equal weight to its two syllables and investing the word with startling malice. 'You'll be too grand for the likes of us, then. I'm sorry I spoke.'

Her face burning, Tessa had extricated herself from the shop under the cold stare of the other woman. Not very sharp, she reflected ruefully, to have got off on the wrong foot with the locals already.

Miserably she had walked back to the empty house, full of uncongenial tasks that she really ought to tackle. It was then she realised she was still clutching the card Hannah Guest had given her. Marnie Evans' workshop was on up the valley, she had said, about ten minutes. On an impulse, she decided to wake Boris up and go.

The card had a line-sketch of the cottage, and it wasn't hard to find, with its steeply pitched roof, thick white-washed walls and little workshop attached. Marnie Evans with her snub nose and her sunny smile greeted her as if they had known one another all their lives.

The spare interior of the cottage was one room open to the rafters, with kitchen and bathroom tacked on at the back. There was a bed covered with brightly-coloured cushions and pushed against the wall to act as a sofa, and a huge pine table in the middle which, on the evidence of the clutter on its surface, served as drawing board, office and food preparation area as well a social centre.

Over a cup of coffee, Tessa had got round to telling her of the recent bruising encounter.

'Bloody woman,' Marnie said dispassionately. 'I should never have let her have any of my stuff – she charges an arm and a leg in commission and barely sells a thing. But she's so unpleasant that everyone agrees to what she wants so as to get away from her sooner. And her sister's arguably worse. The Unholy Trinity, I call that lot – Mother, Daughter and Hannah Guest. Only the daughter, Bronwen, is the one who's invisible. You never seem to see her in the shop.'

Cheered in spite of herself, Tessa laughed. 'I like it. But what worries me is that they're going to tell everyone in Llanfeddin valley that I'm a stuck-up cow and then they'll all hate me. But perhaps that's paranoid.'

Marnie looked back at her, her smoky-blue eyes sardonic. 'Do you want the good news or the bad news first?'

Warily, Tessa asked for the good news.

'The good news is that what they say won't make any difference. The bad news is that they weren't going to like you anyway. Oh –' as Tessa looked shocked – 'don't take it to heart. They don't like anyone who moves in. I'm Welsh and I speak Welsh, but they don't like me – which, unless it's a problem of personal freshness that no one's liked to mention, is because I come from Cardiff and spent a few years in London.'

'Mrs Guest said "London" as if she were swearing,' Tessa said gloomily. 'How did you come to live here anyway?'

'Ah.' Marnie looked down into her mug of coffee. 'Well, why does any girl do something totally bloody stupid?'

'Ah,' Tessa said in her turn. 'Who is he?'

'Was he, as far as I'm concerned.' Marnie's short laugh did nothing to conceal her hurt. 'A lovely young doctor, he was. Paul Arkwright – he's a rugby lad with the soul of a poet. We belonged to the same amateur dramatic group in London, and stepped out together for a bit. Then when he got his job at the hospital here it seemed a good idea to both of us for me to return to my Welsh roots as well.'

She paused, and Tessa prompted her gently. 'But it wasn't?'

Marnie sighed. 'Oh, it was brilliant to start with. It was so brilliant my mother had started marinating the currants for the wedding cake. Then he met Willow.' There was acid in her voice as she said the name.

'Willow?'

Marnie laughed again, shortly. 'Willow Lampton. Nurse at the hospital, very beautiful, very cold, and the biggest man-eater in town.'

'Oh Marnie! What happened?'

'She had him as a pre-dinner snack. And my mother needed counselling. Well, what do you do with four pounds of marinated currants? But it's history now.' Dismissing the subject, Marnie got up. 'Have another cup of coffee and tell me about your painting.'

So something good – something very good – had come out of that first disastrous visit, but the Gavin Guest business had made things much, much worse, and now she avoided going into the shop if she possibly could.

Still, how long could it take to buy two pints of milk? She opened the door and went in, trying not to gag at the smell, which was now in her mind so deeply associated with unpleasantness.

From behind the counter, Mrs Rees shot a look at her, and then looked pointedly away. There were two women customers there too, who looked round and stared at her slowly, insolently, then turned their backs once more.

The third woman was someone Tessa had never seen before. She must have been well into her sixties, but she was still a very good-looking woman with a fine pale complexion and fair hair which was well-cut but unashamedly turning grey. Her clothes were good – cream silk blouse, natural linen skirt with a light Burberry open on top – but so understated that it looked almost as if she had chosen them to avoid making any personal statement.

The woman was at the post office counter being served, if you could call it that, by Mrs Rees. 'And half a dozen first-class stamps, please,' she was saying in a cool, impersonal voice which held no trace of a Welsh accent.

Mrs Rees said nothing in reply, only pushing the stamps under the glass. She scribbled something on a piece of paper and thrust it at her.

Glancing at it, the woman counted out some money; that too was accepted in silence.

'Thank you so much, Mrs Rees. Good afternoon.'

With apparently imperturbable serenity she turned and left the shop. As Tessa grabbed her two pints of milk and went to pay, she heard her speaking to the dog.

Mrs Rees came over to the checkout, rang up the price, took the money and gave her change, also without speaking. As Tessa thankfully hurried out into the fresh air, she heard the mutter of Welsh start behind her.

Chapter Two

The rain was coming down with a vengeance now. Boris didn't like rain; when it got wet enough, the engine always started to cough and splutter, and the wipers tended to wheeze like someone who has smoked sixty a day for forty years, and stick halfway across. She was banging the windscreen to start them again when she saw the woman and the dog just ahead of her.

Even the dog was looking depressed by the rain, his ears flat to his head and the silky coat dripping. The woman had fastened her raincoat, but she had nothing on her head and, Tessa thought, she was walking a little stiffly, as if suffering some discomfort.

She pulled up as she drew level, leaned across and wound down the window.

'Do you have far to go?' she called. 'You're both getting soaked – can I give you a lift?'

The woman looked startled, as if this was the last thing she would have expected. 'Oh – you're very kind. But I have the dog, and we're both very wet—'

'Don't worry about that, for goodness' sake!' Winding up the window, Tessa threw open the door. 'This isn't the sort of car where you worry about wet dogs, and anyway we're friends already – look!'

The dog had hopped unhesitatingly into the car, where he sat on the floor by the passenger seat twitching the tip of his tail, but the woman hesitated. 'I'm Agnes Winthrop.'

It seemed strange that she should insist on introductions in the pouring rain, but Tessa said politely, 'How do you do? I'm Tessa Cordiner. Do get in, before you get any wetter.'

'Well, thank you.' She got in, wincing slightly. 'I must admit, I am grateful for a lift today. My back, like the rest of me, isn't as young as it used to be and I completely misread the weather when we set out.'

'Where do you live?'

'It's on the right, about three quarters of a mile further on.'

'Goodness!' Tessa laughed. 'I'm impressed – you're very dedicated. I live just here –' they were passing the house as she spoke – 'and I'm afraid I pop into the car at every opportunity if I'm not actually jogging or something.'

'Of course, it's not an option I have.' She spoke stiffly, but Tessa, banging the wipers again, didn't notice.

'Oh, don't you drive?' she asked innocently.

Agnes Winthrop went very still. Then, 'Ah,' she said, 'you don't know who I am, do you?'

'Should I?' Tessa shot her a puzzled look.

'I'm sorry, I just assumed that no one in the valley could possibly not know.'

The bitterness in her voice made Tessa feel uncomfortable. 'Oh, don't worry,' she said lightly. 'If they're spreading nasty rumours I'd never hear them. I don't like gossip and they don't like me.'

'You were kind enough to give me a lift and I wouldn't like to feel I had accepted it under false pretences. I am a drunk driver who killed a man, and I have spent two years in prison. I have a driving ban for the next five years.

'This is the house now. You can turn in the driveway here. Thank you so much.'

She opened the door almost before the car had stopped and got out, the dog leaping nimbly out beside her. Without looking round she walked away through the teeming rain and disappeared into the big Victorian house.

★

Chrissie Webb sat back on her heels, sniffed, then drew the back of the grubby hand holding her trowel inelegantly across her nose, leaving a muddy smudge on her face. She glanced at her watch – five o'clock. It was starting to rain more heavily now, and anyway it was time she stopped and got changed into something at least a fraction more respectable before Susannah's disgustingly elegant mother brought Charlotte back from riding the ponies at their place. She'd have to ask the woman in for a drink, even though on past experience that would, depressingly, be a slimline tonic. You couldn't possibly actually *want* a slimline tonic; it wasn't so much a drink as a calculated reproach.

She scrambled awkwardly to her feet. Max, the old black Lab which had been lying on the grass nearby also got up, arthritic but alert to his mistress's every movement. She patted his broad head as he came to her side and straightened her back, painfully.

Chrissie surveyed what she had done with the delicious, weary satisfaction that follows physical labour. The wide, curving herbaceous border was coming up to its best now, and it was worth every bit of the considerable investment of her time, thought and energy. The drifts of yellow daisies were like pools of sunshine on this dull day, with the sky-blue Himalayan poppies behind to set them off, and for once the white foxgloves had seeded themselves in exactly the right place. Nowadays she got more pleasure from her garden than from anything else in her life that didn't come in a bottle.

She collected her tools together with reluctance, rubbing them shiny again with the rag she carried in her back pocket, before laying them neatly in the trug. She gathered up the corners of the PVC groundsheet and carried weeds and clippings over to the compost heap, then went to put everything away.

Chrissie's potting shed was as neat as her husband Richard's surgery, which probably came of having started out as a nurse, even though it hadn't lasted long. She'd always been, as they put it at that time, more interested in getting her M-r-s than her SRN, and when the answer to her maiden's prayer came along, in the form of Richard Webb – then young and romantic – she was down on her knees to thank heaven almost before the proposal was out of his mouth. They were well matched, both from backgrounds they wanted to escape, and she was just the sort of supportive wife that every small-town GP needed in those days.

She sighed as she went into the house, Max padding at her heels, up to their bedroom with its pretty views over the valley and the huddle of houses that was the hamlet of Llanfeddin. Stetford despised its isolation, but she found it restful. You could quietly escape the coffee mornings which seemed to flourish like ground elder in small towns and the lunch parties where women toyed with frilly red lettuce leaves then shrieked at their own depravity in accepting a teaspoonful of pudding from their hostess – who no doubt scoffed what was left after they had gone in tablespoonfuls every time she opened the fridge door. You didn't have to look polite while everyone discussed the *only* place to go to on holiday this year, or the boutique stocking the cloned outfits they all wore.

She was much more interested in the earthier gossip purveyed by the Llanfeddin Stores along with the groceries, despite Richard's irritable reminders that the supermarket products were cheaper, fresher and more varied. There was an edge to it, an unpleasantness, even, that held a deplorable fascination, and anyway she sometimes – well, quite often, actually – thought it might be wiser to walk rather than to take the car, and as a result was one of their most valued customers. And if they talked about her too, behind her back, about the number of bottles of gin that found their way into her shopping basket, at least she could be sure they wouldn't meet Richard at a party and feel that they had a duty to tell him.

No, Llanfeddin, mercifully uncolonised by the middle classes, suited her nicely. It wasn't likely to change, either; there were only a couple of other houses of any size in the valley and neither of those had a paddock, that essential accessory for anyone aspiring to country cred.

The trouble was, the less she had to do the less she wanted to do. Once she had enjoyed the bustle and involvement and sense of importance of being the doctor's wife, but everything happened at a flashy new health centre now, with God knew how many receptionists and something called a practice manager, for heaven's sake, and elaborate answering services, like 'Health Centre, Tracy speaking, how may I help you?' Or, 'Press one for colds and flu, two for broken limbs, three for imminent demise and all the buttons at once for nervous hysteria.'

She had relished answering the phone, reassuring anxious patients and keeping the difficult ones out of Richard's hair without upsetting them. She'd been a star among the partners' wives; everybody said so.

No one said she was a star now. In her shower, she seized the shampoo and lathered her short, practical crop of brown hair flecked with the first signs of grey. She scrubbed her hands too, though there was dirt in the nail beds from gardening which was engrained now, and three nails, Chrissie noticed dispassionately, seemed to be broken. There was another layer of fat round her stomach since the last time she looked, too. She'd never given much thought to her figure until now, when middle age had started its dastardly demolition job and every time you glanced down in an unguarded moment you were treated to a spectacular practical demonstration of the long-term effects of gravity. Sometimes she vowed to diet, work out, give up alcohol and wear gardening gloves. Oh yes, and write a best-selling bonkbuster while in her idle moments she hacked into America's military secrets by way of Richard's laptop.

Richard, unfairly, was still looking good. His hair was greying and he had spectacles but women at dinner parties eyed him flirtatiously and exerted themselves to chat him up, while her own dinner partners might converse politely enough, but moved through for coffee afterwards with ill-concealed alacrity. Not that she minded. Most of them could bore for Britain, with a good chance of making the European team.

She had always suspected that Richard had discreet affairs; she hadn't blamed him, particularly, or even cared very much by now, and took considerable pains not to find out. What, after all, did she have to gain from divorce? If she was trapped in a loveless marriage, it was at least a gilded cage that held her. He didn't beat her up in private, or humiliate her in public, much, and she would lose her financial security, her house and her beloved garden in exchange for what? The freedom to work as a doctor's receptionist, perhaps, at a salary which would be about the size of her present housekeeping allowance. If it was a choice between making compromises for comfort or plain-speaking her way to poverty, she was the third wise monkey. She'd been poor and she'd been well-off, and she seriously preferred well-off, preferred it to the point where she'd do whatever she had to do to keep it that way. Like not enquiring too closely when he said he had an evening meeting.

He was at one tonight, or so he said, before he went on night duty at the surgery, so he wouldn't be here to interfere with whatever plans she might have for the evening, once Charlotte was in bed.

Chrissie towelled herself dry and pulled on a dress she had bought years ago in Laura Ashley. It was her favourite because the label said size twelve, but since it had no waistband and a lot of material she could still get into it and pretend. She never wore it when Richard was at home; he didn't approve of comfort dressing, but he wouldn't be home tonight, he'd get something to eat in town.

Oh damn, she'd forgotten Susannah's mother. Susannah's mother was better groomed than her own ponies, and pencil slim, naturally. Perhaps the Laura Ashley wasn't such a good idea after all.

Chrissie surveyed herself in the mirror as she combed her damp hair back into place, then shrugged. What was the point? The woman wouldn't be impressed whatever she put on, so she might just as well stay as she was. Letting Susannah's mother have the fun of despising her, and telling her friends afterwards how Chrissie Webb had let herself go, could be her good deed for the day.

When she came back downstairs it was almost six o'clock and there was a green bottle in the drinks cupboard in the sitting room singing her a sweet siren melody. There was time for a quick one before the others arrived, and if she chewed parsley afterwards from the pot judiciously kept on the kitchen windowsill no one would be any the wiser.

Chrissie poured a stiff measure of gin into a heavy tumbler and sketched a vague benediction over it with the tonic bottle. As the liquid comfort slipped smoothly down her throat she sat back on the sofa feeling the reassuring sense of detachment begin to return. She had always coped in the past and there was no reason to suppose she wouldn't cope with whatever the future might hold. As long as the money for gin didn't run out.

David Cordiner laid the five bunches of white daisies carefully along the back seat of his car, then drove on towards the police station. At least he had got back from Wales in time to buy them before the flower shop closed; they were Tessa's favourite flowers, and today was the first anniversary of the break-in at her London flat which had brought them together. He rather hoped she had forgotten; a little surprise celebration would cheer her up, and he had bought a bottle of Cava at the off-licence as well. It was hardly going to solve the problem though, was it? He sighed.

Guilt was a habit of thought David slipped easily into, like a hair shirt which had from constant wear become a discomfort he would have been uncomfortable without. He had been introduced to it early, as the only child of a widowed mother; during his first marriage it had been the price he paid for putting work before his wife, to avoid having to change either his attitude or his job.

Of course, he had known almost from the start that Lara was a mistake. He had been twenty, she nineteen, and neither of them smart enough to know the difference between lust and love. When Lara left him for a better prospect, he could have walked away, wiser but undamaged – if it hadn't been for Matthew. He couldn't even fight her for custody, with his hours of work.

Matthew was fourteen now, and since David's remarriage he had refused to see his father. That was Lara, naturally: Lara, deserted by the man she had selected as her next meal-ticket, embittered and spiteful, was determined to punish her former husband for finding happiness without her. Even if it meant depriving her son of his father, warping his mind . . .

He groaned as he switched on the wipers. The rain seemed to have followed him all the way back from Wales.

Oh, he wasn't blameless. He could see now how selfish he'd been when he was high on the excitement and importance of work at the Met, permanently overstretched, right on the cutting edge. 'I'd rather you had a mistress,' Lara had hurled at him once, bitterly. 'I could compete with another woman.'

He had reacted as angrily and defensively as any man accused of infidelity, but it was true; working had been considerably more attractive than being at home.

Now, of course, it was most definitely the other way round, which, paradoxically, was one of his present problems. The Marches force wasn't exactly the Met, was it, and the slowness of life in this place was getting to him, like being forced to adapt to a toddler's pace when you are longing to stretch your legs and stride out.

He'd looked forward to the challenge of taking over Operation Lambchop, designed to tackle a drugs problem which was becoming endemic in isolated Welsh valleys down lanes where the dogs barked at every farm you passed and your target knew you were on your way half an hour before you got there.

That was what had drawn him here, after all. The Marches didn't normally either attract or need high fliers, which was how his inspector had described him when they'd discussed the move as a route to early promotion. David had been keen to have the chance of running a major investigation like this.

Yesterday they had got a snout's whisper that a young constable out at the further edge of their patch was involved. George Barker, the Superintendent, had been rattled, but in fact it was looking distressingly straightforward. They'd got authorisation to tap his phone before David went out to speak to him this afternoon, and he was willing to bet a pint of Boddington's to a glass of Tizer he had flustered the plump, shifty-looking boy enough to make him panic and hand them all the evidence they needed before the night was out.

And that would be Operation Lambchop wound up. No extensive, absorbing undercover work, with intelligence gathered and pubs staked out and ultimately a trap painstakingly set which when sprung would, with luck and good judgement, have the man you had been hunting within its jaws. No sense of satisfaction at having outwitted your prey. George would be delighted, of course, and it would do wonders for his own reputation which had suffered a bit as a result of the Gavin Guest fiasco, but it was, in a sense, an appalling anticlimax. The drugs would move on to someone else's patch for a bit, and he'd be left dealing with break-ins, petty fraud, the occasional domestic – small town stuff, like Gavin Guest, where they would probably end up having to drop the charge.

He'd nobody to blame but himself. It wasn't just the promotion; part of it had been – he blushed to confess it, even to himself – the Londoner's romantic dream of the cottage in the country, the roses round the door, the patter of tiny feet and children romping and playing old-fashioned games in the sunshine of safe meadows instead of the squalor and temptations of the London streets. He thought of Matt, and shuddered.

And Tessa too – what had he done to Tessa, whose glowing eyes were shadowed now with the marks of strain? There were things they didn't talk about any more, worries they didn't share, and it was damaging. What could he do to improve their domestic situation which couldn't, he thought – naïvely – be very much worse?

As he parked his car, he decided to ask George's advice. He respected George; he was a Shropshire man who couldn't understand how anyone could possibly want to live anywhere else, and though he described himself, with monotonous regularity, as 'just an old-fashioned policeman' he was a shrewd observer and his knowledge of his own back yard was unsurpassed. Yes, he would ask George. He would have the answer – if such a thing existed.

★

When Megan Griffiths went into the nurses' cloakroom at the end of the day shift, Willow Lampton was there already. She had seen Willow leaving the canteen ahead of her so she wasn't really surprised, but Megan pulled a naughty face behind her back. She was a rounded, cheerful girl with bright brown eyes; she enjoyed her work and was a first-class nurse, but she did dearly love a chance to catch up with whatever the hospital gossip might be when she came off duty. Well, she wouldn't get any change out of Willow Lampton – and what sort of a name was Willow anyway? She'd feel a right idiot if she was called something like that; she even felt stupid having to say, 'Hello Willow,' just now.

Willow responded with the cool, superior smile which had got her the reputation of being stuck up. She didn't have many friends, well, girlfriends anyway, but she was good at her job in a clinical, efficient style which was worlds away from Megan's good-hearted bossiness.

Willow had taken her cap off and unpinned her hair, which she was now brushing rhythmically in front of the big mirror. It was lovely hair, certainly, Megan thought enviously as she followed suit and attacked her own mop with a wide-toothed comb. It was long and silky and straight and a wonderful pale gold colour that looked as if it might be natural. And you certainly couldn't get it to look that natural when it wasn't on a nurse's take-home pay.

'Had a good day, then?' Megan said too brightly. She always felt at a disadvantage with Willow, who seemed unnaturally comfortable with silence.

'No worse than usual.' Willow went over to her locker and took out a black linen-look dress on a hanger, hooked it over one of the coat pegs and unzipped her white uniform dress.

Megan averted her eyes. That was another thing about Willow she found embarrassing; her lack of inhibition. If there was anyone else in the cloakroom, every other nurse would huddle in a toilet cubicle to struggle out of their uniform and into off-duty clothes. Going around half-naked in public wasn't nice, and anyway she for one wasn't about to expose the three little rolls of flesh around her midriff to anyone, thank you very much. Least of all to Willow, who was standing now completely unselfconscious in her white lacy bra and satin slip. She was small and slight, and though she had high, full breasts there wasn't a millimetre of excess fat on display as she put on the black dress – expensive, it looked, and you could tell it was good taste even if it was the sort of thing Megan would have dismissed as dreary on the dress-shop rails.

Willow was at the mirror now, deploying eye-pencils and fluffy brushes with an expert hand. Megan watched with interest while she took out her own compact and patted the puff across her nose and cheeks. She'd somehow never quite got the hang of what you were supposed to do with brushes.

'Going somewhere special tonight?' she asked as Willow fastened on pearl beads and gold earrings.

She wrinkled her slim straight nose. 'Not really,' was all she said, and for just a second her eyes met Megan's in the mirror, then slid away. She had funny eyes, Willow; it would be hard to say what colour they were, sort of greyish, like water almost, but with that sludgy-green eye make-up they looked quite green, though other times you would swear they were blue.

Willow was packing the cosmetics away into her make-up bag, then finally fished out a little red flask of perfume and sprayed it all round her neck and shoulders. Eau Dynamisante, Megan noticed; it was very popular and she had tried some in a shop, but she liked something more feminine. She'd stick with the Anais Anais her Gwyn had given her for Christmas.

'Bye.' Willow, giving a brief smile directed at but not connecting with Megan, went out.

Alone in the cloakroom, Megan risked whisking out of her uniform and into her T-shirt and leggings without retreating into a cubicle. She just made it before the door opened again; it was, she was delighted to see, Siân Griffiths from Men's Surgical.

They had been at school together, and dropping automatically into Welsh Megan told her about Willow and her little black dress.

Siân was predictably intrigued. Willow, who was renowned for being secretive, was a constant focus for gossip.

'I wonder who's the lucky man who's going to get the benefit. You know we all thought a while ago that she was having a bit of a fling with that nice Doctor Arkwright? Well, Jane Lucas is sure he's been dumped. Looking ever so glum, he's been.'

'Never last long, do they?'

'Not if someone better comes along. She's working her way up, that's what I reckon, doing pretty well too. She's come a long way since that Gavin Guest up Llanfeddin, hasn't she?'

'That's right! I'd forgotten about him.'

Siân giggled. 'Bet she'd like everyone to forget about him. She wouldn't like it to get about that she'd had a taste for the rough stuff, what with him on a charge and all that.'

Megan went back to the original speculation. 'But who do you suppose it is tonight?'

Unpinning her cap, Siân shrugged. 'We'll probably never know, will we? Gets her fun out of having secrets, she does.'

'Get her into trouble one day, that will,' Megan said wisely, with the comfortable righteousness of one whose life is an open book, albeit one unlikely to sell at the airport as a beach read.

The door swung open and, as another nurse came in, they switched effortlessly back into English to greet her. Siân grabbed clothes from her locker and took refuge in one of the cubicles as Megan said, 'Well, Sue, how's the new registrar in casualty, then?'

Chapter Three

Her mind still on the strange encounter with Agnes Winthrop, Tessa backed Boris into the steep drive, forcing him shrieking up and round the curve to leave room for David's car when he got back, whenever that might be.

Then she switched off the engine, took a deep breath and steeled herself to confront whatever might be waiting for her today. There was usually something: a dead bird lying in the path, perhaps, or flowerheads snapped, or a bottle smashed on her doorstep.

On the really bad days, it was Gavin Guest suddenly revving his motorbike at the end of the drive, raising his hand in mocking greeting as he went slowly past just as she got out of the car. It was really bad, because she knew that meant he had been lying in wait, watching for her return. At least she had been spared that, for today at least – spared the sick, helpless feeling that he was playing with her, playing at letting her escape, like a cat torturing a fieldmouse . . .

But she couldn't afford to let herself think like that. She must simply take each day as it came, and looking about her as she hurried through the rain to the front door she couldn't see anything untoward. That would have been reassuring, if it didn't leave her wondering what fresh nastiness they might have planned for later.

Tessa let herself into the dimness of the hall, locking the door carefully behind her as she always did now before switching on the huge glass lamp on the low table. She could smell the hint of dampness that they could somehow never manage to get rid of, despite log fires and state-of-the-art central heating, and tried not to think, as she had been tempted to do recently, that even the very stones oozed hostility. The only sound was the drip-drip-drip of water from the eaves. Like the dripping of the Chinese water torture. Like the endless, spiteful—

'Self-pitying wimp!' she told herself fiercely, because feeling sorry for yourself was an indulgence she despised. She busied herself, going through to the kitchen, making a pot of tea – weak Earl Grey to take away the taste of Dorothy's witch's brew.

Tessa took her mug and sat down at the kitchen table with her back to the window as if to shut out the rain and the dripping bushes and the brooding hill at the back. As always, there was a sketch pad and a drawing pencil lying there, and from habit she began to doodle.

Her work wasn't going well, which was yet another reason for her depression. She had worked at it doggedly, but in the cool, grey-green light here the palette of strong citrus colours and blues and purples which she had found so exciting didn't sing; they looked harsh and brassy instead of vibrant. And as for the charming little ink-and-watercolour street scenes, animated by the wry, affectionate observation which was her trademark – well, there wasn't a lot to observe around here, wittily or otherwise, except perhaps on market day, but wealthy and sophisticated buyers wouldn't exactly queue up for scenes from provincial life. And it was impossible to lie when you were painting; even she didn't like what she had managed to produce, because it came across as critical rather than affectionate.

Under her idly-moving fingers a sheep took shape, and then another, becoming absorbed, she gave one a look of Dorothy, another a sheep-face like Mona. The woman who already looked like a Pekingese was a challenge, but one which she triumphantly surmounted.

Tessa surveyed her work with a grin of pure mischief. They could have that for their stupid craft stall, if they liked.

Then she thought of David, and sighed. No, perhaps not.

She had just crumpled it up and shied it in the general direction of the kitchen bin when she heard a noise outside, and she stood up to look. There were figures in the field outside, half a dozen boys wearing baseball caps with scarves wound round their faces, yelling and capering. A jeer went up when they caught sight of her.

Tessa groaned, feeling infinitely weary. She wasn't actually afraid of them – not like Gavin Guest – and this was presumably just another example of Llanfeddin's idea of harmless fun for the kiddies, but being hated was like suffering from an illness; it drained your energy and made it hard to think about anything else. And living here meant that they had her trapped to torment as they pleased, like a caged animal being baited.

She hadn't told David about it. Any official action would make things worse, not better, and being impotent to protect her would make him feel even worse than he did already about his responsibility for the situation.

She tried to be practical. Perhaps if they couldn't see her, it would spoil their fun. She took her mug of tea and shut herself into the hall where there was a tubby blue chair in the corner next to the lamp. There was a small bookcase there too with some old favourites in it, and she picked out *The Secret Garden* and sat down, trying to ignore her misery and the noise outside. The other thing she was trying to ignore was an inner voice she refused to recognise as her own murmuring the dangerous question, 'Is love really enough – for *this*?'

Paul Arkwright came wearily down the steps from the hospital just as Willow Lampton swept past in her black Fiesta. He caught a glimpse of the pale hair, the delicate profile, the smart black dress and gold earrings which told him she was going out for the evening. The shaft of agony which pierced him was so sharp that he stumbled on the last step, barely saving himself the humiliation of sprawling in the wake of her passage.

He had learned to steel himself over the last couple of months to the chance meetings around the hospital, to hearing her say,

'Hello, Paul,' in that breathy voice which still had the power to make the hairs on the back of his neck stand up, to seeing her smile that artlessly seductive smile which no longer held a promise for him.

But this was an unguarded moment. He had been on call for almost forty-eight hours, and his tiredness was so all-encompassing that it left no space for self-control. Paul could muster no resistance to this pain; it became part of the sick light-headedness and the sense of unreality which were the physical manifestations of his exhaustion.

He got himself into his car – Willow had liked it, a sharp little BMW coupé which was costing half his disposable income in repayments – and sagged forward, his head against the rim of the steering wheel. He had tried so hard to pretend he had got over it, but he hadn't; like malaria, it lay dormant for a time but the infection was still there, in the blood stream, ready to flare up without warning. He might spend the rest of his life trying to cope with a recurrent fever of despair.

He hadn't believed her at first. They had just made love at his flat – ecstatic for them both, as he thought – when lying back against the pillows she told him that this was the end. 'I need my space, Paul,' she had said in that soft, cool, emotion-less voice.

Uncomprehending at first, thinking it was some kind of joke – though Willow never joked – he had sat up, staring at her, the blood draining from his face. 'What did you say?' he demanded, then 'Why? Why?'

She would not be drawn. Evading his clutch she slid calmly from the bed and into her clothes in her usual neat, economical style while he raged helplessly. When she went to the door he, feeling foolish in his nakedness, could not go to stop her.

'Listen to yourself, Paul,' was all she said at the last. 'I can't stand being shouted at.'

And she had let herself out, as if that was some sort of expla-nation, as if he had ever shouted at her before. As if there wasn't another man waiting for her, and another, probably, when she tired of him.

How often he had replayed that scene mentally, thinking what he might have done, might have said, to change her mind! It flashed before him now, but instead of familiar despair there came the first tiny flicker of anger.

He sat up, recognising this healthier emotion as if it were some rich gift unexpectedly bestowed, nursing it, feeding it till it flared into the red fire of pure, beautiful rage.

'She's a bitch. You know that,' his friend Andrew Lomax had said as they sank whiskies together through one interminable night and Paul poured out his anguish and pain like a man spewing desperately and vainly to void some poison from his system. He had mouthed agreement but he hadn't felt it until now. Now he felt it, right to the core of his being. Bitch! Bitch!

It was all at once strangely clear that to free himself he must confront her, give form to his renunciation and voice to this new achievement of contempt.

Paul Arkwright started the powerful car and gunned it out of the parking area and on in pursuit down the road she had taken.

They had gone at last. Tessa stood up, shaking her head as if to dislodge unpleasant thoughts, then set *The Secret Garden* back in its slot on the shelf with a certain tenderness, even if on this occasion its particular brand of magic had failed.

Today it had been just a bunch of kids being stupid. It was unpleasant enough, but that wasn't what gave her nightmares, made her lock the doors and windows, prevented her from enjoying the garden or wandering in the surrounding hills.

It was funny, in a sick sort of way, that having lived all your life with the dangers of London – the threatening beggar in the underpass, the weirdo muttering and glaring at you in the deserted carriage on the late-night train, the walk home afterwards when the only sound louder than the clicking of your heels on the pavement was the pounding of your heart – that it should be in this quiet valley that you first met raw, naked, gut-wrenching fear.

Fear began as a prickling in the back of your neck, a discomfort sometimes between your shoulder blades when you were out in your back garden or working in the little glassed-in studio. It grew as you found yourself constantly scanning the bare, innocent hillside, or watching the foliage of trees and bushes for tell-tale movements, seeing none.

Fear was telling yourself your uneasiness was imagination at first, then neurosis. Fear was not telling David, because you thought you might be going mad. Fear was dreaming about eyes – hot, probing, greedy eyes – which gleamed from the corners of an unidentified, shadowy maze full of nameless terrors.

It was fear, not courage, that had prompted her at last that afternoon to go out into the garden and scream, 'I know you're out there, you bastard! You've seen me – now let me see you!'

There was silence, nothing but silence once the echoes died. No movement, no sound. She waited, her eyes raking the implacably tranquil scene more fiercely than ever. At last, feeling foolish, she turned.

And he was there. Two feet away from her, standing on the path by the house. Tall. Muscular. Good-looking in a sharp, wolfish way. He was smiling an ugly, predatory smile and his light brown eyes were narrow and too bright. They had an animal avidity, like the eyes which had haunted her dreams.

She screamed. He lunged. She side-stepped, diving towards the back door. Her arms flailed like windmills, striking out at him as his hand grazed her elbow. Then he caught her wrist, but with terror-born violence she chopped the edge of her hand down, loosening his grip enough to get her inside, with the door shut before he could put his weight against it. His shoulder thudded against the panel as she turned the key.

It was fear which lent wings to her feet as she locked the front door, wrestled with the old-fashioned locks in the inside doors, then dialled David's number with hands that could barely hold the phone, waiting for the sound of breaking glass, the next assault.

It didn't come. And by the time the first patrol car arrived, three minutes ahead of her frantic husband, he was gone.

He hadn't been hard to trace. She was barely half-way through her sketch – smudging the lines with her trembling fingers – before one of the local men exclaimed, 'Gavin Guest' and they were off down the road to the house in Llanfeddin where he lived with his mother Hannah to pick him up.

He was more than happy to assist them with their enquiries. He had heard the lady shouting hysterically as he passed on an innocent walk. He was sorry if he had frightened her, if his soothing gestures had been misinterpreted.

He'd been on the edge of a dozen different offences. Too smart to get caught, they told David, and in the absence of George Barker – away at a meeting – it was he who took the decision to remand in custody. 'An identifying glimpse,' he begged Tessa as she told him her story. Something, so that they could prove stalking if not assault. But she hadn't *seen* anything. She'd felt plenty, but she hadn't even been certain then that it wasn't her imagination, so it wasn't exactly evidence.

Next day, the magistrates were sufficiently impressed by his brief's description of him as 'a young man of good character', to let him out on bail. That had been a month ago, and Tessa found that since then she and David had become the villains of the piece.

An orchestrated series of letters to the local paper accused the new inspector of over-reaction and personal bias, which had caused all sorts of problems since in the modern police force attracting bad PR took precedence over incompetence, indolence and even probably downright corruption as the ultimate sin. There was no way of proving it, of course, but Tessa knew this was the Unholy Trinity taking its revenge. The petty persecution which had relentlessly followed, and the silence treatment in the shop – a charming Llanfeddin tradition, judging by the way they treated Mrs Winthrop as well – was a continuation of their campaign.

Tessa prided herself on being tough-minded, and she believed George Barker's kindly assurance that she was safe because Guest knew he was under suspicion. At least, she accepted it intellectually; emotionally – well, that was something else.

With a blind instinct for the soothing power of routine, she went back into the kitchen to start preparing supper. She had been planning a chicken salad – every policeman's wife knows that food must either cook in five minutes, keep hot indefinitely, or be eaten cold – but looking out at the dismal, unalleviated grey of the sky she decided that a curry would be more cheerful. With poppadoms – you had to feel more cheerful cooking poppadoms as they puffed up so magically and crinkled in the hot oil.

Tessa had just started chopping the onions when the door bell rang. Nowadays, never sure what might confront her when she opened it (once a dainty pile of manure, another time a shot rabbit, bloody and still warm) the sound made her heart miss a beat and turned her knees to rubber. Her fingers, as she struggled to put on the chain before she opened the door, were shaking.

The relief, when she saw who stood on the doorstep, showed in her face. It was Marnie Evans the silversmith, her best, indeed her only friend here, with an old waxed jacket tented over her head and her nimbus of soft brown hair frizzing wildly in the damp.

'Hey, lighten up!' she cried, shaking the rain off her jacket and dumping it in a heap on the floor of the porch. 'You're in a Welsh valley now, *cariad*, not darkest Notting Hill!'

'Tell me about it,' Tessa said with an attempt at jauntiness, but there was a quiver in her voice which made Marnie spin round and look sharply at her, her broad grin fading.

'What's the matter, Tess? Not Gavin Guest again? Oh, hang about – it wouldn't be something to do with the flower of Llanfeddin's youth who were playing silly buggers in the road as I came along, would it?'

'Might be.' Tessa grimaced. 'Oh, they're just mucking about, ramming home the point they're on his side. Like everyone else. It's Llanfeddin's favourite hobby.'

Marnie was always forthright. 'Rotten bloody bastards, that lot. Rubbish, they are, just the same as he is. Get David to round them up and teach them to mind their manners.'

Tessa shuddered. 'You're joking! It's bad enough already, without making it worse.'

Marnie put an arm round her shoulders. 'Now, wasn't it lucky I noticed David's car wasn't there and decided to scrounge a cup of tea? Come and tell me all about it.'

Tessa led the way through to the kitchen. 'It's not tea I need,' she said feelingly, getting out a wine box and setting two glasses on the kitchen table. 'And you can start by teaching me to say "bluddy" the way you do — I think it would relieve my feelings. And here's to the valley,' she said ironically, raising her glass.

To Marnie she poured out the sad story of perpetual harassment, and felt the better for it. 'I don't really want to tell David, you see. He's feeling badly enough already, poor guy, without piling this on. He's taking all the blame, even though coming here was a joint decision. A lousy joint decision, OK, but I was in on it too.'

'That's insulting, in its way,' Marnie said after consideration. 'That's treating you as if you're a child who isn't responsible.'

'Oh well — he doesn't mean it that way. It just hurts him that he can't make everything perfect for me, and anyway I love him and I don't want him to be more upset.'

Marnie sniffed. 'You're a disgrace to the sisterhood. How many times do I have to tell you that it does men good to suffer? Keeps them out of trouble, like golf, only not so expensive.'

Tessa sighed. 'Marnie, I'd just be playing into their hands if I made any sort of formal complaint, because it's all trivial things. Like when I have to go into the shop for something — they won't speak to me but sometimes they talk Welsh to each other and make it quite clear they're talking about me.'

Marnie groaned. 'Oh, that's a nasty trick all decent Taffies are ashamed of. I'll teach you to tell them to piss off in the vernacular and you can leave them wondering how much you understood.'

'I'll take you up on that. Oh, and by the way, do you know someone called Agnes Winthrop?'

'Agnes Winthrop? *Cariad*, nobody knows Agnes Winthrop. Keeps herself very strictly to herself. Not that you can blame her, really. With the treatment she gets around here, her prison sentence was probably the least of her punishment.'

'What actually happened?'

'She was driving home from a dinner party with her son – he's a consultant at the hospital, divorced, I think, and she housekeeps for him – and a motorcyclist pulled straight out of a side road under her wheels and was killed. He was seriously drunk at the time, but the problem was that she was fractionally over the limit, so –' Marnie shrugged.

'But could she have done anything about it, if she hadn't been?'

'Apparently not. That was why it was such a comparatively light sentence.'

'An awful thing to have to live with, even so.'

'It hasn't been helped by the fact that the victim was a distant cousin of one of Glynis Rees's cronies – well, just about everyone is, come to think of it – which gave her a wonderful excuse to indulge in her favourite hobbies of torture, oppression and victimisation. I bet she went to the early James Bond movies and reckoned that the SMERSH agents were a pathetic bunch of wooses.'

'I gave Mrs Winthrop a lift today, and she was quite chatty, until she realised I'd done it without knowing about her. I think I'll go round and see her tomorrow. I need all the friends I can get, and we can swap notes on our experiences at the hands of the Unholy Trinity.'

'You do that. There's nothing so uplifting as finding a companion in misfortune and slagging off your oppressors.

'I'll have to go. I'm off to an exhibition in Birmingham for the next couple of days and I haven't sorted out what I'm taking yet. But don't let the bastards grind you down.'

Tessa was laughing as she waved good-bye to her friend, and went back to her cooking.

Willow had not seen Arkwright as she drove off in the black Fiesta which had eighty thousand miles on the clock. She hated that, hated all the economies forced upon her, like the cheap black sandals instead of Ferragamo, and the fake pearls and fake gold earrings instead of the real thing.

As always when she thought about it, her chiselled mouth set in a hard, angry line. It was Hal's fault, of course; other girls had smart little cars and good clothes and fathers they called Daddy, but she had to be the one landed with Hal, who was an aging hippie eking out an existence on a tumbledown small-holding and with no money for a good school or expensive training for his daughter.

The local comp and a nurse's diploma was hardly a launching pad for taking the world by storm, but it was the best that was offered to her. Sometimes she really hated Hal. Quite a lot of the time, actually.

She had thought of modelling, naturally. Thought of little else, in fact, but she didn't need anyone to tell her she was nine inches too short for the catwalk. She paid hard-earned money for a portfolio, but the camera did not love her neat, delicately-formed features as it did the wide faces and strong bones of other, plainer girls. 'Chocolate-box is right out this millennium, ducky,' one agent, a spotty yob in a greasy leather jacket, had told her brutally.

Indeed, she didn't like more than two or three of the studies herself. In the frozen abstraction of a still, her neat mouth was exposed as being thin and mean, the space between her striking eyes as too narrow. She looked cold, and hard, and ruthless. Well, they did say that the camera never lied, and no one had ever accused her of being nice.

So she'd had to make her own way as best she could. And at least she'd done quite well out of one little sideline. Unconsciously, her lips curved in a small, ugly, greedy smile; that had paid for good hairdressing and a few decent clothes, and putting the squeeze on might bring in a little more. But she knew it would only be a little more, and it was risky; with the goose becoming increasingly fretful the supply of golden eggs could stop at any time.

No, there was no doubt about it, it was important that things went well this evening. If she played her cards right, this just could be the answer to all her problems. She must see to it that the choice was hers to make – even if she still wasn't entirely sure what that choice should be. It would be dreadful to settle for this only to discover later that you could have done still better for yourself . . .

Willow caught herself furrowing her smooth brow and pushed away the frown with her middle finger. Time was still on her side, after all; she must play it cool, get it absolutely right. That was the important thing. Still, it couldn't do any harm to be particularly charming this evening.

If only she could be allowed just one tiny glimpse of the future. It would be so much easier to bear her present privations if she knew there were good times ahead.

The hospital was on the outskirts of Stetford. She drove towards the town making refinements to her favourite fantasy about money and clothes and travel, happily unaware that God's kindest gift is ignorance of what the morrow may hold.

SESSION TWO

Friday 24 July

Session Two

'I can't think why I'm here. I don't like talking about the past. There isn't any point that I can see.'

'What happened after your parents got back from hospital?'

'I told you, I don't see the point of talking about it. You can't make me.'

'No, of course not.'

'Are we just going to sit here, then?'

'For a while.'

'Oh, this is ridiculous!'

'Was your father still angry with you?'

'Yes — oh, for goodness' sake, I'll tell you and we can get it over with.

'When they came back She was clinging to his arm, holding her bandaged hand up for sympathy just as if she was one of the spaniels.

'I went to stand on the gravel, to face them when they got out. "Stand with me," I said to my brother again, but he slithered away and vanished.

'My father helped her down from the high seat carefully, as if She might break. "Go and sit down," he said to her. "Go in and sit down, and I'll come and make you a cup of tea in a minute."

'Her small puffy feet in their silly shoes scrunched on the gravel. Then there was only silence, I remember, apart from the cawing of the rooks in the trees high above.

'It was a damp spring day and I was frightened — sick and cold with fright. I didn't want him to be my enemy too, to have to stop caring

about him as well. He stared at me, and his eyes were bright and fierce, but I stared back without flinching.

'He sighed then. "Talking won't mend anything, will it? Seldom does, to my way of thinking." And he took my arm. It wasn't painful, but then I didn't struggle. That would have been beneath me.

'The dogs set up a barking when we went into the yard, of course. Jess and Nell were his two black Labrador bitches, lovely dogs, with big square heads and tails as broad as an otter's. Jasper and Meggie the spaniels started squealing and leaping at the bars as usual.

'They were old-fashioned dog runs, solidly built on a stone base with rusted wires close set on top. He opened the middle one. Old Sultan's cage, that was – the old black dog who'd died six months before.

'I walked in and turned to face him as he shut the door, fished out a padlock from the pocket of his patched tweed hunter's jacket, then snapped it into place.

'As he walked away, the dogs' demands for attention died into disappointed silence. Jess – she was old and wise – could always smell trouble; she whined softly at me and Nell came to try to push her muzzle through the wire. Across the yard the ferrets were unsettled too. They padded to and fro in the hutches which always had that sharp, rank, musky smell, with their eyes glowing red in the shadows.

'Then the dogs began to bark again a few minutes later. He was coming back – thought the better of it, then, had he? I felt nothing but contempt.

'But I wronged him. He was carrying a piece of cardboard, the side of a packing case. He didn't say anything, just held it up for me to read. THIS ANIMAL BITES, it said in her thick black capitals, and he propped it against the door of the cage then went back inside.

'I felt my face begin to burn, a hot, painful red. At the kitchen window She, my enemy, was standing watching, smiling, no doubt.

'The kennels faced the road. Before long, one of the children from the next-door farm – no friend of mine – came past on his bicycle. By Monday morning, every child at school knew.

'Oh, it got to be quite a popular outing, to cycle past the Keeper's cottage on a weekend. The punishment never varied, though the captions did.

'Can I go now?'

Saturday 11 July

Chapter Four

In the night and the silence, his breathing seemed very loud, very heavy, almost as if it were hanging about him like a vapour trapped beneath the arching branches of the trees overhead. Straining his ears for any threatening sound, he could not hear even the perennial rustling of the leaves in this windless hush. Somewhere behind him a night bird cried suddenly, the sound ripping shockingly through the stillness.

The moon had risen at last, huge and golden, almost at the full. It lent welcome light to his passage as he followed the unmade path through the trees. Underfoot, the ground was wet and muddy after the recent rain, sucking noisily at the overlarge boots he was wearing, so that lifting each foot was an effort.

His every instinct shrieked, 'Hurry, hurry!' yet he dared not. Careful, he told himself, careful. He had left her car on the safe, unrevealing tarmac of the car park at the bottom, well-screened from the quiet road behind a bank of shrubs; the tell-tale boots he would bury among the contents of some random dustbin in the town below. What he must guard against was the predatory branch of a bush or a tree which like a grasping finger might snatch a fibre, trap a hair.

But then, caution would have dictated that he did not take a step beyond that safe, unrevealing car park. He was taking chances with every moment that passed on this steep path up to the common. His throat constricted; he forced away any consideration of his present actions.

Who would ever have believed she could have been so heavy? Such a little, slight thing, such slender wrists and ankles, such a tiny waist! Yet his arms ached desperately as he bore her along, so delicately perfect in the moonlight with her stiffening neck back against the blanket over his arm and the golden hair – its colour bleached now to moon-silver – falling smooth and heavy almost to the ground.

He had been sobbing as he started out on this terrible journey, but now it had become a question of physical endurance. Another ten steps, another . . . She seemed to be growing heavier with every step he took, as if with the weight of increasing guilt.

He knew exactly where he must go: it was only fitting that he should leave her where they had been happiest together. They had listened to the larks filling the clear air above them with honeyed melody, watched the meadow blues dance among the rough grasses, looking out over the Shropshire plain where it faded away below them into purple distance. Yes, it was only right that he should take her there.

Doggedly he staggered on. Another step. Another step, with the pain of arms and shoulders a distraction from the deeper pain. At last he could see the edge of the trees, was coming out on to the open common which was his goal.

Under the moon it stretched broad and empty. The leaves of the furze bushes were patches of heavy shadow, and the Queen Anne's Lace which edged an old tumbledown dyke like the foam at the edge of a breaking wave, gleamed faintly in the darkness. Over to the west, a house on the hillside had a light still burning, and below on the plain the street lights of the villages and small towns made pools of unnatural light.

At last he could lay her down, easing the screaming muscles in his back and shoulders. At some physical cost to himself, he set her on the ground with infinite care – though what could she feel now? – and smoothed out the blanket in which he had held her wrapped.

The blanket had been his protection, keeping her from contact with his clothes. Now it was a serious risk; he knew he should remove it, to be discreetly disposed of, like the boots. But it was her protection now, warm and soft; how could he leave her to lie cold on a bare hillside?

The dry, harsh sobs, welling up again, choked him. Now he looked at her face, at the closed eyes with the dark fans of lashes, the lips just slightly parted as if in sleep, so serene, so peaceful. Oh, the pity of it, the pity of it!

In a paroxysm of anguish he smoothed a tendril of hair back from her face and tucked the blanket round her, covering the bare arms and the short black dress and the narrow feet with their smart black sandals still strapped in place. Half-blinded by sudden tears, he stumbled across to the wall, tearing brutally at the plants growing there, snatching clumsy armfuls of the delicate blossom.

He strewed it about her, the green-white flowers framing her neck and face no brighter than the luminous pallor of her skin and hair. He stood for just a moment, looking at what he had done, then doubled over, falling to his knees with a shuddering, drawn-out groan, as if his soul were at that moment being torn from his body.

Five minutes passed, perhaps, then he stood up again, and hunched as if battling against some invisible tempest, plunged unsteadily back the way he had come.

He did not look round again to where she lay in her curious shroud, composed in death as in life, while the cold dew started insidiously forming on her waxen skin and the flowers which lay about her head like a bridal wreath began to wilt and die.

'Has Nurse Lampton called in sick?'

Sister Morley's voice rose incredulously on the word 'sick' as if this were some modern indulgence invented by the nurses of today who fell so sadly short of Miss Nightingale's exemplary standards. She was famously as volatile as a mercury detonator, and this morning her spectacular bosom was heaving and her ice-blue eyes sparkling with temper.

It was Saturday morning. Two of her regular auxiliaries were on holiday and the one replacement the agency had sent (male, which didn't go down well with Sister either) was going around behaving as if he'd never seen a bedpan before and wouldn't know what to do with it if he had. Then there had been two emergency admissions overnight for which the proper paperwork was missing, and now Nurse Lampton – whom Sister had always suspected of dumb insolence without being able to prove it – hadn't appeared for her shift.

Standing in the doorway of Sister's office, Megan Griffiths exchanged glances with her fellow victim Nurse Smith, who was giving a heartfelt if not entirely convincing impersonation of someone who isn't there.

'No, Sister,' Megan said submissively. 'Not that I know of.' She almost imagined she could hear the fizzling of the flame racing along the fuse wire before the explosion came.

'This is quite intolerable! How can I possibly be expected to run a ward – a crisis ward like cardiology, mark you – without a proper complement of staff?

'We would never have *dared* not to turn up for work, whatever our excuse. Matron would have seen to that, I can tell you. And what will happen if I report her to the hospital manager? The silly little man will wring his hands and talk about the Unions.'

Megan bit her lip, trying hard not to commit the fatal error of smiling. The hospital manager was a small, harassed-looking man with a slightly pink nose who always made her think of a white rabbit, and it was not uncommon to see him scurrying down a corridor and whisking out of sight just ahead of some senior member of staff who would be striding along with a purposeful expression, only to stop, baffled, when the trail went cold.

Pausing for breath, Sister Morley glared at the meekly bent heads of her subordinates. 'Well, you haven't time to stand here gossiping all day,' she said unfairly. 'Nurse Griffiths, you get on to Personnel and tell them I *must* have somebody up here right away – though why I imagine that will do any good, I can't think.

'Now, there are three beds to strip and change, and Mr Winthrop's coming in at ten to have a look at Mrs Owen, so you'll have to get her ready for that. And Mr Blyth in the men's section is being discharged, so he'll have to be dressed with his things packed ready for his daughter to pick up. You start with that, Nurse Smith, and Griffiths can join you to do the beds, then report to Staff Nurse to see what else needs doing.

'I'm just going to start the medication round. And I don't know what you're standing there for – weren't you listening to what I told you to do?'

'Yes, Sister, sorry, Sister,' they chorused, then fled to their separate tasks.

When they met up again over the bed making Sister was mercifully back in her office marking up medical notes.

'Phew!' said Sally Smith. 'What a cow! No wonder she has staff shortages when she goes on like that. I really thought she would start spinning round and round then disappear in a flash and a puff of smoke. Thanks, Willow Lampton – we owe you one.'

'Wouldn't like to be her, though, would I, when she decides to come back, ill or not.'

Sally snorted. 'She was perfectly all right yesterday. If she's really ill, I'm Posh Spice.'

Megan, her round face flushed with exertion, nodded. 'Mind you, though,' she said mysteriously, lowering her voice and leaning closer towards her bed-making partner as they straightened the top sheet, 'she could be feeling a bit upset this morning.'

'Upset? How do you mean? Not as upset as she'll be once Morley's finished with her, that's for sure.'

'I left here to go home just after her last night, didn't I, caught the half-past six bus. Well, when we were going past the lay-by – you know the one, just before you go into Stetford – guess whose car was parked there, with Doctor Arkwright's car parked right in front of it. They were both out of their cars standing in the rain, see, and you could tell he was yelling at her. I don't *know* what it was about, but—'

'No prizes for guessing, though.' Sally straightened up from her bed making to give this high calibre item of gossip the respectful attention it deserved. 'I heard she dumped him suddenly, and he was ever so upset. How was she taking it?'

Megan gave her a 'need-you-ask' look. 'You know what she's like. Cool as a cucumber, she looked, just acting superior same as usual. That was all I saw – couldn't really ask the bus to stop for a closer look, could I?'

'He'll probably feel better for having got it off his chest, poor guy,' Sally observed. 'You never know, it might even mean he starts looking for a replacement.' She winked. 'Maybe I'll go and see if I can bump into him by some freaky coincidence.'

'I don't think he'll be in today. He was on call yesterday and Siân Jenkins mentioned he'd done a couple of days.'

'Oh, I can wait, I can wait!' Sally laughed incautiously, then smothered the sound, bending hastily to remake a perfect hospital corner as Sister, looking daggers, sailed down the ward with Mr Winthrop the consultant, a tall, distinguished-looking man in his early forties, here to check that the emergency admission last night was recovering satisfactorily. As if, under Sister Morley's care, she would have dared to do anything else, like die to spite her.

After they had passed, Megan, greatly daring, whispered, 'I could quite fancy him, couldn't you, if he didn't always look so serious.'

'Well, if all your patients were likely to drop dead at your feet with a heart attack if you got it wrong, you'd find it hard to see the funny side. And that business with his mother, too – can't have been very nice for him, can it?'

Megan nodded. 'He's a good doctor, though,' she said approvingly as John Winthrop, in defiance of Sister's enraged glare, sat down on the bed and took his elderly patient's hand in his.

Sally gathered up the soiled sheets while Megan went on to the next bed. 'Well, Mrs Watson, how are we today, then? Feeling better? Oh, I'm sure you are, really.'

'Yes, now. Today,' Tessa Cordiner said as the estate agent, a plump, lugubrious man who looked as if the concept of immediate action was taking him well out of his professional depth, made a steeple of his fingers and leaned forward in his swivel chair. Its spring gave a protesting 'pyoinng!' as his fleshy rump shifted.

'This is a very – er – *sudden* decision, Mrs Cordiner,' he said ponderously. 'You've only been in the house – what – three months?'

For 'sudden', Tessa thought, read 'hysterical and over-reactive'. 'Three months too many, Mr Jarvis,' she said crisply. 'Now, you must have the details on file—'

Pyoinng! went the chair. 'Wouldn't it be better to come in with Inspector Cordiner, just to chat this through, before we make a decision we might regret?' He employed the nursery pronoun winsomely. 'I must confess, I did hear that there had been a few – er – local difficulties, perhaps we might call them, and sometimes you ladies can become a little, well, emotional, perhaps . . .'

I hate him, Tessa thought. I hate him, and I hate them all, with their Fifties' attitudes and their pernicious gossiping. Keeping her temper with some difficulty, she said, 'No, I don't think *we* need trouble my husband. The house is in joint names, after all, and we know, don't we, that he is a very busy man whose time is at a premium. Since he is perfectly happy to leave arrangements in my hands, perhaps we could get on with making them now? Unless, of course, you have some sort of a problem with taking instructions from a woman—'

'No, no, dear lady!' Pyoinng, pyoinng! 'Far from it, I do assure you. Great admirer of the fair sex, as my wife would tell you—'

So there wasn't enough business around to let him be choosy, even about hard-to-shift properties like this one. Coldly, Tessa observed him run his finger round the edge of his collar where it was biting into the solid flesh round his neck, and contemplated the Hamlet solution. But they hadn't perfected the vaporising gun yet, had they?

Eying her as nervously as if he could read her thoughts, he said, 'Just let me – er – find a form—'

Somewhat against her better judgement Tessa submitted. She had no reason to suppose any of the other estate agents would be any better and he at least had the measurements and photographs to hand. She arranged, with some force and in the face of protests at this unseemly haste, that someone would come that very afternoon to erect the 'For Sale' sign, and left abruptly as he struggled to his feet to a positive volley of plaintive pyoinngs.

However, when she emerged into pale sunshine her cheerful mood returned. It had been such a relief when David suggested that they should cut their losses and try to sell the house. Over the bottle of Cava they had each confessed to trying to sound idiotically unbothered about the whole sorry mess, in case the other might construe criticism as reproach. They promised one another solemnly never to be so fatuous again, and indulged in an orgy of savagery about the things they most hated about the house, the village, the valley and their neighbours, which had done them both a power of good.

Despite her promise – which of course she had meant, absolutely, with all her heart – she hadn't actually told David about the daily persecution. There wasn't anything he could do about it, and there was no point in distressing him when any day someone might come along with an offer for the house and the problem would be solved.

Admittedly, it had been empty for some time when they bought it, but surely, as David said, they weren't the only suckers around and perhaps next week someone would find that it exactly met their requirements, though neither of them could quite imagine what such requirements might be.

Again, neither of them precisely thrilled to the notion of moving into Stetford, but with any luck the natives wouldn't be actively hostile.

'After all, with my contacts on the Friends of the Hospital Committee we should have it made,' Tessa pointed out solemnly. 'And I'm sure George would start grooming you for Rotary—'

After that things somehow degenerated in an entirely

satisfactory way, and they hadn't got round to eating the curry until almost midnight . . . Tessa smiled reminiscently.

She had been up early this morning, though, baking her batch of scones for the Friends of the Hospital Coffee Morning – well, two batches, actually, since the first batch turned out looking not so much like scones as like sponges – the bathroom kind. The second lot weren't precisely Delia Smith either, but that was her best offer and, if it wasn't good enough, Dorothy's butter-cream angel cakes would just have to be deployed to prevent disgusted punters deserting in droves.

Tessa looked at her watch. Half-past nine – perhaps she should fetch her scones from Boris in the car park and take them across to the Territorial Army Drill Hall where, for the coffee-morning set – Stetford's answer to café society – the event of the year would take place in an hour's time.

When she opened the big wooden door she thought for a moment that it must have started already. There were women everywhere, behind stalls, spreading card tables with effusively-embroidered tea cloths, setting posy vases down on the tea cloths, arranging wedding china tea sets beside the posy vases . . . Then there were other women coming along behind, making subtle adjustments to the position of the sugar bowl and milk jug, tweaking a modest rosebud into prominence, straightening chairs which had already been aligned with mathematical precision. How, Tessa wondered, as she and her scones weaved their way across to the kitchen, would they ever find room for the paying public?

In the centre of the kitchen, a long table stood crammed with boxes and trays of scones and Really Nice cakes: luscious chocolate layers, fancies of pastel-coloured fondant, sponges bejewelled with cherries and studded with nuts, dainty scones so fragile that a puff of wind might reduce them to a rubble of buttery crumbs.

Tessa's own scones seemed somehow to have got even larger and flatter on the walk over from the car park. Looking about her for somewhere to set them down – behind that boiler over there, perhaps – she heard Mona's voice hail her.

'Ah, Tessa! There you are! Good girl. And you've brought your – ah – scones.'

The pause, as her eye fell on the tray, was involuntary, and she went on hastily, 'Now, what can we find for you to do, I wonder?' She looked about her; two women appeared to be engaged in a struggle over one plate of cakes, and Mona sighed. 'It's just that people get so *possessive*—'

Tessa was shocked to hear her own voice say, with shining sincerity, 'Well, actually, I have an appointment I must go to just now. I'll be back later, of course—'

Mona's relief was obvious. 'Of course, dear. Oh, Dorothy –!' She hurried off importantly to join a battalion of ladies being treated to a little touch of Dorothy, in bright pink silk jersey.

It wasn't *exactly* a lie, Tessa told herself as she scuttled to freedom. She had sort of planned to go and see Agnes Winthrop . . . Well, perhaps it was a lie, but if she'd stayed to be patronised for an hour sooner or later she'd have snapped and people would have been upset and if the end justifying the means was good enough for the Jesuits it was good enough for her.

Even so, to ease her conscience she felt she'd better go to see Mrs Winthrop now. It seemed unlikely she would want to go to the coffee morning, but perhaps she would like a lift into town for shopping.

She returned to Boris in the car park. He coughed self-pityingly once or twice, but started all right, and for once she didn't feel the usual leaden misery as she headed out of town, up past the edge of the common and into the hills. It was warm enough for her to open the window and as they sped up the gradient at a heady twenty-eight miles an hour she was singing cheerfully. When you didn't have a radio you had to make your own in-car entertainment, and 'The Sun Has Got His Hat On' seemed entirely suitable, as long as no one was listening.

Mrs Winthrop's house certainly was in an isolated position. It must be tough to have to rely on her son – who, if he was a doctor probably worked long hours – for any sort of motorised transport. She must be a lady of considerable character not to have insisted on selling up and going to live in the town.

Or perhaps she couldn't find anyone who wanted to buy it. On this unwelcome thought she swung the car into the drive where she had turned yesterday.

The house was built more generously than any of the other houses in the valley, with big windows and large rooms. There was a vestibule with a Victorian mosaic tiled floor, and the white front door had a frosted-glass panel.

At her touch, the brightly-polished brass door bell rang loudly. Waiting on the doorstep Tessa turned to admire the view, reflecting that from this vantage point, with the sun shining, the valley looked almost as deceptively attractive as it had the first time she saw it.

She turned back. There was no sound from inside the house, no sign of movement. She hesitated, then rang the bell again.

There was still no response; after a few more minutes, Tessa went back to Boris with a sense of anticlimax. Did Mrs Winthrop, perhaps, never answer her door? She could certainly sympathise with the siege mentality.

Of course, it was perfectly possible that on such a lovely day she might simply have gone for a walk, and indeed as Tessa drove back home she caught a glimpse of two figures walking towards her up near the ridge that bordered the valley to the west. One was a dog, and the other might have been a woman, though the distance was too great to be certain.

Tessa felt a little deflated. There was at least half an hour to put in before she need go back to the coffee morning; perhaps she should go back to the house and do all the things she hadn't done before she came out, in her anxiety to get the house put on the market. After all, someone might want to view it this very day, and it wouldn't do if they were put off by dirty breakfast dishes and an unmade bed.

She was leaving Boris with an affectionate pat on his bonnet – he really did seem to have turned over a new leaf these days – when she heard the phone ringing. It took her a moment or two to get the door open, but for once she was in luck. It didn't stop before she managed to pick it up.

★

'Someone's been churning up the path here, haven't they?'

They were plodding up in single file through the trees on the familiar path leading to the common, as they did at some stage in most weeks, he a little ahead but matching his pace to hers. He did it instinctively now, since they had been walking together through forty years of married life.

She glanced down at the deeply-indented footprints in the drying mud on the path, but said only, 'Mmmm,' saving her breath for the climb. It wasn't quite as easy as it used to be, and she was thankful when the trees started thinning and there was the promise of level ground on the plateau where the common opened out.

'Quiet today, isn't it?' he said. 'Only that one car in the car park; you'd've thought more people'd be out Saturday morning, lovely day like this after all that rain.'

They both stopped and turned, as they always did, to admire the view. Below them, bathed in sunshine, stretched the Shropshire plain, clear all the way over to the Wrekin and beyond. Overhead, the larks were shouting as if there were a prize for the lustiest singer, and the gorse flowers scented the warm air with their subtle fragrance.

He sighed contentedly. 'Beats me why people go wasting money on foreign places, with this on their own doorstep. Couldn't get anything nicer than this, no matter where you went.'

It was what he always said when they came up here, but she, recovering her breath, assented as eagerly as if this dismissal of Paris, the Grand Canyon, Sydney Opera House, the Taj Mahal, and even the Earth as viewed from Space were not only reasonable but a proposition she was hearing propounded for the first time. On such foundations are long and happy marriages built.

'Course you couldn't. Lovely, that is,' she said, and he echoed, 'Lovely,' and then they smiled at one another in perfect satisfaction.

'Let's go this way today,' he said, pointing to his right and setting off without waiting for her nod of agreement. She followed him a little more slowly, looking down over the common as it sloped away past the old wall. She clicked her tongue disapprovingly.

'Would you look at that?' She pointed to the foot of the wall, where the clumps of Queen Anne's Lace had been broken down, as if someone had trampled them. Some even lay uprooted in the long grass. 'Disgusting, I call that. No reason why you shouldn't pick a few flowers, if you want, but that's vandalism, that is.'

He was walking a few paces ahead; he stopped suddenly and turned, lowering his voice.

'Sssh! Someone's sleeping over there, would you credit it? Just wrapped in a blanket over there, sound asleep.'

She peered past him to the anonymous figure bundled up on the turf, then clicked her tongue again. 'It'll be one of those hippies, I shouldn't wonder. Taken those drugs, more than likely. Stands to reason – wouldn't be asleep this time of day, would you, if you hadn't of?'

'Stoned, they call it.' He prided himself on keeping up to date.

'What'll we do? Might be violent, you never know.'

'Asleep now, anyway. I'll take a look-see.'

'Just you be careful, Bill.'

He walked up to the motionless figure, exaggerating the confidence he felt because he knew her eyes were on him from those few meek paces away.

Wrapped in the soft grey wool blanket the girl looked very peaceful, very beautiful, very still.

Too still, and her skin had an unhealthy waxen bloom. Her blonde hair was wet with dew, and there about her face were scattered wilted strands of wild flowers. That was all strange, very strange. His heart missed a beat; he gulped, feeling suddenly giddy, took a step back to steady himself.

She noticed the stagger instantly, on perpetual watch for any hint of the only possible threat to their loving partnership. 'Bill!

Are you all right, Bill?' Her voice sharpened in panic and she lunged towards him.

'Yes, yes,' he said, sounding almost tetchy in his effort to recover himself swiftly enough to protect her. 'Don't look, Maggie, don't look.'

But she was beside him, grabbing for the warm assurance of his hand. She gripped it convulsively.

'Oh dear goodness,' she said softly. 'She's dead, isn't she, Bill? She's dead.'

Chapter Five

Feeling as if the breath had been knocked from her body, Tessa put down the receiver, then picked it up again at once to phone David.

The switchboard put her through, but a woman's voice answered which after a second she identified as belonging to WDC Sue Watson, one of David's team in the CID. She liked Sue, a sparky girl with hair cropped short as a schoolboy's and a lurid taste in hair colour – flaming orange, the last time Tessa had seen her.

'Sue? Is that you? It's Tessa here. I was really wanting to speak to David.'

'Oh – Tessa!' The girl's manner sounded strange, not at all like her usual ready friendliness, and for a moment Tessa felt uncomfortably that somehow she had managed to do the wrong thing.

'David isn't here just now,' Sue went on, without volunteering any further information. 'I could try leaving a message for him, if you like.'

'I'd much rather speak to him myself.' Tessa heard her own voice sharpening slightly. 'Can I get in touch with him, or can you tell me when he'll be back?'

'No, I'm afraid not.'

She definitely sounded distracted; perhaps there was some crisis at that end as well. Doing her best not to sound like a nagging wife, Tessa said, 'I'm really very anxious to speak to him, but don't worry, Sue, I'll ring back later. Though I'd appreciate it if you could put a note on his desk asking him to phone me as soon as he can.'

'Sure, Tessa. 'Bye.' The phone was put down almost before she could reply.

Was there the smallest chance that she would remember to do it? Somehow Tessa doubted it. Sue clearly had a lot of other things on her mind, and presumably so too did David. And with Marnie in Birmingham she couldn't even seek the comforting haven of her cottage to talk about this latest disaster.

Patience was never, even at the best of times, one of Dr Richard Webb's more obvious virtues. Intolerant by nature, he had chosen a career where authority was seldom questioned, and in both his personal and professional life he was accustomed to having the crooked made straight and the rough places plain to free him to pursue his important medical duties. Or his interests, like golf or shooting. Or his whims, which were many and distinctly varied.

Unfortunately, it didn't seem to be anyone's responsibility to see that the roadworks' traffic lights were not against him when he was completely shattered after a night on duty. He swore savagely, and stopped.

He had expensive tastes and was extremely particular about his appearance, but his Gieves and Hawkes suiting was rumpled and his Egyptian cotton shirt was sticking to him as if it were common polyester. Behind his Pierre Cardin spectacles his eyes were red-rimmed and drooping with fatigue.

The last straw, he thought as he glared at the intransigent light which was standing between him and blessed oblivion, this is positively the last straw. He found he was seeing weedy camels with their knees buckling under the weight of the massive haystacks on their backs, and had to shake his head to jerk himself out of this symbolic dream.

Yet wasn't it almost a relief to be able to think of nothing except bed? Correction, a bath and then bed. Provided he didn't fall asleep in his bath and drown – though he was close to feeling that eternal sleep was a tempting prospect.

But then, what dreams might come?

The light changed and he shot away, aware that his speed was unwise, but not caring. Probably some meddlesome fool was even now devising a machine to measure disqualifying levels of exhaustion; his count this morning would undoubtedly be enough to put him off the road for months.

Chrissie was in the kitchen when he came in at the back door. He noted coldly that she was clearing the breakfast dishes with the flustered air of one who had guiltily leapt to her feet as the door opened, noticed too her clumsy attempt to conceal a glass showing the tell-tale dregs of Alka-Seltzer. She had the sweaty, queasy look of someone battling with a hangover.

'Gosh, you look rough!' she greeted him with a painful attempt at heartiness. 'Did you have a bad duty night?'

'There is some other kind?' he said acidly. 'I'm off for a bath and bed – keep the place quiet, will you? I'll switch off the bedroom phone.'

'Do you want me to cook you some breakfast first?' she offered, swallowing hard, and for a second he toyed lovingly with the sadistic pleasure of watching her struggle with bacon and eggs. But the need for sleep was too imperative.

'No,' he said brusquely, and went out. Then he stopped, and went back into the kitchen.

'You are remembering about the Friends' Coffee Morning today, aren't you?'

Chrissie looked stricken. 'Oh Lord, I'd forgotten all about the ghastly thing.'

Richard pursed his lips. 'I suppose you've also forgotten to bake for it,' he said. 'I have a position in the town, you know; it doesn't look good if my wife does nothing for charity, especially a medical charity like this.'

'They always have far too much baking anyway,' Chrissie said defensively. 'I'll send them a donation – it'll be a lot more useful.'

'We're not made of money, you know,' he said tartly.

'Surely you can find something for the stalls instead – bric-à-brac, or some paperbacks perhaps. In any case, you'll have to go and make my apologies.'

Ignoring the look of sick dismay on his wife's pallid face, he went out again, having delivered his instructions. Sometime, when he was feeling stronger, he would end this ridiculous charade and send the woman to dry out before she became a major public embarrassment. Perhaps they could do something about the way she looked, too. It offended him, with his taste for elegance and sophistication and expensive luxuries. Too expensive, some of them – but he must wipe those thoughts from his consciousness. The glory was long departed from those one-time, forbidden delights, and the dream was dead and he was sick at heart and old. And tired.

The post was lying on the doormat in the front hall, and he picked it up to leaf through it. Bills, bills, bills and more sodding bills. His tired mind shied away from the problem. At least there wasn't a grey envelope addressed in a neat black script to deal with.

As he hauled himself wearily upstairs he could hear the noise of the television in the sitting room. That would be Charlotte, glued to some unsuitable video, no doubt, despite the fact that he'd directed that she shouldn't be allowed to waste her school holidays like that. Satan, as he tended to say with the air of one coining an epigram, finds mischief for idle hands, and Chrissie should be finding Charlotte sensible, constructive things to do.

Still, at least it was quiet, which just at the moment was all he cared about. He reached the bathroom and ran a hot, deep bath, dropping his clothes on the floor for Chrissie to deal with later. At last, with a groan of relief, he got into bed and shut his eyes.

It seemed only seconds later that, like a grappling iron, Chrissie's voice hauled him from the depths of sleep.

'Richard! Richard! I'm sorry, but you've got to wake up.' She was shaking his shoulder; outraged, he sat up, trying to open eyes that seemed hermetically-sealed to try to make some sense of what was happening.

'What the hell –' he mumbled, his tongue thick in his mouth.

'It's the police, Richard. They said they need you to go up to the common.'

'Oh God,' he whimpered, collapsing back into his pillows. 'Oh no, no!'

'Well, I *said* you'd been on call all night, but they weren't interested. They just said you were needed because you're the official police surgeon, and you had to come. They wouldn't say what it was about. Do you want some tea, or something? You look ghastly.'

He forced himself upright. His face was grey with the shock of the sudden waking, his neat hair was tousled and his pyjamas, navy smartly piped with red, were buttoned askew. He swung his legs over the edge of the bed and sat there, his head buried in his hands. It felt like the worst sort of hangover.

'Tea, yes, tea, perhaps. I certainly need something.'

'Do you want a slug of brandy in it?' Chrissie offered, and he raised his head to glare at her with revulsion.

'Oh, what a wonderful idea! Did you think of it all by yourself? That would be just what I need to make life perfect – brandy on an empty stomach, and breathalysed when I get there. Make some tea – plain tea – will you, then look out some clothes for me while I go and stand under the shower and try to find my head.'

Tessa waited half an hour, then tried phoning David again. This time the switchboard told her flatly that he was unavailable, and she left another message, knowing better than to ask further questions which wouldn't be answered anyway. It was probably something to do with the drugs bust he'd been talking about, but it could hardly have happened at a worse time.

She should really have been getting back to the coffee morning by now, but with this on her mind she simply couldn't face it. No one would notice her absence, anyway.

She desperately needed to talk, if not to David at least to someone. It wasn't easy trying to keep things in proportion when the only dialogue you could have was with the rebellious inner self which had already flirted with treachery.

She had friends in London, of course, but she found herself out of tune with them these days. 'Poor love, how on earth are you surviving, out there in the sticks?' was the opening to most conversations, and Tessa, hackles rising, responded by being implausibly upbeat at unnecessary length about everything. She wasn't on the circuit any more, of course, and gradually the regular gossip sessions had dwindled into sweetie-I've-been-meaning-to-call-you-for-ages phonecalls.

It would be too much of a temptation to disloyalty to talk to any of them. And even her mother, usually reliably available, had let her down by being away this week on grandmotherly duties cooing over her sister's newest small in Canada.

So with Marnie away, there was no one. She'd just have to pretend to be all grown up and work it out herself, somehow. Unless—

Perhaps Agnes Winthrop might be back from her walk by now. Tessa wasn't sure what she would say to her, if she was, but at least it would occupy the time until she could reasonably dial David's number again. At worst, she might find herself snubbed, but she should be inured to that by now. So spurning Boris she set out briskly on the walk to the Winthrop's house.

When she rang the bell this time, she heard movement almost at once, and Agnes Winthrop opened the door. The dog ran out past her, frisking round Tessa's feet as he recognised a friend.

Mrs Winthrop's expression was forbidding, although on seeing who her visitor was she did smile politely, if distantly.

'Mrs Cordiner,' she said. 'Good morning.'

Tessa's heart sank at the chilliness of the reception. She hadn't quite made up her mind whether to say she had come to pay a social call, or to tell the simple truth, and had hoped to take her cue from the other woman's tone. If she did that now, the appropriate response would quite clearly be to make her excuses and leave.

But she wasn't going to. Nor could she bring herself to insult the dignified woman in front of her with a social lie.

'I've come to beg for your help,' she said bluntly. 'I find myself in a desperately difficult position and I badly need to talk to someone. I can't get hold of my husband and there isn't anyone else.'

A remarkable transformation came over Agnes Winthrop's face.

'My dear,' she said with what appeared to be genuine warmth, 'come in, come in.'

When Richard Webb emerged from the little wood, escorted by the uniformed officer who had greeted him and checked his identity at the car park, there were two men standing awkwardly at a little distance from a muffled shape which was lying on the slope of the hill overlooking the plain below.

'Over there, sir,' his guide said unnecessarily, and at the sound of his voice the men spun round.

He recognised George Barker, the Superintendent, one of his own patients whom he had also known socially for years. Barker was a big man, heavy without being seriously overweight and fit enough to have no problem with the police requirement of being able to cover a mile and a half in twelve minutes. He had high colour, though, and his uniform always seemed to be straining across his barrel chest.

'Richard!' Barker called importantly. 'Over here!'

Webb had a headache that felt like iron hands squeezing his skull and a queasy stomach. He wondered irritably where the stupid bastard thought he was about to go – on a hike along Offa's Dyke?

'Yes, George, I rather thought it might be.'

The other man, tall and slim and in plain clothes, said formally, 'Good morning, Dr Webb. Thank you for coming so promptly. I'm sorry we had to drag you out when I gather you'd only just come off night duty.

'All we need from you really is official confirmation of death and then we can let you go. The police pathologist is on the way, and he'll make a full examination.'

Webb recognised him too – Carpenter, Cornwall, some name like that – from a party at the Barkers'. The new inspector – stunning wife – oh yes, that was it.

'Cordiner.' He spoke the name with simple satisfaction at having tracked it down through the mazes of his beleaguered brain. 'What's the situation?' He had so far averted his eyes from what lay only a few yards away.

'The oddest feature,' Cordiner said, 'is that it's almost as if she had been laid out for burial, flowers strewn and so on. But she looks entirely peaceful, there doesn't seem to be a mark on her, and certainly no sign of a struggle. Though we can't investigate, of course, until the photographer's been to do his stuff.'

'Suicide, I reckon.' To Barker, being robustly incapable of being in uncertainties, mysteries or doubts was a positive virtue in a police officer. 'Got depressed or something, the way girls do, comes up here, sets it all up to look romantic, then takes something and lies down. To punish some young man, no doubt. They watch far too many films, that's their problem.'

Cordiner frowned. 'There are some aspects –' he began, then broke off. 'Sorry, Doctor, don't let us hold you back.'

At the best of times, Webb didn't like corpses, but there was no putting it off any longer. He swallowed hard, and with Barker and Cordiner respectfully a pace behind walked across to stand over the shrouded figure.

The warm scents of summer were all about him, and in the stillness, he could hear a lark singing somewhere high above their heads. Everything else, even time itself, seemed in suspension, waiting for him to break the silence. Webb looked down.

'Good grief,' he said heavily. 'It's one of my patients. Willow Lampton.'

With a surreptitious sigh of relief, Chrissie Webb sat down at an empty table in the far corner of the TA Drill Hall. Mercifully the ladies of her acquaintance were all sitting at tables oversubscribed already, allowing her to pantomime greetings without being obliged to join them.

She had made a dutiful round of the stalls, handing in her own unwanted bits and pieces and buying other people's even less appealing discards, which would do for handing in next year. She had also, of course, given them a cash donation; Richard need never know.

She was feeling better now, even quite tempted by the prospect of coffee and one of Dorothy's Ladies' famous cakes. She was just being competitively served by two helpers when she saw the young registrar, Paul Arkwright, come into the hall. They had met at a party a couple of weeks ago, and she wondered if he would acknowledge her.

Theirs had been a curious encounter. It was at a large drinks do at the handsome Georgian house (with paddock) belonging to one of the senior consultants. Richard had become absorbed in a group of men discussing shooting – possibly, thought Chrissie, the most uninteresting subject in the world apart from other people's dress sizes, which was what the women were talking about.

At least the wine was flowing freely. Chrissie held out her glass for another refill from one of the circulating waitresses, then unobtrusively slipped out through a glass door into the deserted conservatory. Plants were often more interesting than people – certainly than these people – and she had just stopped to commune with a magnificent bougainvillea when the door just behind her was suddenly flung open, catching her on the shoulder.

'Oh – I'm sorry!' A young man stood in the doorway, a pleasant-faced young man, tall and loose-limbed with untidy brown hair. He was, she noticed, looking tired, dispirited, and not entirely sober.

He was very penitent. 'I'm really terribly sorry! Did I hurt you?' He bumped into the door as he tried to shut it.

'No, not at all,' she assured him, amused.

'Well, thank goodness for that. You see,' he confided, 'I'm afraid I'm just a little bit drunk.'

'So am I,' Chrissie said. 'I'm drunk because I'm bored. What's your excuse?'

'I'm drunk because I'm depressed. Why are you bored?'

'Why are you depressed? Let's sit down here, shall we, and I'll tell you if you tell me.'

'No, I've got a better idea. You sit down, I'll fetch another bottle, and then we can talk.'

By the time Richard came looking for her at the end of the party, Chrissie had heard Paul's life story, about Marnie and Willow and the general mess he felt he had got himself into. She had listened, without presuming to give advice, and they hadn't ever got round to her boredom problem, but she didn't mind that. Boredom was boring even to talk about, and she had enjoyed his confidences. It had even made her feel almost like a fully paid-up member of the human race.

She was gratified now when Paul, spotting her, at once waved and made his way over.

'Anyone sitting here? Oh good.' He sat down as one of the bored ladies pounced, with a triumphant glance at her slower companion, to serve him with coffee.

'How nice to see you again,' Chrissie said. 'Nice, if unexpected. Are you a closet coffee morning freak?'

'Well, not exactly, but the hospital puts a three-line whip on this one. And you have to say the food is good.' He eyed the plate on the table hungrily. 'This is breakfast. Yum!'

Chrissie laughed. 'You're looking a lot better than you were the last time I saw you.'

He finished his mouthful. 'I can't tell you how much better. You were brilliant the other day – I'm sure I didn't thank you properly.'

'Think nothing of it. It was the most interesting conversation I've had in weeks. No, make that months. Tell me what's happened to improve things.'

'Today, as they say, is the first day of the rest of my life.' The words were flippant, but his tone was entirely serious. 'Last night, I did what I should have had the guts to do long ago.'

Chrissie raised her eyebrows. 'Willow?'

'Willow. I don't know, something just snapped. I'd been on call for a couple of days, and maybe being completely shattered let me see things more clearly. I had simply had enough – finish. Willow Lampton is out of my life forever, and—'

Chrissie became suddenly aware that two of the hovering ladies had moved in closer, and she could almost see their ears flapping. She jerked her head warningly and murmured, 'Earwigging!'

'What? Oh, I see.' Embarrassed, Paul turned pink. 'Er, well, er—'

'They've certainly managed to get a good turnout today,' Chrissie said brightly, in a clear, ringing voice, conducting the conversation into safer channels as disappointed, the eavesdroppers drifted further away. 'Quite a few people from the hospital, I think, aren't there?'

Paul turned to look about him. 'Yes, quite a lot. Oh, and there's Andrew Lomax – that's a surprise. He's a solicitor, and this is hardly his scene. He's probably looking for me. Andrew!'

The young man who came over was a cheerfully chaotic individual with a sunny nature and a ready smile.

He wasn't smiling today. Paul, just about to perform the introductions, saw his expression and frowned.

'You're looking a bit grim, Andy. Are you all right?'

His friend sat down heavily, not appearing to notice Chrissie. 'You haven't heard, have you?'

'Heard what?'

'About Willow.'

Paul's face hardened and there was contempt in his voice. 'Willow! I don't want to hear about Willow. As far as I am concerned, Willow Lampton is history.'

'Paul, shut up. She's dead.'

The noise of the hall ebbed and flowed around them. Somebody laughed. Somebody else coughed. The words Andrew had spoken made no more sense than the babble of mingled voices.

'I don't understand. What do you mean?'

'She's dead, Paul. Everyone's talking about it. They found her up on the common this morning.'

Paul turned white, as if the wound he had so confidently declared closed might have opened again, agonisingly, and Chrissie became unnaturally still.

'It's all over the town. No one seems to know quite what happened, suicide perhaps. Of course there are the ghouls talking about murder, but—'

'Murder!' The involuntary exclamation came from one of the eavesdropping women. She covered her mouth guiltily with her hand, but her eyes were wide and she and her companion exchanged appalled, significant glances.

It was just after half past twelve when Hannah got home for lunch to her neat little cottage. It was ideally situated, only a hundred yards from the Llanfeddin Stores and not much more from her sister's house, right in the heart of their domain. Not much could happen in Llanfeddin that she didn't filter through her net curtains.

The cottage represented her profit on a ten-year investment in matrimony. Cheap at twice the price, her ex-husband had said in the embittered letter which accompanied the sizeable cheque, and it wasn't her problem if he'd been forced to sell half his farm to buy her off.

It had let her take a quarter-share in her sister's business, with enough over for the domestic luxuries – modest enough, she considered – that she craved as compensation for ten years spent in a two-hundred-year-old farmhouse with oak beams, draughts and spiders.

She shut the imitation Georgian double-glazed front door quietly, and the thick pile of the red-and-gold-patterned Wilton carpet muffled her footsteps as she crossed the hall. Gavin's bedroom door was shut, and if he was asleep and she woke him – well, he was unpredictable, was Gavin.

Hannah never admitted, even to herself, that she was actually afraid of her son. She certainly wasn't afraid of anyone else.

Over the years of growing up with an overbearing elder sister, she had honed her tongue into a razor-edged weapon, so that even Glynis treated her with a wary respect, and Gavin's father had been left with psychological scars as marked as the sabre cuts seaming a dueller's cheek.

Yet somehow it had never worked with Gavin. He was impervious, lacking the emotional crevices in which a poison dart could lodge. He took after her father and Glynis in having a forceful character, but allied to it was something else – something she didn't like to think about.

The door to the lounge was open and he wasn't slumped in front of the thirty-two-inch TV on the cream leather couch. He hadn't been in the kitchen, either: there were no dirty plates and pans and crumbs of toast and packets of butter left to sully the mosaic tile surface in her de luxe pine kitchen.

Hannah went over to switch on the kettle. Was he still in bed, or had he gone out – or even never come in at all? She'd slept soundly last night, hadn't heard him come back on that old motorbike of his, and sometimes he stayed with that woman in Stetford for days at a time. Perhaps one fine day he might even move in with her permanently.

Not that Hannah didn't love him. Of course she did. Naturally. He was her son, wasn't he? He'd never been an easy child, though. Always on the fringes of trouble, always getting out of it with the quick excuse or the smart answer. He was clever, Gavin was, and he could have made something of himself, if he'd ever tried to keep a job for more than a week or two.

Glynis was always telling her how lucky she was, comparing poor Bronwen and her mongrel brood unfavourably with her strong-willed, good-looking nephew. But Bronwen had her own council house, and Glynis didn't have to live with them, did she?

Plenty of mothers would be delighted that their grown-up son still wanted to live at home. But somehow she'd never thought that when he was twenty-seven she'd still be supporting him, and cooking and cleaning and doing his laundry (and finding it crumpled up back in the laundry basket if it wasn't done to his liking) – and going to her purse to find that twenty pounds had somehow disappeared.

And then there was that business with the policeman's wife. Hannah had been shaken by that, no doubt about it. There had been something in Gavin's eyes as he gave his slick explanation . . .

Not that she'd said anything, of course. Glynis, aflame with indignation, had run the hate campaign with even more than her usual righteous fervour, and Hannah, as always, had added her modicum of sweet poison. The charge, according to Gavin's lawyer, was all but completely discredited now, so that was all right, wasn't it?

The kettle boiled. Hannah looked longingly at the weekly magazine she had brought in with her. 'Second Time Around – How to get your (Next!) Man,' it said on the cover, and she really fancied the rare treat of sitting out in the sunshine with that and a cup of coffee and a sandwich. But if Gavin was just going to appear, wanting his breakfast—

Was that him now? She heard his bedroom door open and shut, and her son appeared in the kitchen doorway, barefoot and in his night attire of black T-shirt and grey boxer shorts.

He was looking as rough as she had ever seen him, his eyes sunken and bloodshot, his complexion pasty under the heavy stubble, but she knew better than to comment.

'Morning,' she offered with the tentative air of a bather using his toe to test water suspected of being at sub-Arctic temperature.

He grunted. 'Kettle boiling?' he said, and as she went to make coffee for him slumped on to a chair at the table. The morning paper was lying there; he edged it round to peer at the headlines, then pushed it away again.

'What do you want for breakfast?' Hannah set the mug of strong black instant coffee down in front of him.

'What do you think?' He shut his eyes as if it were painful to keep them open.

She fetched the frying pan. 'What time did you get in

last night? You were very quiet – I didn't hear you.'

The silence which greeted her remark was so intense and so prolonged that she looked over her shoulder at him. He was sitting up, and the bleary eyes were fixed on her with an expression she could not read.

'Well, you wouldn't have, would you? Getting forgetful, you are – must be old age.'

Was that menace in his tone? Confused, she stammered, 'What – what—'

'Did you watch the telly last night?'

'Yes – there was a film—'

'What was it?'

Bewildered by this unprecedented interest in her activities, for a moment her mind did indeed go blank.

'I can't remember – oh yes, wait. It was an old Clint Eastwood. *Every Which Way But Loose*, that's right. But Gavin, what do you want to know for?'

'That's good. I've seen that. Anyone come in?'

'No, nobody. But—'

'So it was just the two of us, having a cosy evening at home, watching it together.'

Hannah went cold. 'Gavin, what've you been doing, then?'

He got up and came over to her, standing too close. He hadn't showered or brushed his teeth; the rank smell of sweat and stale alcohol seemed almost as aggressive as his looming, powerful presence.

'I haven't been doing anything, Mam. How could I, when I was here with you? Wasn't I?'

His eyes were glittering, and she swallowed nervously.

'That's – that's right, Gavin.'

She felt, rather than saw, tension go out of him. He lounged away and sat down again. 'What did you give me for my tea, Mam?' His thin smile, so like her own, mocked her.

Hannah moistened her lips. 'Chicken roll. Chicken roll and salad.'

'And what did I have for sweet? I hope it was one of my favourites?'

She thought of her own meal. 'Creamed rice. Cold, with jam.'

'Yeuch! That muck! I can't think how I put up with it.'

He was playing with her now, and she, who had so often taken secret pleasure in the delicate tormenting of a victim, squirmed helplessly in her turn.

'All that,' he went on, 'and a lousy night on the telly. What a devoted son I must be, when I could have been having a night out with my mates.

'You going to keep me waiting all day for my breakfast, then?'

Her heart thumping, she turned back to the frying pan and put in four sausages.

They had only just begun to sizzle when the front door opened and her sister's voice called, 'Hannah! You in the kitchen, then?'

When she appeared in the doorway, it was obvious that she was big with news. Her heavy face was animated and her sallow cheeks flushed with exhilaration.

'Well, whatever do you think!' She had been speaking in Welsh, but seeing Gavin (who had failed CSE Welsh, a feat reputedly more difficult than gaining a first at Oxford) continued in English.

'They've found a body up there, on the common, haven't they? And who do you think it is?'

She inserted a fine rhetorical pause, but barely left time for any response. 'That Willow Lampton, isn't it! Dead!'

Hannah dropped the fork she had been using to prod the sausages. Bending down to pick it up she took longer than was strictly necessary, to allow the return of the blood which had drained from her head. She heard Gavin's voice saying flatly, 'Dead? Willow Lampton?'

'Oooh, Gav, you knew her, didn't you? Forgotten that, I had. One of your girlfriends, wasn't she, before she went posh and took up with doctors instead?'

'That was years ago.' He got up and went across to the door. 'So what happened to her then, Auntie Glyn?'

84

'They're not sure, are they? Might be an overdose, might be suicide maybe. Well, asking for trouble, that girl was, with all her notions and the airs she gave herself too – and no better than she should be, either.'

Then, perhaps recalling her own position in a glasshouse of extreme fragility, she abandoned her assault on Willow's reputation and hurried on.

'Lying on the common, she was, all got up with flowers round her neck. Sounds like drugs to me, with that hippie father and all.'

With the flourish of a jazz musician, Glynis finished her solo spot, expecting her sister's improvisation on the theme she had stated, but Hannah seemed disappointingly preoccupied with her cooking.

'I'm going to get dressed, Mam. I'll be back in a minute.' Gavin went out and at the cooker Hannah turned the sausages with a hand that wasn't quite steady. Suicide, she kept telling herself, suicide.

'How did you hear, anyway?' Her voice sounded calm enough.

'Jennie Wilson's mam and dad went up there for their usual walk and found her, didn't they. Jennie had to go and fetch them – poor souls, shocked, they were, and him not too good with his heart. And the whole place swarming with those police vans and cars and all, isn't it.'

'But what are they needing all that for? Just an overdose, by mistake, most likely. The way that Hal Lampton keeps his fences, he could have left his nasty stuff lying around anywhere. And with her always so busy thinking about the next man, she could have put it in her tea.'

Encouraged by this return to form, Glynis readily agreed. 'But look you, they don't *know*, do they? Not actually *know*, not until they get in all their reports and examinations.'

'Know what?'

Glynis sucked her teeth in pleasurable speculation. 'Well, you never know, do you? Could be murder, couldn't it?'

Hannah had just cracked an egg. As she turned to stare at her sister in horror, it broke, landing on the pristine surface of her Amtico floor.

'That's a fine mess you're going to have to clear up,' Glynis said in Welsh, surveying it.

To Hannah, distractedly mopping up, it sounded like an echo of her own thoughts.

Chapter Six

In Agnes Winthrop's garden, birdsong from the surrounding trees and the clear, delicate cadences of falling water from a little stream mingled to make tranquil summer music. The varied greens of the lush grass and foliage, emerald through to sharpest lime green, were almost painfully vivid in the brilliant sunshine.

Jake the dog was lying at his mistress's feet, stretched out in luxurious abandon on the warmed stones of the patio outside the Victorian conservatory. Through its open doors a bee buzzed importantly and with the air of arriving for a business meeting landed on the waxen lip of a richly-scented white flower before, throwing dignity to the winds, he forced his plump body up inside the narrow trumpet, wriggling like someone struggling into a pair of skin-tight jeans.

Sitting in one of the green wicker chairs, Agnes watched his antics as she listened to her guest. She was a good listener; she said little, but her silences seemed to Tessa supportive rather than judgemental, and she was surprisingly easy to talk to.

'You know the "Phew, thank you, God, that was a narrow escape" feeling?'

Agnes's laugh seemed to have been surprised out of her, as if she seldom had occasion to be amused.

'Well, that was about the level of thought I gave to being Matthew's stepmother. Of course, I made all the right noises, about how sad it was that I didn't have the chance to get to know him, and how dreadful it must be for poor David to have his child reject him. Oh yes, and what a cow Lara must be to do this. But if I'd been straight with David, or even myself, I'd have admitted that she was doing me a good turn – David all to myself and a touch of the moral high ground as well. All pretty despicable, really. And now – well, now—'

She paused. Agnes leaned forward to refill her cup with coffee. 'Go on,' she said calmly. 'You won't shock me.'

Without warning, Tessa's eyes filled with tears and she fished for a handkerchief.

'Oh, it's miserably selfish, I know. He's only a kid and he's had a rotten time through no fault of his own. I ought to be eager to love him because he's David's son and dying to do what I can to make things better. It's just – well, David's all there is for me here. I'm trapped in this bloody awful place where everyone loves to hate me and I feel victimised and spied on and scared and I can't even paint any more. The one thing that stops me tunnelling out and escaping back to London is my life with David.'

She was twisting her handkerchief into a tight, furious rope.

'And – I know this sounds horrible, but I can't help it – I despair at the thought of sharing our scarce, precious time together with a teenage delinquent with a chip on his shoulder the size of Big Ben.'

'Who is it that you're so angry with?'

At the quiet question, Tessa bridled. 'Angry? What do you mean? I'm *upset*, but—'

Agnes gestured towards the evidence in her hands. Tessa frowned, looked down, stared, then flushed scarlet.

'Oh, I see. Yes.' She thought for a moment. 'I wish I could say I was angry with myself. I would be, if I were a better person.

'But it's David, of course, isn't it, only I haven't let myself admit it. I'm angry because I hate his past life casting a shadow on our nice, pretty, romantic little twosome. I'm angry because I need to talk to him, and he hasn't phoned. And I'm not only angry, I'm terrified at the thought of coping with a surly teenager all through the school holidays while David's out at work. And I'm probably even subconsciously furious with him for bringing me here in the first place, even though it was as much my decision as his.

'And yes, I do know that I'm being totally unreasonable and childish and pathetic, but you did ask.'

By now the maltreated handkerchief had become wholly inadequate to its purpose. Agnes went to fetch a box of tissues from the house and Jake, distressed by her distress, made her laugh through her tears at his anxious attempts to lick them off her cheeks.

Shamefaced, Tessa accepted a handful of tissues, mopped her face and blew her nose. 'Thanks. And thank you, Jake, it's OK. I've stopped now – good dog. Agnes, I'm so sorry – I had no idea I was going to do that. Gosh, how embarrassing.'

'Not at all. I'm sure it's done you good. And it's – it's something of a novelty for me these days to be able to play confidante.' She seemed almost to have to force herself to say something so intimate.

Tessa bit her lip. 'Here am I, moaning away, when it's actually much worse for you than it is for me. Living here like this, I mean, not able to escape.'

A faint, sardonic smile crossed the other woman's face. 'Oh, there are many things much worse than this, believe me. But bad experiences bring with them rich and strange gifts. Detachment, for one, and clear-sightedness. I have no confusion at all now about what is important to me.

'The beauty out there,' her gesture embraced the garden, the hills, the arching blue vault of the sky, 'and the freedom to walk in the fresh air, to watch the birds and the wild creatures. That's important, and my dog, and my son, naturally. And perhaps,' she glanced shyly at Tessa, 'the pleasure of finding a friend?'

Tessa leaned across to squeeze her hand, but did not interrupt her.

'But the little things – those silly women in the shop – I genuinely don't care. They amuse me, in fact, with their self-importance and their absorption in the funny, trivial little universe they've constructed for themselves.'

'Like gerbils,' Tessa said suddenly. 'I used to keep gerbils in a tank. All sharp noses and busybodying about in their elaborate sawdust world.'

Agnes laughed. 'Very like that.'

Tessa was taken with her fantasy. 'I can just see Mrs Guest as a gerbil. I must draw a little gerbil Llanfeddin for you sometime. Though I gather Bronwen might have to be a visiting hamster . . .

'But to get back to my practical problem. What on earth do I do with a London child, out here in the country? And it's not as if he wants to come. Lara's rubbing it in that this is a punishment for him, so he's more or less obliged to hate it.'

'Have you thought –' Agnes began, then stopped.

'Go on.'

'I hope you won't think it impertinent of me to say this. But have you considered that he may have done this deliberately, as a way to ensure his father's attention?'

'He'll get that all right. David will go berserk.' Then she sighed. 'Psychologically speaking, I'm sure you're right. So he'll be jealous of me as well.'

'As, perhaps, you are of him?'

'Touché.' Tessa grimaced. 'What a real little sweetheart I am, to be sure. I'm sorry to have inflicted this on you – an unedifying display of the dark side of my nature.' She got up. 'After this, you may be so horrified that you never want to see me again.'

'Far from it. It's been a long time since I've had a conversation like this with anyone. Except Johnnie, of course.'

As it had done before, her voice softened as she said his name. Tessa said tactfully, 'I hope I may meet him sometime.'

'Of course you shall. He hasn't had an easy life, my poor Johnnie. He lost a child, and then his marriage broke up. Sometimes I think he's quite a lonely man.'

'He's lucky he's got you. You're a very wise lady. May I really come back?'

'Yes, of course. At any time. And bring your Matthew – I'd like to meet him. Fourteen isn't an easy age, either to be or to live with, but Johnnie was very interesting at that stage.'

Then she hesitated, as if uncertain whether to go on.

'I haven't talked about this for years,' Agnes said slowly, almost painfully. 'Johnnie isn't my natural son, in fact. He was my late husband's son, but I became his mother when he was ten, and he has been the most wonderful thing in my life. So perhaps you may find that your Matthew is actually a treasure rather than a burden.'

Tessa was very touched. 'Thank you for telling me that. It's something for me to hold on to – even if Matthew doesn't sound as if he's exactly on course to be a consultant cardiologist! And don't think I won't shamelessly impose on your good nature.'

'Jake and I will take him for very long, exhausting walks.'

Tessa laughed, then sighed. 'I really will try to make the best of it. But something tells me it isn't going to be easy. Thank you for the coffee, and for everything else too.'

Purged, that was what she felt, Tessa decided gratefully as she set off on the walk home. It was as if admitting her anger had shaped all that unacknowledged ill-feeling into a positive force, and seeing someone else who had overcome far greater difficulties than the ones she was struggling with was an inspiration.

When David phoned, she would be able, now, to break the news of his son's disgrace with real sympathy and unselfish understanding. There was probably a message from him on the answerphone right now. And miraculously, she could feel an idea for a painting coming on.

Brimming with the milk of human kindness and fired with the creative urge, Tessa quickened her steps.

Despite Sister Morley's tight-lipped instructions, Megan Griffiths hadn't the slightest intention of hurrying back from her lunch break. Not likely, when Sister had been so late in letting her go that there was no one to gossip with in the canteen, and all that was left was cheese salad.

In solitary state, Megan ate it with a bad grace. She didn't have anything *against* cheese, exactly, or salad for that matter, it was just that it wasn't what she would call a proper dinner. So she bought a chocolate bar and a magazine from the WVS shop and reprehensibly went out to sit on a bench in the sunshine, nibbling and reading an article headed 'How to look Ten Pounds Thinner – Tonight!' for as long as she dared.

If Sister noticed, she decided, she would say that she wasn't a slave, she had rights the same as anyone else, and a full hour for her lunch was one of them. It sounded quite impressive as she rehearsed it in her head, marching defiantly back to the ward.

She was not, however, prepared for the reception awaiting her. Sister was hovering at the entrance to the ward, her face flushed with agitation; she came in for the attack like a falcon swooping to fall like a thunderbolt on some hapless pigeon.

'For goodness' sake, Griffiths, what sort of time do you call this? Where have you been? We've had people hunting for you for the last half-hour.'

'I'm sorry, Sister. I – I felt a little faint and went out to get some fresh air,' Megan said, instantaneously rejecting the peroration on human rights in favour of this finely-judged mixture of meekness and mendacity.

'In there.' Sister pushed her unceremoniously into her office. 'The police want to talk to you.'

'The *police*!' The colour left Megan's rosy cheeks as the alchemy of terror transformed a base lie into twenty-four carat truth.

In Sister's office, a swarthy tough-looking man in a short-sleeved shirt and grey cotton trousers was sitting at the desk, on which a girl with alarmingly orange hair and a mini-skirt was perching. There wasn't a uniform in sight, and Megan stared in bewilderment from one to the other.

They pulled out ID cards and introduced themselves, Detective Constable Watson and Detective Sergeant Pardoe. Detectives! That made it worse. Without waiting to be asked, Megan sank on to the one remaining chair.

She moistened dry lips. 'What have I – what did you want to speak to me about?'

She had almost said, What have I done? Dreadful, that would

have been, as if she thought she might have poisoned half-a-dozen patients. Oh goodness, perhaps she had!

It took a moment to grasp that her reputation was unblemished, and a little longer to absorb the humiliating fact that she, Megan Griffiths, was probably the last person in the hospital to hear about Willow Lampton.

WDC Watson waited patiently while Megan uttered appropriate cries of shock and distress before, glancing at her notes, she said, 'Nurse Evans – she's a friend of yours, isn't she? She suggested that you might have been the last person in the hospital to talk to Willow. Would that be right?'

Soothed by this elevation to significance, Megan assured them of her ready co-operation. This was gossip given official status, gossip as a civic duty.

As a connoisseur in these matters, however, she realised that however willing the source might be, the content was sadly weak. The constable made a few brief jottings in her notebook – Willow had seemed just as usual, she was all dressed up, she hadn't said where she was going – but Megan could sense that she had lost her audience. The sergeant's eyes were visibly glazing over.

He got to his feet. 'Thank you, miss. You've been very helpful. We mustn't keep you – that boss of yours seemed pretty keen to get you back to work.'

The girl slid off the desk as Megan pulled a face. 'Can I just check that time with you? It was a bit after six o'clock when she left the cloakroom, is that right? And you didn't leave with her, or see her drive off in her car?'

Megan was shaking her head regretfully, when she remembered.

'Oh, but I did see her after that, didn't I! It went right out of my head, with the shock, see.'

DS Pardoe sat down again. WDC Watson fixed her bright hazel eyes on Megan's face.

As she told them of Willow's encounter with Dr Arkwright, she had no cause to complain of lack of attention from her audience.

★

Willow Lampton's room affected David Cordiner as her body had not. He had been a little troubled by his earlier reaction; the peaceful corpse, like some marble effigy on a seventeenth-century tomb, had spoken to him of mortality, not ugly death. It was only here, among the relics of her life, that he sensed her restless spirit.

On her dressing table, open jars of face cream still showed the marks of her fingers, with the tissue on which she had blotted her lipstick crumpled beside them. Expensive-looking under-wear had been discarded in a silken pile on the floor and a cupboard door hung open with a jumble of shoes half in, half out. Dresses were tossed down carelessly on a chair, as if submitted to a brief scrutiny and then rejected. Cordiner was no expert, but she seemed to have a surprisingly extensive wardrobe for someone living on a nurse's pay.

A paperback with a lurid cover lay, its pages splayed to keep the place, on her bedside table. The bed itself was unmade, the sheets still crumpled by the weight of her body, and in the hollow of the dented pillow were a few blonde hairs. Squarely in the middle of it was placed a packet of contraceptive pills; she had been meticulous about that, at least.

He had tried to keep an open mind. Suicide, Barker had proclaimed authoritatively, and Cordiner had done his best to accord that opinion the respect due to senior rank and long experience. The trouble was, it was a conclusion he had dismissed whenever he saw the flowers. She hadn't done that herself. He doubted whether it was even physically possible.

No, someone had scattered them about the dead girl – sweets to the sweet – in some sick and sinister private ceremony.

And this most certainly wasn't the way she would have left her room if she had intended never to return.

Still, he searched dutifully for any note. Feeling uncomfort-ably like a voyeur, he riffled among her filmy teddies and lacy slips and panties and bras. He found her nursing diploma, dog-eared and shoved negligently into the bottom of a drawer, which probably told you how she felt about it. Some nurses framed theirs, but the only things framed in Willow Lampton's bedroom were three photographs of herself, in studied and striking poses.

There was a large envelope holding what looked like receipts and statements neatly in one drawer along with notepaper (expensive, grey deckle-edged), a few business letters and documentation for the car they had found in the car park at the common, which was probably, even now, being subjected to forensic examination. She didn't seem to have kept anything very personal – old birthday cards, programmes, that sort of sentimental stuff.

It was hot in the little room under the eaves of the rundown cottage where she had lived with her father, and a blue-bottle was buzzing impatiently on the windowsill where the paint was flaking. She had not aired the room before she left, and along with the perfume of her cosmetics it held a heavier musky undertone – the lingering scent of her living, breathing, sweating flesh. To a parent, or a lover, that could only be unbearable.

He opened the window to dispel that last, ephemeral trace. The bluebottle escaped, and a butterfly he had not noticed spread its painted wings and wafted out and away into the sunshine. The symbolism caught at his throat.

When he went downstairs, Hal Lampton was sitting at a table with a garish oil-cloth in the cheerless kitchen of the cottage he rented along with the hundred-acre hill farm. There was a sweetish smell, like cheap aftershave, which Cordiner would have had no difficulty in identifying even if Lampton's name had not figured in the Operation Lambchop list, but it was hardly the moment to mention this.

Lampton was a big man running to seed, with jowls like a bloodhound and a bloodhound's bloodshot eyes. His greasy grey hair was receding at the front but long at the back and gathered into a straggling pony tail. There was a cold cup of tea on the table in front of him, a milky film settled on its surface, and he was looking at it as if it were a novelty of uncertain provenance.

A policewoman, trained in bereavement counselling, had been sent out earlier to help break the news; she had returned to the police station seriously put out at having her expertise not only rejected, but despised.

Lampton had been no more welcoming to Cordiner in the afternoon, but had agreed, indifferently, to his search of Willow's bedroom.

Now, Cordiner held out the pile of items he had abstracted. 'May I have your permission to take these in for examination, sir? I'll give you a receipt, of course.'

The vague, bleary eyes focused on him briefly. 'Take what you bloody well like. *She* won't be needing them any more, will she?' He had not shaved today, and his faded Jimi Hendrix T-shirt looked as if it, too, had led an eventful life.

'I'm sorry.' Such a hopelessly inadequate remark, but what else was there to say? Scribbling the receipt, he added, 'There are a few things we'll want to ask you, but I won't trouble you further today.'

He set the form down on the table and was turning to go when Lampton burst out, 'What happened? Who did this to her, tell me that?'

'I'm afraid we don't know the cause of death yet, sir.'

'Suicide, that moronic woman said this morning.' He laughed suddenly, incongruously. 'She didn't know much about my daughter, did she? Willow was far too fond of her pretty little hide to damage a hair of it.'

Cordiner had said, I'm sorry, already. What else was there to say in response to that, he wondered desperately, that wasn't positively insulting? Fortunately, Lampton did not seem to expect a reply.

'We've lived here, just the two of us, for the last ten years, ever since my wife took off. God knows where she is now.'

Lampton's grimy fingers pushed about some tell-tale stubs in the ashtray in front of him. 'I owed Willow a roof over her head – and it should have been more than that, according to her – but we didn't get on. She never made any secret of her contempt for me. Fair enough – I've never claimed to have been much of a father. But then, I didn't think she was much of a daughter either. She was hard as nails, Willow, only interested in money and what she could get out of people.'

He paused again. 'We didn't, I suppose, like each other very much.'

There was another long, uncomfortable silence. Then he said, with a ghastly attempt at a smile, 'That should make it better, shouldn't it? But it doesn't. It makes it worse.'

Tears gathered and began to trickle down the seamed lines of his cheeks.

Cordiner said awkwardly, 'Look, is there anything I can do? Anyone I could contact – family, friends, a neighbour—'

'I have no friends, my relatives hate me and my neighbours are a pernicious set of gossiping harpies. Just sod off and leave me alone, will you? Shut the door as you leave.'

There was nothing Cordiner could do, except obey.

He drove away soberly, his mind on the tragedy of family estrangement and inevitably, painfully, on Matthew.

Painfully, but briefly. There were too many other considerations to waste time on the insoluble problems of his personal life. George had put him in charge of the case, at least until after the post mortem tomorrow had pronounced officially on whether it was suicide or murder. He'd have to go to that, and try to look as if it wasn't the first time he'd been in a mortuary. Try not to pass out or throw up, come to that.

It was murder, of course, whatever George might think. And if it was murder, it would be a major operation – national press, TV probably, given the off-beat angle – and they would probably want to pull in a senior man to front it, from Wrexham perhaps, or Shrewsbury or Wolverhampton. Wrexham, most likely; he'd met the Detective Chief Inspector there, and he was all right.

The last thing he wanted was to be diverted to the other case that had come in this morning – a break-in at a cash and carry in Stetford. Normally he would have taken charge of that, but he'd despatched DS Owen to deal with it. He was a sound officer, more than capable of dealing with petty crime, and even

if they had got away with £20,000-worth of drink and ciga-
rettes, petty crime was all it was.

Owen certainly didn't need his inspector to hold his hand,
and for Cordiner it would be intolerable to be moved off the
most challenging criminal investigation ever likely to come his
way on this patch. George had told him proudly that the last
murder in Stetford had been a domestic where the husband
confessed immediately back in 1975.

Well, he had twenty-four hours to establish a grip on the case
which would make him indispensable, whoever took charge.

Cordiner felt the old, addictive adrenaline surge as he headed
down into Stetford, mentally listing the next stages. Sue and Joe
had been at the hospital: they might come back with all sorts of
goodies. He'd have to contact Willow's bank, get all her statements for the past year, say, and run them through against the
papers he'd taken from her drawer, to check his impression that
she'd been living above a nurse's means. And she hadn't been
subsidised by her father, that was for sure.

Lampton would have to be properly interviewed, of course,
and whatever friends the girl might have had. Particularly
about the men in her life; Webb had indicated that men had
featured very significantly in Willow's short existence. It also
sounded as if she might have made enemies; jealous women,
perhaps?

But her laying-out did not speak of hatred. Again, his
thoughts turned to the wilted white flowers. What had
prompted that? If it were indeed a man who had killed her, what
did that say about the sort of man he was?

A romantic, presumably. A homicidal romantic. But how
did you recognise a man with a romantic nature? He wasn't
going to wear it like a wild rose in his buttonhole. In fact, most
men would conceal that side from everyone except the woman
they loved almost as rigorously as they would conceal a homicidal streak.

As he came up to the roadworks, the lights turned to red.
While he waited, he fished in his pocket for a pen and a scrap
of paper to jot down a few reminders, and came upon the

message they had thrust at him as he passed the front desk earlier. 'Please phone your wife,' it said.

Damn! It had gone right out of his head. He'd better remember to make a quick call when he got back; he was definitely going to be late tonight. He turned it over and scribbled on the back, 'Bank statements. No diary? Check car (handbag)?'

He was just about to add 'Phone Tess', when the lights changed and he had to move off. His mind was racing now. For instance, could Hampton's relationship with his daughter be so bad that he might have killed her himself? The flowers could be a token of repentance, paternal sorrow . . .

Reaching home breathless after her brisk walk, Tessa grinned when she saw that Mr Jarvis had been better than his word, and the 'For Sale' sign had been erected in the garden during her absence. Could it be that he was anxious to forestall any further encounter with her? Just seeing it standing there, in token of her eventual release, made her feel even more positive and optimistic as she let herself into the house.

There was no message from David on the answerphone.

He must be out on some very important case, Tessa told herself firmly. He probably hadn't even been back to the station to collect her message.

But usually, he phoned her once, at the very least, in the course of the day.

Still, the picture was bubbling up ever more strongly in her mind. A mood piece, done *alla prima*, in one session. She hurried through to the studio to set up a primed canvas on the easel, then went to sort out tubes of paint for her palette. She was frowning over two shades of green when the phone rang, but she went to answer it eagerly.

It was Lara again. Suppressing her irritation, Tessa explained politely that no, David hadn't phoned yet, but she would get him to ring back whenever she could make contact.

'Back to his old tricks, is he?' the sharp voice at the other end of the phone said with – was it? – a hint of triumph. Tessa ground her teeth.

Back in her studio, Tessa selected Payne's grey, Monestial blue, yellow ochre, viridian and Alazarin crimson, which she would mix with black to a dark, angry red. With her other preparations made – the turps, the rags, the brushes – she seized a number 12 long flat hog, a wide, blunt brush, and began laying on the first sweeps of colour with firm, fluent, passionate strokes. Powerful, angry strokes.

In no time at all, Tessa was completely absorbed in her creation. So absorbed, that although once or twice she absently put up her hand to the back of her neck, as if to rub away a mild irritation, she did not turn her head to scan the hill and the trees beyond.

Chapter Seven

Colour was slowly leaching out of the sky when at last Tessa set down her brush, wiped her hands on an oily rag and stepped back from her easel. Narrowing her eyes, tipping her head first to one side then the other, she assessed her finished painting.

The tones were sombre, the forms abstract, but the swirling, textured brushstrokes were authoritative and powerful, savage energy trapped in paint. It had worked.

She knew it was good. It had felt right, from the moment she had taken the deep breath and the first sweeping stroke. It just might be the best thing she had ever done, deeper, stronger, born of pain. She was comfortably certain that Roddy Anselm would hail it as another step forward in her development as an artist. Best of all, there were other foetal paintings rapidly growing in her fertile brain, demanding to be given life.

At last, the disabling block she had been suffering from had been swept away, and now she acknowledged the lack of integrity which had erected a barrier between herself and her art. She had refused to be truthful, until today. God bless you, Agnes Winthrop!

Tessa found she was shivering in the aftermath of creative tension. It took a conscious effort to relax her rigid jaw, and she rolled her neck and flexed her wrist and fingers. Her right arm would be stiff tomorrow, but she had suffered in a good cause.

Caught up in the race to finish she had not noticed the encroaching darkness and was suddenly aware that she could hardly see. She switched on the light and then, blinking in the sudden brilliance, studied her watch.

Ten past eight! Good gracious, David was *never* as late as that coming home, if he was on a normal shift. And still he hadn't phoned.

For the first time, she felt unease. Was it possible that something had happened to him? His colleagues might have assumed that he had gone home, while she was fuming because he was still at work and all the time—

Tessa was inclined to worry almost as a hobby, the way some people do needlework, embroidering a ten-minute delay into a road accident, a funeral and long lonely years of widowhood with impressive speed and dexterity. She toyed a little with the idea of David ambushed somewhere, kidnapped and helpless, but even she couldn't make a silk purse out of such unpromising material. He'd become absorbed in something at work and never given her a thought, that was all.

She cleaned up, and wiped off the splashes of paint she always seemed to collect on her face and hands. When she had washed, she went to the kitchen. There was salad waiting to be prepared for supper, but she was damned if she was going to have it meekly ready for whenever he deigned to appear.

She wasn't hungry, herself. She sat down at the table, picked up a newspaper and tried to concentrate on its contents, while determinedly not thinking about David and stopping her foot from tapping. She had never been good at patting her head while rubbing her stomach either.

She was terse when she took Lara's fifth phone call. The fourth had been to give Tessa a different number because she was going out; this was to say she had come back in again. By now Tessa had no doubt at all that Lara was enjoying herself.

It was twenty-five to nine when she heard David's key in the door. For the first time in their married life, she didn't go to greet him.

It was a wasted gesture. David didn't even notice, coming bursting into the kitchen with an apologetic smile. He kissed her. On the cheek.

He was physically there beside her, but she could see that his mind was still elsewhere. He didn't look directly at her, or meet her eyes. And was it her imagination, or was the smell of the police station still clinging to his clothes tonight, that smell which suggested derelict humanity and dust and smoke-filled rooms? She had never noticed it before.

'Darling, I'm so terribly sorry. I've been trying to get a minute to phone you all day, but all hell's broken loose. I can't tell you what it's like.'

He was loving every minute of it, though. He was still on some professional high as he spilled out fluent excuses like a naughty child chattering to avoid reproof. Tessa recognised, with cold misgiving, that it was Lara's husband who stood before her, not her own.

'I won't have a drink. Is supper ready, by any chance? I don't know at all how long I'll get – if something crops up I'll have to go back in. We've got a body on our hands.'

Icily, Tessa said, 'By that, do you mean that someone is *dead*?'

He nodded. 'Murdered, in fact. It won't be properly confirmed until after the post mortem tomorrow, but the more information we get the clearer it becomes. I'm in charge meantime, though of course once it's official they'll probably decide I'm too much of a new boy to handle it, for PR reasons if nothing else.'

'How inconsiderate of them.' She spoke lightly, sarcastically. He hadn't noticed her tone before; would he notice now?

Apparently not. He had scanned the table, glanced hopefully at the oven, then opened the fridge, which he was studying with evident disappointment that his supper was not sitting ready, awaiting his pleasure.

'Can I make a sandwich with this?' He held up a packet of ham. 'The thing is, I may be called—'

'Yes, you said that. Fine. I'll fetch some lettuce to go with it.'

Out of the corner of her eye she caught the look David gave her, a little ashamed, a little nervous, perhaps. Did he expect her to get out a rolling pin?

'This – dead person. Who was it? What happened?'

She had fetched the bread, was, out of habit, spreading it for him. Reassured, he took her place at the table.

'It's quite an off-beat one. A young local girl – a nurse, as it turns out – very pretty, completely unmarked as far as the pathologist could see on initial examination, lying bundled in a blanket over on the common. And the weird thing was, there were wild flowers scattered all round her.'

What had Tessa expected, when he said murder? A knifing in a late-night drunken brawl? A mugging? A domestic fight in Stetford's roughest housing estate? Not this – certainly not this.

The face she turned to him was white with shock. 'A girl? On the common, here?'

She had dropped the knife she was using, took a step towards him. When he got up, she expected him to take her in his arms, to reassure, to protect. Instead, he went past her to the work top to finish making the sandwich.

'Yes, just on the slope looking out over the valley. Very peaceful.' He was entirely matter-of-fact about it.

'And you didn't warn me? A young woman has been murdered half a mile away, and after all that happened before, you didn't think of telling me to be on my guard?'

He shook his head dismissively. 'Sweetheart, if I thought there was the slightest danger, of course I would have.' He sat down again and bit into his sandwich. 'This isn't a random assault by some maniac on a killing spree. She looked as if she'd fallen asleep.'

'Gavin Guest,' Tessa said stiffly. 'Have you forgotten Gavin Guest?'

'Not his form.' It was a professional response, authoritative and patronising. 'You needn't worry about that. He simply hasn't got the profile – or the style, come to that. You couldn't really imagine Guest strewing flowers now, could you?'

She was so angry she couldn't speak. She had never, after the age of seven, inflicted physical violence on another human being, but her hand was going out, apparently of its own volition, to a pottery mug she had left upside down on the draining-board, when the telephone rang.

David was on his feet instantly. 'I'll get it—'

'Shut up and listen,' she interrupted brutally. 'It's probably Lara. I wanted to break this to you gently, but you didn't give me the chance. She's phoned five times today to try to tell you that Matthew's been picked up for shoplifting. She's sending him here tomorrow to stay with us for the summer.'

The news hit him like a jug of water thrown over a drunken man. Looking at her husband's face, white and stricken, Tessa tried to feel truly sorry for him and was dismayed to find that she couldn't, quite.

The moon was full and particularly bright tonight, seeking out the chinks in the curtains and even penetrating the curtains themselves. In the greyish dusk the bedroom was clearly visible, but the colour values were different so that it looked like the ghost of its daytime self, lifeless and bleak.

Tessa was asleep, lost in sleep with childish abandon, her cheek pillowed on her hand and her tousled hair a cloud obscuring her face. She had cried, of course; she had cried, and raged and they had talked and eventually in time-honoured fashion had healed their first major quarrel in bed. Or patched it up, at any rate.

Too shattered to sleep, David listened to her soft, even breathing with tenderness which he tried hard not to taint with envy. How long was it since he had been able to sleep like that? Five years, ten? She only sighed and turned over as he slipped quietly out of bed and went downstairs.

The atmosphere of the house was chill and unwelcoming, even on this mild summer night. He did not switch on the lights; he went to sit in the ancient, sagging armchair that stood in the corner of Tessa's studio at the back and stared unseeing out into the shadowy landscape.

Matthew, Matthew! He bent forward, put his head in his

hands and groaned. What had they done to their son, he and Lara?

He was fighting to keep it in perspective. A group of lads, egging each other on to shoplift for devilment. Just kids being kids, hardly what you could call a new problem. They'd probably done the same thing in the Dark Ages, nicking apples off the market stalls.

He'd seen it often enough himself, and he knew the form. Pull them in, give them a caution by way of a slap on the wrist to scare them so they wouldn't do it again, and most of them didn't.

Some of them did, though. Some of them were at it again the minute you let them go, hellbent on the sad, inexorable progress to disaster. Those were the ones who didn't scare easily, or the ones who had done it in the first place for darker reasons than devilment. The ones who, when you read the social enquiry reports, had an absent father in eight cases out of ten.

He hadn't meant to be an absent father. Even when Lara left, taking Matt, it had never occurred to him that this was what he would become. There would be weekends, holidays; eventually, surely, things would settle down with Lara so they wouldn't go on tearing the child apart between them.

The easy way out was to blame Lara, blame her selfishness, her unscrupulousness, her spite. It was true that she had chosen to walk out, had poisoned Matt's mind so that she could use him as a weapon against his father.

But that wasn't the whole truth. If he was honest, he knew that it had happened because she was hurting, because conventional marital weapons had proved ineffective against his indifference. With him using his work as an impregnable shield against her, he shouldn't have been surprised that the conflict had escalated into a dirty war.

To his horror now, he could see that the pattern had reasserted itself today. He could have made a quick phone call on one of the mobiles, of course he could. It was just that, caught up in events, he hadn't given his wife a thought until late in the day when he recalled the message he had ignored with the old, familiar stab of irritable guilt, resentment, even, that someone had an inconvenient claim upon his attention.

'You're using your job,' Tessa had flung at him this evening, 'to legitimise your selfishness.'

Neatly, painfully put. He'd better get *that* sorted out sharpish, before his second marriage went the way of his first.

The immediate problem was the inevitability that, particularly in the early, crucial stages, there would be room for little else in his life beyond the investigation. From the humblest constable doing a fingertip search of the common on his hands and knees, to the boss (whoever it might be) directing strategy, they would all be bolting their meals and snatching inadequate hours of sleep in their pursuit of the killer.

With Matthew arriving tomorrow, there was no way to spare Tessa the burden of his troubled child. She had a warm heart, his Tess, and in ordinary circumstances it wouldn't have occurred to him to doubt her readiness to love his son.

But these weren't ordinary circumstances. Tessa was suffering enough as it was, far from the support of friends and family. A sullen, disruptive teenager, jealous of her and resentful of David's absences, could make her life a hell on earth.

Of course, it should have been possible to ask Lara to postpone Matt's arrival, just for a week or so, until the immediate crisis was past, but he knew better than to wave the red rag of professional commitment. She'd spelled out to Matt that he was being sent to his father as a punishment; to give her the chance to tell the boy that his father and his new wife didn't want him would be playing into her hands.

He got up, restlessly, to pace to and fro. In the half light, he almost knocked over the easel where Tessa's canvas was drying.

She hadn't told him she'd been working again, though he should have noticed the smell of paint. He should have noticed, and asked her about it. Her work was at least as important to her as his was to him. He switched on the light to look at it.

It was good. It was seriously good. He wasn't an expert, of course, but he'd had a crash course in art appreciation in the past year, and he had no doubt that this was more impressive than anything she had done before.

Even so, his heart sank as he looked at it. He had loved Tessa's paintings; they were like herself, humorous, sunny, joyful. This canvas was different; there was anger there, and pain and fear, its dark strong colours eloquent of a desperation that she had concealed from him.

The 'For Sale' sign was up outside the house now, and that was the best he could do for the moment. When this was over, perhaps he should just apply for a transfer back to London, even if it meant dropping rank. It would be worth it to get the old Tessa back.

But as he looked at the painting, he knew that she had changed. For her, it would never be 'glad confident morning' again, and though it might make her a better artist, his heart ached for what had been lost. He felt, as usual, guilty, and helpless and dispirited as well.

Suddenly he was painfully tired. It must be getting on for midnight. He ought to go to bed, attempt to get some sleep. Tomorrow would be a long and trying day. He was yawning as he switched off the light.

A movement up on the hill caught his eye. Some animal was moving across it in the moonlight at a steady jog trot; a fox, perhaps, going about his murderous business.

And what would he have seen moving on the common last night, if he had been there to see?

The girl's exquisite face haunted him. Tomorrow, when he saw it again in clinical circumstances, the skull beneath the skin would have become apparent as the long, slow dissociation of flesh and bones began. And she, who had loved elegant dresses and trashy novels and silk next to her skin would be reduced in death to a specimen on a cold slab.

Had she believed in an afterlife? Somehow, he doubted it; he wasn't sure that he did himself. But whether or not there was justice in heaven, Willow Lampton was owed human justice, at least.

Another huge yawn seized him. He stumbled upstairs in the

dark and slid into bed beside his sleeping wife. He heard a car pass, saw the beam of light sweep across the ceiling, then with Tessa's soft breath on his cheek fell asleep at last.

The powerful headlamps of John Winthrop's Mercedes reflected back from the blank, close-curtained windows of the houses it passed, illuminating the full width of the narrow, twisting, valley road. From time to time, bright predatory eyes glinted from the hedgerow or dark scurrying life scuttled in panic across the beam of light.

He had stayed late at the hospital again tonight, only this time without the excuse of a professional emergency. Tonight all was quiet on his wards, and he had dismissed his young registrar, surprised and grateful, to catch up on her sleep, and thoroughly flustered the night staff by making an unscheduled late evening round.

John needed his work tonight, needed it as an anaesthetic to numb the immediate pain. While he was considering the long-term prognosis for the frail child in Ward 7 or checking the details of the coronary bypass he would perform tomorrow on the overweight bus driver in Ward 10, there was no room for personal emotions. Like agony. Like despair.

Eventually, of course, he had to leave, to face the drive home alone with his thoughts in the big luxurious car with its leather upholstery and its sophisticated sound system and the heavy doors that shut with an expensive 'thunk'. The Dead Sea apples of success.

Pain. Despair. They were so much easier to control when you must put on a public face, conceal them behind the mask of calm assurance which you could don like a surgical mask before an operation.

He was comfortable with control. Control was safe. Emotions were dangerous. How many lessons did he need to learn that loving meant suffering?

He had believed himself impervious by now. Perhaps, when he reached forty, he had relaxed his guard. Perhaps, whatever his attitude had been, he couldn't have helped himself.

When Willow Lampton first brought herself to his attention, it was because of her cool competence in a medical emergency. She was an excellent nurse, and he admired that. It was only later he had noticed that she was beautiful.

Cathy hadn't been beautiful, or competent. Cathy had been sweet and gentle and helpless. He had been wary of dependence on another human being, having lost his mother as a child, but he was disarmed by her dependence on him. There had been love, and laughter, and then their tiny daughter to whom he had given his heart, simply and naturally. He should have been cold and wise, protected himself against loving too much, but how could he know that Daisy's days would be so pitifully few in number? How could he have foreseen that after her death Cathy would repulse him so violently, so irrationally? The early lesson, imperfectly learned, was driven cruelly home.

Agnes, as always, was there to pick up what was left of his life, but she couldn't replace a happy family and a future. It took him a long time to regain a rational control over his emotions.

There was nothing rational about the raging desire that Willow's cool perfection aroused in him. Nor was it like the love he had for Cathy, tender and protective. He recognised his folly and, alarmingly, did not care, helpless in the grasp of a passion which was at once sexual and aesthetic.

Being neither vain nor a fool, he did not delude himself that if he had been one of the hospital porters she would have given him so much as the time of day. Girls of twenty-six didn't lose their heads over men in their forties unless they had money, status, power. That was his currency, beauty was hers, and he believed they understood each other.

He bit his lip. Oh, it had always been easy enough to be cool and objective in her absence. When she was there, in the utterly desirable flesh, he could only look at her in an enchantment of the senses, and lust, and marvel.

Quoting Browning, he had said to her once, "'How could you ever prick those perfect ears, Even to put the pearl there!'"

He touched a delicate lobe with its pearly stud; she had glanced at him, uncomprehending and uncertain.

'Andrea del Sarto,' he explained. 'Called "the faultless painter". An older, once-successful man enslaved by his young, beautiful but faithless wife.'

She had looked thoughtful, then smiled, though the smile had not reached her extraordinary, no-colour eyes. He saw that, and knew what he had seen, but like del Sarto he was ready to let smiles buy him.

Now he would never see those smiles again, never hear the breathy, enchanting voice, smell the warm perfume of her skin, that skin which now . . . His pathology lectures came back to him with lurid clarity and he gagged, shuddering, then grasped the steering wheel as the car veered towards the ditch at the side of the road.

Control. Control. He must not let his mind wander so. Desperately he focused it on his immediate practical problem, fixing on it as a drowning man battered by waves might cling to a rock even though it lacerated his grasping fingers. What was he going to do about the police? They were bound to take a close interest in someone who was the lover of a woman found dead in suspicious circumstances.

They had been very discreet. As a consultant he had his reputation to consider, and in the hospital – that hot-bed of gossip – he had been careful to treat her with no more than the meticulous courtesy he showed to every other nurse. Surprisingly, she had an instinct for secrecy which matched his own, relished it, even, as if the challenge lent spice to the affair.

Clearly the colleague who had told him the news that was sweeping the hospital had no idea that it had any special significance. John, slipping behind his mask with the ease of long practice, was sure he remained none the wiser.

Perhaps nobody knew. Willow had no confidantes, or even, he suspected, women friends. Perhaps no one would ever find out, to rake over in public what had once been private and precious.

The police always did find out, though, didn't they, if they decided to look? At least, that was the fiction; he was less convinced that in fact they were as infallibly efficient as they would have you believe. But it would only take one local busybody who had spotted her in his distinctive car, one sharp-eyed receptionist at one of the smart, secluded hotels . . . Once you had seen Willow, you wouldn't forget her face. Oh God, no, you wouldn't forget . . .

He swallowed hard, forcing himself back to practicalities. No, however little the hospital might relish one of their consultants proclaiming an affair with a junior nurse, he must go to the police tomorrow and be completely open about the relationship. Answering their no doubt prurient questions would be distasteful, but preferable to having it leaked by rumour and exposed in scandal.

When he turned into the drive, there was as usual a light left burning over the front door. The rest of the house was in darkness, apart from Agnes's bedroom.

She hadn't waited up for him, but he knew she never slept properly until he got home. Aware of how lonely her days could be – though when had she ever complained? – he would usually tap on her door as he passed; she was always awake, ready to listen for as long as he wanted to talk. There had been so many nights when she had listened, back over the years, right back to the time when he had been a bewildered child, still grieving the loss of his own mother in his stepmother's sheltering arms.

Tonight he couldn't talk to her. It was too raw, too horrible, too difficult. He walked past her door and into his own room.

It was the largest bedroom, at the front, with the view which looked right down the valley between the low hills which enfolded it on either side, along the course of the river meandering in its stony bed. Agnes had turned down the bed invitingly, as she always did, but he went instead to the chaise longue in the bay window, where he had sat so often in the difficult past, and stretched out on it wearily. Daisy's death. Cathy's rejection. Agnes's imprisonment. It was amazing that the very cover did not reek of despair.

He had not bothered to put on the light. The moon was almost gone; there would be a couple of hours of starlight before the first streaks of dawn appeared in the summer sky.

Despite his mental anguish he would have wanted to keep vigil. It would have been fitting, somehow, to watch the night away, but there was a man whose life would depend tomorrow on the clearness of his brain and the steadiness of his hand.

Reluctantly he got up again, went into his bathroom and switched on the light to find the bottle of valium he kept for such emergencies. After a brief calculation he swallowed one and prepared for bed.

Sleep came at last in a confused jumble of pictures and images: Agnes, Cathy, a laughing baby, a delicate ear with the pearl set there, 'my serpentining beauty, rounds on rounds—'

The tears welled and spilled down his cheeks to soak his pillow even while he slept.

SESSION THREE

Tuesday 28 July

Session Three

'Do you want to talk to me today?'

'I might. You didn't wait yesterday.'

'If you're not going to talk to me, there's no point.'

'Do you want to hear?'

'Do you want to tell me?'

'Perhaps. Oh, why not? It's dull here. You're not much, frankly, but you're better than nothing.'

'Tell me about the baby.'

'What baby? Who said there was a baby?'

'You said she was pregnant.'

'Oh . . . Yes, She was pregnant. Fat and disgusting.'

'What was the baby like?'

'Ugly. It was hideous, a scrawny purple thing with a head too big for its body. My father's eyes, She said it had, looking at its muddy, cloudy-blue pupils. Fatuous cow.

'My father nursed it when it cried at night, holding it in his huge gentle hands, soothing it against his shoulder the way he had soothed my brother and me too, long ago. I could remember, just, the soft feel of his well-washed flannelette shirt and the faint warm smell of dogs that always hung about his clothes. That was before my mother said he was babying me and I had to learn to stand on my own two feet. She was always trying to turn my father against me. A hard woman, my mother – did I tell you that?

'It was difficult for my brother. He was jealous, because the baby was in the place he used to be able to take on Dad's knee after work.

She wasn't bothering with my brother by then, so I was the one he turned to, more and more. That was good, at least. Allowing myself to care for him was a risk – but you have to take risks sometimes, don't you? And I didn't see how he could betray me.

'*She cooked now, and did more cleaning – easier, really, than forcing unwilling slaves. I learned how to be stupid and incompetent, and eventually She didn't speak to me any more, just kept a book where She entered my sins, real and imagined, to show my father when She was demanding that he gave me the usual punishment.*'

'The cage?'

'*Yes. But he was uneasy, increasingly. He knew enough about training young animals to know that a punishment that doesn't work shouldn't be repeated.*

'*But She liked it, and Dad's problem was that he wasn't strong enough to say no to her, not when She came to break up our family, not now. Not ever.*

'*She liked to watch from the kitchen window while I stood in the cage – or sat, after Dad, without discussion, had put in an old wooden chair – with my face as blank as I could make it. She liked seeing my brother standing by the door pushing his little fingers through the wire for comfort, tears streaming down his face in shared humiliation. He was only little, my brother – he couldn't help being soft.*

'"*Apologise,*" *my father said to me at last.* "*Say you'll turn over a new leaf, make peace with your stepmother and then we can all make some kind of life for ourselves.*"

'*I just looked back at him stonily, and he groaned.* "*Do it for your brother, if you won't do it for me. You're warping his nature. He used to be a happy child.*"

'"*So was I.*" *I turned away, and we didn't talk about it again.*'

'What happened after that?'

'*I don't want to tell you yet. I don't trust you. Why do you want to know?*'

'It might help us to understand.'

'*I'll think about it. Can I go now?*'

Sunday 12 July

Chapter Eight

Usually Glynis Rees hated weekends in high summer, when she opened in the afternoon for passing trade instead of shutting as usual at half-past twelve, but this Sunday she rose promptly, her hopes high for the day ahead. Sensation was to her as addictive as blood to a vampire, and as the heart of village life the Llanfeddin Stores would surely be the centre for whatever gossip, rumour or speculation might be circulating.

She dressed herself with the care of one who feels she owes it to her public to look her best, patting pink powder over her nose and pouchy cheeks, then outlining her small mouth generously with Tea-Rose Pink. She put on her favourite black suede shoes, then walked across to make a final check in the mirrored door of the wardrobe, part of a tortoiseshell melamine bedroom suite which had seen better days.

Lacking Hannah's generous and much-envied divorce settlement, she never had much to spend either on the house or herself, but she'd treated herself to a new blouse last week – shell-pink, imitation crêpe de Chine, real quality stuff – and today seemed ideal for its first airing. She pinned a pink china rose brooch at the neck, then patted the collar tenderly into place.

It was half-past seven when she left the house, and as usual she called in at Hannah's on the way. Hannah was always an early riser, and in a good mood could sometimes be persuaded along to help shift the mountain of newsprint stacked in the shop doorway on a Sunday morning.

Glynis hated the Sunday papers. She hated the endless sections and supplements and inserts, sorted by her to be binned unread, mostly, by their purchasers. She hated the fat, opulent magazines, pursing her lips at the skinny, half-naked girls and the louche young men, the bleak, minimalist interiors and the voguish food made from ingredients unknown to Llanfeddin.

Rubbish, she called it, in the ringing tones of righteous indignation, but her distaste had deeper, unacknowledged roots. Llanfeddin values, Llanfeddin opinions, were those she dictated, and these Sunday glimpses of a wider world eroded her power base with their unstated suggestion that what Llanfeddin thought might not be so important after all. And the tabloids, with their menu of salacious scandals, could only blunt local appetite for the more modest fare which was her stock in trade.

She was in the entertainment business – that was why her customers were prepared to pay the prices she charged for their tins of baked beans and their sliced white. And if they lost interest in what Owen Griffith's mother's cousin had said about Barry Jones's divorce, that was her livelihood gone.

Today, however, she was feeling more charitably disposed towards the Sundays. She would have time to trawl through them for every shred of information about their own home-grown news story, particularly if Hannah could be persuaded to lend a hand. That shouldn't be difficult today.

So it was a surprise, as well as a disappointment, to find Hannah still in her dressing gown, with dark circles under her eyes and the air of one who has slept badly, hunched round a mug of tea at the kitchen table.

'What's the matter, Hannah – you ill, then?'

From shadowed eyes, Hannah shot her sister a malevolent glare. 'Ill? Why should I be, then? Sunday morning, isn't it – don't have to be up and dressed this hour.'

It was not often that Glynis could claim sartorial superiority over her younger, smarter sister. She prinked the collar of her new blouse and said, sisterly candour overcoming caution, 'Well, look like something the cat brought in, you do.'

Hannah's eyes narrowed dangerously. 'All dressed up your-self, I see. New blouse, and everything.'

Glynis patted her bosom fondly. 'Got it in Moreton's in the High Street, didn't I? Wasn't cheap, I can tell you that.'

'Pink!'

At the monosyllable, Glynis bridled. 'And what's wrong with that, then?'

Hannah achieved a little, silvery laugh. 'Oh, nothing. I was just remembering what our Mam used to say – "A very *young* colour, pink." She was good on colour, our Mam.' Then pausing just long enough to be sure that she had destroyed her sister's pleasure in the new garment, she added sweetly, 'Probably things are different nowadays anyway. Want some tea?'

She got to her feet, and Glynis was saying, 'Haven't time, have I?' when the kitchen door opened and Gavin Guest came in.

The two women stared at him. He was shaved and smartly dressed, in chinos and a deep blue shirt faithfully pressed for him by his mother. At the look of astonishment on their faces he smiled his thin-lipped, humourless smile.

'Look like two cows with their cud taken away, you do,' he said.

Hannah seemed nonplussed; it was Glynis who, switching to English, spoke. 'Well, never seen you up this time before, Gav.'

'Got things to do, haven't I, Auntie Glyn? Got a business appointment in town I got to get to, haven't I?'

Hannah said dully, 'You'll be wanting your breakfast, then.'

'I'd best be going.' Glynis got to her feet. Addressing Hannah, she said, without much hope, 'Don't fancy coming to help me sort the Sundays, do you? Could be interesting today, I reckon.'

To the further astonishment of his mother and his aunt, it was Gavin who responded, 'Well, I'd like to help you out, Auntie Glyn. Give me ten minutes while my mam makes me a cuppa and a slice of toast, and I'll be right with you.'

Disappointed of her sister's company, Glynis brightened. There was no doubt about it, a scandal shared was a pleasure doubled.

'I'll go on then, Gav. See you in a minute.'

As she hurried out, he called after her, 'Now don't you go doing any heavy lifting, Auntie Glyn.'

For a fraction of a second she suspected mockery, but dismissed the thought. He was a good boy at heart, was Gavin, and always with a soft spot for his Auntie Glyn.

He didn't arrive, of course, until after she had carried in all the bundles of paper – grasping them awkwardly because she wasn't really built for bending and she was trying to keep the soft smudgy ink off her blouse – and separated them all out along the counter with eager anticipation.

It was a serious blow. Not one carried the story in any prominent position. Having gone through them all, the best she could come up with was 'Girl Found Dead' as a short item in an inside column of the *Sunday Times*. By the time Gavin arrived, she was seething with indignation.

'Call themselves investigative journalists, they do, and this is the best they can manage!' she said bitterly. '"Girl Found Dead" – can you credit that? And not a thing I couldn't have told them myself.'

Gavin was soothing. 'Well, you're on the spot, aren't you, Auntie Glyn? And nobody ever knows more than you do. I tell you what, they should employ you as one of their stringers, they should.

'But look, you went and carried in all those heavy bundles when I said I'd do it. Didn't get that smart blouse messy, did you now?'

Glynis simpered. 'Well, you're here to help me sort anyway,' she said, thinking balefully of Bronwen who was probably at this moment spooning mushy cereal into one of the ever-open mouths at the breakfast table. Bronwen, she was apt to say in acid tones, took after her father, whereas Gavin was his maternal grandad all over again.

Even looked like him, he did, though it was hard to imagine Gavin as the pillar of the Chapel her father had always been. Still, even she had heard the rumours about her father – followed the Laughing Man in his day, as they called it round here . . .

And look at Gavin now, sorting through the papers for her and even checking to make sure she hadn't missed anything, pausing now and then to check thoroughly. He was a good lad, was Gavin.

Then, of course, he'd said he had to go – someone to see before this appointment, whatever it was. Probably that woman down in Stetford, but she'd given him a fiver out of the till anyway. She'd always spoiled him a bit, and she couldn't really stop now.

Outside, Gavin Guest revved up the old motorbike with its disabled silencer, and roared off in a cloud of fumes. Ignoring the speed limit, he had wound it up to sixty before he was out of the village, but even so he took time to turn his head and give a wink and a salute to the grotesque stone by the roadside.

Tessa was painting again, working with controlled haste and ferocious concentration, holding her brush in her teeth while she manipulated a painting knife, using deft economical strokes to mould and define the paint already thickly applied to the canvas.

Her mood was different today. Today she was angry with herself, for a whole variety of reasons. She felt older, too, much older even than she had yesterday – when she had believed she had taken a giant step towards maturity – for a whole variety of reasons, many of which related to being childish and selfish and spoiled.

The colours were less sombre, with a palette of acid yellows and limes – sharp, sarcastic almost. She was trying to strike a balance between spoiling her painting with impatience by working too quickly and being compelled by events to stop before she had captured the essence of her thoughts. She could refine it later, over shorter snatches of time, but she was desperate to set down what she felt this morning without interruption.

She'd meant to get up early. She'd meant to make David a proper breakfast, partly because it was unlikely he'd bother with lunch, and partly to show that even if he wasn't perfect after all, and neither was she, she still loved him just as much as, and arguably even more than, ever.

She'd planned to be supportive and understanding and un-demanding, instead of throwing infantile and pathetic tantrums. When at last they'd stopped yelling and started talking and he'd told her about the girl's bedroom and the sad, hopeless father, she'd felt ashamed of herself. His first appointment today was at the mortuary, and reading the dread in his face – though he hadn't talked about it – she'd vowed to send him off freed from domestic concern and reassured that she would cope with Matthew, of course she would.

And then once he had gone, Tessa would have made an early start to her painting, got in a three- or four-hour stretch before she needed to go and sort out her stepson's bedroom.

But she hadn't, had she? She'd slept through David getting up and going off to work, slept until a finger of sunlight from a chink in the curtains edged its way up the bed to shine teasingly in her face at half-past nine.

Why couldn't he have wakened her? That had been her first, unjust thought, but of course David would have been doing his best not disturb her. Damn, damn, damn.

When she got downstairs at last, there was a note on the table. 'Eat your heart out, Picasso!' it said across the top, and then, in an ineptly-drawn border of what were probably smiling daisies, 'Not only are you beautiful, utterly desirable, clever and funny but you are one helluva painter and I love you to distraction. I WILL PHONE YOU LATER. Signed in blood, D.'

Tessa had smiled, of course, and pinned it to the top of her easel as she worked, but there can be few things more exasper-ating, when you are brimful of generous impulses which you have through your own negligence and weakness failed to implement, than to have the object of your intended benevo-lence do something generous and graceful for you instead. Double damn, twice.

David phoned at half-past eleven. 'Ah, the Sleeping Beauty has awakened, has she?' The cheerfulness was forced and unnatural.

Without rehearsing her excuses, Tessa said simply, 'Was it awful?'

'Yes,' he said heavily. 'Worse than that. But I didn't disgrace myself.'

'And is it murder?'

'They seem to think so.'

He did not elaborate; reminding herself that he was a policeman on duty, she did not press him.

David went on, 'Now, about Matt. His train's four twenty-five, isn't it? I'm going now to do a couple of interviews, but I'll make time to meet the train and bring him out. I'll have to dump him on you and leave, I'm afraid, but—'

'Sure,' Tessa said hastily. 'No problem. Once you've introduced us, we'll be fine.' Thank heavens she wasn't going to have to find a child she couldn't confidently recognise and explain to him that his father's work was so important that he couldn't meet his son for the first time in a year.

'Good girl.' Relief and gratitude were evident in his voice. 'Now, have you got a pen? I'll give you the number of the mobile phone I've taken today, so you can get in touch if necessary.'

'That's useful,' she said, scribbling.

'I must go – oh, how's the painting?'

'Thanks for your note.' She hoped he could tell from her voice that she was smiling. 'Sometime, when we're old and grey, which is probably the next time we'll get the chance for a quiet tête-à-tête, I'll tell you all about it.

'But I'm sorry about your breakfast.'

'My breakfast?'

'The lovingly scrambled eggs you were supposed to have, served on heart-shaped pieces of toast to show how much I love you.'

She could certainly hear the smile in his voice. 'Me too,' he said, and rang off.

Tessa glanced at her watch as she went back to the easel. Oh God, was that twenty to twelve? She had decided she must stop at one, and make Matthew's room a bit more welcoming.

She had barely picked up her brush when the phone rang once more. It was unlikely to be David again, and she swore.

Wiping her hands inadequately on her painting shirt, she picked up the receiver, leaving a smear of burnt sienna. It was probably Lara. She really didn't want to talk to Lara.

It was a female voice, but one she didn't recognise, one which sounded as if the speaker was chewing gum at the same time.

'Is that Mrs Cordiner? This is Karen from Jarvis's.'

For a moment it meant nothing, then she remembered the board outside the house. 'Oh yes – yes of course.'

'Mr Jarvis said to phone you,' Karen went on, her tone suggesting that this had proved an intolerable intrusion on her personal life. 'Wants to bring someone to see your house. All right?'

All right? Looking wildly round her disordered kitchen and remembering her unmade bed, Tessa groaned inwardly. But the words 'beggars' and 'choosers' did come forcibly to mind.

'Goodness, that's quick,' she said hollowly. 'Yes of course. But there's no need for him to come – I'll be here anyway.'

'I think he said they didn't have a car, or something.'

'Fine. Oh, what's the name?'

'Didn't say.' There was a long pause, then a sigh. 'D'you want me to find out, then?'

Tessa could almost hear the nails being varnished at the other end. 'It doesn't matter. I'd hate to trouble you.'

'Fine. Tarra.'

Tessa replaced the phone with exaggerated care. She wanted to smash it down, scream with rage and frustration, but it wouldn't do any good. She tore off her overshirt, crumpled it into a ball and threw it down at the foot of the easel on which she had been about to create the best thing in art since the Sistine Chapel. It was probably now, to use the technical artistic term, completely buggered.

They could be here in less than twenty minutes, twenty minutes in which she must make the house look absolutely irresistible. If she could swing it, they might be out of this hellish place in six weeks. There was a lot riding on this.

Flowers and coffee, they always said, but that was perhaps assuming you had made the bed, washed the dishes and hoovered first. Flowers were out of the question, but she wasted precious moments hunting for coffee beans.

In the end, she shovelled a couple of spoonfuls of instant in a pan and put it on to heat while she went upstairs to comb her hair, with the result that the windows were still open to dispel the smell of charred coffee when the doorbell rang.

WDC Watson had been summoned to pick up her inspector from the mortuary, where he had gone with Superintendent Barker early this morning for the post mortem on Willow Lampton. When she drew up, Cordiner was on the pavement, just finishing making a call on a mobile phone. He looked pale and strained.

'Thanks, Sue,' he said as he got in. 'The Super's gone back to the Station, but I wanted to get on with the interviews without delay.'

'Is it murder, sir?' The young constable's urchin face was alive with eagerness.

Cordiner sighed, reminding himself that she, after all, had not spent the past three hours watching unspeakable indignities being inflicted on the body of a girl no older than she was herself.

'Oh yes, it's murder,' he said heavily. 'All the signs of asphyxiation are there – congested lungs, pinpoint haemorrhages in the eyes and brain and on the surface of the lung. Probably, they think, because someone smothered her.

'And they think, from the lack of any sign of a struggle, that she was doped, probably with flunitrazepam – they market it as Rohypnol—'

'The date-rape drug? There's been a lot about it in the papers.'

'That's right. Roofies, they call them, and they're available on the street, if you know the right people. Puts the victim in a trance-like state where they're incapable of resistance. It comes in soluble, tasteless form, so you'd never know it was in your drink.'

'What's it prescribed for?'

'Pain, insomnia – it isn't on the NHS prescribing list because there are cheaper alternatives, but it isn't exactly hard to get hold of. The other problem is that it's assimilated into the body quickly, and the testing for it is difficult. They're making an educated guess that this is what was used.'

'Wouldn't be difficult for a doctor to know that and get hold of the stuff, would it?'

'Spot on.' Cordiner rubbed his hand tiredly across his face. 'So let's go and chat to young Doctor Arkwright, shall we? Flat somewhere in the High Street.'

'Ninety-three,' she said absently and drove off with her brow furrowed in thought. 'So if all the evidence is so shaky, how come they're saying it's murder?'

'They can't find any natural explanation, and then there's hypostasis.'

'Taking me right out of my depth there, boss.'

Cordiner almost smiled. 'Just thought I'd show off some of my painfully-acquired scientific knowledge.

'When blood circulation stops, apparently, the laws of gravity operate and it settles in the lowest blood vessels. So if the stains aren't consistent with the position you find the body in, it's been moved. We found Willow lying flat; the marks say she was in a sitting position for some time after she was killed, then moved before rigor mortis stiffened the limbs.'

'As it might be, in a car?'

Watson had a good, quick brain; a useful officer. Cordiner nodded.

'As it might be, in a car. And of course, she and Arkwright were both at their cars when the nurse saw them.'

'Have they any idea of the time of death?'

'That, at least, they can be fairly definite about. A body

temperature estimate is tricky, apparently, because she was moved, but with the stomach contents –' he broke off abruptly and Sue, casting him a sympathetic glance, saw sickly colour come into his face. But he went on, 'They could tell she'd eaten no more than three hours before she was killed, and the nurse's evidence is that she was in the canteen at five-thirty.'

'That would tie in with Arkwright too, wouldn't it?'

'Almost perfectly, if, say, they went on for a drink after their meeting. We'd better get someone to check round the pubs – she was pretty enough to be memorable, even if they didn't know her.' He fished a notebook out of his pocket and jotted down a reminder. 'Still, from bitter experience I have to tell you that it's seldom that simple.'

They were turning into the High Street now. A little hesitantly, Sue Watson said, 'If you don't mind me asking, will you be in charge of the enquiry, boss?'

Cordiner shook his head. 'Too much of a new boy. It might be Bryan Pugh from Wrexham – he's a good man. Or someone from Shrewsbury, perhaps. Just as long as they don't take me off the case when they arrive, send me to deal with the break-in at the cash and carry instead.'

'Oh, they won't do that,' she said earnestly. 'They'll need you on this. And anyway, Owen has it in hand. Someone said something that made him think there might be a drugs link, so he's comparing the list from Operation Lambchop with the list of employees—'

'Good man!' Cordiner was impressed, as well as relieved. 'It would be useful to get that one out of the way quickly, because unless someone comes holding their hands out for the cuffs to be put on we're going to need everyone we can get over the next few days.'

She drew in and parked neatly in a space outside number ninety-three, then got out and followed Cordiner up a narrow staircase between the shops. On a tiny first-floor landing there was a bell marked 'Arkwright'; he pressed it, and they stood waiting.

'No reply. He must have gone out,' she suggested.

Cordiner frowned, looking at his watch. 'Ten to twelve. They said at the hospital he wasn't on duty today, so he's probably still asleep. At that age you can sleep through anything.'

He leaned on the doorbell a little harder, and after a moment or two was rewarded with sounds of movement.

A groggy voice mumbled, 'All right, all right, I'm coming,' and then the door was opened.

Paul Arkwright, unshaven and bleary-eyed, in a T-shirt and boxer shorts, had clearly just stepped out of bed.

He focused on them with difficulty, then frowned. 'What d'you want?'

'Police,' Cordiner said crisply, flashing his warrant card. 'Detective Inspector Cordiner and WDC Watson. May we come in?'

Taking advantage of Arkwright's confusion he stepped forward so that the younger man had little alternative but to step aside.

'In here, sir, is it?'

He was deliberately hustling him. They were valuable, these minutes when you managed to catch a suspect with his defences down. Sometimes it got you straight answers, and if it wasn't exactly cricket – well, they weren't exactly the MCC.

Pushing his hands through his rumpled hair, Arkwright padded after them into the tiny sitting room and slumped on to the sofa, yawning and shaking his head to clear it. Sue Watson went to draw back the curtains, which were still shut, and opened a window to dispel the smell of stale cigarette smoke and last night's beer. A fair number of cans lay discarded about the room, and judging by the demeanour of their reluctant host it seemed likely he had accounted for his share.

'I'm – bemused,' he said.

'I'm sorry, sir. I'm sure you are. But it's quite simple, in fact. Can you tell us in detail about your relationship with Willow Lampton?'

He sat up very suddenly, as if shocked into full awareness. 'Willow! Oh my God, I'd forgotten—' He bent forward to put his head in his hands, and groaned.

With a nod, Cordiner cued Sue. She said at once, her voice gentle, 'You were pretty crazy about her, weren't you? Were you gutted when she gave you the push?'

He raised his head slowly. 'Well, I was certainly infatuated with her, at one stage.'

Observing him meticulously, Cordiner saw that there was wariness in his eyes now, and recalled regretfully that he was dealing with someone whose professional life dictated that you should come rapidly from sleep into full, intelligent wakefulness.

Arkwright was choosing his words carefully now.

'I was also, quite clearly, "gutted when she gave me the push", as you so elegantly term it. But that was some time ago. And I had fortunately worked through it to the point where I realised that this was the best thing that could possibly have happened to me.

'My friends had been telling me all along that she was merely out for all she could get, and recently, I'm happy to say, I had come round to believing they were right.'

'Meant nothing to you now, is that what you're expecting us to believe?' There was a sneer in Cordiner's voice.

'No, Inspector, I didn't say that. Please don't put words into my mouth.' It was a steely, measured response. 'I was both shocked and saddened yesterday when I heard about her death. She was very young and very lovely—'

He broke off. Sue said softly, 'But surely, you must have had a bit of a grudge against her? Surely you could hardly help being jealous of whoever was the new man in her life?'

'I told you, I'd got beyond that.'

'Then why,' Cordiner snapped, 'since you had reached such a happily dispassionate state, were you seen in a violent argument with her in a layby on Friday evening?'

That rocked him. His eyes widened in shock.

'Of course, the gossips at work,' he said. 'I suppose, if I told you—'

He looked up and met Cordiner's eyes, hard, clear and unwavering. Predatory.

'There's no point, is there? You won't believe anything I

tell you, and I'd be a fool to say anything more without my solicitor present.'

Cordiner said stiffly, 'Of course, if that's your decision. Though if it's a simple matter of an explanation which could clear the whole thing up, it seems a pity to waste everyone's time.'

'Come on,' Sue said coaxingly, 'if you can put yourself in the clear, we'll be delighted.'

As Arkwright looked from one to the other, Cordiner realised, with some annoyance, that he had underestimated him. Dealing with ordinary decent criminals of limited intelligence left you ill-equipped to tackle someone who dealt on a daily basis with the crises of heart attacks and car accidents and violent schizophrenics. His own recent experience of a post mortem was one of the nastiest things he had had to cope with in years of police work; to this lad, that sort of thing was all in a day's work and he would go straight home and enjoy a hearty meal afterwards. He would do well to remember that, when he found himself thinking of Arkwright as a decent young fellow.

Arkwright smiled, wrily. 'Oh, do me a favour, Inspector. Surely the nice cop – nasty cop routine went out with *Dixon of Dock Green*. No, I think I'll just wait till I have professional advice.'

'As I said, it's your decision, sir. Then we'll just wait until you have contacted your solicitor, and then we can continue this down at the police station.'

He was bright, but he wasn't that tough. His cheeks lost colour and he looked very young and very scared.

'All – all right,' he said. 'I'll make my phone call and then get dressed. With your permission?'

He made them an ironic bow, and a moment later they heard him say, 'Andrew? Yes, I know you were asleep, but I've got a bit of a problem—'

Chapter Nine

There was no doubt about it, she was tasty, very tasty indeed, he thought, as Tessa Cordiner opened the door, her cheeks flushed from some sort of exertion.

He saw her see him, standing a pace behind the corpulent figure of the estate agent, saw her eyes shoot wide in shock. Her lips parted too, and she drew in a breath as if she were about to scream. She didn't, but she was scared, very scared.

He liked that.

'What is *he* doing here?' she demanded fiercely of the other man.

Jarvis was sweating. It was warm, and he sweated easily. Guest, whipcord-thin himself, eyed the fat pig with contempt as he fished for a crumpled handkerchief and mopped his brow.

'Now, Mrs Cordiner, there's no need to go upsetting yourself. I don't suppose the Inspector's in?'

His tone was not hopeful. Tessa, standing inhospitably in the doorway, said, 'Not just at this moment, no.'

'Gavin is looking at the house on behalf of his mother, isn't that right, Gavin?' He looked round pleadingly for confirmation.

'That's what I told you, yes,' he said ambiguously, never taking his eyes from Tessa's face.

'I realised it might be a little awkward,' Jarvis persisted, 'because of your – er – misunderstanding—'

'Misunderstanding?' Tessa spat out the word.

'Well – er – yes – whatever.' He was floundering. 'That was why I brought him myself, instead of just sending Gavin along to you; I can see that you might not be – well – entirely comfortable, shall we say. And to be perfectly frank, Mrs Cordiner, I don't feel that you can ignore whatever interest in your property there may be.' He was on firmer ground now. 'Mrs Guest is in the shop today, I understand, but if Gavin can carry back a favourable report I'm sure we can manage to arrange a mutually convenient time for her to see it.'

Guest saw Tessa falter, weighing up what the estate agent had said. Then, with her body language screaming reluctance, she allowed them passage, stepping back into a corner of the hall to distance herself from any possible physical contact with him.

With calculation, he took a couple of paces towards her, in pretence of admiring the fine dimensions of the meagre hall, and with relish watched her recoil like a salted snail.

She cleared her throat, a soft, deliciously nervous sound. 'I'll leave you to show him round, then, Mr Jarvis.'

Keeping the estate agent's bulk between them like a barricade, she escaped to the back of the house as Jarvis said with professional heartiness, 'Fine, we'll do that. Let's start upstairs then, shall we?'

Guest was certain she was listening, but even so he raised his voice. 'Yes. What I really want to see is the *bedroom*.'

Jarvis led him into the smaller bedroom first, a rather bleak, narrow, north-facing room which was clearly unoccupied, though folded linen lying on the bed suggested it might be about to be made up.

Guest gave it the most cursory of glances, then walking out on a dutiful recital about the number of power points and the built-in wardrobe, he crossed the landing to the bedroom at the front. *Her* bedroom.

It was simply furnished, but the combination of sea-blues and greens, with deep purple accents among the cushions heaped on a little chair and on the bed, was striking and fresh against walls with a faded lilac wash. There was the faintest hint of lilies of the valley in the air.

One bedside table was meticulously tidy, with a clock, a tray for the contents of pockets and an action thriller. His side.

Guest moved round to the farther side, where the crowded table held tissues, a couple of women's magazines, pens, a comb, and a toppling pile of paperbacks. He picked up the one which lay spread open on the top.

'*Behind the Scenes at the Museum*,' he read out. 'Not a very sexy title, is it, then?' Again, he raised his voice. The walls and floors in houses like these weren't that solid, and he could almost sense her below, moving to shadow the footsteps overhead, her eyes turned up to the ceiling.

'Got some nice stuff here. Classy,' he said, picking up a bottle of Diorissimo, opening it and sniffing appreciatively as he sprayed a little on his forearm. He fingered the tissue that was uppermost in the box, wiping his hand delicately across it. She would put that to her face, tonight.

In the doorway, Jarvis was eying him uncomfortably. 'Don't touch anything,' he told him sharply. 'These are Mrs Cordiner's personal property.'

'I know.'

Jarvis recoiled, took refuge in a recitation about the view over the valley, pointing out of the window while Gavin slid out of the room behind him and shut the door.

In the bathroom, he licked the bright pink toothbrush, rubbed a deep blue towel round the back of his neck, and was fondling a pink velour robe hung on the back of the door by the time Jarvis reached it. He was definitely uneasy now; Guest favoured him with a smile as he continued to stroke the soft fabric.

'We'll go downstairs now.' Jarvis didn't even attempt to point out the new shower, the heated towel rail and the shaving light over the bathroom mirror.

'In a minute.' Guest picked up a cake of soap and lathered his hands extravagantly, leaving dirty soap bubble traces, then wiped his hands on another of the fluffy towels while the other man looked helplessly on. Guest loved helplessness. It made him feel so powerful.

With Jarvis lurching awkwardly after him down the narrow steps, he went, with only a perfunctory glance through the open door at the sitting room, through to the back of the house.

Tessa was standing, as if at bay, with her back to a cupboard in a corner of the kitchen. She met his eyes defiantly, her chin raised and her arms crossed protectively in front of her, but he could see that the slim brown hands were gripping fiercely to stop her shaking.

'Not much security in this house, is there, Tess? No window locks, no alarm system – anyone could get in here in two minutes. You want to get the police out to come and advise you about that, you do. A lot of funny people about, these days.'

He smiled his ugly smile, licking his lips as he saw her flinch involuntarily, but her reply was sturdy.

'There are good sound locks on all the inside doors, if your mother is worried about her safety. And of course, I do have a very direct line to the police.'

'Don't have to tell me that, do you?'

She ignored the gibe. 'Is there anything else you want to see? Perhaps we might save it until your *mother* comes for a proper look.'

She emphasised the word with a challenging look at Jarvis who, sweating more profusely than ever, had edged his way into the kitchen. He did not meet her eyes.

'Well, I've seen where you sleep and where you bath.' Guest lingered suggestively on the words. 'What about giving us a bit of a demonstration back there in the porch? If there's one thing I like, it's to watch an artist at work.'

Even for Jarvis, the product of a lifetime of experience of avoiding trouble, this was going too far. Belatedly taking control of the situation, he said, 'I think it's time we went. If your mother wants to see round, we could make another arrangement.'

For a long moment, Guest did not reply, his eyes lingering insolently on Tess as if he could see naked flesh below her shirt and jeans.

'Maybe,' he drawled. 'But she likes her cottage, does Mam.

I don't know she'd be interested in moving, after all.'

Turning at last, he said over his shoulder, 'I left the bike at my girlfriend's in town, Mr Jarvis. You can give me a lift back there – she's always looking for a bit of excitement on a Sunday afternoon – if you get my meaning.'

As he slouched out, he could hear the estate agent's bleating excuses.

'I do apologise, Mrs Cordiner. I trust you don't think I was any part of that, it's just – not an easy property to sell, you know, have to take every chance that offers—'

Then Tessa's voice, slipping out of her control, 'Just get him out of here, get him out!'

Looking shaken himself, the estate agent waddled down the path and wedged himself behind the wheel of the car.

'You really shouldn't have put me in that position, behaving like that,' he said feebly, disapproval emanating from every sweaty pore.

Ignoring him, Guest stared straight ahead, humming under his breath. Somehow he knew, as if he could see her, that Tessa was upstairs in the bathroom at this moment, kneeling on the pink and white mat, being sick.

It had been, as Glynis had surmised, an unusually busy Sunday for the Llanfeddin Stores. People came in for a newspaper and lingered to chat, then browsed in the gift shop as if they were afraid to leave before whatever was going to happen happened. They did good business for the first part of the morning.

The only problem was, there was nothing new to say, and as the day wore on, anticipation soured into disappointment. The most significant excitement was the arrival of Sandra Jones who, having been away the day before, arrived in the shop in a state of unsullied ignorance as tempting as virgin snow. It had taken the full force of Glynis's personality to prevent anyone else from having the pleasure of telling her.

Apart from that, it was a normal routine Sunday and by midday the shop was quiet again. There were only two women picking up forgotten essentials for Sunday lunch when Hannah, lacking customers and standing bored by the window at the front of the shop, said sharply, 'Oh my goodness! That's the police!'

As if practising line-dancing, the four women swung round as one to face the door as it opened. Assailed by four sets of staring eyes, PC Pickering and PC Lloyd paused on the threshold. Pickering took an instinctive step back; Dai Lloyd, native of the next valley up, took his cap off and grinned.

'Mrs Rees, Mrs Guest, ladies. How are you all today?'

Glynis drew her breath between her teeth importantly. 'Shocked, Dai *bach*, that's what we are, shocked.' She shook her head with suitable solemnity, but the excitement showed through like the flash of a red slip under mourning. 'Dreadful business, this, we've all been saying.'

Lloyd turned to wink, improperly, at his more stolid companion.

'Now I like to hear that, Mrs Rees,' he said with matching gravity. 'Shocking it is, indeed. It's good to know we have right-thinking people up here in the valley to help us in our task. Public-spirited, that's nice.'

Unconsciously, Glynis licked her lips, removing the last of the Tea-Rose Pink apart from the small fleck clinging obstinately to one of her front teeth. She lowered her voice portentously.

'Is it – murder, then, Dai?'

'Murder, Mrs Rees?' The young policeman's eyebrows shot up in a pantomime of innocent amazement. 'I don't know about any murder. We're just here to check out one or two addresses with you. We're wanting to have a little chat with a couple of the lads. About the break-in at the cash and carry Friday night.'

The change in Glynis's expression was so ludicrous that Dai did not register the much more subtle change in her sister's demeanour. She straightened up as if a weight had been removed from her shoulders, and simultaneously her eyes sharpened to narrow, defensive slits, boding ill for the oblivious young man.

'You mean, you haven't heard about it?' he was saying with ill-considered glee. 'Well, well, you're slipping here in Llanfeddin, isn't it? It's been the talk of Llanrhimmon for a couple of days now.'

Pickering, with a warning glance at his colleague, cleared his throat. 'Er – am I right that one of you ladies is Mrs Guest?'

Hannah stepped forward, small, neat and composed, with a smile sweet enough to bring on toothache. 'I am, Constable. What is it you were wanting, then?'

'We were hoping to see your Gavin. At home, then, is he?'

'In town,' Hannah smiled. 'Got some business there today.'

'On a Sunday? Works hard, then, does he?' Dai's tones were mocking. 'We just wanted a word with him, see, him and Alun Jenkins of Colwyn Cottage.'

Glynis, resenting being trifled with, leapt to the attack. 'This is another of these false accusations you're trying to pin on our lads, is it? If that Inspector is picking on our Gavin again, there'll be trouble, I promise you.'

'Now, who said anything about accusations?' Lloyd was wondering innocently, when Hannah, smiling still, stepped forward with one of the notebooks decorated with Welsh wildflowers taken from her stock, and a ballpoint pen shaped like a leek.

'Have to do this right, don't we?' she purred. 'Let's just have your names and numbers before we start our little chat. I know you, of course, Dai Lloyd, but just let me copy down that number on your smart uniform. Just to keep the record straight, isn't it.'

Pickering winced visibly, and even the insouciant Dai looked unsettled.

'No need for formalities, Mrs Guest,' he tried to placate her. 'All unofficial, this. All we want is a few words with the lads, just see if they can give us a bit of help with the enquiry. You know Alun Jones works at the cash and carry—'

'My Gavin doesn't.'

Lloyd rubbed the back of his neck. 'No, no, that's right,' he said hastily. The two policemen exchanged glances, each looking to the other for a lead in an interview that was turning unexpectedly sticky. Taking his courage in both hands, Pickering went over the top.

'Just for the record, Mrs Guest, would you have any idea what your Gavin was doing, Friday night?'

Hannah's hesitation could have been a natural pause for recollection. Then, 'He was with me all evening,' she said flatly. 'Came in for his supper and stayed watching the TV all night.'

'And later on?' Pickering might be uncomfortable, but he knew his job.

'Watched the late-night film, didn't he? And I'd've heard him if he'd gone wandering off in the middle of the night. Sleeps right next door to me, doesn't he – hear him if he so much as turns over in his bed, I do.'

The two men exchanged glances. 'You're sure about that, I suppose, Mrs Guest?' Lloyd said.

Her eyes, as she dimpled up at him, were cold as a rattlesnake's. 'As sure, Dai, as I am that your Mam bought that jelly that got her first prize for preserves in the Stetford show. And now, if you'll excuse me—'

She went to the back of the shop, leaving the young constable with his face aflame.

'Well, I expect you'll be wanting to try your luck with Mrs Jenkins now,' said Glynis with malicious satisfaction. 'Second cottage on the right, it is, beyond the shop. But mind how you go. She's inclined to be sensitive, is Jane. Not understanding, like we are, about the difficult job you lads have to do. Maybe you'd better let your friend do the asking, Dai *bach*; you know what they say about the Llanrhimmon folk – mouths big as codfish and their feet made to fit in them.'

It gave Glynis some satisfaction to see them retreat, routed. But the shop had emptied again, and Glynis tidied up a few things left on the counter with a sigh.

It looked like being just another long dreary Sunday. Hardly worth putting on her new blouse for.

★

The tips of Robert Arkwright's ears were a deep, embarrassed pink, Cordiner noted dispassionately, as he ushered the young doctor before him through the heavy glass doors into the police station.

'Oh sir – message for you,' the desk sergeant hailed him and leaving WDC Watson to direct Arkwright to the waiting room the inspector took the memo and scanned it.

A Mr John Winthrop was, apparently, anxious to speak to him, either here or at the hospital where he was a consultant. Cordiner flicked the paper with his thumb and reflected.

Arkwright's solicitor was on his way here, but then it wouldn't do them any harm to cool their heels for a bit – the middle classes always got usefully twitchy in a police station. And he hadn't been to the hospital where Willow had worked yet.

He called Sue, suggested tea, sympathy and stalling, then arranged for Winthrop to be told he would be with him shortly.

The building, a Victorian cottage hospital originally, was now a labyrinthine sprawl with, as far as he could see anyway, no coherent ground plan. He lost his way twice, blundering through Ear, Nose and Throat (noisy children with weary, ineffectual mothers) and Orthopaedic (cheerful young men on crutches and elderly ladies with slings and plaster casts) until, directed by a series of unnaturally cheerful receptionists, he found himself at last in Cardiology.

Here the waiting areas were hushed, with an unmistakable atmosphere of tension. As the nurse to whom he had introduced himself ushered him into Mr Winthrop's consulting room, a man with a papery, unhealthy complexion and an anxious-looking wife at his side raised his eyes from the dog-eared magazine he was pretending to read and tiredly watched him go in.

The room was a modern box, featureless, with cream walls, grey carpet and vertically-slatted blinds. There were no photographs displayed on the large, bare wooden desk, not so much as a pot plant or a letter-opener; even the plastic pens in the plastic pen-tray were hospital issue, and the most personal thing Cordiner had seen was the plastic nameplate on the door bearing John Winthrop's name with a string of impressive-looking initials after it.

Winthrop's greeting was cool and impersonal as well. He was a tall man in a well-cut suit made up in an unobtrusive tweed. Pale grey shirt, subdued blue tie, greying hair, neat features and a self-effacing manner – nothing at all that stood out in any way, Cordiner noticed. His handshake was firm, though, and his voice was pleasant, quiet but confident. If you were an anxious patient, you'd feel reassured.

'How very kind of you to come here, Inspector.' He motioned him to one of the seats opposite and sat down himself in the chair behind the desk. 'You must be very busy. I thought I might have to come to you.'

Though his manner was calm, he had picked up one of the pens from the tray in front of him and was fiddling with it. He was nervous, definitely nervous.

Intrigued, Cordiner murmured some platitude about the importance of a doctor's time, then with a calculated lack of finesse, said, 'What did you want to tell me?'

As the other man hesitated, watching the pen spinning between his well-manicured hands, Cordiner pressed him. 'You knew Nurse Lampton, did you?'

Without lifting his head Winthrop said, almost inaudibly, 'Yes. Yes I did.' Then he looked up and with some surprise Cordiner saw that his eyes were very striking – deep blue, and fringed by dark lashes as long as a girl's. When you actually looked past the 'I'm-just-part-of-the-furniture' manner he was a very attractive man.

'It's – it's very hard for me to talk about this,' he said, his agitation confirming his words. 'Perhaps I should start by explaining that we – she and I – had, well, an understanding.'

An understanding? When was the last time Cordiner had come across that phrase outside the pages of a Victorian novel? Was this guy for real? With deliberate bluntness he said, 'Do you mean you were having an affair with her?'

Winthrop looked down again. 'You could say that. We had been lovers for a couple of months. But – but what I was trying

to convey to you is that this wasn't just a casual relationship. I
had asked her to be my wife.'

Cordiner blinked, a token of complete astonishment. 'And
she went along with this?'

Abruptly Winthrop got up and turned to stare unseeing
between the slats of the window blind.

'I think so, yes. Probably. But with – Willow,' his voice
shook on the name, 'it was never quite as simple as that.'

'Forgive me, sir, I don't quite follow.' Sometimes the
smartest thing to do was, as his Scottish granny would have said,
to play the daft laddie.

'She was very – private. You could never tell exactly what
she was thinking, exactly what she would do next. It was part
of her allure, that core of mystery.' Then he sighed. 'You never
met her?'

Brutally, he said, 'Only in death.'

The man winced. 'I – I can't think about that. I'm sorry.' As
Cordiner had intended, he looked all at once more vulnerable.

'What did you want to tell me?'

'Well – just that.' The doctor seemed surprised. 'I thought
you would feel it was something you should know—'

'And you didn't think we would have been informed already?'

Winthrop looked taken aback. 'Were you?' he said, but as
Cordiner gave nothing away, went on, 'we thought no one
knew – we were very careful—'

'Why?'

'Well, hospitals, you know,' he said vaguely. 'Gossipy places,
and doctors have to be particularly careful about scandal. Willow
hated the idea of people picking over our relationship, and we
both had our reputations to think about—'

He was retreating behind the shutters again. Cruelly,
Cordiner said, 'From what I can gather, Nurse Lampton's
reputation wasn't exactly fragrant. You must surely have known
you weren't the first.'

The dark blue eyes blazed with an unexpected passion.
'Arkwright, I suppose. A young man without the grace to take
no for an answer.'

'Was he forcing himself on Nurse Lampton?' Cordiner invested the question with elaborate indifference, but Winthrop backed off with an animal's instinct for unspecific danger.

'No, no, I'm sure he wasn't, not in that sense. Willow said he was taking it badly, though . . .'

That cock wouldn't fight. Changing tack, Cordiner asked, 'And when was she to make up her mind about your proposal?'

There was no mistaking the pain which twisted his mouth. 'This weekend,' he said huskily. 'She would have said "yes" this weekend.'

'Confident, were you?'

Without answering, Winthrop fumbled in his pocket and produced a small box of tooled red leather. He snapped it open, and on a bed of cream velvet a large cabochon ruby in a modern setting of white gold glowed dark with internal fires. 'Yes,' he said heavily.

If Willow Lampton had seen it, from what he knew of her it would have been a very substantial inducement to consent. 'I – see,' he said, considering, as he watched Winthrop put the ring away.

'And did you see her, sir, on Friday?'

'I passed her in the corridor late on Friday afternoon. I was with a colleague; I smiled and we said hello. Just as if she was any one of the nurses I work with. I – I didn't know—' He stopped, turned away again.

Cordiner produced a notebook and pen. 'May I just jot down your movements for the rest of the evening, sir? If you can recollect?'

'Readily. I was here, working in the office after my clinic. My registrar was on duty, and I was on the point of going home at about eight o'clock when she called me about a woman brought into casualty with a coronary thrombosis. I went across there, got her condition stabilised and had her admitted to the cardiac ward. I had just got her settled when another patient came in – indigestion, as it transpired, but I kept him in for observation overnight. So it was well after eleven o'clock when I got home.'

'Thank you.' Getting to his feet, Cordiner smiled. 'Your hours sound just about as irregular as ours do, sir. Was there anything else? No? Well, thank you for your co-operation.'

He left Winthrop staring once more out of the window. The man and woman in the waiting room looked up again as he left, and as the nurse said, 'Mr Martin? You can go in now,' he saw the wife blanch as she squeezed her husband's hand and watched him go in, probably to learn whether the latest series of tests confirmed what they both already knew. Cordiner didn't envy Winthrop his job.

'Good doctor, is he?' he asked the nurse with a jerk of his head at the closing door.

She stared at him, with the expression a Catholic priest might assume on being asked whether the Pope knew what he was doing. 'Excellent,' she said frostily. 'The best you'll find.'

'I'm happy to hear it.' What was it about doctors that made their subordinates think they were infallible, and why didn't the same dispensation operate for police inspectors? 'Now, Mr Winthrop said he had admitted a couple of people on Friday night. Can you direct me to the ward they would have gone to?'

Sister Morley, alerted by internal phone, was lying in wait for him, bristling in advance at the notion that a mere policeman would have the effrontery to demand confirmation of what a *consultant* had told him.

'Checking up on Mr Winthrop, I hear,' she greeted him aggressively, without pause for identification, introduction, or question. 'I was on duty until nine o'clock, but because there was an emergency I stayed and walked down with Mr Winthrop when he left just after eleven – though of course if you doubt my word it's a simple matter to show you the patients' records—'

'Perish the thought, Sister,' Cordiner said solemnly, and recognising mockery she shot him a killer look from her light blue eyes.

'In any case, I am at a loss to understand why you should

imagine *Mr Winthrop* would have anything to do with a junior nurse like Lampton—'

'I understand that they were about to become engaged.'

He told himself that lobbing this conversational grenade was a professional use of shock tactics, but he couldn't deny that there was a certain reprehensible personal pleasure in watching the senior nurse's reaction.

She gasped, and the already high colour in her cheeks seemed to spread outwards, until her whole face was an alarming brick-red.

'Lampton!' she exclaimed. 'That little tramp!' Then she paused, collecting herself, and laughed harshly. 'But of course, that's just the sort of gossip people invent all the time about consultants. You don't want to believe everything you hear in a hospital. Who told you that rubbish?'

'Mr Winthrop himself, in fact.' But he didn't have time to waste enjoying himself like this. 'Would she have confided in any of the other nurses, do you suppose?'

'Not confided, no. Barely civil, Lampton. Thought she was a cut above everyone else, goodness knows why.

'But if there was a rumour going the rounds, Nurse Griffiths would know all about it. If she could be persuaded to dedicate half the energy to her work that she does to trawling for gossip we could solve the staffing crisis overnight.'

'Is she here?'

'You'll find her through there – but no more than five minutes, mind. Tell her I'm waiting for her to take someone down to X-ray.'

Megan Griffiths, who was standing with her arms folded comfortably across her ample bosom and deep in a Welsh conversation with an elderly patient, jumped visibly as she heard Cordiner's footsteps behind her.

'Oh my goodness!' she cried, as he flashed his warrant card. 'Thought you were Sister, I did. Gave me a nasty turn, I can tell you.'

He drew her aside. 'She isn't in the most cheerful frame of mind, but she's allowing me five minutes. Can I ask you, quickly, if you had heard that Willow Lampton was about to become engaged?'

Megan's brown eyes went rounder still in pleasurable surprise. 'Engaged? Who to?'

Cordiner evaded the question. 'You don't know?'

It was a challenge to her skills. Megan considered. 'Well, not Doctor Arkwright. She'd definitely finished with him. And there were rumours ages ago about her and another doctor, but he was married so it wouldn't be him. But on Friday night, when I saw her all dressed up, Siân and me were just saying we didn't know who she'd picked for her next victim.'

He noted the term. 'But she looked as if she was going out for the evening?'

'Oh, definitely. Black dress, pearls, perfume – but who was it? Do you know?'

She deserved her reward. 'Mr Winthrop.'

'*Mr Winthrop!*' He would have said it was impossible for Megan's eyes to become rounder still, but he would have been wrong. She was also, uncharacteristically, at a loss for words.

'I take it you didn't know about it, then, any more than Sister did? She certainly seemed reluctant to believe it.'

Megan snorted. 'Jealous,' she said succinctly. 'Always fancied him herself, didn't she – wouldn't let any of us so much as speak to him on the ward. Ever such a nice gentleman he is too – but – Willow!'

Sister's footsteps echoed down the ward, and Megan jumped again. 'She'll be in a worse mood than ever, now. I'd better go. I'm just coming, Sister,' he heard her call as he followed her more slowly out.

So Winthrop, the man who was sure Willow was about to marry him, had been at the hospital that evening. And on the evidence that Megan had given before, Willow's encounter with Robert Arkwright did not look pre-arranged. For whom, then, had Willow put on the black dress, the pearls and the perfume? He was thinking hard as he made his way, after only one false cast, back to the car park.

Chapter Ten

As he went back into the police station, Cordiner looked anxiously at his watch. It would never do to get absorbed in an interview and forget about picking Matt up from his train. Still, it was only three o'clock – plenty of time.

The desk sergeant was on the watch for him. 'The Super wants to see you,' he said.

'Now? Or do I have time to talk to Arkwright first?'

'Now. He's looking a bit edgy. But maybe you'd better have a word with Doctor Arkwright's brief – Sue says he's getting stroppy. First time in a police station, she reckons, and doesn't know the ropes.'

Cordiner frowned. 'Is DS Pardoe in?' and as the man nodded, said decisively, 'Right, tell him and Sue to go ahead. I'll join them once the boss has finished with me. Set it up, will you?'

George Barker was frowning as his inspector came into the office, but when he saw who it was his face cleared.

'David! Good man! Come and sit down. How's it going?'

Cordiner pulled a face. 'Hard to say, yet, sir. A lot of strands to pull together—'

Barker nodded. 'Right, right. Well, David, it's up to us. They're going to dump this on our plate.'

It was totally unexpected. Cordiner's heart gave a thump of – what? Excitement, elation? Terror?

'I thought they had decided to bring in someone with a bit more experience from round about.'

'They were. But it's the usual story about manpower. They've got a major fraud investigation in Shrewsbury and a nasty rape in Wrexham, and everyone's at full stretch.'

Cordiner tried to collect his wits. 'What about Chief Inspector Rackham? His name was mentioned.'

'In Florida, on leave. So it's you and me, lad. You mainly, I have to say, and I know you won't let me down.'

'I'll certainly give it my best shot, sir.' Then he laughed. 'Sounds a bit *Boys' Own Paper*, that, doesn't it? Thank you very much – I'm, well, honoured, I suppose, once I get over the shock.'

Barker smiled. 'The thing is, the Chief Constable wants to meet you. It's not a vetting – the decision's made, but he says he'd feel more comfortable knowing the man in charge.

'Luckily, as it happens, he's been across in Wales at a convention and he's going to look in here on his way home in about an hour's time.'

'Fine,' Cordiner said automatically, his mind racing. 'That'll give me time to sit in on the interview with Arkwright – we brought him in earlier—'

Then he stopped. 'Four o'clock, did you say?'

'Four, quarter past. He can't spare very much time, he said. Half an hour will probably do it.'

'Sir, I'm afraid there's a problem—'

Barker looked at him sharply. 'Then fix it, David. I've stuck my neck out in saying you can handle this, and I can tell you that when the Chief Constable takes the trouble to come to a small town police station to see a junior police officer, you don't tell him it isn't convenient. Right?'

'Right, sir,' Cordiner said hollowly.

In the corridor outside, he groaned. What was that saying, about being ground between the upper and the nether millstone?

With dragging feet he went to make his phone call.

★

Clammy and shaking, Tessa rose unsteadily from the pink and white rug, swilled her mouth with water and spat into the bathroom basin. Her eyes fell on the bar of soap with the grubby rings of foam he had left on it, and shuddering she picked it up between two fingers and threw it away. Then she ran her own hands under the tap, splashed her face; she dried her hands on the dark blue towel, and buried her damp face in it.

Then seizing the bright pink toothbrush she scrubbed at her teeth, scrubbed and rinsed and scrubbed and rinsed until her gums were sore.

Her eyes were still watering. She went through to the bedroom and grabbed a tissue to wipe them. She still seemed to smell disgusting; the bottle of her favourite Diorissimo was there on the dressing table, but she had caught a whiff of it on Guest when he came downstairs, knew he had touched it, used it.

She picked up the expensive bottle and dropped it in the waste-bin. She could never bring herself to wear it again, never. To her the delicious, flowery, innocent scent would forever reek of fear and lechery.

It had been a sort of rape. The thought occurred to her, to be dismissed sternly as melodramatic, but indeed she knew that his invasion of her home had been a calculated violation. And now he knew the layout of the house, knew where she worked and ate and slept, had inspected the doors and windows.

She could have extra locks fitted, of course, an alarm, a panic button . . . But windows could always be broken, and how long would it take for any police response to reach here? Could she ever be at ease alone in this house again?

Tessa wouldn't be alone, of course. At least Matthew would be here – and how contemptible it was that now for the first time she welcomed the thought.

She had almost stopped shaking and slowly she walked downstairs. Once she would have been rushing to phone David, her cry to him for comfort and protection as instinctive a reaction as the visceral disgust which had just convulsed her. But it seemed a long time since she had been naïve enough to believe that David – or anyone else, for that matter – could kiss and make it better.

She would tell him about it, of course, but she was no longer confident that she could make him understand. How, in cold words, could she explain what Gavin Guest had done? He had come to the house, used her soap, sprayed himself with her perfume, made suggestive remarks, all in the presence of a third party. Put like that, her reaction seemed paranoid.

David would be sympathetic and try to be reassuring, but after yesterday she had been forced to realise, painfully, that David's priorities did not, after all, completely coincide with her own.

Even so, when the phone rang and she heard his voice, Tessa's heart lifted. 'David, oh David,' she said, and the tears weren't very far away.

He didn't notice. It was, she recognised bleakly, the policeman speaking. He sounded guilty, apologetic and phoney.

'Darling, I don't know how to tell you this. I'm terribly sorry—'

Flatly, she supplied the end of his sentence. 'But you can't meet the train.'

'I'm afraid not. It's—'

'I thought you said you had fixed it.'

'Well, I had. But the thing is –' He paused. 'Well, they've put me in charge of the investigation.'

What did he expect her to do – cheer? 'Even if you're so frightfully important now, surely you can take half an hour off for your son?'

'It's not that. Of course I would, normally.' There was a hint of exasperation in his voice now. 'But the thing is, the Chief Constable wants to see me just at the time I was going to fetch Matt.'

'Can't you explain to him?'

There was no mistaking his irritation now. 'No, Tessa, I can't. I've been given an order, and there's nothing I can do about it.' He sighed. 'Look, it wouldn't really take that long for you just to pop down and fetch him, would it?'

'That's not the point!' Tessa cried. 'This is about Matthew, not me. It's like a slap in the face – you can't even take the time to come and meet him. You know that.'

There was a brief silence, then David sighed again. 'I know, of course I know. I wouldn't have had this happen if I could possibly avoid it. I'll come up whenever they've finished with me – tell him that—'

With intent to wound, she said, 'We won't hold our breath. Now, how shall I recognise him, I wonder? There's that photograph of him on the bookcase, the one where he's five years old – I can have a look at that. Or perhaps you can give me a description of what he looks like now instead.'

He sounded wretched. 'He's dark, dark eyes, round face – though of course that may have changed. And I'm not sure how tall he is—'

Knowing she was being unfair, not caring, she snapped, 'You don't even know what the poor bloody child looks like, do you? Oh, I suppose we'll manage somehow.'

Then she slammed down the phone and burst into tears, not knowing herself whether they were tears of rage, of misery or of shame.

But there was no time for that. It was after three o'clock already, and Matthew's bed wasn't even made up. Sniffing, and wiping her eyes like a child with the back of her hand, she addressed herself to the task of making the dark little room cheerful for a child who would arrive feeling ill-used and unwanted. There were some art posters at the back of one of the cupboards in the studio . . .

It was good for her to have something to do instead of brooding over Gavin Guest or her row with David. She pinned up the posters, found a mirror and positioned it so that it improved the light. She cut some roses and thrust them into a jug to put on the windowsill, then raided her bedroom for cushions to throw on the bed. She even disconnected her beloved stereo system from the studio and installed it, trying to stifle the unworthy thought that she hoped he might properly appreciate her sacrifice.

When she had finished working at breakneck speed it was quarter to four, but the room did look bright and welcoming. He might consider it was sort of a chick's room, but that was the best she could do, and no one could say she hadn't tried. Pausing only to tug a comb through her hair, put on some lipstick and grab her bag and keys, she hurried downstairs and out to the car.

She mustn't be late. 'Come on, Boris,' she murmured as she turned the key in the ignition. 'Go for it, lad!'

With a sputter, a wheeze and an apologetic cough, Boris's engine died.

Blotting out the sun, Richard Webb's elongated shadow fell across the flower bed where Chrissie was engaged in a highly satisfying operation to repel an invasion of ground elder. Feeling, as usual when he approached her without warning, obscurely guilty, she hastily sat back on her heels and pushed her hair off her face, unconsciously leaving a muddy smear. Max, the old Lab who was lying at her side, struggled up in protest as his patch of sunlight was usurped.

Richard didn't normally come to seek her out in the garden. His favoured Sunday afternoon occupation was commandeering the newspapers and retreating with them to his study where he would be undisturbed until Chrissie came to tell him tea was ready.

But today he had been uncharacteristically restless and fidgetty. He had fetched the papers early today, but had seemed to tire of them quickly. When the phone rang, he had been the first to reach it, and then been needlessly terse with Susannah who was phoning to invite Charlotte over. And after lunch instead of retreating to his study he had announced that he was going out for a walk.

'Take Max,' Chrissie had suggested, but he had sent a contemptuous look in the direction of the dog at her feet and said, 'Too old and too fat.' Chrissie winced. Was it only the dog he meant?

He was back now, but he didn't look as if the exercise had given him any particular satisfaction.

'Were you thinking of making tea today,' he said brusquely, 'or is that too much to ask?'

Chrissie looked at her watch. 'Goodness, is that four o'clock already? Yes, of course.'

With a longing backward glance at the ground elder – so nearly vanquished – she and Max followed Richard into the kitchen.

She washed her hands, switched on the kettle, fetched a tin of biscuits. As she got the mugs out of the cupboard he said, so casually that the remark screamed significance, 'Have you been along to the shop today?'

Chrissie stiffened. Had somebody told him, or did he suspect, her convenient arrangement for procuring the comforting green bottles?

'No,' she said defensively. 'No, I haven't.' She hadn't needed to; there was still one left at the back of the cleaning cupboard, and anyway she was always very cautious when Richard was at home.

'I just wondered if there were any more news about that poor girl on the common? Your friend Mrs Rees is usually the fount of all knowledge.'

'Oh, did you go along there on your walk?' Chrissie asked innocently. 'I would have thought there would be policemen there you could ask.'

Richard's face darkened alarmingly. 'What on earth makes you imagine I would do such a vulgar thing as going to gawp at the scene of a crime?' he demanded angrily.

Chrissie hastily backed off. 'Sorry, no, of course not. It was just when you asked me about the talk in the shop. Usually you're pretty scathing about Mrs Rees.'

'For God's sake, it was a casual remark, all right? I was surprised, if you really want to know, that you'd managed to get through Sunday without finding you'd forgotten something you needed.'

'Organised for once,' she said brightly as the kettle boiled and she went to warm the pot.

Richard made no reply. A moment or two later, however, he got up, frowning, and went over to the kitchen cupboards, opening a couple to rummage inside in a haphazard sort of way.

'Do we have any olives?' he asked suddenly.

'*Olives?*'

'Yes, olives. I just thought I might make dry martinis tonight. I haven't had one in ages.'

Dry martinis! Why on earth should he think of that? Usually, if she ventured to suggest having a drink on a Sunday night, he looked down his nose and pointed out that there had been wine with Sunday lunch. As if that had anything to do with it, as far as she was concerned; it was wearing off already, and with Richard acting so peculiarly what she needed was a quick swig of something to clear her mind. Dry martinis . . . Was it some kind of elaborate trap for her?

'Well, fine. If you like.' Surely that was noncommittal enough?

'So I'll need olives. I can't see any.'

'I don't think we've had an olive in the house for months. Probably not since the last time you had a dry martini.'

'Well, why don't you pop along to the stores and see if Mrs Rees has some tucked away somewhere?'

'I'm sure she won't. Olives aren't exactly a big thing in Llanfeddin.'

'Go and see anyway. It's worth a try, and if you go now she'll still be open.'

With the bemused feeling of someone expected to join in a conversation without having heard what topic was under discussion, Chrissie left him with the teapot, took her bag and hurried out. Max, delighted at the unexpected walk, padded along behind her panting a little in the afternoon sunshine. He waited politely outside while she went in, ensured that the Llanfeddin Stores did not, in fact, have a secret olive cache, and came out again.

She really didn't know what to think. She almost expected to see Richard tailing her, skulking behind a bush, trying to catch her out. But there was no sign of him and indeed when she got back he was still sitting at the table where she had left him.

'Well?' he said, looking up sharply as she came in.

Chrissie shrugged. 'No olives. I didn't think they would.'

She had turned to lift the cosy and pour the tea, did not see her husband's hands tighten convulsively on the edge of the table. He kept his tone light.

'And what did the evil old bat have to say today?'

She stared at him. 'Richard, I didn't stop to talk. You were waiting for your tea—'

He got up as if he could bear to sit still no longer. 'It's probably bloody well cold by now anyway,' he said, and went out, slamming the door.

As always when things were difficult, Chrissie thought longingly of the cool green bottle. It produced that wonderful comforting fuzziness which stopped her trying to work out what was wrong when the answer, whatever it was, was unlikely to make her happy.

But Richard might come back in as suddenly as he had left, so she contented herself with substantially stiffening her tea from the bottle of cooking brandy, always conveniently to hand in the cupboard next to the cooker.

It wasn't as good, but she was thankful she hadn't risked getting out the gin because minutes later the door opened without warning, and there was Richard. Smiling.

'Chrissie, I'm sorry. I don't know what's got into me today.'

He was switching on the charm. Why, she wondered dispassionately? Even when he wanted something he didn't usually make the effort.

'There have been a couple of things at the surgery that have been bothering me,' he went on, 'and I still feel completely washed out after my night on duty. I didn't get much sleep last night.'

She knew that was true, of course. No one else could sleep in a room with Richard, if Richard couldn't. He had groaned, flung himself to and fro in bed, snapped on the light to read, got up to fetch a glass of water. And anyway, her principal ambition in life was to be allowed to take things at face value.

'That's all right.' She gestured at the teapot. 'Are you sure you don't want some? It's still hot, actually.'

'Oh yes, why not. And are those some of your shortbread biscuits? Excellent!'

He took one, bit into it thoughtfully, then said, 'You know, Chrissie, I've been thinking. We never see people nowadays, and I'm sure it's not good for you to be isolated. Goodness, we don't even know our neighbours properly.'

Chrissie looked at him doubtfully. 'I can't think we'd have much in common with the Llanfeddin people—'

'Oh, I don't mean that. But there are people like that consultant – Winthrop, isn't it? – and his mother, and that girl we met at the Carltons', a silversmith, I think she said she was. They all live in the valley, and that police inspector and his wife along the road. We really ought to know them better. Why don't you ask them in for a drink?'

And she had worked so hard at her isolation! Reluctantly, she said, 'Well, I suppose—'

'Why not? Just a casual, short-notice drink among neigh-bours, nothing elaborate. Maybe they could come tomorrow – Monday afternoon's usually quiet, and I haven't got an evening surgery.'

He'd obviously been working this out. Perhaps that explained the bizarre business with the olives.

'Oh, were you planning to give them dry martinis? I couldn't think why on earth you wanted to make them tonight.'

She did not notice the infinitessimal pause before he said heartily, 'That's right, yes. It's been on my mind that we should do a bit more entertaining. You won't forget to buy olives tomorrow, will you – we'll just have to make do without them tonight, won't we?' He laughed. 'And then after that perhaps you might phone round?'

He went out without finishing either his tea or the biscuit. Chrissie sat on at the table, sipping at her mug of tea-flavoured brandy.

Even that couldn't blot out the fact that Richard was up to

something. It didn't, thankfully, seem to have anything to do with her drinking, as she had guiltily thought at first. Could it be the silversmith, perhaps – Marnie? She was a very attractive girl, vivid and amusing. It wouldn't be surprising.

Chrissie looked down at her baggy jeans, with the muddy patches on each knee, at her cracked hands and blackened, grimy nails. She couldn't blame him, and as long as it was discreet, unthreatening—

Then she remembered Paul Arkwright. He had sounded so wistful about the broken relationship, and they'd made a lovely couple. She could ask him for drinks tomorrow too, throw them together . . .

The unlikely Cupid got to her feet, rinsed the mugs and put the lid back on the biscuit tin. Then she hurried joyfully back to the ground elder.

In his study with the door shut, Richard wasn't smiling any longer. His face was grim: he knew he was behaving irrationally, and sooner or later even Chrissie was going to start asking questions.

He glanced across the room at the telephone, sitting innocuously on the table by the fireplace. He had been resisting the temptation to pick it up all day.

'This is the police surgeon,' he could say. 'I was wondering what progress had been made on the Willow Lampton case—'

They would probably tell him, that was the frustrating thing. But he couldn't be sure that they wouldn't think it was odd that he should be so anxious . . .

He had taken a risk in going across to the common this afternoon; one of the policemen guarding the area might have recognised him. 'Funny,' he might have said, 'I wonder why the police surgeon was hanging around today?'

But he couldn't bear any longer not to know what was going on, and climbing from the other side to the slope above he had been able to look down on the polythene tent they had erected over the place where her body had been, and the men fanned out searching the immediate vicinity. He shivered. It certainly looked like a murder investigation. But he didn't *know*.

The Rees creature probably did by now, and if Chrissie hadn't been so dimwitted . . . He groaned.

It would be in tomorrow's papers for sure. And then if they could get Cordiner round for a drink tomorrow, it would be perfectly natural, in his position, to chat about the case, find out his way of thinking, subtly of course. Then he could work out his strategy accordingly – it should be easy enough for someone of his intelligence to keep one jump ahead of the plods.

The trouble was – his stomach lurched – if they started digging . . . Perhaps they would decide it wasn't murder, after all.

For form's sake, Tessa turned the key once more in the ignition, but it was no surprise to hear nothing more than a dead 'click'. Boris's statement had turned out to be final, not to say terminal.

It was tempting to beat on the steering wheel, scream with frustration, but she was too short of time to indulge in unconstructive emotion. She leaped out of the car and hurried back into the house.

Llanfeddin boasted a taxi – only one, but then it was only one she needed. As she dialled the number she breathed a fervent prayer that no one had been inspired to hire it for a Sunday visit to their auntie in Wales.

Apparently the gods were smiling.

'Immediately?' a woman's voice said. 'And what address?'

When she gave it, there was a long, cold silence. Then, 'I'm afraid he won't be able to take you,' the voice said, and then the line went dead.

It took a moment for Tessa to understand. This was part of her punishment for daring to accuse Gavin Guest, yet another feature of Llanfeddin's organised campaign of persecution. They had declared her an outcast. Would they, she wondered wildly, leave her where she lay in the gutter if she crawled there bleeding and begging for their help?

She bowed her head and clasped her arms about her tightly

with a dry sob. They had got her caged here now, caged and help-less, with no escape, an easy prey to their implacable hostility.

And now David's son was going to arrive at the station in a strange town and find no one there to meet him – a child who was feeling resentful and unwanted anyway, a child who might do anything . . .

There would be plenty of time for self-pity later, Tessa told herself fiercely. Just at the moment there was a pressing practical problem to deal with.

Rapidly she reviewed the possibilities. David was incom-municado. A taxi from Stetford could easily take twenty minutes to get here, and if she set out to hitchhike any passing neigh-bour was more likely to run her down than to give her a lift. There was Mrs Winthrop, of course, but she didn't drive—

Marnie, she thought suddenly. Could she, by any blessed chance, be back from her trip?

The cheerful voice saying, 'Hi there!' at the other end of the phone, and promising immediate rescue, brought tears of sheer relief to her eyes.

Tessa was waiting on the road at the foot of the drive when the battered blue van, exotically emblazoned with silver scrolls, drew up a few minutes later.

'What time is the train?' Marnie demanded as Tessa scram-bled in and slammed the door, then slammed it again as it failed to catch.

When she told her, Marnie shook her head. 'We won't make it, obviously. Still, at least I should get you there in time to prevent him phoning Childline and accusing you of neglect. Hold tight for chills, thrills and hopefully not spills – here we go!'

As the elderly machine roared valiantly into action, Marnie said, 'I didn't realise you were expecting your stepson.'

'I wasn't,' Tessa said tersely, and filled her in on the back-ground as the van bucketed round corners to which Marnie took an artistically impressionistic approach.

'And of course, with the murder, David's got his hands full already,' she concluded.

'Murder?' Marnie took her eyes off the road to look at her

in astonishment, as a result adopting a line for the next corner which was almost catastrophically interesting.

'I'd have broken the news more gently if I'd realised you didn't know,' Tessa said when she got her breath back. 'It happened on Friday night. Willow Lampton. Oh, watch out!'

Correcting just in time to avoid an on-coming car, Marnie said, 'Willow Lampton! Oh God, how awful. Not that she wasn't courting trouble, mind you, but – murder! Who – who do they think did it?'

'Don't ask me. I'm only married to the guy in charge of the investigation.'

Tessa told her what she did know, but Marnie's response was so muted that her friend cast a sharp glance at her.

'Oh – you don't think your young doctor—'

'He isn't my young doctor, and no, of course I don't.' It wasn't like Marnie to snap; she drove on in silence for a minute then burst out, 'But oh, Tessa, what if she drove him to it? She was such a bitch, that woman. She got pleasure out of torturing people.' Then she added, 'Not that it's anything to do with me, of course.'

'Of course not,' Tessa echoed diplomatically. 'Anyway –' she hesitated, then said in a rush, 'I'm sure it's Gavin Guest. I said that to David, and he just brushed me aside. He wouldn't even listen. And today Guest even came to the house – it was horrible –'

Marnie listened, then said gravely, 'Do be careful, Tessa. He's a bad man, everybody knows that. And he's been clever enough to get away with it for years, but sooner or later—'

They were just reaching the station now, and Tessa looked at her watch.

'Twenty to five. Brilliant! I thought it would be worse than that. Taking my life in my hands is a small price to pay.'

She jumped out and shut the door on Marnie's indignant protests. At least, with all the fuss, she hadn't had time to agonise over the difficult encounter which lay ahead.

Chapter Eleven

'Well, what did you make of all that?' Paul Arkwright said tiredly, hoping for reassurance. The police interrogation had been an ordeal, but if it had served its purpose in convincing the police of his innocence it would have been worth every agonising minute.

Andrew Lomax took a long pull at his beer and stretched back in the sagging armchair, his long legs reaching half-way across the floor of Paul's tiny sitting room.

'I don't know, Paul. I just don't know. The trouble is, I'm seriously out of my depth here. Tomorrow I think I should phone someone who's got experience of dealing with the police. One of the guys who did law with me, Damien Burgess, went into a criminal practice in Birmingham—'

'You don't think they've finished with me, then?' Paul could not conceal his dismay at the lawyer's response. 'I answered all their questions – in fact, I told them everything I could think of. Surely they can't believe I've got anything to hide?'

Andrew sat up again. 'You see, the problem is I'm not even sure whether that was the best thing to do. Perhaps I should have told you to say nothing at all.'

'But surely—'

'Oh, I know, I know, the great British justice system, we're all on the same side and all that. Fine, provided you're dealing with decent straight coppers who are only interested in getting at the truth.'

Paul looked at him in horror. 'And you don't think they are?'

'Oh sure, sure. As far as I could tell it was all straightforward enough, and of course if I'd thought anything different I'd have stopped you.

'But if you talk to someone like Damien, he'd make your hair curl. They all have efficiency targets these days, and cutting corners is just part of the job. He'd probably say you should tell them as little as possible.'

'Well, thanks,' Paul said bitterly.

'Look, I don't mean that exactly. They're decent enough around here, I reckon, and I still think you did the best thing in the circumstances. And anyway, maybe we'll be able to find someone to say they saw you coming home, or heard you moving about your flat, or something. I'll chase around tomorrow asking questions – you're on duty, aren't you?'

Gloomily, Paul nodded. 'Just for the day.'

'I'll catch up with you sometime tomorrow evening, then, but I've got to go. I promised my mother I'd be home for supper tonight. All I'm saying is, if they pull you in again get someone like Damien in on the act. And don't say anything more without getting advice. OK?'

It was very quiet after Andrew left. The little sitting room was dark and not particularly comfortable, which usually didn't matter because he spent so little time in it alone, but tonight its effect was depressing.

Tonight he was alone, very much alone. Outside, he could hear voices in the street, the voices of people out for a walk, for a meal, for a drink. Andrew was on his way home for a family supper. None of them were under police suspicion for murder.

Perhaps it felt like this when you were told you had cancer. You were marked out as different, apart, alone . . .

He switched on the television, but as he surfed the channels the programmes seemed almost offensively fatuous, and he switched it off again. He could phone his parents in London, of course, but he couldn't bring himself to worry them, probably needlessly. He had to stand on his own two feet – but he felt young, and vulnerable, and very scared.

He was tired, too, but it wasn't the sort of tired where you could go to bed and sleep for twelve hours. He shut his eyes, then opened them again.

If only he had stayed faithful to Marnie, none of this would have happened. He thought longingly of her now – her bright eyes, her wide generous mouth, her gutsy infectious laugh. Willow's had been the charms of darkness – sensuous, exotic and ultimately sickening. Marnie – Marnie was wholesome, like fresh linen and warm bread and clear spring water.

He glanced at the telephone, tempted, but what was the point? What could he say, that wasn't contaminated before he said it by Willow's poison?

At least there was one consolation; Matthew wasn't hard to identify. He was alone on the platform, sitting on a well-stuffed kitbag, his head bent. He looked forlorn, despondent, and Tessa's heart went out to him.

'Matthew! Matthew!' she called, hurrying over.

He looked up, and for a fraction of a second she could see relief on the unformed adolescent features. Then he got to his feet, and scowled.

He was at the growing stage, as awkward in movement as a foal not yet used to unfolding its legs. He was much darker than his father, but he had David's well-shaped head and narrow, intelligent face. One day, when his complexion settled down, he might be quite good-looking with those very striking dark eyes, now glaring at her stormily.

Tessa hesitated. She couldn't possibly kiss him; that would be both impertinent and phoney. But shaking hands with your stepson seemed equally unnatural, particularly when his hands at the moment were firmly tucked into the pockets of his distressed jeans. She contented herself with saying, 'I'm Tessa. I'm so sorry to keep you hanging on like this – my wretched car packed up just as I was ready to come and get you.'

He barely glanced in her direction, picking up the bag and setting off towards the exit.

'Where's Dad?' was all he said, over his shoulder.

'He sends his apologies. He's really upset not to be here, but he's just been put in charge of a murder investigation and the Chief Constable insisted on seeing him just at the most inconvenient time. He's coming whenever he can get away.'

The still-childish mouth tightened. 'Same old Dad!'

They came out through the station archway on to the pavement at the same time, if not precisely together.

'Which is the car?' he asked, looking past Marnie's van drawn up neatly on the double yellow lines in front.

Tessa indicated. 'One of my friends was kind enough to come to my rescue when the car wouldn't start.'

'*This?*' he stared at the dilapidated vehicle disbelievingly as Marnie got out smiling.

'Hi! You must be Matthew. I'm Marnie.'

He ignored her. 'It's only got two seats.'

'Oh, I'll get in the back,' Tessa said hastily.

Marnie eyed them both, amused. 'No, no. Matthew won't let you do that, will you, Matthew? He'll heave his bag in and then he can sit on it. Lucky you're wearing your old jeans!'

'They're *designer*,' he began furiously, then recognising mockery, stopped. Giving her a death stare he clambered resentfully into the back of the van, making a production out of clearing a space among the boxes stacked there so that he could sit down.

He volunteered only one remark on the journey, as they turned off the main road and into the valley – 'People live in places like this? When do we drop off the edge of the world?' – to which there didn't seem to be any very adequate reply.

Marnie dropped them at the foot of the drive, waved aside Tessa's heartfelt thanks and drove on.

As the noise of the van's engine died away, the silence seemed to close in like the wake behind a ship. Somewhere a bird was chirping, and the leaves overhead rustled in a breath of wind, but there was no other sound. The road was empty of cars and the view of the valley and the surrounding hills was unbroken by any sign of human habitation. Tessa saw the boy stare about him, noticed him swallow convulsively, and again felt that surge of pity.

'Have you spent much time in the country?' she asked gently.

'What would I want to do that for?'

She led the way up the drive. 'As a matter of fact, we feel we made a bit of a mistake, moving out here.' She gestured towards the 'For Sale' sign. 'It's just that bit too isolated. Though there are good things about living in the country – pretty views, lovely walks—'

'Have you got a dog?' His voice sounded quite different as he asked the question.

'I'm afraid we don't.' She unlocked the front door and opened it to let him through in front of her. 'Do you like dogs?'

'They're all right. We had one once, but we had to give it away after –' Then he broke off. 'Can I phone Mum?' he said, and his voice was harsh again.

'Of course. Let me show you your bedroom first, then you can phone while I make tea.'

Matthew looked disparagingly round the room she had so anxiously prepared, dropped his bag on the floor then went downstairs to the phone in the hall. As she followed him down she heard him say, 'Mum? Yeah. Well, she was late and he didn't bother to come at all. How long do I have to—'

Tessa went into the kitchen and shut the door. This wasn't going to be easy, but she didn't feel like blaming him. The blame lay squarely with David and Lara, who had both put their own needs before the happiness of their child, and she felt angry on his behalf. He'd even lost his dog as a result, hadn't he?

Perhaps they might get a puppy.

Matthew slouched into the kitchen looking more surly than ever and sat down at the table without looking at her.

He ate four crumpets and drank two cans of coke while she sipped a mug of tea, but the conversation didn't exactly flow. More for the boy's sake than his father's, Tessa emphasised again how important the meeting was. Matthew showed a flicker of interest when she talked about the murder situation, but even

that topic soon became mired in the quicksands of his determined indifference.

Matthew was getting obviously restive. With a certain
desperation, she said brightly, 'Half-past five. David shouldn't
be long now. He said it would be quite a short meeting.'

Matthew got to his feet. 'Can I go out?' he said. 'Or are you
supposed to keep me locked up here so I don't get into trouble?'

If being out when his father got back was intended as
deliberate provocation, that was between him and David. She
was tired of making diplomatic noises.

'Matthew, I'm nobody's keeper. And if you can find trouble
out here to get into, I will personally award you a prize for in-
genuity. And if it's fun, you can tell me about it so I can try it
out for myself later.'

She almost surprised a smile out of him. The corners of his
mouth quivered before he got them back under stern control.
Hands still in his pockets, he lounged out of the kitchen with a
contrived swagger and she heard the front door close.

So he had a sense of humour as well as a liking for animals.
She didn't feel as dismayed as she had done before she met him,
despite the adolescent sulks and the black looks. It was up to
David, of course, to decide how he was going to handle the
shoplifting business, but if Matthew was bad – as opposed to
confused and angry and hurt – she would eat David's uniform
cap, badge and all.

And she hadn't thought about Gavin Guest once since they
came in. Perhaps she had got things completely out of perspective, from being here on her own so much. Perhaps she was
over-refining on what were, after all, unpleasant but childish
tricks, and stupidly offensive behaviour. Perhaps all she needed
was something else to worry about, and Matthew looked ideally
suited to fill that slot.

David Cordiner came out of the Superintendent's room and
glanced at his watch.

The Chief Constable had been disconcerting: a blunt, hard-bitten Northerner who had asked a few abrupt questions, seemed satisfied enough with the answers, and showed no inclination to prolong the interview for social reasons.

'You need extra manpower,' he said, 'and a Press Officer. I'm sending you Peters. She's a seasoned operator, journalist herself once, and she'll keep them off your back. The rest is your job.'

And that was it. No hiding-place. An opportunity for triumph, or disaster. And it did not seem likely that the Chief Constable would have Kipling's even-handed approach to the outcome.

Back in his own office, David glanced at his watch again. Tessa would have picked Matt up by now, and she wouldn't be expecting David's return for at least another half hour. He had crucial planning to do for tomorrow, and he was very curious to know what Pardoe and Watson had made of the rest of the Arkwright interview. Then if he sorted out some files to take with him, he could work on at home, and unless anything unexpected came up he wouldn't have to come back in again until tomorrow morning . . .

When he reached his car eventually, it was after half-past six. Feeling harassed, he slung his briefcase in the back and drove off.

He shouldn't be leaving now. He should be sitting round with Pardoe and Watson, discussing, speculating, arguing. Tonight was the calm before the storm; there would be no time tomorrow, once the bandwagon started rolling and the snow-drifts of reports started piling up. And while the chat might seem inconsequential, that was how a good investigation took shape. Where you made your breakthrough, sometimes.

Instead, here he was driving home to a disaffected wife and a delinquent son, feeling guilty because he was leaving as well as guilty because he hadn't left sooner. It was a dismally familiar feeling.

He should be working out how to deal with Matt, since all his agonising last night hadn't achieved anything. But how could he, when he couldn't even conjure up the boy's face, hadn't even managed the most basic 'Wanted'-style description for Tessa?

David flinched. He'd see Matt, he'd react. That was the best he could come up with, and with deplorable relief he switched back to more constructive considerations.

Tomorrow he would have all that extra manpower to deploy. They must have their details first thing so they wouldn't be standing expensively about waiting while he decided what he wanted them to do. Widen the search at the common, check the car park area, interview locals, hospital contacts, school friends. He'd have less time for leg-work himself, which was a pity. Reading and analysing and sifting – that would be his major task now.

Then he was backing up the drive and he couldn't duck the problem of Matthew any more. He let himself into the house.

Today he noticed that Tessa hadn't come to meet him when she heard his key in the lock. She'd be with Matt, probably. He listened for their voices. They weren't in the sitting room – in the kitchen, probably—

David opened the door, a smile prepared and his lips ready to form the words, 'Matt! Good to see you!'

Tessa was alone in the kitchen, sitting at the table reading a magazine. She didn't get up.

'Goodness, the Chief Constable kept you a long time,' she said coolly.

He didn't correct her, but went over to kiss her cheek. 'Where's Matt? Upstairs?'

'Out.'

David's eyebrows rose. 'Out? What on earth has he found to take him out at this time?'

'He's gone for a walk, I imagine. He wanted to go, and I didn't feel obliged to stop him to wait in for you. Always supposing I could.'

'Well no, of course not.' But it was an anticlimax, and the atmosphere in the room was decidedly uncomfortable. David moved restlessly round the kitchen, noticed the salad prepared and the steaks waiting to go into the frying pan. 'When did he go?'

'About half-past five.'

'And it's getting on for seven! Well, Matt must have changed a lot in the past year if he's into country walks. Are you sure there isn't an amusement arcade in Llanfeddin we don't know about?'

The joke fell flat. Tessa said uneasily, 'I know it's a long time, but I can't see that he could find anything too terrible to do out here.'

'How – how was he?'

Tessa grimaced. 'Hostile, I suppose, would be the best way to describe it. But then, we didn't exactly get off to a good start. Boris broke down, the Llanfeddin taxi is clearly part of the Unholy Trinity mafia and charmingly refused to come. I don't know what I'd have done if Marnie hadn't been back from Birmingham and able to come to the rescue.

'But by then, of course, we were late, and Matthew wasn't much impressed by that, or by the standard of the transport provided. And naturally he wasn't precisely thrilled that you weren't there.'

'No, I can see that. I'm sorry. And I apologise for my son.' It came out cold and pompous; he didn't mean it to sound that way.

'Oh, don't apologise for Matthew.' Did he imagine it, or had she put a faint stress on the name? 'He doesn't like me at the moment, but I rather like him. I think there's a good kid in there somewhere, but I'm not sure that it's actually struggling to get out as yet. And when it does it's going to be some struggle.'

'So what time do you think we can expect him back?'

'David, I don't know. Perhaps I should have given him a deadline, or something, but I'm not very practised at dealing with teenage boys.'

She sounded irritable, and he could hardly blame her. She went on, 'I told him you said it was a short meeting and you wouldn't be long, and at half-past five he just got up and said he was going out. Perhaps he's waiting until he's sure you're home before he comes back, just to make his point.'

'I see. Do you want a drink?'

Without waiting for an answer, he fetched two glasses and a

bottle of wine, uncorked it and poured it out. He found some peanuts, tipped them into a bowl on the table, and sat down. He took a handful of peanuts, a sip of his wine. Then he said, 'Do you think he's run away?'

'Oh, don't say that!' Tessa sighed heavily. 'I can't deny the thought was beginning to occur to me. But I couldn't stop him leaving the house, could I?'

'Of course not. It's not your fault.'

'But how could he do it, from here? I had enough difficulty, goodness knows, without Boris, and it's a long way to walk to Stetford. Anyway, you'd have passed him on the road, wouldn't you?'

'He might have tried to hitchhike—'

When the phone rang they both jumped up, but Tessa was nearer the door. David followed her through to the hall.

'Oh hello, Agnes,' he heard her say, and disappointed went back into the kitchen again.

But when Tessa came back she was smiling. 'Relax! Matthew's all right. That was my friend Agnes Winthrop from up the valley. She's quite an impressive lady – her son's a consultant at the hospital.'

'Yes, I've come across him. And?'

'Matthew's at her house. She was out walking her dog – he's gorgeous, a cheerful springer spaniel called Jake – and Matthew and Jake struck up an acquaintance. He's keen on dogs, isn't he?'

'We had one, a rather sporty little dachshund. But Lara felt she had to get rid of it after they moved to the flat.'

'Yes, he told me. Well, he and Agnes got into conversation about dogs, and one thing led to another. She's a good person to talk to – I can vouch for that – and he's still there. She asked if he wanted to stay to supper, and he said yes, but she wasn't to tell us—'

'*What!*'

'Well, I think his idea is that we should be made to go through agonies of uncertainty about what had happened to him. She managed to sneak to the phone while he was out in the garden, trying to train Jake to die for Arsenal, apparently, but I promised I wouldn't tell him she'd given him away.'

David glared at her. 'Well, that seems to me a very peculiar attitude. She could have tried just sending him home—'

'And what makes you think he would have meekly done that? For goodness' sake, David, he's a very upset, mixed-up child—'

'He's a very rude, inconsiderate little monster.' He gestured towards the food she had prepared. 'You had supper waiting ready for him—'

'Oh no! Leave me out of this!' Her voice was rising, dangerous.

Angry himself, partly in reaction to his earlier anxiety, he ignored the storm signals. 'All right. Purely from my own personal point of view, then, he's a rude, inconsiderate little monster. We've both been worried; in another quarter of an hour I'd have been out combing the place for him, and then I'd have had to report he was missing, waste police time – and a right idiot I would have looked, wouldn't I? I don't see why the woman is encouraging him—'

'She isn't! She just phoned us, didn't she?' Tessa's eyes were sparkling with temper. 'David, could you do me a favour and forget you're a policeman, just for ten minutes? Do you think you could manage that?

'I don't actually care if you might have looked foolish to your colleagues. As a matter of fact, I don't give a stuff if it might have wasted half an hour of police time. I pay enough for it. Is that heresy? Oh, wash my mouth out!'

She drew a deep breath, then said more temperately, 'David, you have a job, that's all. It's not a religious vocation. If that was what you were looking for, you should have been a monk, not had a son whose life is in a fair way to being ruined because he can't rely on a father who will put his needs before the demands of the job. Do you know what the first thing he said to me was? "Where's Dad?"

'I do understand how important a murder investigation is, so spare me the heavy explanation. But I do just wonder if you did actually come running home the minute your interview with the Chief Constable was finished?'

David hadn't blushed in years, but now he felt his face turn a childish crimson and even his ears start to glow. 'I thought, if I just finished up one or two things, then I wouldn't have to go in afterwards—'

'I'm sure that was terribly sensible. I'm also sure that if you're honest with yourself you'll admit that it was a lot more appealing than coping with poor Matt's problems. And you see, you had said you would come dashing out the minute the meeting was over, and you didn't come. That's what you said you would do, and you didn't do it.'

From force of habit he began defensively, 'You don't understand—' But as he said the words, he could feel the chasm opening up in front of him, a black abyss of misery and misunderstanding. He had stood on that brink before, and, God forgive him, he had not cared enough to draw back. He cared now.

Under her clear, accusing gaze his own eyes fell and he said humbly, 'You're right. I'm sorry. That was a promise I didn't need to break.'

'But do you hear what I'm actually saying? I wouldn't presume to speak for Matthew, of course, but I do appreciate how demanding the job is. I didn't marry you expecting to have a husband who worked nine to five. What I find hard to accept is being the less favoured option.'

David saw her mouth quiver and, aghast, went over to put his arms round her. 'Never that, my darling,' he said, then, aware with shame that his statement was not as wholly truthful as he would have liked it to be, added, 'but sometimes it's difficult—'

She turned her head into his shoulder, but she didn't cry. 'It's not easy for anyone,' she said, her voice muffled. 'Gavin Guest came to the house today.'

'Guest?' He held her away to look at her in concern, then listened gravely as she tried to explain what he had done and how it had made her feel.

'Hmmm,' he said when she had finished. 'He's a smart

bastard. What can one possibly do about that? And it's hard to know whether it's more than a malicious attempt to wind you up.'

He sat down beside her, and she leaned forward earnestly. 'David, what about the murder? Why do you think he shouldn't be connected with a violent crime, right here on his doorstep?'

David sighed. 'It goes without saying that we have to keep an open mind. And as of tomorrow I've got a much bigger force at my disposal, and I'll certainly see to it that someone checks him out.

'But you know what I mean when I talk about psychological profiling—'

'Of course. It's in every crime series on TV.'

'Right. But just because it's a telly cliché, it doesn't mean that it doesn't work. And the style simply doesn't fit with anything we know, or even suspect, about Gavin Guest. Willow Lampton wasn't grabbed violently, as you were. She wasn't assaulted. She didn't have a mark on her.

'Not only that. Alun Jenkins, who is one of Guest's little Llanfeddin chums, works at the cash and carry that was broken into on Friday night, and we're pretty sure he was behind it. So it's more than likely Guest was too.'

'I see,' Tessa said thoughtfully. 'I suppose I ought to feel re-assured, but I'm not sure that I do. So who do you suspect? Have you got a front runner?'

'No. It's far too early, far too many questions still un-answered. Though there's a young doctor who's definitely in the frame—'

'Not Marnie's Paul Arkwright?'

'Well, that's his name, but—'

'He was more or less engaged to her before Willow came along.'

'Was he, indeed.' David pricked up his ears. 'He didn't mention that.'

'You don't really think he might have done it, do you?' She sounded startled.

'Nice young doctors don't do that sort of thing, you mean?

I'm afraid nice young doctors have been known to do just that. Not that I'm saying he did, of course—'

'But what do you *think*?' Tessa demanded.

'I didn't sit in on the whole interview. Joe Pardoe thinks he's capable of it, Sue Watson thinks he isn't, and Joe thinks Sue's swayed by the fact that he's a bit of a hunk. And that's about as far as we've got.'

Tessa got up to start cooking the steaks. 'It must be difficult not just to see it as a professional challenge. To remember that out there is someone who killed a young girl, who might be planning to kill again.'

David said soberly, 'No, that's a thought that is permanently at the back of my mind. And if they kill again, I have that person's death on my conscience, because I wasn't clever enough, or painstaking enough or just lucky enough to get to them first. But if I let myself dwell on that, I wouldn't be able to think straight, which wouldn't help anyone. So I have to concentrate on the practical problems, and otherwise – well, just get on with life.

'Like laying the table and fetching the mustard for the steaks – French or English?'

It was getting on for ten o'clock when Matthew set off for home. He started jauntily enough along the dark road, whistling at first, but somehow in the night and the silence the thin sound he made was not reassuring after all.

But Matt Cordiner knew how to handle himself – didn't he? The sky wasn't pitch dark, after all, there was a moon, and he could see the lights of the houses and the village on ahead. But there were no street lamps to show him where to put his feet; he stumbled once or twice, and the night noises from the fields and hedgerows spooked him. The small rustles, the occasional inexplicable crack of a twig nearby had him looking round over his shoulder at nothing. When he startled a bird, asleep in the hedge, and it whirred out at him with a startled squawk, his own heart raced in sympathy. Twice he had to climb on to the verge as cars came past, and dazzled by the headlights he could only stand transfixed like a fugitive trapped by a searchlight's beam.

He half-expected one of them to be Dad, out searching for him and furious. It had seemed a good idea to scare him, punish him, by disappearing, but now the confrontation was looming he did wonder weakly if he might just have gone over the top. His last demonstration of defiance was what had landed him here in the sticks, and if they had phoned Mum and she'd been worried she'd go ballistic too.

He hesitated as he reached the house. But there was a light on outside, and he didn't much like the sort of darkness they kept here in the country.

Both cars were in the drive; they weren't out looking for him, then. Obscurely disappointed, he tried the front door. It wasn't locked.

The hall was in darkness, but he could see the frame of the kitchen door outlined in light. With dragging feet he went across and opened it, squaring his slight shoulders as he did so, as if to withstand a hail of verbal blows.

After the threatening darkness outside, the kitchen looked particularly welcoming. Dad was working at the table with piles of paper spread about. She was perched at the end with a big sketch-pad propped on her knee and a pencil in her hand. They looked comfortable together.

He didn't want to think about that. He stood in the doorway, licking his lips nervously.

They had both looked up as he came in. They didn't look wracked with anxiety. They smiled.

'Hi, Matthew,' she said tranquilly. 'There you are!'

His father pushed back his chair, got up and came over to hug his son. 'I was beginning to wonder what on earth you were finding to do out there. Good to see you, Matt. This is where I don't say, "Goodness, how you've grown", right?'

Matthew stood rigid within David's embrace, rigid and furious. What the hell was this? He'd prepared himself for rage, furious questioning, the Where-do-you-think-you've-been-till-this-time-of-night? crap. He even had the sneering answer ready. 'What do you care, anyway? I'm old enough to do what I like.'

Perhaps they did think he was old enough. It seemed strange that this was an unwelcome thought.

Ungraciously he made no reply, freed himself, then went to slump in a chair by the table. He put his hands in his pockets and stretched out his legs in a pantomime of ease.

'Are you hungry?' she asked. 'It's a long time since tea.'

He would have liked to ignore her, but couldn't, quite. 'Er – no. Got something from Mrs Winthrop,' he muttered.

'Mrs Winthrop? Oh, I'm glad you met her. She's an interesting person, isn't she?' The woman sounded brighter than anyone would be normally; you'd think she was in a play or something. 'And Jake – Jake's brilliant, isn't he?'

'Jake's cool. And I've nearly taught him to die for the Gunners.' He had let himself be betrayed into enthusiasm; he stopped short and scowled.

His father said, 'Matt, I'm really sorry not to have met you at the station today. There was some excuse for that, but afterwards I should have dropped everything and I didn't. I should know better than to make promises and not keep them.'

Once again, this wasn't in the script. It had been clear in his head: he, hurling defiance and reproaches against an angry father who had never – his mother still banged on about it – seen anyone's point of view but his own. It had played well in his head, had even seemed quite dramatic and impressive when he ran it past Mrs Winthrop.

Now he looked down sulkily and shrugged. 'Doesn't matter.'

'Well, we more or less managed.' Tessa made a rueful face. 'Not that Marnie's van is exactly a stretch limo, I'm afraid. But David, I'll have to get someone out urgently to see Boris.'

'Boris, bizarrely enough, is what Tessa calls her car,' David explained to Matthew. 'I'll give Ron a ring at the garage that services the police cars and see if he can do a rush job.'

'No, I'll give Ron a ring and mention your name,' Tessa said firmly. 'I'm learning my lesson. The chances that you will remember tomorrow are somewhere between zero and zilch and until I get Boris fixed we're stranded, I'm afraid, Matthew.'

'That's no big deal.' It was good to be able to brush her off. 'Mrs Winthrop says if you're training a dog you have to, like, do it every day. And she knows where there are these fox cubs and we might, like, take a picnic or something. So count me out.'

He knew he sounded offensive, and it was gratifying to see Dad bristle. He'd always been very hot on good manners, had Dad.

But she didn't even seem to notice – thick-skinned, or what? 'Great!' she said. 'Oh, and we've got an invitation for tomorrow evening – drinks along the road at the Webbs'.'

As David looked alarmed, Tessa laughed. 'Oh, don't panic. I told Chrissie you'd be tied up. But she said to bring you, Matthew – she's got a daughter about your age.'

Oh, fantastic. That was all he needed. Some freaky kid wished on to him. He saw his father shoot him a sympathetic look, but refused to be disarmed. 'Do I have to go?'

'Oh yes, I think so,' David said before Tessa could reply. He was smiling, but his tone made Matthew decide not to argue the toss. He remembered that tone.

Tessa got up. 'I'm going to have an early night. Are you sure you don't want anything to eat before I go, Matthew?'

'I'm going to make a cup of coffee,' David said. 'There's Coke in the fridge, isn't there, and we'll probably raid the biscuit tin. You and I have one or two things to talk about, don't we, Matt?'

Matthew's heart gave a leaden 'thump' as his step-mother made her smiling good-nights and went out leaving father and son together.

SESSION FOUR

Wednesday 29 July

Session Four

'*Why did you go away yesterday?*'

'You didn't seem to want to talk to me.'

'*I didn't say that.*'

'You didn't say anything.'

'*I might have, if you'd stayed.*'

'What would you have said?'

'*You're trying to be clever now. Trying to trap me. I don't like to be trapped.*'

'It's your decision, what you want to say.'

'*You want to hear, don't you? You want to hear about what happened after the baby was born. You said you did.*'

'If you're ready to tell me.'

'*Perhaps I'm not.*'

'It's up to you.'

'*Why do you want to know, anyway?*'

'It might help us to understand.'

'*You said that before. But you won't. No one can understand, not really. No one ever has. No one. Not even my brother.*

'"*Do you hate the baby?*" *he asked me one day, as we stood throwing stones in the broad stream that meandered through the wood at the back of the house.*

'"*Oh yes, I hate the baby,*" *I said. I was skimming stones and I made a round flat one skip across the pool, glinting in the early summer sunlight. There were dragonflies too, brilliant shimmering blue dragonflies. I remember the dragonflies.*

'"Is it –" he said hesitantly, picking up a stone himself and throwing it clumsily so that it sank. "Is it all right to hate the baby?"

'I skimmed another stone before I replied. Perhaps he wasn't so soft and silly after all.

'"Remember Dad telling us about the cuckoo?"

'He screwed up his face uncertainly. "Sort of."

'"It lays its egg in another bird's nest with the other eggs. Then when the chick hatches it takes all the food and then it pushes the other chicks out of the nest."

'He remembered. "What happens to them when they're pushed out?"

'He was anxious. I can picture him, turning his little face up to me. I held his gaze. "Nobody looks after them, and then they die," I said slowly. "The baby's like a cuckoo."

'His eyes – big brown eyes like my mother's – were rounder than ever. But he didn't cry. I'd managed to teach him that, at least.

'After that, for a while, there was a sort of uneasy calm. When we weren't at school, we kept out of her way – I made sure of that. We slipped in at meal-times when my father was there, sat silent then slid away like wild things to the secret dens we'd made in the woods behind the house.

'In a strange way, I wasn't unhappy. I had cut my father off, you see, and my brother and I had each other – "forever and ever", as he still liked to say.

'The cuckoo baby was still purple and ugly but more active now, doing all the messy, noisy unpleasant things babies do. They're disgusting creatures, babies, aren't they? Revolting, I always think.

'My father was looking tired and sad and somehow older, but it had been his choice. He'd betrayed us just as surely as my mother had. They both made their choices, just the way She did, and the consequences were their responsibility too.

'They had made me into a freak show, and apart from my brother I had no friends at school. Children hate freaks; they're like rooks who'll peck a white rook to death if it tries to join the flock.

'One day, I lashed out at one of my tormentors. It was a lucky blow. He had a black eye for a week and his mother complained to the teacher. He asked me why I had done it, but I could read the verdict in his face before I could say anything, so I didn't bother. What would have been the use? He was against me anyway, like all the rest.

'In any case, it wasn't much of a punishment, being kept in after school, sitting with my arms folded among the empty desks in the schoolroom that always smelled of dust and old gym shoes, while the teacher ignored me pointedly and marked exercise books.

'At last he dismissed me. Outside it was a mild, sunny autumn day and the leaves were just starting to drift down, I remember; I made one or two half-hearted tries at catching one, but the chances of gaining a happy day next year – as the superstition had it – were so remote that it hardly seemed worth the trouble.

'My brother, of course, had gone home at the usual time, and thinking of him I quickened my steps. I didn't trust her not to do something spiteful when I wasn't there to protect him, and I hoped he would have had the sense to go off and hide.

'He hadn't. I saw him through the hedge in front of the cottage, sitting on the little square of grass. She wasn't there, but the baby was, lying on a rug in the sunshine, kicking its legs. As I got closer I could hear him talking. I stopped and bent to a gap in the hedge so I could peer through.

'The baby was mouthing at him, a stupid, meaningless grimace, but he obviously thought it was smiling. And he – he was smiling back, letting it make random grabs at his fingers with the fat pudgy hands that looked like hers.

'Suddenly, I was icy cold, as if the sun had gone out and the sky had turned black. Before my eyes the baby, which was still no more than a thing, was turning into a person, where he was concerned. And when it really was a person, would he still want to be mine, "forever and ever", or would he betray me too?

'When I turned in at the gate She was watching and I knew that this was her doing. She looked deliberately, meaningfully, from me to my brother with the baby on the grass, then back again. She smiled, a cruel, triumphant smile.

'She thought She had won. She thought She had stripped me of everything at last, broken me. That I was nothing, just as She had intended right from the start.

'When my brother saw me, he broke off guiltily. He scrambled to *his feet, came over, fawning like a puppy, pawing at me.*

'*I ignored him, ignored her. Walked past the house, walked so fast he couldn't catch up with me.*

'*I heard her voice calling him back, but he was still stumbling along behind me crying, "Wait for me! Wait for me!" And I knew he wasn't lost to me altogether. Not yet.*

'*But unless I did something, something strong and terrible, he very soon would be.*'

'I have to go now.'

'*What do you mean? I haven't finished. I enjoyed talking to you today.*'

'I know. I'll see you again tomorrow.'

Monday 13 July

Chapter Twelve

'What on earth makes you think you should go wasting money in Marks and Spencer's, just because you've asked one or two of the neighbours in for a casual drink?' Richard Webb said disagreeably. 'They won't be expecting much – a few crisps and nuts would do, and if you wanted you could cook a few sausages, couldn't you? If it wouldn't run away with too much of your day?'

He had come down to breakfast looking for an excuse to lose his temper. It had been another awful night: horrible dreams when he managed to fall asleep, horrible thoughts when he woke again ten minutes later.

He was feeling liverish, he told himself, after too many of the sample martinis last night. He didn't want to consider the other explanation.

'Richard, you make it sound as if asking these people was a whim of mine. It was you who suggested it, remember?'

Chrissie was looking offensively bright this morning. She usually did, on a Monday, when Richard was leaving to face the backlog of patients built up over the weekend. Probably because she'd have the gin bottle out before he had even cleared the drive.

'Well, of course I remember,' he blustered. 'I thought it would be nice for you, get you out of yourself a bit.'

He couldn't exactly say to her that if Cordiner wasn't going to come they might as well scrap the whole thing. Especially when, during his wakefulness in the small hours, he had realised that even if he were, a couple of dry martinis would hardly make an experienced police officer loose-tongued about the progress of the investigation. Nor was a very public ten-minute conversation going to change the Inspector's mind about the direction in which it should proceed.

The morning paper thudded through the letter box, and his heart missed a beat. There must have been a press release by now, surely? He stopped himself leaping to his feet to fetch it; Chrissie would definitely think it odd that he should suddenly perform the chore which was hers every other morning.

Today she was provokingly slow, finishing making the coffee before she plodded through, the dog as usual at her heels, picked it up and then came back. She seemed to pause in the hall; was she reading the headlines herself?

Richard looked down at his bowl of healthy high-fibre cereal doused in pale blue skimmed milk with distaste. It looked like nothing so much as shredded doormats, and tasted that way too. In the interminable minutes while he waited to learn the police verdict on Willow Lampton's death, he found himself wondering whether the present misery of eating the filthy stuff was really worth it for more of the same throughout a hideously protracted old age.

Chrissie laid the paper in front of him, then sat down to spread her thick slice of toast with butter and then chunky marmalade.

He picked it up, unfolded it with a practised shake and spread it flat on the table beside him, apparently with his usual calm.

The *Telegraph* was not given to sensationalist front pages. 'EU slap to Blair' was the main story, but there at the bottom right-hand side was a discreet headline, 'Mystery of Woman's Death'.

He read it through, his heart pounding now. In its customary measured terms, the paper described the circumstances in which Willow Lampton's body had been found, including the odd touch of the scattered flowers. It told him nothing he did not know already, until he reached the final paragraph. 'Despite the curious absence of any signs of violence on the body,' it said, 'the police are treating the death as suspicious.'

'Murder.' He said it aloud, then recollected himself as his wife said blankly, 'Sorry?'

'Er —' he cleared his throat, which seemed somehow constricted, 'there's a report here on Willow Lampton's death. It sounds as if they're thinking it might have been murder.'

'Oh yes. They were saying that on Saturday at the coffee morning. Poor thing – she was one of your patients, wasn't she?'

Richard looked across at her, looked at her thick, crepey neck and thought wildly of closing his hands around it, tightening his grip, squeezing and squeezing—

He got up abruptly, pushing aside his bowl with the cereal which had swollen to a murky, lumpy paste.

'I'd better get going,' he said. 'Monday's always a heavy morning surgery.'

'Fine,' Chrissie said, pouring herself another cup of tea and stretching across for the newspaper. 'See you this evening. There will be eight of us, I think, including the children – the Winthrops have refused, so it's ourselves, Marnie Evans – oh, and that nice young Doctor Arkwright we met at the Jamiesons. Susannah's staying the night, of course, and Tessa Cordiner's bringing her stepson – I told you that, didn't I? Inspector Cordiner can't come, obviously.'

'Obviously,' he echoed hollowly, going out.

Perhaps it got better once you accepted that there was absolutely nothing you could do. There was that experiment, wasn't there, done years ago before animal rights and all that sort of thing, when they wired up two sets of rats, and the ones that couldn't avoid the electric shocks survived while the ones with buttons to press that might stop them died in a matter of months, riddled with stomach ulcers.

Feeling twinges in his own stomach, though that was probably hunger, he drove off.

David Cordiner had gone off to work rather earlier. He was on his way to Stetford by seven o'clock, leaving his wife in her dressing gown and his son, at least judging by the sounds emanating from his bedroom, sound asleep.

He was just picking up speed as he drove out of the village when he noticed, as he passed the old carved stone, the flash of something white in the ditch. Frowning, he drew up, then walked back.

Once again, there was a piece of paper weighed down with a stone as if in tribute to the offensive, leering face above. It was soggy: it could have been there for days, of course, without his happening to notice it. He fished it out, then smoothed it open.

It was another drawing like the one he had seen that first morning in Llanfeddin, clearly by the same unskilled hand, the style like that of some monstrously perverted child. This time it was drawn in some sort of liquid ink – roller ball, perhaps – which had spread and smudged in the damp.

Even so, the agonised helplessness of the female body subjected to unspeakable indignities by the brutalist male figure was sadistically portrayed with crude, graphic eloquence.

He had thought himself hardened to most things, but this turned his stomach, and he held it away from him as if the very touch of it might contaminate. Perhaps, in any case, he should have picked it up with tweezers; forensic had some extraordinary techniques these days, and it would certainly be advisable, if possible, to establish the identity of someone with an imagination as sickly lurid as this. The paper was very wet, though. He could hardly believe that anyone would be able to resurrect the delicate greasy imprint left by the sweat on a fingertip.

Still, there was a plastic bag in the car and he fetched it, bagged the loathsome thing and put it out of sight in his briefcase with some relief.

When had it last rained? Not for a day or two, as far as he could remember, though it had been wet on Friday evening. Anyway, paper lying in a ditch for a few days would be wet through even with dew, so that probably didn't help. He got back into the car and drove on.

Inevitably, Gavin Guest came to mind. He was certainly sadistic enough to enjoy torturing Tessa. She had had a night-

mare last night, thrashing about and sobbing: when he roused
her she had muttered something about being trapped before
falling asleep again. She hadn't mentioned it this morning;
perhaps she wouldn't even remember.

The trouble was, personal involvement made it impossible
for him to be objective, as George Baker had brutally pointed
out before. Perhaps she had been neurotic and he overprotective
and Guest was merely reacting – unpleasantly enough, for sure
– to being wrongly accused. It was theoretically possible. And
what was certain was that he hadn't the slightest valid reason to
connect him with this obscenity.

Anyway, it would be up to the laboratory now. He couldn't
think it had any bearing on the case in hand, and he put it out
of his mind.

He yawned, a huge, exhausted yawn that made his eyes
water. It had been after two last night before he had got the rotas
mapped out and decided on what he would say at the general
briefing this morning. He didn't, however, grudge the time he
had spent with Matt after Tessa had left them.

He wasn't sure about the PR effect, if you could call it that.
Matt was still glowering when he went to bed, and David was
thankful to think that the public-spirited Mrs Winthrop would
be keeping him out of Tessa's hair today.

But after talking to him about the shoplifting episode, David
had felt at once relieved and ashamed. Relieved, because it was
obvious that Matt had been unhappy doing it and was even more
unhappy about it now. Ashamed, because it was part of a pattern
of behaviour designed to shock and upset, but above all to force
him to engage with his son.

When Lara told him Matt didn't want to see him, he had
been wrong to accept that. He should have exploded, refused to
permit it, shown the rage and pain he actually felt so that Matt
wouldn't be able to believe that his father was content to walk
out of his life with a philosophic shrug.

They had all paid for that mistake, but at least David had
worked it out now and it wouldn't happen again. And Tessa,
bless her golden heart, had been prepared to look beyond

the rudeness and rejection to the sad child within.

She had insisted on getting up to make David's breakfast this morning – though giving him a rain-check on the heart-shaped toast with the scrambled eggs – and at least she would have painting time today, thanks to the good offices of Agnes Winthrop.

His mind went to her son, John. He wasn't at all sure what to make of John Winthrop. He was a hard man to read, and in a way he was sorry he wouldn't be at the Webbs' drinks party tonight to which according to Tessa they seemed, curiously enough, to be inviting Willow's two most recent lovers. Did the Webbs realise that? Did the men themselves, come to that? It could prove an interesting encounter, if they both accepted, and he had managed to persuade Tessa to promise, if somewhat warily, that she would report back afterwards. He hadn't told Tess about Winthrop's involvement with Willow; he wasn't sure whom Winthrop had told, and it could be embarrassing with Agnes.

He arrived in his office expecting an hour or so of peace before the day shift arrived, but to his surprise the door opened a few minutes later and DS Owen Owen put his head round the door.

'Sir? They told me you were in, and I thought I'd stop by to give you the good news.

'They had me out of my bed at five this morning, didn't they, because they'd found a hired lorry up on a forestry track about ten miles away there, with all the cash and carry stuff right there inside.'

'Well, that's a bonus we didn't expect.'

'Oh, it gets better, sir, I tell you! What do we find on the floor in the cabin but a video card giving Alun Jenkins's name and address – one of the Llanfeddin boyos—'

'I know him. Mate of Gavin Guest's.'

'That's the one. Nice of him to leave his calling card, isn't it? And some good recent prints on the door handles and steering wheel too—'

'Guest's?' Cordiner asked hopefully.

Owen frowned. 'We-e-ell, you might reckon that, but according to Dai Lloyd yesterday his mam Hannah says he was with her all Friday night. Definite about it, she was, not to say downright nasty.'

'Would she lie?'

'Would a salmon swim if you dropped it in the Teifi?'

Cordiner laughed. 'You can try your luck with the prints, anyway, and see what happens when you lean on young Alun. Well done, Owen. It's good to think we'll be able to wrap that one up anyway.'

'Any leads on the murder yet, sir?'

'Nothing much. Today we should make a bit of progress, with all the extras coming in.'

'That's right, my cousin Ifor from Wrexham phoned me last night to say he was coming across.'

Cordiner sighed. 'Let's hope it pays off, that's all. It's been hard to get any sort of hold on this one. Give me a nice straight-forward domestic any day.'

Tessa sat on, huddled round her second cup of coffee after David had gone, conscious that she shouldn't be sitting there in her dressing gown, conscious that she should be dressed by now and in her studio slinging paint around.

Judging by the muted sounds of deep and enjoyable sleep she wasn't going to be bothered by Matthew for an hour or two. In fact, it sounded as if getting him on his feet in time for Agnes's picnic lunch might be quite a challenge. And after he'd gone, Tessa would have the rest of the day to herself as well.

So why was she still sitting moping here? I'll go when I've finished my coffee, she promised herself, then undermined the resolution by topping it up from the pot with the excuse that she needed the caffeine to get her going.

She had slept badly, and woke with her mind still clouded by vague half-memories of distressing dreams: she was impris-oned, tied down with ropes or behind bars, she was surrounded by sticky filaments like a spider's web which clung even closer when she tried to break free.

Even in the bright light of morning, she shuddered. You didn't need to be a Freudian to pick up the psychological symbolism; she had gone to sleep wondering how on earth she would manage her life if she couldn't instantly find someone to fix Boris. Trapped in this bloody place, bound to it by the sticky cords of love—

Oh, for goodness' sake! She jumped up, drained her coffee, cleared the dishes and went upstairs to shower as quietly as she could, dressed and came downstairs ready to start work. She reminded herself of what her art tutor, the original Boris, had always said, pointing to a reproduction of Rodin's 'The Thinker': 'That was a guy who sat around waiting for inspiration to strike, and look what happened to him.'

Downstairs in the studio she considered the canvas on the easel, prepared her palette and started doggedly to build on what she had done yesterday.

It didn't flow. After half-an-hour's work she stepped back to survey what she had done, and knew that she had ruined it.

With tears springing to her eyes she took it down from the easel and propped it with its face to the wall, not caring that she smudged it. On a better morning, perhaps, she could paint over it, recapture the vision . . . perhaps.

But she was determined not to be beaten. Gritting her teeth, she fetched the sketches she had done the night before and flicked through them. They weren't bad, in fact.

Encouraged, she pinned one to the easel and began to scale it up. The work was mechanical rather than inspirational: gradually it began to soothe her and she became absorbed, started to develop and elaborate the original conception.

So it was the more infuriating when she started feeling uncomfortable. Once she put her hand up to rub the back of her neck; twice she glanced beyond the wall of windows, without giving it much thought. The third time, when she felt impelled to look over her shoulder, she realised what was wrong.

Someone was out there, watching her again.

Either that or she was losing it to such an extent that they should take her away and put her in a home for the bewildered. It was only nine o'clock in the morning, for goodness' sake.

Outside, three sheep on the hill were nibbling grass with their usual neurotic assiduity. The trees were waving gently and the thick leafy foliage of the bushes which fringed the field rippled innocently in the same breeze. Or was someone making the branches move? She stared with painful intensity, her eyes raking the leaves for any betraying sign.

Was he there, staring back, relishing Tessa's awareness of his presence?

He had taught her before the unwisdom of stepping outside to put her suspicions to the test. He had made her feel, even here in her own home behind a locked door, exposed and vulnerable. She didn't care any more if he would enjoy seeing that she was afraid. She fled the studio.

With her heart thumping she locked the inside doors and stood still in the dark centre of the house and bowed her head. Whether it was by being there in the bushes outside, or by forcing his way inside her head, it was Gavin Guest who had caged her here.

He couldn't see her now. But then, neither could she see him. Was he moving stealthily round the house, seeking out some weakness he had discovered yesterday, inserting a knife silently to prise open a flimsy catch? If she opened the studio door, would he be there outside the windows? Was he in already, noiselessly listening to her roughened breathing from the other side of the door?

Tessa shivered. At least she had known not to try to make her escape in Boris. She could have been there, with no hiding-place, turning the key vainly in the ignition again and yet again, more and more frantically while he circled closer and closer, savouring her helplessness, playing with his prey until he picked up a stone and—

This was ridiculous, hysterical and childish. Painted devils, she told herself harshly. Imaginary terrors. Don't be such a pathetic fool!

It wasn't her style. Cheerful, she had always been, and confident and practical, feet firmly on the ground. Whatever had happened to the Tessa who was famed for having her head together?

Llanfeddin had happened. Llanfeddin with its prejudice and its persecution and its cold black heart. The Unholy Trinity – the jokey name didn't seem so funny any more.

If she allowed herself to be spooked like this they would have won, wouldn't they? She was damned if she was going to let the bastards win.

And the comforting thought occurred to her that she was not, in fact, alone in the house. She had forgotten Matthew was there upstairs, there to be roused if she found that her fears had substance. She certainly didn't fancy waking him to tell him she had a funny feeling that someone was watching her, which rather put things into perspective.

There was the telephone too, of course – wasn't there? In sudden panic Tessa snatched up the receiver and when she heard the dialling tone cradled it to her as affectionately as if it were a kitten making that reassuring purr.

She'd been planning to phone Ron at the garage anyway. The arrival of a sturdy mechanic would discourage any prowler, if prowler there was, and after that Boris would be fixed and her link with the outside world restored. The only question was how soon Ron could be persuaded to come, and she was prepared to use the leverage of David's position shamelessly.

It worked. Less than half an hour later Ron, a morose-looking man, was outside with his head under the bonnet of the car doing unmentionable things to Boris's innards. She had unlocked the doors, Matthew had surfaced and had groggily indicated that he would be prepared to let her supply him with bacon and eggs.

Presiding over the frying pan with the fragrance of sizzling bacon in the air and the kitchen window open to the breezy sunshine and the fluting of a blackbird in the apple tree in the garden, Tessa felt her mood lift. It was all so domestic, so normal . . .

Was it possible that her anxiety had been a hangover from those unpleasant dreams? It was hard to recapture something as nebulous as the feeling of being watched, and recollecting the artificial terror she had induced in herself afterwards, she was no longer absolutely sure.

'Matthew!' she called. 'Don't be long, will you? I'm putting your egg into the pan now.'

As she turned to fetch the egg, her eye was caught by a flash of something white in the garden, a sheet of paper, blown in no doubt from the road or someone else's dustbin. She was just about to go out and pick it up when a gust of wind caught it and twirled it merrily away into the bushes.

Tessa shrugged, then turned back to break the egg into the frying pan.

'Well, naturally they want to play with things, don't they,' Hannah Guest said, her voice vibrant with sympathetic sweetness. 'That's all right. Know what they're like at that age, don't I?'

She beamed at the harassed-looking young mother in her unwisely yellow shorts and crumpled T-shirt, whose three children all under the age of six were roaming free range about the craft shop fingering everything within their reach.

The woman smiled back gratefully, tucking her stringy hair behind her ears. 'It's ever so difficult in a caravan,' she confided. 'It's our first time, and we thought they'd just play outside nicely.' She sighed heavily. 'But they're not used to it, I s'pose, coming from Liverpool, and there isn't a telly. So I have to keep taking them out to give their Dad a bit of peace.'

'Of course if they break anything,' Hannah paused delicately as a rough pottery mug, unpredictably heavy, slipped from the four-year-old's grasp to shatter on the floor, before continuing smoothly, 'you would have to pay for it.'

'Damon!' his mother cried in dismay. 'You naughty boy! Look what you've gone and done now! I'm ever so sorry. How much is it, then?'

'Have to look it up in the catalogue, won't I?'

Hannah went over to the neat desk in the corner and selected a ring-bound price list, for shelving systems, as it happened.

'Seven pounds,' she declaimed, running her finger artistically down a column.

'*Seven pounds!*' Damon's mother paled visibly. 'Are you sure that's right?'

'Oh no, I'm sorry. Misread it, didn't I?' She hesitated just long enough to watch the woman's face brighten. 'That was the pottery bowl. Seven pounds fifty, that one is.'

Sensing drama, the children had fallen into a silent group round their mother. Damon's lip was trembling ominously.

'Seems a lot, just for a mug,' his mother ventured bravely.

'If he wanted to break one, look, he could break one for one ninety-nine in the supermarket.' Hannah made no attempt now to conceal her vicious satisfaction. 'It's a craftsman makes these – none of your mass-produced rubbish, is it?'

'Well, it'll be stopped out of your pocket money, Damon, that's what. And I don't know how I'm going to tell your Dad.'

The money was produced from her battered purse and Damon set up a miserable wail as the dejected family trailed out.

Glynis, observing from a detached distance, approached her sister. 'Not very nice to them, were you, then?' she said in Welsh. 'Won't be back after that. And I thought it was two pounds fifty, the price for those mugs.'

Hannah tucked the money away in the till. 'Price is what I say it is,' she said harshly. 'Won't learn a lesson, will they, if it's cheap. Children need to learn the way to behave, don't they? Sooner the better.'

Glynis, assuming reproach, bridled and stalked away. Bronwen should have been in today, but she'd phoned to say that one of the children was in bed with 'flu. Glynis had given up on examining her excuses too closely, even if she was fairly certain it wasn't one of the children and it wasn't with 'flu.

But she was wrong in thinking that it was Bronwen who was on Hannah's mind, or responsible for her particularly sour mood.

Gavin had got up and gone out early this morning, which was unsettling in itself. Normally Gavin came in late and treated the morning the way ordinary folk regarded the middle of the night.

He'd been in a funny mood yesterday evening as well, laughing too much and being what her mother would have called 'above himself'.

Hannah knew he hadn't slept much last night, because she hadn't either, and she had heard the video on loud in his room every time she had woken up. She had tried not to listen to the sounds coming from it.

She hadn't gone through to ask him to keep it down. She'd gone in once when he was watching a video not long ago to give him a pile of ironed shirts and hadn't liked what she saw, hadn't liked it at all.

They'd taken Alun Jenkins down to the police station in a van, first thing this morning. Hannah was almost hoping, once they'd started twisting his arm and got him talking, that they'd be back for Gavin.

The report from the pathology lab was waiting on Cordiner's desk when he got back to his office, much later than he had hoped. It had all taken up so much time: the briefing session, the supervising of the disposition details, welcoming the very competent – and very attractive – press officer, reporting to George Barker. It was mainly this that had thrown his timetable; George was twitchy, and just a bit inclined to stand on his dignity as officer officially in charge. Keeping him on side probably wasn't a waste of time, it just felt like it.

Cordiner leafed through the pages, the masses of technical detail using terms he didn't understand, but as far as he could tell it didn't give him much more information than they had given him verbally yesterday, until he got to the last paragraph.

They had managed to track down some new forensic test devised by Scotland Yard for the detection of Rohypnol in low concentrations, and were able to confirm positively that it had indeed been present in Willow Lampton's body.

That didn't, of course, show how it had got there, but it was suggestive. It cleared up the mystery about the lack of any struggle, and it was the kind of good solid evidence which brought a smile to the faces of the Crown Prosecution Service.

Local pharmacies, then – how many prescriptions had they filled for it in, say, the last three months? And did the hospital dispensary stock it as a pre-surgery anaesthetic? He scribbled a memo and attached it to the file, then tossed it into his 'out' tray.

The next half-dozen reports he speed-read. Dull stuff, and none of it helpful except as more background to Willow's life. He yawned, then yawned again.

It would be fully another twelve hours before he could hope to catch up on his sleep. Strong black coffee, that was the answer. He picked up the next file and carried it over to scan while his electric kettle boiled.

Now this was more to the point – Willow's bank statements for the last twelve months. He'd been waiting for these. Forgetting about the kettle, he went back to his chair and spread them out on the desk.

Would this explain the disparity between her standard of living and her nurse's salary? He ran his eyes down the neat columns.

There was her salary, paid in by the Hospital Trust on a regular date every month. Little enough, considering the responsibility the job entailed.

Surprisingly, given the evidence of consumption he had seen in her room, she seemed not to spend all that much. There were sizeable fortnightly cheques to a hairdresser, standing orders for a loan and insurance for her car, modest cash withdrawals and a few other cheques for small amounts, which left her more or less in the black at the end of the month.

Cordiner frowned. She had a room full of expensive clothes, cosmetics and shoes – how had she paid for them? He checked again: no, there were no credit card payments listed.

Very odd. Perhaps she had a deposit account somewhere. He hadn't seen a savings book among her belongings, and they had said there wasn't much beyond cosmetics and a purse in the handbag they had found in the car, though they hadn't sent in a detailed report yet.

Somewhere on his desk there should be the file of papers he had brought from her bedroom. It took him a few minutes to locate it, but then he tipped out the contents of the foolscap envelope on to the desk.

She'd got the money to buy clothes from somewhere. The top two receipts, for £125 and £140 respectively were for dresses bought from two of Stetford's most expensive clothes shops. He frowned again.

Among the papers spilled out on the desk, a heading caught his eye. It was a heading all too depressingly familiar to him: it came from the credit card company he himself used.

So she'd had a credit card after all, in her purse, presumably. Not only that, she paid it off monthly. Using what for money? Well, they could get the card company to check how it had been paid. He picked up the phone and put Sue Watson on to chasing that up, then sat back, thinking.

Even if she did have, say, a building society account, where had she got the money to put in it? Not from her father, that was for sure.

Perhaps one of her lovers was in the habit of giving her little cash presents. But she didn't keep her lovers for long, and even at a cursory glance through the papers lying on the desk he had noticed a credit card account dating back more than a year.

Perhaps she was on the game, or drug dealing, and kept her profits in a secret account. But the police usually knew all about the people involved in stuff like that, and anyway that was hardly her style.

Blackmailing was. Everything he had heard about Willow Lampton – from her father, from John Winthrop, from Paul Arkwright, from the plump nurse, whatshername, and even from the blandest of the reports on interviews he had read this morning – she was cold-hearted, mercenary, manipulative and scheming.

So who was she putting the screws on, and what about? And

was she squeezing him – or her, come to that – hard enough to make murder seem the only way out?

Cordiner searched out the credit card statements and arranged them systematically. Some were missing, but on the face of it, it looked as if her spending was rising as the months passed. The early amounts were in the three-hundred-pound region; latterly, they were nearer five.

You could get pretty desperate, trying to find five hundred pounds out of taxed income. And if she kept raising the stakes . . .

You only blackmailed someone when you were intimate enough to know their secrets, so who had she been close to? Winthrop, of course, and Arkwright, but they were both relatively recent relationships.

Willow was famously discreet about her intimates. Though there was something niggling away at the back of his mind, wasn't there, something someone had said . . . If he could only pin it down.

It wouldn't come. Well, they should get information on the method of payment quite soon; if not today then surely tomorrow. That would with any luck open up a fresh avenue to follow.

With a sigh he picked up the next report, and started yawning again. Coffee – of course. He went to switch on the kettle again.

Chapter Thirteen

'I just came along to thank you for having Matthew last night – and today, of course.' Tessa was standing in the front hall of the Winthrops' house. 'He's obviously very excited at the thought of seeing the fox cubs – trying to be very laid back and cool and not quite managing.'

Agnes Winthrop smiled. 'I only hope they oblige by appearing today! It was pure luck that I saw them yesterday. I happened to approach up-wind, and there they were playing outside the den. The most entrancing little creatures!'

'It's a very kind thought to take him. Here's a small contribution for the picnic. He's cheaper to keep for a week than for a fortnight, as the saying rather quaintly goes – I would have thought everyone was, actually.'

Agnes smiled, shaking her head at the bag of plums Tessa was handing her. 'My dear, you shouldn't have done that. I can't tell you what a pleasure it is to have a boy with a hearty appetite to feed again. And Matt's a delightful young man.'

Matthew, after greeting his hostess as comfortably as if they were old friends, had gone through the house to the garden for another training session with Jake.

'I'm so glad he's shown you that side,' Tessa said. 'I must say, I envy your skill. You've obviously struck exactly the right note with him.'

'He's not like this with you?'

'We-e-ell,' Tessa pulled a face. 'I don't like telling tales out of school. And this morning has been better, certainly. He's still wary of me, but more as if he'd promised himself to keep his distance than as if he was doing it from inclination.'

'Now that is strange. The first thing I thought last night was what an open, friendly child he was, and once we started talking it was as if we had known each other all our lives. It was Jake, of course, who broke the ice. Matt's besotted about dogs, isn't he?' She hesitated. 'One never, of course, knows quite how much to believe of what a child tells you, but did his parents really get rid of his dog because they were divorcing?'

Tessa shifted uncomfortably. 'I don't think it was *quite* in those terms. After the divorce, Lara and Matthew were living in a flat and I think she felt it was impossible to keep it.'

'I see. Losing the dog has gone deep, though, hasn't it? And it's your husband, whether rightly or wrongly, whom he blames.' Agnes paused, then said delicately, 'He's afraid of your husband, isn't he? Is he – is he a harsh man?'

'Harsh!' Tessa was indignant. 'He spent hours last night when he was exhausted anyway and had more work to do just talking and talking to Matthew. And given the way Matthew was behaving last night, that must have taken endless patience.'

'Oh, I am relieved to hear that! After Matt left I kept thinking about him – he'd told me about the shoplifting – and wondering what your husband would do, being a policeman, you know—'

Tessa said stiffly, 'I'm sorry you were concerned. David is a loving and gentle father and even as a policeman doesn't go beating people up.'

'Oh, forgive me!' Agnes put an apologetic hand on her arm. 'That was a crass thing to say. Please don't be offended – I didn't mean it to sound impertinent and intrusive, as indeed it did. I'm – I'm not really at my brightest today.'

Looking at her sharply, Tessa saw the marks of strain on her face, the pale, papery skin, the blue shadowy marks round her eyes and felt guilty at her own readiness to take offence.

'Agnes, I didn't notice how tired you were looking. I'm the

one who ought to apologise. Look, you should be resting. I'll take Matt away—'

'Oh please don't, please. I've been looking forward to having him today to take my mind off this dreadful business.'

It took Tessa a second to realise what she was talking about, then she said soberly, 'Yes, it's very upsetting, isn't it?'

Agnes set down the bag she was still holding on the hall table and sank into a chair beside it. 'You don't know, do you?' she said tragically. 'I wondered if you were just being tactful. But of course I didn't know either, except that she was a young girl and it was all very sad.

'But then Johnnie told me he'd been in love with her, and they were about to become engaged.'

'Engaged!' Tessa too sat down. 'No, I hadn't heard that. Oh, how dreadful for him!'

'He's – he's beside himself. In a quiet way, of course; out-wardly he's quite calm, but I know him too well and I can see it. And he won't even talk to me.'

She was crying now. 'Always before – after the baby died, after Cathy left him – he's always come to me and I've listened hour after hour and gradually over the months – years, even, I've helped him to draw out the poison.

'But now he's bottling everything up and I'm so afraid. He barely looks at me, just goes into his room and shuts the door. He shuts me out, Tessa. I've lost him.'

'Agnes, it won't be for ever.' Tessa tried to find consoling words. 'He probably needs time to himself to come to terms with another tragedy in his life. You'll be able to help him in the way you always have, later, once the first agony passes.'

Taking out a white linen handkerchief, the older woman dabbed at her eyes then blew her nose fiercely, pulling herself together almost visibly.

'I'm sure you're right.' She made the polite response, but Tessa could read desolation in her face as she went on with determined brightness, 'And I must say Matt has been something of a life-saver. It's been wonderful to feel useful to someone, and to have today's outing to plan—'

'Come on, Jake!' Matthew came running into the hall, his face alight with pleasure and the dog close at his heels. 'Look, Mrs Winthrop! Watch this!'

Jake's eyes, luminous with greed, were fixed avidly on the packet of dog-treats held in his young instructor's hand.

'Die for the Gunners, Jake!' Matthew commanded, and the dog, with an air of weary resignation, rolled over on his back with his paws in the air.

'Good boy, Jakie, we've won the Cup!' Jake, miraculously resurrected, leapt up for his reward and Matthew knelt to embrace him, fending off an extravagance of licks.

The two women exchanged smiles. 'That's excellent, Matt,' Agnes said. 'You have a real way with dogs, obviously.'

When Matthew beamed, he looked much younger than his fourteen years. 'Are we going now?' he asked, with a sidelong glance at Tessa which suggested she was definitely surplus to requirements.

'I'm on my way. Matt, please could you be back at about half-past five so you have time to change and go to the Webbs?'

Matthew pulled a face, but at a surprised look from Agnes said hastily, 'Yes, all right.'

'I'll keep my eye on the time.' Agnes walked to the door with Tessa. 'Matt, pick up the two haversacks in the kitchen and fetch Jake's lead please. We can't let him rush at the fox cubs.'

'You – you won't be going to the party yourself, will you?' Tessa asked. 'Chrissie said she was asking you both.'

Agnes shook her head, and the look of desolation was there again. 'No, we never go about much anyway, and now, of course – well, Johnnie's hardly been home from the hospital at all these last few days.'

Tessa went home so deep in thought that she forgot that she had earlier been dreading the walk back along the lane alone. There was still a breeze so that the occasional rustle behind the hedgerow was natural enough, and if twigs cracked without obvious reason, she was unaware of it.

Poor Agnes. There was so little in her life now. And poor John Winthrop, dogged by tragedy. She wondered if David knew of his relationship with the dead girl. She should probably tell him, but it was an uncomfortable position to be in. It felt like spying on your friends, and though she had already promised to report back on the drinks party tonight, she wasn't happy about it.

She was even less happy when she reached the drive to find that Ron, his long face more morose-looking than ever, was packing up his tools and wiping his hands on a greasy towel with almost symbolic thoroughness.

'Nothing I can do,' he said gloomily. 'It's a part, see, and we don't carry parts. Not for an antique like this, anyway.'

'Oh no!' Tessa was dismayed. 'So what happens now?'

'Beats me. Buy another car.' He laughed, then, as if the sound had taken him by surprise, stopped abruptly. 'Well, might come to that.'

Tessa's shoulders drooped. There was no way, just at the moment, without even an income from her painting, that they could afford another car. 'Surely there must be someone specialising in parts for old bangers?'

Ron scratched his nose, adding another oily smear. 'Might be somewhere in Birmingham, I s'pose. I'll check at the garage – but don't hold your breath. Might mean phoning round dozens of places, just on the off-chance. Could take weeks. Months, even.'

He said it with a sort of glum satisfaction, and just for a moment Tessa felt she might kick first him, then Boris, then burst into tears.

'Not that we were *eavesdropping*, of course.'

'Oh no, not *eavesdropping*.'

The two middle-aged ladies who were sitting on the edge of their chairs in front of DS Pardoe's desk, as if they might catch something from too much contact with the furniture, had obviously consulted together over the ticklish problem of what one wore for a visit to a police station.

They had opted for dressing down, in so far as their wardrobes permitted such an option, one in green check leisure trousers with a plain green shirt sporting a green-check flower in the middle of her ample bosom, the other plumper one in pale blue slacks with a check overshirt. Outfits bought specially for foozling relentlessly round the local golf course, Joe Pardoe surmised with the bitterness of a serious golfer who has suffered all too often.

'Of course not,' he reassured them solemnly in answer to their protestations. 'It's just that sometimes you really can't help overhearing something, isn't it?'

Gratified to find him so perfectly understanding that he had even spoken their next line for them, they nodded in vigorous unison.

'It was the way he said it, you see. It sent shivers down my spine, didn't it, Edna?'

'Oh yes, Maureen. And mine. "Last night I did what I should have done long ago," he said – and you should have seen how he looked!'

'"Something snapped inside me," he said. "She's out of my life forever." That's right, isn't it, Edna?'

'Then you remember, when his friend mentioned that poor girl's name, Willow – it's an odd sort of name that, isn't it? I couldn't really fancy it – Willow. But anyway, when his friend said, "Willow", Doctor Arkwright said – and he looked so black, I'll remember it as long as I live, it made me feel really funny – he said, "That Willow Lampton! She's history."'

'"History as far as I'm concerned," he said,' amended Maureen.

They both looked across at Pardoe with identical shocked expressions and round eyes under the same shade of pale blue eyeshadow.

'So we talked it over and decided it was our duty to tell the police. Though of course,' Edna tittered, 'neither of us has ever been in a police station before.'

'Well, I hope it hasn't proved too unpleasant an experience.' Pardoe favoured them with one of his more saturnine smiles; both ladies recoiled slightly.

'Now, if you can just take me through that once more, I'll

get it all down. He was sitting with Mrs Chrissie Webb, the doctor's wife, you said?'

They were more than happy to repeat their story.

'Will we have to appear in court, Sergeant?' Edna asked at the end.

'Oh dear!' murmured Maureen, her hand at her throat as if she were horrified at the idea, but from the glance they exchanged Pardoe reckoned they were planning their court outfits already.

'I'm sure we needn't trouble you,' he said. 'It's very helpful to us to know this, of course, but what you heard him say isn't actually evidence that he did anything.'

He saw their faces fall as dreams of witness-box stardom vanished. 'Now, if I could just take you back to the waiting room, I'll get someone to type up your statements for you to sign.'

They followed him out of the CID room and through the corridors, glancing eagerly in at any open door as if they were tourists on an African safari hoping to be lucky enough to spot some exotic species in its natural habitat.

As he showed them into the waiting room, Maureen said in hushed tones, 'Will any *criminals* come in while we're waiting?'

'No, no, madam, certainly not.' A wicked impulse made him add, 'Not without chains and leg-irons, that is.'

As he went out, he heard one say to the other doubtfully, 'That was a joke, wasn't it?'

On his way back to type up his report, Pardoe hesitated. This could be an excuse for dropping in on the Inspector, because like everyone else he was curious to know how the investigation was progressing.

When he opened Cordiner's door, DS Owen Owen was with him.

'Sorry, sir. If you're busy—'

'No, Joe, that's all right. Come in. Owen's just got the cash and carry break in wrapped up, and he's just going to charge Jenkins and his little chums.'

'Fancy that! "Speedy" Owen, they'll be calling you around here.'

Owen grinned, getting to his feet. 'Job satisfaction, they call it, Joe *bach*. You wouldn't know about it.'

'Was Guest one of them?' Pardoe asked with interest. 'It would be the cherry on the cake to wipe the smirk off that offensive bastard's face.'

'Funny you should say that – just what the boss and me were saying ourselves. No, Jenkins won't budge from his story that his mate Gavin wasn't there, and with the alibi from his mam as well, we're stuck, isn't it? Pity, though.'

'Thanks, Owen. Oh, by the way,' Cordiner leaned down and took something out of his briefcase, 'can I ask you to chase this up for me? Something I picked up by that creepy carving in Llanfeddin – nasty stuff, the second one I've found there. Thought it might be an idea to let them check it for prints, not that I'm optimistic. There's no particular rush, but I do get the feeling this is someone we should know about.'

Owen took the drawing in its plastic covering and glancing at it, pursed his lips in a soundless whistle. 'I take the point. OK, sir.'

Pardoe, who had glanced at it too, grimaced. Cordiner was looking, he noted, very tired.

'How's it going, boss?'

'Oh God, I wish I knew!' Cordiner gestured helplessly at the paper in front of him, which had piled up in the in-tray as the day wore on. 'I've spent the whole day directing operations from the incident room and reading reports here, and you don't get a feel for it when other people are doing all the leg-work. It's a bit like playing on one of those fairground machines when you're trying to pick up the fake gold watch with the remote control grabbers which only go sideways.

'They've bused in all this extra manpower today, but not one of the reports I've seen has come up with anything new or useful. Which is probably reasonable enough, except that I keep thinking maybe if I'd been there I'd have thought of the question that would have solved the whole thing. Don't tell me, I know it's unfair.'

He rubbed his hand across his face in his customary gesture

of weariness.

'Boss's prerogative,' Pardoe said cynically. 'They can always kid themselves they would do it better. Make the most of it!'

Cordiner said wrily, 'If you say so. I don't suppose you've got the lead we're all looking for?'

'I can't say it's anything new, sir, but it is further confirmation of Arkwright's attitude. Straws in the wind, if you can describe two Stetford matrons that way and keep your face straight.'

He repeated their story, and mentioned Mrs Webb. 'Arkwright may have said something more to her. I might go out to Llanfeddin and have a little chat with her.'

'Chrissie Webb? Oh, hang on – what time is it? Half-past six? I'll do that myself. We were invited there for drinks, and I refused, but I daresay they won't mind if I put in an appearance. Then I'll snatch a bite of supper at home, which will put me in good with Tessa, and come back here after that to cope with the joys and delights of my in-tray.'

He got up, rubbing his face again. 'I only hope we have something to show for the outlay by this time tomorrow night. Make your hair stand on end if I told you the sort of hole these two days are making in our budget. Remind me why I'm doing this, Joe.'

Pardoe grinned sardonically. 'You wanted the job, you got it, boss. Me, I only have to do what I'm told.'

Cordiner groaned as he went out of the door.

It wasn't hard to tell, as you entered the Webbs' drawing room, that this was a social occasion which was dying on its feet.

Chrissie had greeted David Cordiner at the front door with pleased surprise, and he had managed to snatch a word with her before they went through to join the others.

She had, he reckoned with an expert's eye, had rather more than a couple of drinks, but she was handling it with only a hint of alcoholic detachment. She was certainly clear enough to describe in detail everything Paul Arkwright had said to her at the coffee morning, and to put it in the context of their previous conversation.

For good measure, she added a pungent denunciation of the two harpies who, she claimed, had just about climbed on to the table between them to eavesdrop. She was also adamant that Willow's death had come as shocking news to the young doctor.

'He was poleaxed,' she said firmly. 'Laurence Oliver couldn't have looked that convincing, not without the lights and the greasepaint. And if you're mistaken enough to charge him, I'll say that in the witness box as many times as they'll let me.'

David smiled at her. 'I'm sure you would. Thanks, Chrissie, that's most helpful. Now I'll put on my other hat and try to be a good guest. It's kind of you to invite us – and to include Matthew.'

'Oh, he's made a terrific hit. The girls dragged him off like tigers preparing to share a particularly toothsome goat. I hope he's surviving.'

On the evidence of the decibel level of the music pounding behind the closed door she indicated, David gave it as his opinion that Matthew would be in his element, and was she quite sure she had the characters of tiger and goat the right way round?

They were laughing as they entered the room, otherwise so unpromisingly quiet.

There were only four people there; clearly the Winthrops had refused, which on reflection was hardly surprising. Paul Arkwright was standing just inside the door engaged in a low-voiced, intense conversation with Marnie Evans, whose dark blue eyes were fixed hungrily on his face.

'Their attitude just seemed to be that whatever I said, I had to be lying,' he was telling her as David came in, but he stopped abruptly, his face turning a dark, embarrassed red. His changed expression made Marnie turn round; seeing David she gave him only the curtest of greetings.

Damn! he thought, smiling back as if oblivious to her coolness. He was used to the cold shoulder, but would it be extended to his poor Tess as well?

She was standing across in the window corner with Richard Webb. Tessa's body language, with arms folded across her body, and head half-turned away, was defensive, while his was predatory. He had positioned himself between her and the room, so that in order to escape him she would have had to push him aside, and he was standing too close. Not a sensitive man, it appeared; he seemed to be exerting himself to charm her, oblivious to her discomfort and the heightened colour in her cheeks.

David's entrance afforded relief. Catching sight of him, Richard broke off without excuse and came across to him immediately, while Tessa, giving her husband a brief, glittering smile, escaped to join Marnie and Paul.

'David, my dear fellow!' Richard greeted him heartily, shaking his hand. 'How good of you to make time to come! Let me get you a martini - *specialité de la maison*, and I flatter myself it's a pretty lethal concoction.'

'I can readily believe it.' Why was it that the man's greeting sounded as if he had studied etiquette from a book which laid excessive emphasis on bonhomie? 'But just something soft for me, thanks. I'm afraid I won't be able to stay long – I've got work to do later.'

'Of course, of course.' He led him across to the drinks tray, fussing about alternatives. Chrissie brought over a tray of somewhat shrivelled sausages; David, hungry by now, took a couple before she took them over to the group by the door.

Richard gave David a mineral water and poured himself another martini from a glass pitcher, then dropped in an olive.

'Well, how's it going, then? Ready to lock anyone up yet?'

He laughed at his own facetiousness, but David didn't. 'Oh, it's still all in the very early stages. Lots more hard work to be done, I'm afraid.' He moved towards the window and looked out. 'What a beautiful garden you have here. A lot of work, though.'

No, Richard wasn't going to take the hint. 'Chrissie's hobby,' he said dismissively. 'But tell me, what has the path lab said? I take it this is a murder investigation?'

'Oh, yes.'

'I'm surprised, you know. She looked so peaceful I rather assumed it was suicide. You can't tell, you know, before you do the post mortem in cases like that.'

Well, he probably felt he had to cover his back. David murmured agreement.

'When is the inquest? I haven't had notification yet.'

'Wednesday, I understand.'

'Right, right. Have the boffins been able to fix the time of death?'

David hedged. 'Well, you know how hard it is to be exact about these things.'

The other man downed his martini in one gulp, making David glance at him with suddenly awakened interest. Was that a nervous reaction, and if so, why? He stopped trying to change the subject.

'You said she was one of your patients, didn't you?' he said casually. 'Did you know her well?'

'Good gracious yes, since she was a child.' He glanced away as he spoke. 'Hang on just a moment, I'll be back, but I see there are people over there dying of thirst.'

Very interesting indeed. Rather than going across to Tessa and the others, who seemed to be engaged in a rather self-conscious conversation about films they had seen, David hovered at the window waiting for his host to return.

Richard had refilled his own glass too, and his flushed face was confirmation that his boast about the lethal nature of his cocktail had not been an empty one.

'Just between you and me, old man,' he said, moving closer to David and lowering his voice, 'and I'm not breaching patient confidentiality here, because it's common knowledge, poor little Willow was a bit of a tart. High-class now, of course.' His 's's were becoming faintly slurred. 'But she wasn't always. She was into some pretty rough trade before she decided to better herself – local lads not a million miles from here. If I were you, that's the line I'd follow.'

'Local lads?'

'Oh, no names, no packdrill.' He winked clumsily. 'Just a word to the wise, eh?'

'Absolutely.' Doing his best not to show his distaste, David drained his glass. 'Well, I hate to break up the party, but work, you know—'

'Of course, of course.' The other man did not seem anxious

to detain him, and Tessa, seeing him move, was not slow to detach herself from the other group.

'Thank you, Chrissie,' she was saying in a bright, unnatural voice. 'It's been good to have a chance to get to know you better. Now I suppose I'd better go and dislodge Matthew.'

She went out ahead, and by the time David reached the hall there was a deputation waiting: Matthew was standing sheepishly between a brunette in white jeans and a cropped top who had apparently hit puberty early and was certainly making the most of it, and a pretty younger girl with fair hair and a radically abbreviated mini-skirt.

'Mummy,' said the fair girl, 'Matt doesn't have to go home yet, does he? He could stay to supper too, couldn't he?'

'*Please*, Mrs Webb,' begged the brunette.

Chrissie laughed. 'There's certainly no problem as far as I'm concerned. Unless you've got supper for him already, Tessa?'

'Heavens, no!' Tessa's laugh sounded brittle to David's ears. 'I was going to plan the menu on the way home. And we couldn't hope to compete with the company.'

Matthew rewarded her with a brilliant smile, and the trio retreated into the room. As the Cordiners made their polite farewells, the music began to throb again.

They walked in silence to David's car. As he drove away he glanced at her set face. 'Was it bad?' he asked gently.

'Terrible,' she said, and burst into tears.

He could soothe her and be sympathetic, but there was no magic wand he could wave to make the problems disappear. After her passion of tears she wasn't angry – he would almost have preferred that – but retreated into what he recognised wretchedly as a sort of mute, helpless despair.

Supper was a constrained meal. Finally David said, 'Tessa, my love, I did warn you that being a copper's wife was tough.'

'I'm not blaming you. Of course you told me. But I didn't expect – all this. It's as if I'm being forced to choose sides.'

'This is unusual. I promise you we'll do a radical rethink about the future whenever this investigation is over.'

'But how long is that going to be?' she cried. 'There was a

lot I was prepared for, but not creepy Richard Webb trying to come on to me to get a line on the police investigation.'

'Did he, indeed?'

'Oh yes, and what got to me more than anything was that he seemed to think I was such an airhead, or would be so dazzled by his charm, that I wouldn't notice he was doing it.

'But it was worse with Marnie. It would never have occurred to me that my best friend would find it hard not to blame me because she thinks you might be about to arrest the man she loves. I am obviously expected to stop you, or something. "Oh Paul, can't anyone convince them that you're innocent?" she said a couple of times, and there were no prizes for guessing who she meant by "anyone".'

'I take it he's been forgiven,' David said drily.

'Oh, she was cold and distant with him at first. For all of ten seconds.'

The mild joke helped, and then the story of the rest of her day poured out, about the verdict on Boris and her conviction that she was being spied on again.

David listened gravely without interrupting until she had finished. Then he said, 'Boris is the easy part. I'll phone the garage owner and see if we can speed things up. And OK, so we can't afford just to go out and buy a replacement, but we can certainly manage a taxi when you need to go shopping. You mustn't be reduced to suffering at the hands of the Unholy Trinity.

'But Guest – you asked me if it's just your imagination, and I don't know what to say about that.' He sighed. 'Be very, very careful, my darling, and if you catch so much as a glimpse of him hanging about here, dial 999. Not my number – that way there can't be accusations of personal bias. And stalking's a crime now.

'At least you've got Matt around. That should help a bit.'

'If I can tear him away from his harem!'

He left, reluctantly, to go back to his office. He had said nothing to her about the drawings, but he did check that the windows and doors were secure before he drove away.

SESSION FIVE

Thursday 30 July

Session Five

'*You're late. I've been waiting for you to come.*'

'I'm sorry. I was detained. Were you anxious to talk to me?'

'*You left early yesterday as well, before I was ready to finish.*'

'I'm sorry about that too.'

'*I think you did it deliberately. I think you think that if you make me wait, I'll be more anxious to finish my story. But you haven't understood, have you?*

'*I want to finish it, because, you see, you've heard it all, right from the very beginning. You know that She was trying to kill my soul, and that She left me with no choice but to defend myself. If I tell you the rest, will you stay to listen?*'

'Yes, of course.'

'*You didn't yesterday. And it's a long story.*'

'I won't go until you're finished.'

'*I'll trust you. I have to trust you, because no one else knows. No one else could possibly understand, but I've explained to you.*

'*I carry no shame or guilt for what happened. These I lay to her charge now, just as I did then.*

'*She wanted to snare my brother, steal him from me. And he was so little, so soft, I couldn't be sure of him. I had taken the risk of allowing myself to love him; he mustn't betray me now. Not the way my father had.*

'*So I had to bind him to me, you see, with bonds stronger than love. I had to bind him to me with the bonds of guilt and fear so that we would be together with no one to come between us. Forever and ever.*

'I was only nine years old – did I tell you that? Only nine years old, forced into doing these unchildlike things.

'"I have a secret," I said to him next evening. "I know something bad. Something terrible."

'We were sitting in one of our dens under a beech tree, and it wasn't quite dark. But all the warmth had drained from the light and his face shone pale and frightened as he turned to me.

'"They're going to turn us out," I said. "They don't want us because they have the baby now. The cuckoo baby."

'His face puckered, but he knew by now that he shouldn't cry. "What - what will we do, then?"

'"It's the baby, you see. If the baby wasn't there, Dad would want us again. And maybe She'd go away too."

'"But the baby is there! She—"

'"It," I corrected him fiercely. "It's there now, but I know how we can make it go away. Magic!"

'He stared for a moment, then looked away, and I could see he was torn. Had it gone too far already? I held my breath.

'"What – what will you do?" he said at last.

'"Not me. It has to be you."

'He looked at first alarmed, then terrified. "But I'm only little. Why do I have to?"

'"Because you're the boy. I'm –" and I had to swallow hard, because even for this purpose it was a bitter admission, "I'm only a girl, and girls aren't so important."

'He preened a little at that – it doesn't take much, does it, to flatter a man whatever age he is – and before he could think too much about it I swept him along.

'I made a sort of game out of casting our spell, collecting the black bird's feather and the three white pebbles and the seven handfuls of beech-mast from the floor of the wood.

'Then we arranged them in a special pattern on a large flat stone in a little clearing – he was enjoying himself now – and I made a magic, a singing magic with words that weren't words and pictures you couldn't see sketched on the air with my hands.

'And we danced, faster and faster in among the trees round and round until we were dizzy and fell in a heap. Then I grabbed him and spoke in a low, mysterious voice.

'"Now is the time. Now you must do it. You must say, 'I hate you cuckoo baby, go away,' three times, and then spit on the ground."

'It was almost dark by now, but I could see that his eyes were bright with the excitement of the new game. He did as he was told with no further prompting, shouting it so loud I was almost afraid that they might hear him.

'Then I spat on the ground too, and I told him the spell was complete.

'He seemed a little quiet that night after we went to bed in the room we shared. "Shall we play hide-and-seek tomorrow?" I suggested, as if that was just another game like the one we had been playing, and he cheered up at once. He prattled happily about it until sleep overcame him. But I lay in the darkness, listening to them in the room next door with the baby, refining my plan until I too fell asleep.

'We played hide-and-seek the next night, and the night after that. It was my brother's favourite game at that time, especially as dusk gathered and there was that delicious childhood frisson of imagined fear as you were hunted, then caught – can you recall that feeling?

'We didn't talk about the spell again. He might almost have forgotten it – or at least banished it to the limbo of things we choose not to remember.

'The weather was still warm, but sultry now. The baby was fractious in the sticky heat and She was leaving their bedroom window open to the cooler night air when She put it to bed after supper. By the third night, when we played hide-and-seek again, I had it all clear in my mind.

'It was almost too easy. I could hear my brother counting laboriously up to one hundred as I sped through the wood up to the house. They were talking in the kitchen; She was laughing her silly, high-pitched laugh as I climbed over the windowsill.

'It was a doll lying there on its stomach, no more than that. It didn't move or struggle when I put the pillow over its head very, very gently. I only had to hold it there for a few minutes, you know, that was all. It didn't seem a terribly significant action, somehow. It looked just as it had before when I left. Only still, quite still.

'My brother managed to find me hiding down by the stream at the bottom of the wood rather more quickly than usual.

'After the baby's funeral we came back to the house for the funeral tea – made by the neighbours, I think, who stood about sampling each other's baking and talking in hushed tones about other cot deaths they had known.

'My brother and I lingered uneasily on the fringes, he clinging to my hand. He never mentioned the spell, but he had been sleeping badly, waking up with nightmares and needing me to comfort him and cuddle him back to sleep.

'My father had wept at the graveside but She hadn't shed a tear, standing as still and pale as one of the marble monuments. She repulsed him, almost angrily, when he tried to draw her into their shared grief.

'When the neighbours left at last it was late and dark. My father sat by the fire, his head bowed. She was standing silent at the window, staring out at nothing. Ignored, my brother and I quietly got ourselves to bed.

'He cried under his covers, but he was tired and soon sobbed himself to sleep. But I lay awake, hearing my father move at last, urging her to come to bed. I don't think She replied; I heard my father groan, then walk to their bedroom and shut the door.

'There was no sound for a long, long time. The moon was full, I remember; I could see the form of my brother in the bed across from me, still shaken in sleep by the occasional sob.

'Then the door opened and She was there, outlined in the light from the room outside. She closed it behind her and her dark dress disappeared into the shadows, leaving only her face and her pale bare arms gleaming spectrally in the moonlight. My stomach lurched.

'She came over to my bed. "You're glad now, aren't you," She spat at me in a low, fierce voice. "You hated her. You wanted her dead."

'Her eyes glittered, brilliant with the madness of pain. What was there to say? I said nothing.

'She grabbed my wrist, yanking me upright. "Get up, and don't make a sound."

'I could have called for help. My father would see that She was unstable, dangerous; would protect me, but in a way revenge was her right, just as self-protection had been mine. There had been no hint of suspicion, yet at some visceral level She sensed what She could not know.

'I went with her in silence, out of the room, out of the house, in my cotton pyjamas and my bare feet.

'With frantic haste She dragged me over to the yard, to the inevitable cage. The dogs stirred, but they were sleepy and scenting familiar humans did not bark.

'She pushed me in and snapped the padlock shut. "Stay there till you freeze," She said, and I have never heard such hate in a human voice. "If you die of cold, that will be fair. Why should you be alive and my baby – my baby—"

'Her stony face crumpled and She fled back inside the house. I heard her screaming, scream after scream, then through the window I saw my father come hurrying into the kitchen. Eventually the screams settled to harsh sobbing, and I saw him leading her through to the bedroom. The light in the kitchen went out and I couldn't hear her any more.

'Thick cloud was covering the moon now, and it was very very dark. It was so dark that the air seemed almost thickened by it, and there was no wind. The strong familiar animal smells were all about me, and the dogs were settling back to sleep; I heard the soft grunt Jess gave as she moved her arthritic leg and the rustling of a restless ferret in one of the hutches. Then there was silence.

'I was cold as I stood there, almost naked in this bowl of darkness. No light, no sound.

'I could still summon rescue, of course. My father was sad, but not demented with grief as She was.

'But something within me told me to bear it stoically, for the sake of absolution. Oh, don't mistake me – I was only nine years old, after all, and what I had done was to defend myself.

'She said it might kill me, and I thought perhaps it would. In this strange vacuum of the senses I felt I could meet my judgement. So there in the night and the silence I stood, still as a stone. I fainted at last, I think, and my father found me in the early morning, before it was actually too late.

'After that She went away. At no small cost, I had saved myself from her, and it was just the three of us again. Just the three of us, the way it had been before.

'Yet like a malevolent army in retreat, She had poisoned the well *before She left. Somehow I never got close to my father again, and my brother – well, he never seemed really happy, always quiet and withdrawn.*

'I blame her for that. If She had never come into our lives, everything would have been different, everything, right up until now.

'So you see, it wasn't my fault. And if there was sin, I expiated it that night, and as I said, I feel no shame or guilt. Not about anything. Always, I have only done what I needed to do. To survive, you understand, just to survive.'

Tuesday 14 July

Chapter Fourteen

It was the early hours of the morning when Gavin Guest arrived home. Hannah, in bed but unable to sleep, heard his return. He hadn't taken his motorbike and she hadn't heard a car draw up that might have dropped him. Where could he have been, late at night in Llanfeddin?

Not at Alun Jenkins' house. Alun had been round earlier looking for him, saying he hadn't seen him in days. He was out on bail, he told Hannah.

'The pigs wanted me to finger Gavin for it, didn't they, but I told them I hadn't seen him all night. Not that they wanted to believe me – got it in for Gav, isn't it?'

She looked at him, at the poor skin and lacklustre eyes of the drug-user. She was pretty sure Gavin wasn't into that, at least.

'Just between us, Alun,' she said, 'just between you and me, straight. So as I know what to say, if they ask me again – was he there?'

Alun's reaction was unmistakably genuine. 'Oh no, Mrs Guest. Honest. Gav doesn't need that sort of money, does he. Got more sense than some of us, look. I didn't tell them a word of a lie about Gav.' Then his pathetic, pinched face lit up in a grin of pure mischief, and with a pang she recognised the child she had known before he became possessed by this modern demon. 'Couldn't put my hand on my heart about the rest of what I told the bastards, though.'

'Thanks, Alun.' She tried to look as if this was the answer

she had been hoping for. 'I'll tell him you were looking for him. Get him to go round your house tomorrow, maybe.'

Now, Gavin was making no attempt to be quiet. He whistled as he had a shower, slammed his bedroom door, and then she heard the video start up, so loudly that she could hear the sound-track of the film. She put her head under the pillow so that she didn't have to hear the horrible sounds.

At last she fell into a doze, but whenever she woke again throughout that interminable night she could hear that he hadn't gone to bed, that he was moving about, going through to the kitchen, to make tea perhaps. And always the noise from the video.

When was he sleeping? He was getting up early, and he didn't seem to be tired: indeed, yesterday morning he had been full of energy and his eyes, far from being heavy, were almost feverishly bright.

Hannah was too afraid even to think of reasons why that might be.

Hannah was not the only woman who was wakeful that night.

In her elegant bedroom, Agnes Winthrop stood at the window which looked down between the low hills enfolding the valley on either side, along the course of the little river meandering in its stony bed.

The silent room behind her had faded with the light until she seemed to be standing alone in a darkness without bound-aries. The moon had gone down; only once did the headlights of a passing car stab the shadows with a long finger of brightness.

Before her blank, unseeing eyes the sky changed from the grey-purple of dusk to near-darkness, then lightened to the cold colour of steel, before the first refracted rays of the sun would warm it again to honey gold. Her heart too felt cold, cold as the light, cold as the stones in the river below, cold as the ancient hills about.

Johnnie hadn't come back until nearly eleven. At the hospital, he had told her tersely when she went down to the hall to meet him, but she had seen the damp smears of mud on his shoes. At the common, she suspected, but his expression forbade further questioning.

'Have you had anything to eat?' she asked him, but he hadn't replied, walking away from her towards the stairs.

'Can't we talk?' She hated pleading, but he had not even hesitated in his reply.

'Please, Agnes,' was all he had said, and walked away from her, silent, into his bedroom, shutting the door quietly behind him so that he divided the silence in his dark room from the silence outside as she stood on the upstairs landing with her hands still outstretched towards him.

Slowly, she lowered them. He had closed another door, too. She knew, with the bleakness of total certainty, that she couldn't reach him now. After all these years, after all they had been to one another, he had gone beyond her now, out of her reach.

So she had looked at the sky and the hills, and she had thought and thought, a still monument to bleakness and desolation.

As the sun came up, a thrush from the shrubbery in the garden sang its poignant double song, question and answer.

Agnes had spent all night considering the question. Now, on the thrush's breath, the answer came clear.

David Cordiner set down the phone after his conversation with Megan with a mirthless smile of satisfaction. It was amazing how much more clearly you could think after a night's sleep; that was the conversation he had been trying, and failing, to recall yesterday. For the first time, and not before time either, he felt with a flicker of optimism that he had a trail worth following.

That was good, since all the searches at the common had come up with seemed to be fag packets, empty bottles, discarded chewing gum and polystyrene takeaway trays, none of which had any demonstrable, or even probable, connection to the crime.

The prize exhibit had been the cast of a size 9, Barbour Wellington boot print, one of a series on the path. The experts, apparently, with their usual helpfulness, thought that the depth of imprint might indicate a man carrying a body, but couldn't rule out a woman with very large feet or a fat man struggling up on an innocent early morning stroll on Saturday morning, before the path had dried out. Well, it could be useful corroboration once the detective work was done but unless they happened upon a similar boot in suggestive circumstances, it wasn't going to get them much further.

Apart from that, they had isolated a couple of strands of hair and a few fibres from the blanket she was wrapped in on a twig three feet off the ground, but that didn't tell them anything they didn't know already either. The blanket itself was from a chain store.

But Richard Webb, now. That fitted. The girl was not only very young but his patient, and the rules about that were strict; a complaint from her would get him struck off. Fertile ground for blackmail, and if the amounts she demanded were increasing – as they were – and there was no end in sight . . . ? He would only need to scribble a false prescription to get hold of Rohypnol.

Webb, from all he knew of him, would take badly to victim status. He would hate being jerked around by someone he would undoubtedly consider to be his social and intellectual inferior. And interestingly enough, last night he had treated Tessa like a bimbo and David like a fool, with the sort of self-delusive arrogance a killer often betrays.

No, Cordiner had no problem at all with Webb's profile. Snuffing out an inconvenient life would be plausibly in character.

Not evidence, though, was it? George Barker, just for one, would flip at the notion of pulling in for questioning a prominent local figure who also happened to be his own GP and the police surgeon without evidence hard enough to cut glass. Perhaps the report from the credit company would provide it.

It was nearly nine o'clock. He gathered up his papers for the day's briefing, riffling through to make sure he had his deployment list. He had worked hard to make sure that all the intensive leg-work was covered, because, barring unforeseen circumstances, his extra forces would vanish on the stroke of nine o'clock tonight, and he'd bloody well better have more to show for it to George Barker than a glass slipper. The inquest, too, was only a day away, and Jan Peters the Press Officer, who was doing a brilliant job of keeping the newshounds in check, would be anxious to have a juicy bone to throw them.

First he must grab Sue Watson and excuse her attendance at the briefing so that she could go and lean on the accounts department of the credit card company. If the gods were smiling, she might even have a result by the time he came out of the meeting.

She did.

The telephone at her bedside roused Tessa from a deep and dreamless sleep, bringing her sharply awake. She squinted at the clock: five past nine! That was ridiculous. She shouldn't be in bed at this hour on a weekday morning. Only people without a life slept this late.

She hoped she sounded bright and brisk as she answered it.

'Tessa?' It was Agnes Winthrop. 'Oh, good morning! It was really Matt I wanted to speak to.'

'Goodness, Agnes, he isn't awake yet. I shouldn't think he'll be up for ages. He was quite late coming back from the Webbs' last night, and on yesterday's form he's not likely to appear much before eleven.'

'I see.' She sounded taken aback. 'Johnnie was always such an early bird at that age, I just assumed –' Her voice trailed off, but then she said, 'I suppose with young people nowadays it's different.'

Only if older people don't phone and wake them, Tessa thought, stifling a yawn as Agnes went on, 'Well, perhaps you could get him to ring me when he does get up? It's another lovely day, and I thought that today after he's done his training session with Jake we might walk the other way at the head of the valley. I've seen a pair of eagles there, and we might be lucky. Johnnie was always very keen on birds.'

'Fine. Yes, I'll give him your message, but I'm not making any promises about when.'

'Thank you, my dear. I'll expect to hear from him sometime later.'

Now thoroughly wide awake, Tessa put the phone down and groaned. This was going to prove a further complication, wasn't it? Agnes, so miserable yesterday, was clearly making some sort of transference from her own stepson to Tessa's, and it didn't take a crystal ball to be able to foresee disaster.

Despite the attractions of the fox cubs, Matthew had been lukewarm about the joys of Agnes's undiluted company when he came back. 'She wanted me to call her, like, *Agnes*, and she's really, well, old,' he had said, screwing up his face. 'It was gross.' And though he might well have developed a sudden interest in bird-watching after last night, it wasn't the feathered variety we were talking about here.

Oh dear, as if life wasn't difficult enough already! Perhaps, she thought as she showered and dressed, Matthew might be persuaded to go along there just for a bit, even if he excused himself from the walk. Agnes had been very kind to him; he owed her something for that.

Tessa was in the kitchen when the phone rang again at half-past nine, but to her surprise before she reached it she heard Matthew's door open and he came hurrying down the stairs in his pyjamas to take the call.

'Hello?' he said breathlessly, then, 'Oh, hi, Susannah!'

Stifling a chuckle, she went back into the kitchen. He'd been expecting her to phone, had he?

A moment later Matthew stuck his head round the kitchen door. 'Susannah says, can I go over there for the day?'

'Well, of course, but we don't have transport—'

'That's OK, Charlotte's mum's taking her over and she's going to pick me up.'

He was in sunny mood when he arrived downstairs, fully dressed, in an amazingly short space of time.

'When is Mrs Webb coming to collect you?' Tessa asked, putting toast in the toaster for him.

'Soon. Quarter of an hour or so. It'll be brilliant – Susannah's got, like, this really cool house, with, like, oh, horses and dogs and things.'

'Cool,' Tessa echoed. It looked as if Matthew wasn't going to be making too many demands on her time after all. Then she remembered Agnes.

'Oh, Matthew, I forgot. Mrs Winthrop phoned earlier. She was hoping you'd go for a walk again today.'

Matthew, who was eating cereal with the vigour and concentration of someone going for a world speed record, didn't look up. 'Well, I can't go, obviously.'

'No. I sort of got the impression that you wouldn't be terribly keen. But what about Jake's training session? You were going to do that every day, weren't you?'

'Oh, it won't hurt to miss one.' Matthew finished his cereal, paused thoughtfully, then refilled his bowl.

'Well actually, Matthew, it's not really Jake that's the problem.' Damn, why did she have to tackle this, and probably sour the atmosphere? 'Agnes is having a bit of a hard time at the moment, for one reason and another, and she was looking forward to you going round there today.'

Matthew gave her that cool, wary teenage look, the one that says, 'Leave it, OK?'

'I can't, if I'm going to Susannah's,' he pointed out.

'No, I suppose not.' Tessa sighed. A lecture on social obligation wouldn't get her anywhere; she took up a fallback position. 'Well, perhaps you could phone her and explain before you go.'

There was a fractional pause, then Matthew got up to fetch his toast. 'Sure,' he said easily. 'I've got a couple of things to sort out in my room – the girls want me to bring some of my hip-hop tapes – but then I can do it while I'm waiting for Mrs Webb to come.'

Tessa had no experience in dealing with teenagers, but it wasn't long enough since she had been one herself for her to have forgotten the tactic. Smile, accept the suggestion, don't disagree, don't argue. Just make damn sure that some-how it doesn't happen. Should she call his bluff and have a confrontation, or make the difficult phone call herself later?

Make the difficult phone call herself, she accepted wearily, waving him off in the car with the Webbs.

When Agnes answered the phone, her voice was bright and eager, but when she heard it was Tessa at the other end, it went suddenly flat.

'I thought it must be Matt,' she said.

Tessa swallowed. 'I'm terribly sorry, Agnes, he's made other plans for the day. The Webbs' daughter has taken him to a friend's house, I'm afraid. I didn't realise they had set it up last night or of course I'd have told you earlier.'

There was no mistaking her disappointment. 'But he said he was coming to train Jake. We arranged that.'

'Yes, I know. He was sorry about that, quite upset.' She crossed her fingers scrupulously. 'But Chrissie Webb had arranged to take them over early.'

'Couldn't you have made him put it off? He could have gone some other time, surely?'

'Agnes, you can't *make* a child do something these days. Especially not somebody else's child, when he's as touchy as Matthew can be. I feel I'm pushing my luck when I ask him to put his breakfast dishes in the dishwasher!'

She laughed hopefully, but there was no answering amusement in Agnes's voice.

'It all depends, though, on whether you want to do it or not, doesn't it? I could see yesterday that you found it awkward and embarrassing that Matthew had chosen to confide in me. I'm sorry if you were annoyed, and I would be even more sorry if that came between Matt and me. We had a glorious day together yesterday, and ours is a very special friendship, you know.'

Tessa winced. 'Of course it is, Agnes,' she said gently, 'and I would never want to get in the way. It's just – well, the young do tend to prefer one another's company.'

There was a frosty silence. Then Agnes said, 'Yes, I see. Perhaps Matt can tell me that himself sometime, if that's really what he thinks. Good-bye.'

Oh God, Tessa thought, the sick misery she kept trying so

determinedly to shake off returning once more. Through no fault of her own, that was another avenue to friendship closed down. Wherever she turned, there seemed to be bars across her way.

For Richard Webb, it came almost as a relief, in a strange way, when there was a tap on his surgery door between patients and one of the senior receptionists, rigid with disapproval, came in with two uniformed police officers behind her.

'I'm so sorry, Doctor, I did *explain* that you were in the middle of a surgery, but they *insisted* –' She favoured the offenders with a withering look.

When Webb got up and said, 'It's all right, Mavis, I've been expecting them to come for me,' she gaped, then gave a little shriek and clapped her hand over her mouth.

The worst part was walking out through a crowded waiting room under police escort. He could feel a Mexican wave of shock swelling as he passed, looking neither to right nor to left, and climbed into the police car.

It was the worst part only until he arrived at the police station, where a couple of lounging photographers sprang to life as he came towards them, thrusting cameras which rattled and flashed offensively in his face, dazzling him. One of the officers paused to say, in answer to their shouted questions, that he was helping police with their enquiries. No, he hadn't been charged.

Then he was taken into an interview room, and the worst part of all was hearing the key turn in the lock when they left him. The sound seemed to shatter the unnatural calm which had possessed him, and his hands started to shake. He gripped the sides of his chair to stop them.

If he had considered it at all, he would have assumed there would be preliminary discussions which would take place in normal surroundings, in an office, perhaps, across a desk. This was totally unexpected. It was bare of decoration and bleak, with the sinister eye of a camera watching him from one corner and recording machines by the table. There were fixed microphones too, almost like the recording studio where he had once taken part in a medical programme. The two rooms had the same dead atmosphere, the same sense of being divorced from the world outside, in some sort of alternative reality. It was strange how different it felt, though, when a locked door stopped you walking out.

It was ten long minutes with only his distressing thoughts for occupation before he heard the door being unlocked and David Cordiner with another man he did not recognise came into the room.

'David!' He hailed him with a ghastly travesty of a social smile, but the Inspector ignored him, going to stand to one side while the other officer, a burly man with a swarthy, pugnacious face, took the seat opposite, put a tape in the machine, started it, and spoke into the microphone.

'Tuesday, fourteenth July. Ten-twelve a.m., Detective Inspector Cordiner and Detective Sergeant Pardoe have entered the room. Interview with Doctor Richard Webb commences.'

Leaning back in his chair, Pardoe surveyed him for a long moment, his eyes narrowed. Trying to soften me up by looking threatening, Webb told himself, but considering that the situation was pretty much as threatening as it could be anyway, that assessment was cold comfort.

'Doctor Webb, there are some questions we need to ask you. Are you prepared to co-operate? You have already been informed of your rights.'

Ignoring Pardoe, Webb looked over his head to where Cordiner was standing, his shoulders propped against the wall.

'They told me I could have a lawyer. Do I need one, David?'

'It's entirely your decision, Doctor Webb.' A correct, impersonal, cold response. 'You may certainly decide not to say anything without taking legal advice, but if you have nothing to hide answering our questions could help us eliminate you from the enquiry, which would be to our mutual advantage.'

'Yes.' In these disorientating circumstances, Webb was finding it more difficult than he would have expected to think straight. Smart lawyers, he knew, could keep people out of trouble, but the only ones he knew were the practitioners in the local firms, and he would back his intelligence against any of theirs. And having the police think you were unco-operative wasn't clever.

'I'm prepared to talk to you.'

'Good.' Pardoe, who had been leaning back in his chair, leaned forward, thrusting his face towards Webb. He could smell cigarette smoke on the man's breath; instinctively he tried to push his chair back, and found it was fixed to the floor.

'You could start by telling us why Willow Lampton was blackmailing you?'

Webb's stomach lurched, but he managed to say coolly, 'Have you any evidence that she was?'

Pardoe bared nicotine-stained teeth in an unappealing smile. 'Well, now, I always get a bit self-conscious saying this, but we ask the questions.'

It was a bit like scoring debating points. He had enjoyed debating at university. 'I think a lawyer would tell me not to answer that.'

'Fine. Perhaps you could explain, then, instead, why you should have been paying off her credit card bills every month? Large bills, and getting larger.'

'Ah.' He had won the point, forced them to reveal their evidence, but much good it had done him. This was what he had been dreading all through these past terrible days when he had cursed his folly in not paying the little bitch in cash, like the whore she was.

There was no percentage in futile denial. 'I admit I made those payments,' he said, then paused, his mind racing. For three days he had tried, and failed, to think up an alternative explanation; he wasn't going to come up with one now.

'I admit also,' he said reluctantly, 'that she was blackmailing me. We had a brief affair, with her full consent – rather more than that – but afterwards, because she was technically a patient of mine she threatened to make an official complaint. If I wanted to keep my career, I had to pay up, and she produced the clever little idea that I should bankroll her credit card spending. I came to suspect that it had been a set-up, right from the first.

'However, I formally and categorically deny that I had anything whatsoever to do with her death.'

'Pretty convenient for you, though, eh Doctor?'

'Convenient, as you say.' He had read somewhere that under interrogation the temptation is always to start talking, to say too much; he clamped his mouth tight shut on the urge to justify himself.

'How were you planning to stop her, then?'

'I didn't. I suppose I hoped . . .'

'Yes?' Pardoe prompted.

'I suppose I hoped she would catch the big fish she was angling for, and wouldn't need the bills paid any more.'

'Hardly likely, though, was it – nice little earner like that? She'd got you by the short and curlies, hadn't she, Doc? If you'll pardon the expression. It's the sort of thing we coarse coppers say, but I wouldn't like to offend a professional man like yourself.'

Webb clenched his fists under the desk, fighting the primitive desire to wipe the sneer off the man's face, while realising that this was a manipulated reaction.

'You're trying to make me angry, Sergeant, aren't you? And you're succeeding, but what that won't do is make me admit to a murder I didn't commit.'

He paused. 'May I clarify the situation? You must forgive me, I'm not really *au fait* with the etiquette of crime. I understand from what the Press were told as I came in that I am merely "helping the police with their enquiries". Does this mean that if I choose not to help you any longer, I can terminate this interview and leave?'

Pardoe was surprised into a chortle; even Cordiner, the shadowy presence at the back of the room, smiled.

'Sorry about that,' Pardoe said, 'but we don't get many laughs around here. It's a nice idea, Doctor, but I'm afraid not. We can hold you without charge for up to twenty-four hours. Longer, if we have good reason.'

'I see.' Webb chewed his lip. 'Then perhaps I would be wiser not to say anything further until I have legal advice.'

Cordiner moved suddenly. Without interest, he said, 'Fine. Arrange a phone call, Pardoe, and book him into a cell meantime.' He made to leave.

Webb cracked. 'Wait! Look, I want to get this sorted out, of course I do. So do you. But can I just ask you one thing which could save a lot of time before we get even more bogged down in hypothetical questions like motive?'

Pardoe glanced at his superior, then shrugged his shoulders. 'OK, be my guest.'

'What time did she die? Do you know? Because although I was out making calls on Friday night, as you may or may not know, there were other stretches of time when I was in the company of witnesses who would be even by your no doubt exacting standards unimpeachable.'

For the first time, Webb sensed uncertainty in the glance the two policemen exchanged. Cordiner said mildly, 'It's a perfectly valid way to proceed. We would have been coming to that. Perhaps you could tell us your movements on Friday night.'

They weren't going to give him any clues about what they knew. He would have to go into it blind.

'My surgery finished around six o'clock. I was in a meeting with my four medical partners until about a quarter past seven, after which we had a working supper in the restaurant two doors along from the surgery, as is our practice after the monthly meeting. We finished at about eight and went back to the surgery together, they then went home and I stayed since I was on call.

'I had a cup of coffee with the duty receptionist, then worked in my office for perhaps half an hour until the first call came in, a bit after nine, I think, but it will be logged.'

He paused, suddenly aware of a change in the atmosphere – or was that wishful thinking? He went on.

'After that, I have to admit, my alibi becomes much less watertight. I have no means of knowing how precise my patients could be about my times of arrival and departure; I can't be very precise myself. My first visit was on the outskirts of town, then

I had a call on my mobile to go to a farm a couple of miles east of here. That was a suspected heart attack; I had the man admitted and then got back to the surgery around midnight. There were another two or three calls, I can't remember exactly, but again it will be logged in the surgery.'

He paused again, looking from one to the other, trying to read their expressions. 'I do see,' he concluded, 'that there are gaps that you could drive a bus through. I can only tell you again that I am being completely truthful when I say I had nothing to do with that girl's death.'

He found he was shaking again. Perhaps he had been a fool to be so open. Now that they knew the times when he could not account for his movements, they would be able to pin it on him to secure a conviction – he'd read about that sort of thing. On the other hand, Pardoe wasn't sneering any more. He was, indeed, conspicuously silent, and Cordiner's voice was flat as he said, 'Can I go over that again, just to get it straight in my own mind? You were at the surgery, or in the company of your colleagues, from half-past five until at least half-past eight?'

'From half-past four until quarter past nine, in fact, but who's counting?' Webb was the only one to laugh this time. Light-headed with relief, he didn't need them to tell him; he knew from the disappointment on their faces that he was in the clear. 'Is that what they've given you as time of death? As precise as that?'

Cordiner nodded. 'Stomach contents,' he said briefly. 'We know exactly when she had her last meal, and the digestive processes had barely started.'

Webb slumped back in the hard, upright chair, letting the wave of exquisite relief wash over him. 'God, I wish I'd come to you three days ago. You've no idea of the hell I've been going through, wondering if you would trace those stupid cheques.'

'Oh, we wish you had too, sir.' Pardoe's smile did not suggest that he was happy.

'Now, am I right,' Webb drawled, his confidence returning, 'that while blackmail is a crime, being blackmailed is merely a matter for considerable sympathy? Yes? And I am now free to go?'

Pardoe got up. 'Certainly, sir,' he said very correctly. There was no trace of the bullying persona now. 'This way.'

Webb paused on the threshold and turned to Cordiner. 'This – this won't go any further, will it, David? It's a dead end in your investigation, after all.'

'I'm afraid I can't give you any definite assurance on that,' Cordiner said, and Webb had the distinct impression that the bastard got pleasure out of saying it. Well, let him! He obviously wasn't having much joy in any other direction.

Chapter Fifteen

There was a leaden silence in the CID room, where Cordiner and Pascoe had gone after setting in train the formalities for Webb's release.

They were alone in the room; Cordiner went across aimlessly to glance at the notice-board with its out-of-date memos and curling safety posters, while Pardoe sat down at his desk and lit up a cigarette.

'We've still got to check out the alibi, boss,' he said in a clumsy attempt at optimism. 'He's such an arrogant sod, he could be lying on the assumption that we wouldn't check up.'

'I think the Super is going to want more for his money than a couple of soggy straws we've clutched at.' Cordiner's face was grim. 'And where the bloody hell do we go from here?'

Pascoe looked up at him with a certain sympathy. Cordiner's first major case, this was, so a lot was riding on it, like the rest of his career. He'd more respect for him than for most; it was tough that this one should be such a bitch.

'We've still got Arkwright in the frame,' he offered. 'He hasn't got an alibi, she'd kicked him where it hurts and he wouldn't have a problem getting hold of the stuff to knock her out.'

'Yes.' Cordiner sighed heavily. 'It's always possible, but you and I both know it doesn't feel right.'

'Mmm.' Pascoe was more reluctant to let the idea go. 'Could be we're letting ourselves be snowed by the fresh-faced innocence act.'

'Oh, I haven't written him out, but . . .'

'Nothing's come in from the reports, sir?'

Cordiner shook his head. 'Nothing substantial. Bits and pieces. The preliminary report on the car's in, and there's a smear of mud which wasn't the same composition as the stuff on the common, but we can't go crawling all round Wales and Shropshire looking for a match. But there isn't anything else; the driver wore gloves, apparently, and they think he may even have put polythene over the seat to protect his clothes.'

'Thinks of everything, this one. Smart.'

'Oh yes, smart. Not your run-of-the-mill stuff at all. This is someone who has worked very hard at committing the unsolvable crime, and I've got a nasty feeling it might be just that.'

'Early days yet, boss,' Pardoe said stoutly.

Cordiner's expression was sardonic. 'Oh, it's awfully sweet and supportive of you, blossom, but you know as well as I do that after seventy-two hours the chances of a successful conviction dwindle to the point where the odds in the lottery look good.

'The only other line I have a mind to follow up is Winthrop. He's a highly intelligent man, plays his cards very close to his chest. He was definitely at the hospital on Friday night, but could he have been out of his office, say, for an unaccounted-for three quarters of an hour? It's all it would take, you know, if he'd arranged to meet her secretly in some quiet place. He said they were always discreet, so she wouldn't think anything of it. Then he leaves her dead in her car in some out-of-the-way spot, drives back to the hospital, and reappears as if he's been in the canteen or across at the ward. In that rabbit warren you could be untraceable for a good long time.'

'But surely, if she was going to marry him—'

'Was she? We only have his word for it. Perhaps she turned him down. If I'd bought her a socking great rock like that and found she'd been taking me for a ride, I'd be seriously unamused. Or perhaps he didn't know about her past, then found out and didn't like it.'

Warming to his theme, Cordiner sat down on the edge of a

desk. 'You see, Joe, I keep coming back to the ceremonial way she was laid out up there on the common. Usually at a murder scene you see all the ugly things – brutality, rage, hatred. But she hadn't just been callously abandoned in her car for us to find, which surely would have been simpler. She'd been laid to rest gently, lovingly even, and I feel if we could understand why, we'd be half way to cracking it.

'Now, if he loved her so passionately that he couldn't bear the thought of her past, if it made her fatally flawed in his eyes, or else if she'd rejected him and he couldn't bear the thought of her with somebody else—'

'Couldn't live with her, couldn't live without her? I like that one, sir. It feels better than Arkwright. A lot better. Still waters run deep.'

Cordiner stood up again. 'Come and grab a sandwich in the canteen – it's after two. Then I have to go and talk to the Super, and at half-past three I've got a meeting with Jan Peters about how we're going to handle the inquest tomorrow. She thinks I'll have to speak to the cameras, grim thought, and she wants to rehearse me.'

Pascoe grinned. 'Some people have all the luck. I wouldn't mind having the lovely Jan putting me through my paces.'

'Keep your filthy lascivious thoughts to yourself, Joe, and get down to the hospital. For God's sake don't go upsetting them, and don't start unfounded rumours about a senior consultant or the Chief Constable will have your guts for garters. And unless you fancy being reduced to cats' mince, steer clear of Sister Morley. Try chatting up the receptionist, find out who was around at the time, who saw him and so on. Let tact and charm be your watchwords, Joe, tact and charm.'

Pascoe contorted his bruiser's face into a grimace. 'Can't I just hit them till they tell me what I want to know? No? Oh, it's just no fun being a copper any more.'

The operation, a delicate one, had been successful, but it was nearly three o'clock when John Winthrop, dripping with sweat, came out of theatre to disrobe and shower. He had been on his feet for four and a half hours. Though that was not unusual, the theatre sister thought when he emerged in his grey suit that he was looking even more than usually drained and exhausted. Poor man, she thought, having heard the hospital gossip, no wonder, with all he's had to cope with. He could hardly be expected to see that escaping Nurse Lampton's clutches was by all accounts the best thing that could possibly have happened to him.

'Have you a busy afternoon ahead?' she asked solicitously, and when he admitted there was a full appointment book for his afternoon clinic, read him a motherly lecture on the need to have a rest and a proper lunch first, whether he kept them waiting or not.

He smiled his quiet, attractive smile. 'You're very kind,' he said, without committing himself to follow her instructions, and set off on the ten-minute walk through the hospital to the Cardiology Department.

His secretary, who also mothered him, produced sandwiches and coffee for him when he arrived, and stood over him while he ate them; it was only after that she permitted the first of his patients to be shown in.

It was half-past six when the last one left. The nurse on duty put her head round the door. 'Your secretary said to say you'd been very late the last two days, and you should try to get home early for once.'

He smiled up at her from his desk, his sweet, weary, patient smile.

'You're all far too good to me. You get off home now; I'm sorry you've had to work so late. I've got quite a bit of paper-work I must get finished, but it should all be over and done with by eight o'clock. Good-bye, nurse.'

When the door had shut behind her, he bent forward, putting his head in his hands. He sat like that for a long time, then, with sudden resolve he sat up. He reached into the drawer of his desk and took out a half-bottle of whisky. He fetched a glass from beside the basin in the corner of the room, then opened one of the cupboards and took out a packet. He carried them over to his desk and set them down in front of him.

He broke the seal on the bottle, poured out a generous measure of whisky, took a mouthful, then pulled the computer keyboard towards him. He began to type, slowly at first, then faster and more confidently.

'The sin which has plagued me all my life is weakness. Courage is a virtue which I most tragically lack . . .'

It was raining heavily now, that steady summer rain which looks as if it is never going to stop. It was cold, too. Tessa shivered in her summer dress as she grabbed her shopping bags out of the taxi which had brought her back from Stetford, then dashed up the path to the front door, her key at the ready. She didn't pause, as she usually did, to check whether Llanfeddin had left another of its charming little surprises for her, didn't see a piece of white paper held down by a stone just to the left of the front door.

The damp chill of the house struck her, as always, even as she heaved the bags in, thankful to be out of the deluge. It was very dark too, and she hurried to switch on the big lamp in the hall.

After she had waved Matthew off that morning she had felt, pathetically, like the child who wasn't invited to the party. It was a thoroughly feeble reaction, and she was ashamed of it. It had been her great dread that she would have to spend her whole summer entertaining a teenager; how could she now even whisper a complaint when he had proved more than capable of entertaining himself? And it was ridiculous to feel, when he had only spent two nights under their roof and had been out all the previous day, that the house felt emptier without him than it had done before he came.

Housework, Tessa told herself firmly. There was plenty to do; after all, the phone could go at any moment to herald the visit of a possible buyer. She even tidied a couple of cupboards, telling herself encouragingly how much easier this would make it for packing-up when the move came. But once she had done all that, and the house was spotless and gleaming with polish, it was barely eleven o'clock and she hadn't an excuse to avoid facing up to her problem.

She couldn't bring herself to go into her studio. She had tackled every other room, but she hadn't even opened the studio door, to expose herself to those naked windows, bare to the hill outside. However much she might tell herself she was being irrational, she just couldn't do it, even quickly just to fetch her sketch block and pencils.

The day stretched ahead of her, hours of achingly empty minutes. David had warned her he would definitely be late, well after half-past nine, he had said, since he had to give a debriefing when the extra forces were stood down at nine o'clock. Matthew wouldn't be back much before six. She couldn't phone Marnie, in the present circumstances, to ask her to drop round for coffee. Agnes had clearly taken offence. Boris was dead. What could she do to escape?

She had pottered in the kitchen a little longer, had a cup of coffee, made a pudding for supper. She really needed to get some groceries in – and David had suggested a taxi . . .

If she went now, she could have a snack in a café for lunch, wander round the shops for a bit, have a cup of tea, then go to the supermarket and get what she needed for the next few days. She could spin that out for most of the afternoon, surely? Without wasting any more time, she had gone to order a taxi from Stetford. If it brought her back around six, Matthew might even be home before her.

But now, from the atmosphere in the house she could somehow tell that Matthew wasn't at home. She called 'Matthew!' up the stairs, for form's sake, but expected no reply.

She went to the answerphone. There were two messages, the first from David, just saying hello, the second from Matthew.

'Oh hi, Tessa!' his voice greeted her. 'We're having supper at the Webbs' again. OK? Oh, and they said to tell you they'd bring me back by ten. See you.'

She pressed the delete button slowly. She had no right to

mind that he wasn't going to be at home to keep her company; she was getting as bad as Agnes.

Four hours. The long evening yawned ahead of her, a threatening void. Though it was still early, the sky outside was a dark, purplish grey and the rain showed no signs of abating. Indeed, a vicious little wind had sprung up, its squally gusts sounding like someone throwing handfuls of fine gravel against the window-panes. Tessa shivered and went upstairs to find a woolly.

There were still the shopping bags to unpack, so she did that. The pizza and chips she had thought Matthew would like now looked thoroughly unappetising, and she put them in the freezer. The pudding in the fridge would keep for another day.

She ought to eat something, though she didn't feel particularly hungry. Scrambled eggs, as the ultimate in comfort food, suggested itself, but before that she would pour herself a glass of wine, take the magazine she had bought and go and find a mindless soap to watch on TV.

She drew the curtains – against the weather, she told herself – before she switched on the lamps, then lit the fire which was laid ready in the hearth. With the noise of the television and the lively crackle of the flames for company, she began to feel warmed and soothed. When she had finished the wine, she made her scrambled eggs and settled back into the reassuring comfort of the curtained room.

At half-past nine, the programme she had been watching in a desultory way finished. She channel-hopped for a few minutes, then switched it off. It wouldn't be all that long now before David or Matthew or both came home.

With the television off she could hear the sound of the storm outside, still lashing the windows in bursts of percussion. It was good to be safe inside, with a fire burning and the curtains drawn so that no one could see you from outside.

And you couldn't see them. Was it some sound from outside that made the horrid thought enter her head? She couldn't be sure, but suddenly the carapace of comfort she had constructed about herself seemed an eggshell illusion. Every outside door might be locked, but her security could be breached by one tap of a stone against a windowpane.

What if, as she sat here in pitiful self-delusion, *he* was out there, prowling about the house, unseen by her? Testing, perhaps, the windows of the studio, waiting until it was fully dark before he made his move?

It must be almost dark by now, on such a stormy night. Her chair was beside the window on the side of the house; she twitched aside the curtain covering it to look out.

He was there. Barely two feet away from her, with only two millimetres of glass between his face and hers. As the light struck them, his eyes seemed to glow luminous, and then he saw her and bared his teeth in a slow, predacious smile. He had long pointed canines, like a wolf.

She had never before looked in the face of pure, naked evil, and her scream held that primeval terror which is as ancient as evil itself.

The cleaners always arrived when the Cardiology Department was closed in the evening not long after eight o'clock. It was a popular slot, with no patients to get in your way or bossy nurses to tell you not to smoke or to make pointed remarks about what you had failed to do yesterday.

This was part of Gladys's patch. She was in charge of the team of three by virtue of having spent twenty years in grudging service to the hospital. She was a bulky woman with high colour who moved with all the vigorous bustle of a bishop walking in procession.

As was their custom when they arrived, bearing their buckets of cleaning materials and pushing a Hoover and a floor polisher, they made straight for the little scullery where there was an electric kettle for the nurses' breaks.

Arriving ahead of Gladys, one of the younger women took down the jar of Gold Blend labelled 'Personal property of Nurse Smithers' from the shelf, while the other, with cheerful disregard for the '5p in the jar per biscuit PLEASE' request, got biscuits out of a tin.

'Just a minute,' Gladys said, a little breathless after the three-minute walk over from Orthodontics. 'Better see if *he's* in again tonight.' She jerked her head towards the door opposite marked 'Mr John Winthrop'.

'Perfect nuisance, he's been, always around the place just now,' she grumbled. 'Never know when he's going to pop out and give you a turn, do you?'

The others nodded agreement with her. They always did. It was easier that way.

'I'll just stick my head in, ask him if his room wants doing. Maybe he'll take the hint.'

They waited in the doorway opposite while she waddled across importantly to knock on the door. Receiving no answer, she mouthed, 'Seems to have gone,' to her cronies, tapped again and opened the door.

'Oh my gawd!' she gasped, clutching at the door handle for support. 'Oh my gawd almighty, take a look at this!' Her florid face took on an alarmingly purple hue.

John Winthrop was collapsed forward over the desk, his arms stretched out in front of him, with a red leather ring box under one splayed hand. There was a used glass and a half-bottle of whisky, almost empty, and an emptied blister pack of pills with their cardboard box. Lying neatly on top of the papers in his out-tray was a sealed envelope addressed 'Detective Inspector Cordiner' in a neat firm hand.

Cordiner commandeered a squad car to take him, with its lights flashing and siren blaring, at speed through the streets of Stetford and out to the hospital. The traffic parted before them like a breaking bow-wave. He had sent another car to fetch Superintendent Barker, off-duty at home.

Pardoe had been instructed to have someone waiting at the main entrance to guide him to Cardiology without delay, and as a result, it was little more than twenty minutes after the 999 call that he arrived at John Winthrop's consulting room.

Outside in the corridor, a small knot of cleaners, nurses and two porters with a trolley were chattering in hushed voices. Another squad car had arrived earlier; a uniformed man appeared from a room on the right, spotted him with obvious relief and said, 'In here, sir.'

He posted the constable who had brought him from the entrance to the Department to control comings and goings, then made his way through the group which fell back as he approached.

Inside the consulting room there were three people: a nurse, standing a little apart, looking aghast and helpless, and two young men in white coats wearing 'Accident and Emergency' doctors' badges. They were in a state he could only describe as frozen confusion.

Their names were Jack and Donald, they told him, when he introduced himself, and they probably didn't look quite so like dressed-up schoolboys when they weren't in a state of shock.

'Am I glad to see you!' Donald said in heartfelt tones. 'That was quick! We've only just given up working on him.'

'We moved him,' Jack blurted out. 'You'll probably say we're not supposed to, but he was sprawled over the desk and we had to try . . .' His voice trailed away.

John Winthrop was laid out neatly on the floor, and he was very clearly dead. His eyes were almost closed, with a faint white rim showing. His shirt had been torn open and there were livid marks on his chest. There was a defibrilator lying abandoned on the floor beside him.

'We tried to get his heart going again,' Donald offered, 'and the senior registrar's on his way across. For what good that may do. But obviously—'

'Obviously,' Cordiner echoed. His eyes travelled from the body to the desk, noting the glass, the bottle, the sad evidence of the ring box. The cardboard packet which had contained the pills was lying face down. He took out a pen and flipped it over.

'Aldomet,' he read out. 'Do you know anything about this stuff?'

'Oh yes,' Jack said gloomily. 'Methyldopa is the active ingredient. It's quite a common hypertensive.'

Catching sight of Cordiner's expression he amplified hastily, 'That means it's used for lowering blood pressure. And alcohol —' he gestured to the whisky bottle and glass — 'would intensify its effects. He'd know what he was doing. He'd just get weak and dizzy and drowsy and then,' he swallowed, 'well, then, everything would just sort of slow down and stop, I suppose.'

'I see. How long would it take?'

Donald stretched out his hand thoughtlessly to pick up the packet, then flinched as Cordiner said sharply, 'Don't touch anything, if you can help it.'

'Sorry. After all that? It would be quick — ten minutes, quarter of an hour, perhaps, before he lost consciousness.'

The nurse, who had effaced herself at the back of the room, cleared her throat. 'Er — sir, did you notice the letter addressed to you?'

'To me?' Startled, Cordiner looked more closely at the fat envelope lying on top of the pile of papers in the right-hand tray. There was the direction: *Detective Inspector Cordiner.*

He was always to remember that as one of the most frustrating moments of his life. He had John Winthrop's confession — for this it must surely be — there in front of him; to know all he needed to know, he had only to pick it up, slit it open and read it.

He said stiffly, 'I can't touch it until it's all been photographed and fingerprinted,' and turned away from the tantalising object.

'Is there any word about the SOCOs?' he demanded of one of the constables who was hovering in the doorway.

'On their way.'

'Right. Well, we can be grateful they had a unit free to send. Nothing we can do now except wait.'

In fact, there was this and that to arrange. Barker arrived, agog, and he had to fill him in on the situation. Another couple of officers had now appeared too, and he set them to taking names and getting statements.

Then he phoned Pardoe to tell him to take charge in Stetford and hold a short de-briefing session, not giving anything much away, then to stand down the large-scale operation as planned.

And then there really was nothing to do but wait.

Chapter Sixteen

As Tessa screamed, her eyes locked with Gavin Guest's. Stiff with fear, she could not move, could not breathe. She would die now, her heart pounding faster and faster until it stopped.

He vanished.

She drew a breath, then another breath. He had ducked down, hadn't he, to find a stone or something. In another second the fragile barrier of glass which was all that separated them would shatter, and he would be in.

Then somehow she was out in the hall, trying to lock the solid wood door of the sitting room with fingers that bent like rubber. Somehow she turned the key just as she heard glass splintering inside.

Nine nine nine. She controlled her shaking hands, picked up the receiver, pressed the numbers before she put it to her ear. It did not connect. Grimly she tensed her treacherous limbs, slammed it down, picked it up again.

No sound. No comforting kitten-purr. Dead. He had cut the line, hadn't he?

He was just on the other side of that door. If he had an axe, she was dead. He would strike her down at the front door, or on the staircase as she tried to flee him, splitting her skull – No, don't think that.

If he didn't have an axe, there was an inch of solid pitch-pine between them. So lock the other doors now, the dining room, the kitchen, the studio. Create her safe space, here in the centre of the house.

He was wrestling with the handle of the sitting-room door. She watched mesmerised as it rattled and turned, saw the door shudder under the impact as he put his shoulder to it. But it did not yield. Then the obscenities started.

Words, she told herself, only words, but they made it hard for her to think clearly. She had to think clearly.

Escape. How long would it take her to get out of the front door? Ten seconds, she estimated, with the adrenaline coursing through her to assist flight. But he would hear the door open, and then how long would it take him to come after her?

She had no car to make a getaway. Out there in the dark windy night, with him hunting her down with superior strength and speed in a killing frenzy, what chance would she have? Even if she reached the nearest house, got to the door to hammer and shriek and plead, could she be sure, here in Llanfeddin, that the door would be opened?

Tessa could feel hysteria building, terror, panic.

Terror paralyses. Panic kills. She didn't want to die. Please God, she didn't want to die.

Breathe. Think. Keep calm. Breathe again, slowly. Think.

She could stay here, with the doors locked about her. It felt as if he had trapped her, huddled sightless while he prowled freely around. But she mustn't think like that. It wasn't a trap, it was her shark-cage. She could hold out here until David came, or the Webbs.

She looked at her watch. Twenty to ten! Was it possible that she could have lived through what seemed a lifetime of horror in less than ten minutes?

It had gone quiet again. He didn't have an axe, then. But she wasn't fool enough to imagine he had given up. He couldn't, now. She had seen him, and either he would kill her, after – she mustn't think about that – or she would escape, or she would be rescued. There was no other way.

Then came the crash of more broken glass, at the back this time, and she knew he was breaking in to the studio. He was bellowing now in rage and pain, screaming about cuts and bleeding, and about making her pay. Then the studio door shook under his onslaught, kicks and thuds and the smash of furniture being hurled against it. The sturdy pine was holding, but Tessa found herself flinching with every blow. She couldn't watch this.

She could go upstairs. The bedroom doors didn't lock, but the staircase was protected by the locked doors in the hall. She would be just as safe upstairs, and there were windows she could look out of.

What if he got a ladder? Well, if he had a ladder she wouldn't be safe in the hall either, and she would feel so much better if she could see what was happening. Less like a rabbit cowering in its burrow while a ferret coursed through the warren.

In Matthew's room, the window was a paler square in the darkness. Directly under her feet, in the studio, Guest was throwing things. Her canvases, probably. Her paints. Her brushes. The personal tools of her trade, things she would have cared about, once.

Again, the noises stopped. What was he doing now? She peered cautiously out of the window, but could not interpret the shifting shadows on this wild night. She strained her ears, but could hear only the rushing sound of wind in the trees.

From window to window she went, screening herself with the curtains as she looked out. Reaction was setting in now; she was cold and shaking and the blood was roaring in her ears, pulsing to the beat of her racing heart. She couldn't see to read her watch, couldn't tell how long might have passed.

Outside, the trees near the house, whipped by the wind, cast weird, sinister, changing shadows, bending and dipping their branches. Bending and dipping, weird shadows, weird shapes—

It felt as if her blood had turned to ice, freezing the breath painfully in her lungs. She recognised what she was seeing just below her, that thickening among the shaken leaves of the old apple tree which grew up outside Matthew's window, the apple tree with its low, hospitable branches.

The amorphous shape moved and stretched. Long, ape-like

arms reached to gain purchase overhead, swinging up through the limbs of the tree with frightening ease.

He had only to break through Matthew's window, and he had breached her stronghold.

No chance to sit it out now. So gain time. Gain the extra minutes which might be the difference between life and a horrible death. Slam Matthew's door. Slam her own bedroom door. Wedge a chair under the handle. Drag over the old pine chest to wedge the chair. Delay him for those few vital minutes while he thought she was still inside. Fling open the window.

Below was a drop in to blackness. There should be soft wet grass down there, but if she broke her leg—

She couldn't afford to think of that. She swung herself on to the window ledge. Rain buffeted her face, borne on the swirling wind.

Behind her, she heard the shocking detonation of glass. He was inside.

She lowered herself by her arms and let go.

As the police officers drifted away to the mini-buses which would return them to their various home centres, there was considerable speculation. Pardoe, acting on his instructions, had said only that there had been significant developments in the case, but would not be drawn.

'I'll get it out of him once you've all gone,' Owen Owen assured his cousin Ifor in Welsh. 'I'll phone you later, *bach*.'

'I'll be home by ten, I should think.' There was no Wrexham mini-bus; the force there was stretched at present with a particularly nasty rape and had only been able to spare Ifor Evans and one other officer. 'It would be good to know we'd got it wrapped up, after all this.'

'Oh, before you go! Mary gave me a present to give you for your Alys's birthday next week, and if I'd forgotten to give it to you I'd be in some trouble, I can tell you. I've got it in my desk, isn't it – take a minute to come and get it, will you?'

The two men, talking family news, went along to the big

general office from which Owen operated. He led his cousin across to his desk, then bent down to open a drawer at the bottom while Ifor Owen waited, his eyes travelling idly across the papers on the top.

'Good grief, Owen!' he exclaimed suddenly. 'What on earth is this?'

Owen straightened up, a beribboned parcel in his hand. 'What's what? Oh, that. Something the boss found up at Llanfeddin – nice lot they are up there. I've to send it away, see if the chaps in the white coats can get us anything off it. Nasty little picture, isn't it?'

As a chapel man, Ifor was not given to strong language, but he said, 'Bloody hell, man, that isn't a picture, that's a bloody diagram!'

Owen looked at it again. 'Was – was the rape something like that?' he asked hollowly.

'Not something like that. Just like that.'

So then the alarm bells were pressed. Ifor Owen phoned Wrexham, while Owen Owen found Pardoe and explained.

Pardoe was feeling aggrieved at being excluded from events at the hospital, particularly since it was, after all, he who had found out that there might, indeed, be gaps in John Winthrop's alibi. He felt disinclined to allow Wrexham to muscle in on their patch and get all the credit without having at least a backup car from Stetford involved.

'Tell them we'll rendezvous at Llanfeddin,' he instructed Owen Owen. 'We'll start with Gavin Guest – he's got the profile, right enough. And in any case, with the number of males in Llanfeddin who can get it up at all, we could sort it out with a house-to-house overnight.'

'Shouldn't we let the Super know?' Owen suggested nervously. 'Or the DI?'

'Got plenty on their plate at the moment,' Pardoe said with provoking discretion. 'I'll get them on the radio later.'

They were in their cars on the way to Llanfeddin by ten to ten.

★

The television drama Glynis Rees had been watching finished at nine o'clock. Sadly flat, she thought it was, but then given the events which had shaken Llanfeddin today perhaps it was only by comparison.

First, there had been the news that they had done Alun Jenkins for the break-in at the cash and carry. Then they had heard he had been released on bail and shortly afterwards his tearful mother Jane had come in on the pretext of wanting to buy a sliced white, but really to slag off police prejudice, brutality, and plain stupidity. And after she had gone, of course, there had been a particularly enjoyable session with Jane's two closest friends, discussing the ways she had failed in the upbringing of her child.

As if that hadn't been riches enough for one day, on top of it had come the truly astonishing news of Dr Webb's arrest, right there in the middle of morning surgery, for Willow Lampton's murder. One of Llanfeddin's older residents, who had been there for treatment on an ingrowing toenail, had come in breathless with an eye-witness account. And him a *doctor*! they had all chorused in pleasurable shock.

All day Glynis had hoped that in this stressful situation Mrs Webb would need at least one of the vital green bottles, but she hadn't appeared. Lying low, no doubt, and no wonder.

Now, as the news came on, Glynis settled back comfortably in her chair. You couldn't expect that the Stetford murder would head the news, but it had made a good splash in the morning papers, and a *doctor*, after all . . .

She watched with growing dissatisfaction the stories on the famine in the Sudan, the parliamentary row over the euro, the scandal of hospital waiting lists. Nothing on the national news. She had almost given up hope altogether when, towards the end of the local bulletin, the newscaster announced that a man who had been helping police with their enquiries in the Stetford murder case had been released without charge. A press statement, apparently, was promised for the following morning.

'And now the headlines again—'

Glynis clicked off the set. Well! *Well!!* And what might that mean? He'd done it, but they couldn't make it stick? He hadn't done it, and they'd got the wrong man? She snorted. That would be typical. Glynis had little respect for the official forces of law and order.

She couldn't bear to wait until tomorrow to discuss this latest development. It was a terrible night out, but she'd just fling her raincoat over her head and pop along to Hannah's. She'd seemed a bit out of sorts today in the shop, short-tempered and not taking her customary part in their successful back-biting double-act, but she'd have been watching the news, surely, and couldn't help being interested in this.

The light was on in the sitting-room window, and Glynis tapped on it as she trotted past, then went into the house, calling a greeting to her sister as she hung her dripping coat on a peg in the hall.

She couldn't hear the telly, and Hannah didn't call back, as she usually did. When Glynis opened the sitting-room door, her sister was motionless in a chair by the coal-effect electric fire, which glowed without giving out heat. Her face was ashen, and there were marks on it as if she had been crying. She had a piece of paper in her hand; as Glynis came in, she jumped convulsively and shoved it down the side of the chair.

'Oh Glynis, is that you?' she said in Welsh, getting up. 'Do you want a cup of tea?'

As an attempt at normal behaviour, it was pathetic. Her hands were shaking so that it was hard to imagine how she would manage to hold a kettle under the tap.

Glynis hesitated. She was, with good reason, wary of her touchy, sharp-tongued sister, and all too often had paid painfully for some thoughtless intrusion into what Hannah considered her private affairs. But she had never seen her sister in a state like this.

She spoke gently. 'What is it, *cariad?*'

It was not their family's practice to use endearments to one another, and it was this unexpected tenderness which broke Hannah's reserve. For the first time in her life she hurled herself into her sister's arms, sobbing and choking out her agony.

When at last Glynis had got her calm enough to be coherent, she listened to the tangled story: of Gavin's demand that she lie for him about the night of the murder, and Hannah's hopes that it was because of the break-in; of Alun's firm denials and her fears because of the episode involving Tessa Cordiner.

It took some time to sort it out, then Glynis said comfortingly, 'But look you, Hannah, you know Alun Jenkins. Half off his head with that nasty stuff most of the time, wouldn't know if his own mother was there, would he? Anyway, he's not going to tell you, go getting Gav into trouble supposing he was there. And that Tessa – stuck-up isn't it? Could go hysterical, just thinking someone common like our Gav might dare to even touch her! He's been a good boy, Gavin—'

Hannah, shuddering painfully, shook her head. She reached down the side of the chair she had been sitting on and pulled out a piece of white paper with a drawing on it which David Cordiner would have recognised.

'Found it in his room.'

Glynis was looking at her sister as she took it. When her eyes fell on it, she gave a gasp that was almost a cry.

'Oh dear heavens,' she said softly. 'It's meant to be that Tessa, isn't it?' and she put up her hand to her mouth as if she feared she might be sick.

'What am I to do, Glynis? What am I to do?'

It was at that moment that they saw, in the space above the curtains, the silent, rhythmical pulsing of a blue light as the police car pulled up outside.

It seemed to take forever, before the scene of crime people got there, and another age while they photographed and dusted the envelope, and photographed again.

In the interim, Sister Morley had arrived, pushing past the constable foolish enough to get in her way with an imperious, '*Don't* be ridiculous, young man, I'm Mr Winthrop's Sister!'

She was not in uniform; the constable, with a sympathetic nod, escorted her to Cordiner who was waiting outside the closed door of the consulting room with a murmured, 'Member of the family, sir.'

At Cordiner's look of surprise, she turned on the hapless young man. '*Nursing* sister,' she snapped. 'Is there no end to your stupidity?' Then she turned to the Inspector. 'I was just on my way off duty when I heard some nonsense about John Winthrop having taken his own life.'

The tone was brusque and dismissive, but her cheeks were flushed and her eyes suspiciously bright. Cordiner looked at her with some sympathy.

'It's too early to be certain exactly what's happened, but I'm afraid it's true that Mr Winthrop is dead.'

The colour vanished from her cheeks, and she seemed to shrink into herself.

'Oh no – not that!' she cried.

There didn't seem to be anything he could say, and barely a moment passed before she visibly pulled herself together.

'What a waste,' she said harshly. 'What a dreadful, dreadful waste. Over a little trollop like that. A great doctor and a fine man.'

Having pronounced his epitaph, she turned. Cordiner heard her say, 'His poor mother! Oh, his poor, poor mother!' as she marched out again.

Then at last they opened the door. George Barker, talking to the hospital manager who was looking more than ever like a white rabbit in his dismay, broke off in mid-sentence and followed Cordiner in.

The prints man said, 'We'll have to test properly, of course, but looking at the prints we have I would say they're all the same, and his own at that. I can't see any suspicious features.' He handed over the sheets of paper.

'I'd be surprised if there were.' Cordiner, with Barker looking over his shoulder, was at last able to read the letter he had been waiting for so impatiently.

It began without preamble.

The sin which has plagued me all my life is weakness. Courage is a virtue which I most tragically lack.

Bear with me, if you will. These are the last sad ramblings of a coward who will be dead by the time you read this.

I do not seek to excuse myself. This is my attempt to understand, on my own account, how it came to this. A final unburdening of my soul, if you like, though I am not a religious man.

As a child I was, like my dead mother, timid by nature. My father bullied me, carelessly rather than maliciously, I suspect, but the result was the same. Agnes quite simply transformed my life.

I don't know how they met. I would guess that he married her because it offered a solution to the problem of having a child to look after and a house to run.

I adored Agnes. She became my mother in all but name, my protector, my adviser, my guide. I had been a lonely child, and now I had a friend who listened to anything I wanted to say, who entered into everything that interested me, who made me feel clever and important and cherished. I was the centre of Agnes's universe, as indeed she was of mine. As, God help me, she still is. You can't choose to withdraw love.

But this – this—

I have found myself in this position, I suppose, because of the accident which sent Agnes to jail. It was not she who was driving, of course, it was I, foolishly, because I knew I had drunk more than I should.

The result would have been the disastrous end to my career. There were no witnesses; it was Agnes who suggested, indeed insisted, that she should take responsibility, and I had never grown out of the habit of allowing her to tell me what I should do. The motorcyclist was blatantly at fault, she said, and she was sure she would be below the limit.

She wasn't, quite. When I opened my mouth to confess, she dug her nails into my hand so hard that she broke the skin. 'Leave it. We're in too deep,' she hissed at me. And to my eternal shame, I left it. She almost seemed to glory in her sacrifice.

That was my greatest, but not my only debt to her. She was with us the night we found Daisy dead, there to hold me when Cathy in the wildness of her grief would not let me mourn with her. After the cremation she claimed Agnes had come over to her and said she was glad, and then Cathy kept making wild accusations, crazy, hysterical charges. I wouldn't listen to anything she said about Agnes. Cathy was barely sane in her agony, and it made no sense.

After that, Agnes was all I had. She was always there to listen, to let me talk myself into some sort of healing. The wound is there – oh yes, the wound is there, still raw and deep, but thanks to Agnes I brought my life together.

When I told her about Willow, she seemed as usual supportive of my plans. She joked about having to make sure this girl was worthy of her darling boy. I must arrange a meeting, let the two women in my life get to know each other without me getting in the way.

You are ahead of me now, of course. She invited Willow to the house for a drink after supper, and I would join them later. As you know, I was delayed and Willow, I thought, would have given me up and gone home long ago.

Her car was still outside. A good sign, I thought naïvely. They must have got on well, to talk so long.

Agnes greeted me at the door. She kissed me. Her usual self. Calm. Welcoming.

I can still remember the cheerful phrase I used. 'Should my ears be burning? You girls seem to have found lots to discuss.'

Her face changed. 'We must talk, Johnnie, before you go in,' she said, and opened the dining-room door.

I followed her in, my heart sinking. I had been afraid of this. I knew, intellectually, that Willow was for me a sort of madness, but one which I had no power to resist. I could not counter the loving arguments Agnes would produce, I could only reject them, and hurt her.

Her manner was practical, her argument logical. She knew me too well to think she could stop me, whatever she said. And if she couldn't, then she would lose me to Willow.

'You have to understand, Johnnie, that you are, quite simply, my life. I am dead without you. If she took you away, she would murder me.'

She said that twice, as if trying to make me realise what she had done. I didn't. How could I have realised, when she stood there so calmly, speaking so reasonably?

She had thought it out carefully, she said as one who claims a virtue. She had used the Rohypnol I had given her months ago to use when her back was painful in bed at night. The girl hadn't struggled.

I think it was only then I grasped what she was saying. What did I do? Gasp, scream, run from the room?

I don't remember. I remember Jake the dog, bolting out of the room, shivering. I remember the drinks tray on the big tapestry stool in front of the fireplace.

I remember Willow, in the high wing-chair by the fireplace. She looked peacefully asleep, with colour in her pale cheeks, she couldn't be dead, Agnes couldn't have—

She was not only dead, she was cool to the touch, and I could even recognise the first stages of rigor setting in. The big tapestry feather cushion Agnes had used to smother her was lying at her feet. It had big cabbage roses on it; I remember Agnes stitching it by the fireside on winter nights.

Such a hideous way to die: imprisoned in your cage of flesh, able to see and hear but unable to speak or scream or move a muscle to save yourself, watching her coming closer and closer—

Agnes told me that I would have to help her now. Her back, she explained apologetically, had prevented her from dealing with the whole thing herself, before I came home.

I think I said then I must phone the police. I remember that her eyes fixed on my face, and that they slowly filled with tears. 'Oh Johnnie,' she said, 'you know I would do anything for you, make any sacrifice. I've proved that, haven't I, over the years. I've done my best for you. Always. Now, though you can't see it yet. But even for you, I can't go back to prison a second time. It would kill me, and I would rather kill myself now. I will, if that's what you want. If I mean nothing to you any more.'

I am not going to tell you I was in shock. I was, as always, weak *and cowardly. Evil. You know by now what I did.*

The details are blurred. Pictures flicker in my mind like movements under strobe lighting. I remember the rain, mingling with the tears on my face as I staggered up that path. I remember that she was surprisingly heavy. I remember laying her where we had sat one summer afternoon when love and sunshine and laughter and hope still existed. I remember scattering flowers. 'Sweets to the sweet.'

Agnes had planned it all, the gloves and the boots and the plastic on the seats. I drove Willow's car while she drove my car behind on the way to the common – like a funeral cortège, I remember thinking – so that it was there to take us away again.

We have never mentioned it since.

I was disingenuous when we spoke, Inspector. I apologise for that. I was buying myself time, still trying to find the coward's way out. Perhaps this is it.

Perhaps I should have decided to leave no explanation. You would have believed me guilty, and closed the case. A life for a life.

In a sense, I owed her that. But I am afraid, I am very afraid that Cathy was right about my darling, darling Daisy. I believe that jealousy has driven Agnes to kill before, and that she may kill again. I believe she is sociopathic.

Put her in the hands of a good psychiatrist – Dr Sara Medlock, if I may presume to make one final professional recommendation – and I believe she may never have to go to trial. I hope she may not, because, as I said before, you cannot choose to withdraw love.

I shall print this out and address the envelope while I wash the pills down with whisky. One never quite knows what the effects will be, but from my reading I trust it will be swift, and uncomfortable rather than agonising. I am, you see, a coward to the last.

The typescript stopped as abruptly as it had begun, with no signature, but across the bottom was scrawled, in the same hand as the superscription on the envelope but markedly less neat, *I said I was not a religious man, but here in the shadows everything is clearer. May God have mercy on my miserable soul.*

Chapter Seventeen

The ground, rising to meet her. The sickening jar as she landed. The treacherous slope dropping away under her feet. Wet grass, mud against her face, the smell of the sodden earth. Rolling, gathering speed. The stones of the rockery at the bottom, rough and hard and dangerous. The cry of pain, suppressed.

Half-stunned, Tessa struggled to rise. Her ankle hurt, and her knee. Her cheekbone was numb and stinging and she could feel blood when she put her hand to it. The tears which mingled with the rain slashing at her face were tears of fear as much as pain. What if she couldn't run, couldn't walk, even . . . ?

She could walk. Limping at first, she began a cautious climb down the rockery, moving more easily as she gained the cover of the wildly-waving branches of the trees on the drive, a shadow now among the shadows. From somewhere, a waste scrap of white paper danced past her on the drive in a crazy ballet with the forces of the storm.

Above the roaring of wind and creaking branches she could hear his attack on her barricade, the crashes which sounded as if he was repeatedly charging the door. The old pine chair under the door handle wouldn't last much longer; she had a minute or two at most, certainly not enough to give her the start she would need to reach the safety of the village. She couldn't risk running, screaming, to the nearest house; they might be out, or deaf, or indifferent.

Bent low under the trees she reached the roadway, scanning with frantic hope along its length in both directions for headlights, but on this stormy night she couldn't see so much as a distant glow in the sky.

She needed cover, then; out here on the road she was naked, exposed. There were no trees here, only an ancient hedgerow on the other side, tall bushes woven thickly together. Behind that, she would be hidden, able to watch him unseen as he had watched her, gaining at least a tiny advantage in this nightmare game.

There was no gap that she could immediately see, and no time to look for one. She began trying to force her way through, praying there was no barbed wire embedded to bar her passage.

There wasn't, but the ancient hawthorns had been planted centuries before as nature's own barbed wire. Their stiff, rasping twigs and vicious thorns resisted her every movement, grabbing at clothes, tearing her skin, impeding her progress until she was sobbing with terrified frustration. The pain she hardly felt.

Trying to control her noisy, gasping breaths, she broke through with one final frenzied struggle, dropping thankfully to her knees behind the thickest bush she could find, just as the light came on in her bedroom.

Through the leaves Tessa could make out Guest's face at the window, a black shape against the light. He was yelling something, but the wind tore his words away.

He wasn't mad enough to jump out in pursuit. Seconds later, she saw him silhouetted against the oblong of the lighted doorway, then he was gone into the darkness of the trees.

She could hear his approach, though, and he was barely ten feet from her on the other side of the hedge. She turned her face away, bending it down on to her chest in case its whiteness showed, praying that no car would come now to illuminate the hedge, holding her in a brief spot of light, and then pass.

She could almost smell his frustration as he strode to and fro, venting his fury in a long, monotonous stream of obscenities. She could not know what visible traces her passage through the hedge might have left, and she could sense he was casting about him now like a hunting dog trying to pick up the lost trail of its quarry. Weak with terror she crouched, trying not to listen to his threats. Still as a hunted hare on its form, she lived an eternity of suspense.

She had gambled that he would believe she would head for the village, for lights and safety. Surely he could not risk delaying his pursuit much longer?

The wind was dropping a little now, the rain easing off. When she listened she could hear the sound of his running footsteps fading in the distance.

Time to move. She set off in the opposite direction, behind the hedge but hugging the road. If she heard a car coming she must be able to stop it, but she dare not break cover otherwise, even though on the level road surface she could make better time. He might turn back at the start of the street lamps, suspicious that she could have so far outrun him. He might turn round, might come up on her unawares.

At last, though, she could give way to the instinct for flight, yield to the primitive urge to put as much distance as possible between herself and her persecutor. It was only when she stumbled alarmingly over a tree root that she became cautious, and went on more slowly over the rough unseen ground.

Longingly she looked back to the house, hoping for the miracle of rescue. She could see by the light that the door was still standing open, but no one was there.

She bowed her head briefly, but this was no time for tears and despair. She had made her escape unaided, and now she must get herself to safety.

The Winthrops' house was a little more than half a mile down the road. That was a long way, in darkness and on difficult terrain, but there was the certainty of shelter, a telephone, security. Even if Agnes still bore Tessa a grudge for, as she seemed to see it, coming between her and Matthew, she wouldn't turn her away. With one last look over her shoulder she resolutely hurried on. The next turn in the road blocked her view.

It was about five minutes later that the pulsing blue light of

Pardoe's police car, coming fast but silently into Llanfeddin, lit up the sky behind her.

'Look, Mum, just let us listen to the end of this one tape, OK?'

Chrissie Webb gritted her teeth. Charlotte had said that twenty minutes ago, when Susannah's mother had collected her daughter. Weakly, Chrissie had acquiesced, even though she was keen to have the driving over and done with. She was pretty careful about not risking a drunken accident. So far, at least.

Her chauffeuring duties had meant she'd had to keep consumption down to one gin level all day, and she was beginning to twitch. Richard had been at home too, oddly enough, ever since lunch-time, and seemed in a curious mood, sort of elated, almost, and showing signs of wanting a serious conversation, which she'd determinedly dodged. Any serious talk with Richard seemed to end in a discussion of her personal inadequacies, and she definitely couldn't face that without a drink. Several drinks, preferably.

'No, Charlotte,' she said with the doggedness of desperation. 'Been there, done that. It's quarter past ten – high time we got Matthew home. Tessa will be wondering what's keeping you.'

'Oh, she won't mind,' Matthew offered hopefully, but Chrissie remained firm.

'We said ten o'clock, so we're late already. In any case, Charlotte, I want an early night myself. And no, before you suggest it, Matt can't walk home by himself, particularly on a night like this. I said I would take him, and I'm going to do that. So just come, please.'

Charlotte pouted. 'OK, OK, you don't have to freak out. We'll be five minutes.'

'No, you won't be five minutes. The car is leaving, now.'

Charlotte jumped up from the floor where she had been sitting, looking strikingly like her father in a temper. 'That's so mean! You're always nagging on about how I have to be polite to your friends and then you're foul to mine.'

Matthew, lounging on the sofa, got to his feet before Chrissie had time to draw breath. 'Oh, chill, Charlotte,' he drawled with effortless authority. 'There's tomorrow, right?'

Then turning to Chrissie he said with disconcerting politeness, 'Thank you very much for a lovely evening,' and went out with Charlotte, shooting her mother a 'drop dead' look, trotting meekly at his heels.

Was there, Chrissie wondered idly as she drove off, any future in setting up an agency for swapping teenagers? Susannah's mother always said Charlotte was charming . . .

'What's that?' Matthew, sitting in the front, was the first to notice the blue glow pulsing in the sky above the village ahead.

'Goodness!' Chrissie exclaimed, slowing to a crawl as they passed the end of the road leading in among the houses. 'Police cars!'

There were three of them, with men standing beside them, clearly in earnest conversation.

'That's Mrs Guest's house, isn't it?' Charlotte, intrigued, pointed to the open door where the policemen were standing.

'Hey, it'll be that murder, won't it?' Matthew leaned forward, trying to make out faces. 'Maybe Dad's there – I could get out and see—'

'Even if he is, Matthew, I can't think he would want you around just now. Why don't I take you home – Tessa probably knows what's happening, and I must admit I'm curious myself.'

She drove on, parking the car in the drive where Boris stood useless, then she and Charlotte walked up with Matthew to the house. With all that was obviously going on, she wasn't alarmed or even particularly surprised to find the lights on and the front door standing open.

'She could be at the village,' Matthew suggested. 'I could, like, just check she's not making thirty cups of tea for people in the kitchen, then maybe you could take me back and drop me off.'

'Well, I'll wait anyway,' Chrissie temporised. They certainly couldn't leave the child here alone if Tessa had gone off to help in some police emergency, and she and Charlotte drifted inside to stand a little awkwardly in the hall.

Matthew tried the door to the kitchen. 'That's funny,' he said. 'It seems to be locked. Maybe she's in the studio.'

That door was locked too, but he turned the key and went in. He froze in the doorway and Chrissie, seeing his unnatural stillness knew a sudden pang of unease.

'Matthew —?'

He turned round, his face white. 'There's — there's a terrible mess,' he stammered. 'Glass, and — and blood!'

'*Blood!*' Chrissie was at his side immediately, her hand on his shoulder, looking over his head into the room beyond.

The state of Tessa's studio was indescribable. Not only had windowpanes been smashed, but the flimsy struts between them had been knocked out as well. Canvases were smashed, furniture broken and knocked to the floor, and there was paint everywhere: metal tubes ground underfoot, burnt sienna and viridian and chrome yellow and cadmium red, bright as blood. Only the blood which had dripped on the window ledge and floor and was smeared on the window ledges wasn't a dramatic colour at all, but a sort of dirty brown . . .

Charlotte began to cry hysterically. Matthew, shrugging off Chrissie's steadying hand, was off up the stairs, shouting, 'Tessa! Tessa! *Tessa!*' at the top of his voice. Chrissie, who had started after him, heard him gasp, then run from one side of the house to the other before he leapt dangerously back down the staircase.

'My window — all smashed in,' he said breathlessly. 'And Tessa's room — there's furniture sort of piled up like a barricade and the window's wide open.'

'Could she have jumped out — trying to escape from someone —?'

Chrissie found the outside light and was halfway out of the door when Matthew pushed unceremoniously past her. They could see the sloping grass under the window quite clearly; the body that Chrissie had imagined lying broken below wasn't there, and it was Matthew who spotted the deep indentations where Tessa had landed. It was all she could do to stop him taking off into the darkness to look for her — to do something, anything.

She grabbed him and got him into the car with Charlotte, now sobbing quietly, and drove back at speed to the centre of the village.

The policemen who had been conferring seemed to be dispersing uncertainly now along the narrow street. Chrissie drew in behind one of the patrol cars, and Matthew leapt out, grabbing a tall, burly-looking man by the sleeve and pouring out his story.

'Take it calmly, son. You'll have to go a bit slower. Did you say Matt Cordiner? And – and is this Mrs Cordiner you're talking about?'

Chrissie joined them. 'I'm Mrs Webb. I was taking Matthew home and we found someone had broken in very violently. There's a lot of damage, and Tessa's not there. We think she may have jumped out of a window to escape from someone.'

'Sergeant Pardoe.' He introduced himself automatically, but his agitation was obvious. 'You mean Mrs Cordiner's out there somewhere now, with him after her?'

She didn't know who he meant, but she said, 'Probably.'

'Christ!' Pardoe turned, yelling a summons to the men who were checking gardens and the little lanes and tracks behind the houses. They began to hurry back.

Under the street lights, Matthew's face was pale but his jaw was set firmly. 'I can help. If Dad isn't here, I ought to be looking after her.'

For a fraction of a second, Pardoe looked at him. 'Oh God, your dad. Yes, of course.' Then he said, 'Look son, that's good, you've got the right ideas. But we don't need anyone else to worry about tonight. Take them back home, madam, will you? Go in, and lock the doors. Shut the shutters as well if you have them, and we'll take it from here.'

As Chrissie, feeling sick, got the shocked children back into the car, she heard him saying urgently into his radio, 'I need as many men as you can lay hands on to Llanfeddin – yes, now this minute – top emergency.'

★

When the storm blew itself out and the wind dropped, it seemed very silent, very dark and very silent, with none of the usual rustlings and stirrings of a country night.

It was chilly too. Tessa was wet through, her hair hanging in damp rats' tails and her teeth chattering with cold and shock. She was limping again as her bruised limbs stiffened, and now cuts and scratches she had been unaware of earlier began to sting and smart.

Tessa had stopped hurrying when the stitch in her side had made it unbearable, and she had been walking now for what seemed a long time. There was no sight or sound of pursuit, which at last gave her confidence to come out on to the road where she started to make better progress. The moon was appearing now from behind the clouds, and that helped too.

When she saw the lights of the Winthrops' house ahead of her, it was with a sense of unreality, as if she had expected to remain forever in this nightmare limbo. As she turned in at the drive the elegant house, with a welcoming light shining above the front door and a comfortable glow behind the curtains of the drawing room, looked so normal, so reassuring, that she had to bite her lip hard to stop herself from bursting into tears of relief.

There was no car outside; John Winthrop must be at the hospital, so Agnes would be alone. Still, they didn't need a protector when a phone call would summon any number of the Marches' finest in a matter of minutes.

Suddenly, she had no reserves of energy left. She couldn't summon up the strength to run those last few yards, batter at the door, scream for help, as she had thought she would. In any case, the calm of the place made a mockery of her fears, and she rang the highly-polished bell and waited as if she had been an afternoon caller.

She heard movement behind the frosted glass of the front door and then Agnes opened it. She looked, as usual, poised and well-groomed, in a cream linen dress, but when she saw Tessa she did not speak or smile.

Bewildered, Tessa sensed hostility in the other woman's

unyielding pose, and the urgent words died on her lips. Then she remembered.

'Oh Agnes, I'm sorry. You're angry with me about the arrangements with Matthew, aren't you? I'll explain, but please, please let me come in. There's a man —' She looked fearfully over her shoulder, as if mentioning him might conjure him up, there in the empty driveway.

After a momentary hesitation Agnes stood aside without replying, but as Tessa stepped properly into the light an exclamation was surprised from her. 'Good gracious, whatever has happened to you?'

There was a gilt Georgian mirror above a Pembroke table in the hallway, and Tessa caught sight of her own reflection — muddy face, scratches, smears of dried blood, twigs and leaves caught in the bedraggled hair and torn sodden clothes. She began to laugh, then found it difficult to stop.

'Please — the front door — please could you lock and bolt it? I'll explain then, but—'

Silently Agnes went out, closed the double wooden doors and secured them, then came in, shutting and locking the glass door too. It was only then that Tessa saw her face, pale and expressionless, without any sign of welcome or sympathy or even interest.

It was more than she could bear. She burst into tears, fountains and floods of tears and sobs and gasps in an outpouring of her pent-up emotions, but through it she still tried frantically to make her peace with the silent woman whose support she so badly needed.

'I'm sorry, I'm so sorry, Agnes. Please believe me, I'm not trying to come between you and Matthew. He's just young and thoughtless and flattered by the girls. And — and I can't bear it if you hate me, because I need help—'

Incoherently, she started to explain what had happened and at last, as if something she had said had brought about a change in Agnes, Tessa felt the other woman's arm round her shoulders.

'It's all right, my dear, it's all right. Now, this won't do. Come along, you're wet through, and there's a fire in the sitting room. You go in there and thaw out while I fetch some dry things and make you a cup of tea. I'll take care of you.'

'The police—'

'Yes, of course, but we'd better stop you getting pneumonia first.'

Tessa allowed herself to be led like a child into the lamplit comfort of the sitting room. Jake the dog leapt up from where he had been lying and rushed over to greet her, waving his tail. She laughed shakily through her tears and patted him.

Agnes installed her in the high wing-chair on the far side of the fireplace, tucked a big soft cushion at her back, then went out. Jake came to lie at her feet with a sigh of contentment, the logs in the fire crackled and in the tranquillity she began to regain her composure. She smudged the last of the tears away with the back of one grubby hand, then wiped her nose on the torn sleeve of her jersey like an urchin. She was still shivering with reaction, but the warmth was so soothing that she could feel her swollen eyelids beginning to droop. Perhaps once they had phoned the police she could beg a bath – hot water and scented soap and fluffy towels . . .

At the sound of the door opening again, Tessa sat up with a start and a cry of undefined terror.

'You've been asleep,' Agnes said. A damp face flannel, a towel and a white bathrobe were piled over one arm and she was holding a tray with two cups of tea and a brandy bottle. She set the tray down on the big tapestry stool in front of the fire. 'Here, mop yourself up with this and then I think you should take off those wet clothes and put this robe on instead. And I've phoned the police. They won't be very long.'

Still feeling fuddled from sleep, Tessa took them gratefully, rubbed the mud off her face and hands, towelled her hair, then stripped off the wet jersey and dress and wrapped herself in the cosseting embrace of velour towelling.

'Now,' Agnes went on, 'I've put some sugar in your tea. Even if you don't usually have it, it's good for shock.'

Agnes still sounded stilted, but Tessa had no inclination to refine upon it. She was dry, she was warm, she was safe, and very soon David would come and everything would be all right. She took the cup Agnes held out to her and allowed her to top it up with brandy. She sipped the brew, then sank back into the chair holding it cupped between her hands, feeling the fiery warmth spread through her.

'Thank you, that's wonderful,' she said, and Agnes at last smiled, a curious, twisted smile, but a smile all the same.

'Drink it up, my dear. There's plenty more.'

Agnes went to sit opposite with her own cup, settling back into the matching wing-chair which cast a shadow across her face.

With her tongue loosened by the cocktail of exhaustion, heat and brandy, Tessa found herself compulsively relating the history of Gavin Guest's persecution, right from her first tentative suspicions up to the horrors of tonight. She had perfect recall of what had happened but now in this quiet haven it began to feel almost as if she was recounting the screenplay of some particularly vivid and melodramatic film she had seen.

Agnes had listened to her without speaking until Tessa reached the end of her recital. It was only then that she looked properly at her hostess, saw that her face was set and grim.

'Agnes, are you all right?' She found she was starting to slur her words – brandy on top of strain and an empty stomach, presumably.

'No, not really.' Her voice was quiet, unemotional. 'Sister Morley phoned me from the hospital tonight. My son, my darling Johnnie, has taken his own life.'

'Agnes!' Tessa gasped with horror, but her own voice seemed to be coming from a long way away. 'How – how awful,' she managed.

'Yes, awful. And I will have no one now, no one.' Her voice was rising; it had a harsh, hysterical edge. 'There could have been Matthew – Matt could have taken Johnnie's place. Matt wanted to, we were friends, you knew that, didn't you, and you hated it. You're a jealous woman, Tessa Cordiner, spiteful, selfish. You didn't want him – he was just a nuisance to you – but I mustn't have him instead, oh no!

'But once you're gone, Tessa, I'll comfort him. He'll turn to me then, just the way Johnnie did. When the baby was gone, my brother – no, not my brother. That was before – Johnnie clung to me, needed me, lived only for me as no one else has ever done. But Matthew will—'

Tessa tried to form the words of protest, but somehow she couldn't get them out. She tried to get up, but there was no strength in her limbs. She realised that there had been no call to the police, that there was no prospect of rescue, and there was nothing she could do. She could only look helplessly at the woman on the other side of the fireplace, at her blank, soulless expression, at the fleck of spittle which had gathered at the corner of her mouth. Even as the shadows gathered in her own mind, Tessa realised that Agnes Winthrop was mad.

Chapter Eighteen

'Well – better go and bring her in, then, hadn't we?'

George Barker, who had read Winthrop's letter over his Inspector's shoulder, was fairly jiggling with impatience. His biggest ever case, this was, without a doubt, and it was going to be a triumph – a prompt arrest on solid evidence. A real feather in his cap. He might even take the press conference himself, despite not having been groomed by the delectable Ms Peters. Any fool could handle a press conference when you were announcing that you had got your man – or woman.

Cordiner sighed, then took the letter back into the room where they were transferring John Winthrop's body on to a trolley. He put the document back on the desk to be tagged as evidence later, and with Barker waiting impatiently behind him watched as they draped a sheet over the face. 'Poor sad beggar,' he said. 'Does his best to be a loving and loyal son to the woman who had looked after him all his life, and it comes to this. If he'd been an ungrateful bastard it wouldn't have happened.'

Barker snorted, unmoved. '"Sooner or later, you must pay for every good deed,"' he quoted. 'Let's go.'

They were wheeling the trolley out now through the hushed group of nurses and cleaners waiting round the door like the chorus of a Greek tragedy preparing to lament the hero. Cordiner, following through in his boss's wake, grimaced as a dramatic wail greeted the sight of the body. He lengthened his stride to get away from the sound.

Outside the heat of the hospital the air seemed particularly cool and fresh. The rain had stopped now, though there were still puddles on the tarmac reflecting the lights in the hospital car park.

The police car was drawn up waiting for them, its engine running. As they got in, the driver said to Barker, 'Have they contacted you, sir? There seems to be a do on up at Llanfeddin just now. They've put out a call for all possible assistance.'

'Llanfeddin?' Cordiner said sharply, as the driver went on, 'Do you want to get up there, sir?'

'It's on the way. I suppose we might as well see what's going on – she's not going to do a runner after all, is she?'

'Of course we do. And step on it.'

The two officers spoke together, and the driver, looking at them in the mirror, asked hopefully if he should make it quick.

Barker groaned. 'Depends how good a driver you are, doesn't it? Oh well, we'll risk it.'

Trying to suppress a grin of satisfaction, the man activated lights and siren and they accelerated off into the dark.

As he had demonstrated on the way out to the hospital, he was very good. Even Cordiner, tortured by terrible anxiety, couldn't have hoped to get there more quickly and smoothly.

Barker, meantime, on his mobile phone, was trying to raise someone who could give him the story, but eventually gave up in disgust. 'All the info anyone seems to have is that they've asked for backup, and Wrexham is involved somehow.'

'Wrexham?'

'Well, exactly.'

There was another police car just ahead of them, also moving fast with lights and siren as they turned off on to the valley road. As the village came into sight they could see that blue lights were flashing there and Cordiner, who had been gripping the armrest so hard that his knuckles were white, forced himself to relax. He had so much feared that the cars would be stopped outside his own house, that Tessa – well, he needn't think about that now.

They turned off and parked in the centre of the village with the other cars, two parked and one which had just arrived. There was some confusion, with people out of their houses to watch the show and a knot of uniformed officers standing together talking.

Barker marched over. 'Who's in charge here?'

He did not recognise the men, who looked at one another uncertainly. 'We're just waiting for the Super from Wrexham,' one said. 'He should be here any minute now.'

'There was a sergeant – Pardoe, I think, from the Marches force who's been taking charge meantime,' another volunteered. 'He's gone along to the house.' He gestured vaguely along the road.

Cordiner went very still. 'The house?'

'Further along. There's been a violent break-in, and we think it could be this guy we want for a rape in Wrexham. The woman's missing.'

Barker, seeing Cordiner's face, said sharply, 'David, you don't know—'

But Cordiner was back in the car and the Superintendent had to hurry to get himself in before it took off again.

As they came round the bend just before the Cordiners' house the driver had to brake sharply to avoid hitting the police cars half-blocking the road, then Cordiner was out and sprinting up the drive to the house with its door open and every light blazing before the car had stopped. Barker eased himself out more slowly. 'And for God's sake, man, go back and direct the traffic. We don't need a couple of police cars written off to add to our troubles.'

'Tessa! *Tessa!*' David yelled as he reached the hallway. 'Oh my God, what's happened?'

The doors were standing wide open on the wrecked studio and the sitting room where there was glass everywhere and chairs overturned.

'Tessa!' he shouted again, as if she might not have heard him.

Pardoe shot out of the studio looking dismayed at the sight of his frantic boss and quickly pulling to the door behind him on the scene of devastation.

Cordiner, with two threatening strides, grabbed a handful of his tunic. 'Pardoe! What's going on? Where is my wife?'

'Sir – it's not as bad as it looks. She jumped out and got away.'

'Got away? Where is she?'

'We – we don't know that yet, sir – oh, here's the Super-intendent.'

There was considerable relief in his voice when Barker appeared and taking in the situation at a glance, went to put a restraining arm round Cordiner's shoulders and pulled him gently away.

'David, take it easy. Let's get things straight and see what we can do. Pardoe, fill me in – briefly.'

Outside, sirens heralded the approach of another police car, but Cordiner did not turn his head, listening with painful attention until Pardoe had finished.

Then he said, his voice dangerously quiet, 'You're telling me that my wife is out there, possibly injured, with a frenzied rapist hunting her, while we're standing here? For God's sake, man, get out of my way!'

He shoved Barker aside and was out, pushing past more arriving officers and was down at the road before anyone could stop him.

The two men exchanged glances. 'Well, what do we do about that?' Barker said.

'There are four men out along the road already so he'll probably meet up with them anyway. But with your permission I'll go after him, sir,' Pardoe suggested. 'I'll take a torch – he won't have one.'

'Right. Good man. Report to the Wrexham boss when he arrives – it's his case, after all.'

As Pardoe hurried off, Barker briefed the two men who had come in and then gave his orders. 'Two of you – the garden and the field behind. Search every bit of cover. You – comb the field opposite. We'll get people ringing doorbells later to see if she's taken shelter somewhere, and they don't have a phone, maybe, but that's not so urgent. If she's with someone at least she's safe.

'Now watch it. The man's seriously dangerous. And report

to me direct, not to the Inspector, do you understand, if you
find – anything. You know what I mean.'

Nodding soberly, the men trouped out.

In the fire, a log collapsed with a sudden crackle in a shower of
sparks. Jake the dog, who had been sleeping on the hearthrug,
started suddenly awake, stared, then settled again.

The girl in the bathrobe did not move. She was slumped in
the corner of the wing-chair, almost as if she were drunk, her
gaze glassily fixed.

In the chair opposite, Agnes Winthrop sat almost as still, her
hooded eyes narrowed in thought. Always before she had
planned these things, meticulously and coldly, but tonight she
had acted on impulse. She didn't like that. It made her feel
vulnerable, uneasy.

She couldn't have planned it, of course. Couldn't have
known that the girl would walk in on her despair, offering a
solution . . .

She frowned. What was it, that solution? She couldn't
remember. What solution could there be to the gaping void that
was Johnnie's death, sucking her down and down in a vortex of
emptiness and agony?

No! No! She had told herself she must not think about it,
that it was past, over, with all the other things she had so effec-
tively blanked out of her mind. She prided herself on her
control, but tonight it didn't seem as effective as usual. She
needed to think clearly, but Johnnie's face kept swimming up,
getting in the way. She knuckled her eyes like a child, as if trying
to rub it out.

The girl, that was it. The creature in the chair opposite,
like that other one. Helpless as a rag doll. A living doll. Living,
as yet.

'Touch your head, Tessa,' she said suddenly. 'Go on, Tessa.
I told you. Touch your head.'

It worked with her too, just as it had last time. Suggestible,
they had described it in the newspaper article which had alerted

her to the possibilities of the tablets Johnnie had prescribed for her to take at night for her back-pain. Loss of motor skills and impairment of willpower was the way they put it in Johnnie's MIMS drugs directory when she checked it out.

'Now scratch your nose, Tessa.' Again, obediently, the girl did as she was told and Agnes laughed, a strange high-pitched sound that went on rather too long. From the hearthrug the dog looked up uneasily.

She found it difficult to stop laughing, had to take out her handkerchief to wipe away the tears of mirth. She needed to think; she had a job to do.

The drug had taken full effect. She would get no resistance from the girl now. Her eye went to the big tapestry cushion on the sofa which had proved so effective before.

Agnes looked at the girl again. Her victim: she liked that word. Was there some emotion – fear, despair – that could be read into those half-focused eyes?

'Do you feel anything, Tessa?' she asked conversationally. 'I wonder if you feel trapped, there in a body that won't respond? Like being in a cage, isn't it?

'They used to put me in a cage when I was a child, you know. Lock me in, to punish me, humiliate me.' Her voice was rising and the dog got up and came over to his mistress anxiously.

'But I punished them, Tessa. I made them suffer more – oh, a thousand times more. I've never told anyone this, but I'm like God. I stretch out my hand and they die.

'Because – I – will – it – so!'

She threw back her head and shouted the last words. The dog at her side whined and pawed at her skirt and without even glancing at him she brought down her hand and chopped hard at his sensitive nose. With a yelp of pain and fright he fled to crouch shivering in a corner.

She couldn't delay much longer. In an hour or so the effects of the drug would start to wear off. But she still hadn't planned what she would do – afterwards. Johnnie would have to help her again. No, not Johnnie. Of course not Johnnie. She knew that, of course she did.

She'd think of something. Afterwards.

Bryan Pugh, the Superintendent from the Wrexham force, was a compact, powerfully-built man with a small black moustache and the brusque manner of a man who has no time to waste on the niceties. He had been briefed by his own men along in the village, and now joined George Barker in the hall of the Cordiners' house, assessing the implications of the destruction with shrewd dark eyes. He nodded a greeting.

'George. Nasty business. No joy yet, I take it?'

Barker shook his head. 'Not so far.'

'I sent for a tracker dog. Just arriving now. The handler's a good man. Good dog too, come to that.'

'Oh, we'll get the bastard all right. It's just a question of whether we've got to him before—'

'Yes. Well, give it our best shot. That's all we can do. Sorry for your Inspector, though.'

'He's taking it hard. Well, you would, wouldn't you? But I'll hand over to you, Bryan. There's no point in me hanging about now, and we've got our own fish to fry tonight.'

Pugh nodded incuriously, and Barker went out into the confusion of lights and voices outside to look for David Cordiner.

He spotted him almost immediately, picked out in the head-lights of one of the cars, with Pardoe his minder hovering uncertainly as he talked to the handler. A huge, shaggy German Shepherd was sitting obediently at their feet.

From the tone of his voice, Cordiner was giving instruc-tions; from Pardoe's manner, Barker deduced that these were inappropriate, and he sighed. He'd have to get David away somehow, and it was a complication he could have done without.

'Yes sir,' the man was saying patiently as Barker reached

them. 'I'll just have to report to the Super up at the house, and then me and Barney'll get right on the job.'

'I'll wait here for you then,' Cordiner said. He was rigid with tension, jumped visibly when Pardoe touched his sleeve to indicate Barker's presence. When he turned, his face was ashen in the artificial light.

'I'm just going to go along with this fellow, after he's checked in—'

Barker sighed again. He was sorry for the lad, of course he was, but he wasn't helping the cause. 'No, David, you're not.'

Cordiner's jaw tightened. 'Sorry, George—'

'Bloody hell, man, it's not up for discussion!' It was not in Barker's nature to be patient indefinitely. 'I said no. You'll distract the dog, and if they found Guest I wouldn't trust you. I don't need the hassle of having my Detective Inspector up on an assault charge. Right?'

The younger man's face was still set and mutinous. 'It's my wife, George. How would you feel if it was Mona?'

'Exactly like you. That's why I'm not taking any chances. You can come with me to bring in Agnes Winthrop or I can take someone else and put you in a car with someone to see to it that you stay there. Which would mean you'd be tying up two men who could be out searching.'

Cordiner glared at him defiantly for a second, then his eyes dropped and he put up his hands to cover his face with a dry sob. 'Oh God, what am I to do?'

'You're a policeman,' Barker said flatly. 'You're going to do your job.'

Cordiner hesitated, but only briefly. Then he took a deep breath and squared his shoulders. 'You've made your point, sir. Let's get on with it.'

He walked over to the car they had come in, got in and started the engine.

Pardoe, still hovering, asked Barker, 'Do you need anyone else with you, sir?'

'No, no, I shouldn't think so. He'll hold himself together

meantime, and I can't see that lifting her is going to be a problem. I'll call in for backup if I need it.'

Pardoe watched the car disappear down the road, then walked back to meet the handler who was coming down the drive. He wanted the way ahead cleared of distractions, and Pardoe volunteered to go ahead of him towards the village and sweep people and cars out of the way. The dog, its feathered tail waving, was sniffing excitedly at the ground as if it had found its trail already.

Feeling something approaching optimism for the first time in this hideous night, Pardoe departed at a jog trot. It was barely five minutes later that he heard the volley of sharp, savage barks and the handler's voice shouting. He doubled back towards them.

The dog, snarling and straining at the lead, was pulling towards the dim outline of a coppice a few yards off the road.

'I've given you the warning,' the handler was shouting. 'Thirty seconds and I release the dog.'

'Don't give the sod the chance,' Pascoe yelled. 'Set it on to tear out his throat!'

'No, no! I'm coming, I'm coming!' There was naked terror in the voice that screamed from the darkness of the scrubby trees and then Gavin Guest, wet, filthy and bloodstained, with a long gash on his face and a gaping cut in his right arm stumbled out into the spotlight of the dog-handler's torch.

Dazzled, he put up his good hand to shield his eyes and found it grabbed into a painful arm-lock behind his back as Pardoe's voice spoke in his ear.

'Where is she, you bastard?'

His arm was jerked again. He swore, kicking out ineffectually, and the voice in his ear said, 'Oh, go on. Resist arrest and make my day.'

He stopped struggling, and as Pardoe frog-marched him back on to the road the torch beam dipped and Guest could see the handler moving away, getting his excited dog back under control.

'Where − is − she?'

Pardoe shouted it this time, but with the dog safely restrained Guest changed his tone. He wasn't afraid of policemen.

'Don't know what you're on about, pig,' he said contemptuously. 'But if you don't let go my arm I'll have you for assault.'

It was perhaps fortunate that several officers were converging on them now, and Pascoe unclenched the fist he had been on the point of smashing into Guest's face. But no one was going to deny him the vicious satisfaction of employing gratuitous brutality as he snapped on the handcuffs and shoved him into the back of a police car.

Superintendent Pugh came down from the house just as they were shutting the door. 'Got him? Good,' he said as the car swerved away with the wail of its siren echoing round the valley.

'Haven't got her though, have we, sir?'

'Helicopter at first light,' Pugh said laconically, and sick at heart Pardoe turned away.

When they arrived at Agnes Winthrop's house, David Cordiner realised that he had no conscious memory of driving there. How curious that you could do that without hitting anything!

He was starting to feel numb now, detached, as if all this were happening to someone else. He found himself making crazy bargains in his head – if I just do this, carry out my job properly, they'll have her safe when I get back – with someone or something, he didn't know who or what.

As they climbed out of the car, the sound of a police car's siren came borne on the air from down the valley and he tensed, ready to leap back into the car. Barker's steely voice stopped him.

'No, Inspector. Job to do, remember?'

They did, of course, and he tried to stifle his resentment at good old George Barker pulling rank to compel his obedience. 'Sir,' he said stiffly and marched to the front door to ring the bell.

This should be a moment of elation for him, the successful wrapping-up of his first major crime investigation. Ironic, really.

'Try again.'

At the instruction from Barker he realised that there had been no sign of movement. He held the bell for longer this time. The double front doors were closed, but there was a light in the hall and behind the curtains of the room to the left. She had to be there; the rest of the house was in darkness.

This time he rang again on his own initiative, leaving his finger on the button for a full thirty seconds. There was still no response.

'Damn! It couldn't just be simple for once, could it?' Barker said irritably. 'Better let her know it's us, I suppose, see if we can persuade her to open up. We've had enough broken windows for one night.'

It wasn't tactful. The nauseating picture of the mess he had glimpsed in Tessa's studio came into David's mind and he almost gagged as Barker, oblivious, went across to the window and knocked on it.

'Mrs Winthrop! Can you hear me? This is the police. We need to talk to you – could you let us in, please?'

He stepped back, waiting. Nothing.

'Mrs Winthrop!' The knocking was harder this time, the voice peremptory. 'We know you're in there, and I insist that you let us in. Otherwise we will force an entry. Do you understand?'

An uneasy silence followed. The two men looked at each other. It wasn't possible, was it, that she'd done the same as he had, that they were talking to a dead woman—

The sound of the bolts being drawn on the other side of the door startled them both and it was they who looked flustered when it opened, not Agnes Winthrop. Neat, self-possessed, she surveyed them calmly.

'I'm sorry not to answer you sooner,' she said, though her tone was one of reproof rather than apology. 'I had hoped whoever it was would go away. I am an elderly woman, and I don't open the door at this time of night.'

It seemed almost impossibly rude to shoulder your way in, even knowing what they knew about her. Cordiner found himself hesitating until an impatient jerk of the head from his superior ordered action.

He did not have to touch her; she stepped aside as they advanced on her, waiting courteously to shut the door behind them, retaining social control. She looked coolly from one to the other as they showed their warrant cards.

'If you have come to tell me the sad news from the hospital,' she said with perfect assurance, 'then you could have spared yourself the journey. Sister Morley was kind enough to telephone me some time ago.'

She bowed her head as if in grief, but her eyes were sharp and watchful.

'Mrs Winthrop, we are very sorry about your son's death. But the Superintendent and I have questions we must ask you. May we go in?'

Cordiner was standing beside the sitting room door and his movement took her by surprise, shattered her composure.

'No, no, not in there,' she cried shrilly. 'The dining room, here—'

Cordiner had turned the handle of the door already, opened it a little. As he did so, a dog shot out, its tail between its legs, shivering, and scuttled through an open door at the back of the hall. Something must have upset it . . .

The chill seemed to catch at his heart first, then his lungs, making it hard for him to breathe. 'I remember the dog bolting out of the room shivering' – that was what John Winthrop had written, describing the horror of his discovery. What if Tessa had sought refuge here – and the woman was, as her son suggested, mad—

He burst into the room. With a paralysing sense of déjà vu, he saw it all just as Winthrop had described it; the rose-embroidered cushion on the floor, the tray on the big tapestry stool, and in the wing-chair—

Tessa, his Tessa. As if asleep, Winthrop had said of Willow, sitting there. The scream he gave was one of animal despair.

He threw himself across the room, taking the limp body in

his arms, putting his lips, as John Winthrop must have done, to his darling's cold cheek—

It was warm. Just dead then; killed, oh God, while they delayed outside? Perhaps there was still hope, something they could do—

It was only then he felt the slow, even breathing damp against his face.

SESSION SIX

Friday 31 July

Session Six

'I didn't think I would be seeing you today.'

'Didn't you? Why?'

'Because I've told you everything.'

'Have you?'

'Everything that I want to tell you. Everything that explains—'

'Explains? Or excuses?'

'I don't need excuses! You, of all people, you who had heard it all, should know that I had every right to do what I did. You know what they did to me. Do you understand? Do you?'

'Tell me about the other baby.'

'What other baby?'

'John's daughter. Daisy.'

'I don't want to talk about it. Nasty little thing, always crying. Silly name. Johnnie wanted to name it after me, but she wasn't having it. Oh no.'

'Did Johnnie love the baby?'

'You're trying to find out if I was jealous, aren't you? If I was afraid he loved her more than me? What an impertinent suggestion – impertinent, do you hear? I've been Johnnie's world since he was ten years old. His mother. His best friend. He needs me there, in his life, forever. Forever! The baby – he hardly knew it. It's dead now.'

'How did it die?'

'I don't want to talk about it any more.'

'I can't understand if you don't tell me.'

'I don't think you do understand. I don't think you want to. I think I'm wasting my time.'

'Tell me about Willow instead, then.'

'*That cheap little tramp! She didn't care for Johnnie, you know – she only cared for what she could get out of him. You should have seen the ring he got for her – ridiculous! It was her idea, I have no doubt, not Johnnie's. Good gracious, he's never even given me anything like that!*

'*But she had trapped him, you see, trapped him like one of these poor foxes that have to gnaw their feet off to escape. Or like a lion in a cage, pushing against the bars till its nose is raw. I wasn't going to let her put Johnnie in a cage.*

'*He couldn't see it then, of course. Well, I didn't expect it – he's a man, after all – but I knew he would be grateful afterwards, that we'd be even closer.*'

'After what?'

'*You're trying to trap me too. You want to lock me up, put me in a cage for ever. You're my enemy. I thought you were my friend.*'

'I'm a doctor. I'm here to listen.'

'*I don't need a doctor. I'm not ill. Johnnie's a doctor, anyway. I want to see Johnnie.*'

'Johnnie? But Johnnie's—'

'*Don't say it!* Don't say it! *You're going to say he's dead, aren't you? You're going to say he killed himself, and I don't like you to say that, because it's not true. It's my brother who killed himself, long ago, not Johnnie, and you're trying to confuse me, upset me.*

'*And I know why. You're trying to keep him from me, keeping him away because you want him yourself, don't you? But you shan't have him—*'

'Agnes, don't. No, Agnes – Constable! Constable!

'No, I'm all right, thank you. Just a little shaken. It was all so sudden – but it was my fault. I should have been prepared.

'I'm sorry that this should have happened, Agnes. Is there anything else you want to say to me, before the constable takes you back to the ward?'

'*I can kill you, you know. I can stretch out my hand, just like God, and you will die.*

'*Because – I – will – it – so!*'

Monday 3 August

Chapter Eighteen

There was a 'For Sale' sign outside the Llanfeddin Stores, David noticed as he passed on his way in to work. The stores had been closed for two weeks now; rather than face the shame, the two sisters had vanished.

The DNA tests were unequivocal and Guest had been advised to plead guilty. At least it would mean that Tessa, and even more that other poor girl from Wrexham, would be spared the ordeal of appearing in court to recount their terror and desperation for his gratification.

Soon it would all be history, once his transfer came through back to the Met. The memory of that agonising night, of his humiliating failure to protect his wife, of his responsibility for all that she had suffered in this God-forsaken place would be just that – a memory.

He passed the carved stone at the entrance to the village with a shudder. The Laughing Man, the locals called him, apparently. One of Gavin Guest's ancestors, more than likely.

Matthew had gone soberly back to his mother in London, and Tessa had been whisked off by her parents. He got bright, unconvincing phone calls from her, telling him how absolutely fine she was, but she wasn't talking about coming back yet. He came home after work to an empty house, where there was nothing to do but relive it all: the wait by the hospital bedside until Tessa woke up, the horror of watching recollection etch her face like acid as it all came flooding back. At least she had no memory of what Agnes had tried to do – a blessed side-effect of the drug. But he could remember – and did.

Work was his only salvation, work early and late. His colleagues were clumsily sympathetic, but there was no one he could talk to. Better not to talk, in fact. Better just to live with your guilt, like barbed wire next the skin. Better not to think about the odds against the survival of your second marriage. Better just to lose yourself in the paperwork – there was no shortage of that.

When he reached his desk, a fresh pile was waiting for him. He took off his jacket, draped it on the back of his chair, sat down and reached wearily for the top envelope.

'Psychiatric report on Agnes Winthrop', the pages inside were headed.

He sat up with sudden interest. He'd been waiting for this: Dr Medlock's pronouncement. She had come to him for an unofficial briefing after the magistrates had commissioned a psychiatric report, and he obliged on the understanding that he would, equally unofficially, get a copy of it. He'd been very impressed with her: a slim, grey-haired woman of indeterminate age, very self-contained, with a wholly deceptive air of diffidence.

'Agnes Winthrop has been shown this report and has theor-etically accepted it, though I cannot be certain how meaningful that acceptance may be,' it began. That was interesting. He skimmed the rest until he reached the conclusion. 'I found convincing evidence of sociopathic disorder and also recorded elements of behaviour which might indicate some form of paranoid schizophrenia,' it said. 'In my professional opinion, this woman is not fit to plead.'

So John Winthrop had been right, then. He would have been relieved at the recommendation, but David wasn't sure whether he himself was glad or sorry. Provided the report was accepted, Agnes Winthrop would spend the rest of her life in hospital confinement and there would be no trial. That was good, surely, and it was inappropriate to feel a sense of anticlimax.

He read the report again, more carefully. It was, as he would have expected, a thoroughly professional production, meticulously observed, clearly reasoned and scrupulous in its clinical conclusions. At the end of it, he had no more understanding of the mind of Agnes Winthrop than he had had at the beginning.

On an impulse, he dialled Sara Medlock's number. 'Thank you for the report,' he said.

'Report?' Her voice was quiet, cool, amused. 'Good gracious, did a copy accidentally find its way to you?'

He smiled. 'Can I buy you a drink after work tonight?'

She hesitated, then said, 'Thank you, yes. Although I think out of town might be wise. I wouldn't like anyone to get the idea that I'm a police stooge.'

He suggested a pleasant country inn he and Tessa had discovered in one of the valleys beyond Llanfeddin, and rang off. At least it would provide occupation for another long, dismal evening.

It was a golden summer night. The inn was quiet, with only one other couple on the terrace which looked out over hills soft as folded green velvet and a little river which talked quietly to itself as it ran over its stony bed.

After David had fetched their drinks, there was a silence which he found awkward but, he suspected, she did not.

'Agnes Winthrop,' he said at last.

'Yes?'

'Why did she do what she did?'

She looked at him quizzically. 'You read the report, didn't you?'

'Yes, but – well, just for a start, how could you be sure she was mad?'

Sara Medlock winced. 'I'm sure you don't need me to tell you that isn't a helpful expression. But in answer to your question, I'm not *sure*, of course. I gather impressions, sift them and analyse them, and on that basis calculate what I consider to be a clinical probability.'

'What's that in English?'

'An educated guess,' she shot back, making him laugh. He hadn't felt like laughing, recently.

'You always have to keep in mind,' she went on, 'that an intelligent patient like Agnes Winthrop can have her own agenda, can be quite cunning enough to manipulate you to her own advantage.'

'But —?'

'But even so, she did seem to me totally incapable of empathy with the sufferings of others – which is in layman's terms more or less the definition of a psychopath, though sociopath is a more accurate term. She also had delusions about power and persecution which could indicate some kind of paranoid schizophrenia, though that's less certain.'

He considered what she had said. 'I suppose, of course, given what you outlined as having happened to her as a child, it's hardly surprising that she flipped.'

Sara shook her head. 'Not the point. A normal person could be warped by circumstances, of course, but it wasn't that way round with Agnes. If you think about her history, the circumstances arose out of seriously abnormal behaviour by her. From earliest childhood she had a distorted, obsessive attitude to her relationships – exclusive, pathologically possessive – and she had no scruples about hurting, damaging or even killing anyone who got in the way of those.

'And think of poor John's baby – oh yes, I'm sure she killed that too, cot deaths are notoriously ambiguous – or her attitude to his engagement. In her own mind, she was acting with perfect logic and total justification.

'But when he took his own life, I think it tipped her over the edge. There were only three people she had ever allowed herself to care about – her father, her brother and her stepson – and two of those had escaped from the relationship by committing suicide. The ultimate, devastating rejection. So at that point the social control she had always managed to maintain began to fragment, and – well, I needn't tell you the rest.

'How is your wife, by the way?'

David's fingers clenched round the handle of his beer mug. 'Oh, I'm sure she'll be fine,' he said stiffly.

Sara didn't say anything, which was disconcerting. To fill the silence, he floundered on, 'I'm hoping to be transferred back to London shortly, and she's with her parents meantime, being pampered. It'll take time, of course.'

'Of course.'

'It's not easy.'

'Not easy for you either.'

He didn't want to talk about it. He would prefer not even to think about it, supposing that were an option.

She wasn't forcing him to talk. She was just sitting in silence, sipping her drink and enjoying the tranquil scene. Not looking at him. Not challenging him—

'She's – she's damaged,' he burst out. 'Damaged, that's the word.'

'In what way?'

'Oh God!' He put his head in his hands. 'When I first saw her,' he said at last, 'the very first day I saw her, I couldn't believe she was real. I'd never met anyone like her. She was – a golden girl. I know that sounds corny, but she had a sort of bloom about her, a sort of shining conviction that life was good and every day was a new celebration. Tessa thought the sun always shone.

'Now, thanks to me, she's lost that. She's had to learn that there are storms and earthquakes and lightning strikes, and she can't go back to what she was before. Ever.'

'But then, the sun doesn't always shine, does it?' Her question sounded almost tentative.

'Of course not. But I did that to her. I brought her here. I should have been able to protect her – I'm a police officer, for God's sake.'

'Tessa isn't a child, though, is she?'

'Not now.'

'She was before?'

He shifted in his seat. 'Well yes, perhaps. In a way. She's had a sheltered life, I suppose you could say, up till now—'

'Would she choose to be a sheltered adult?'

He glared at her, ready to take offence. Then suddenly, he remembered the painting Tessa had done, the one that even he could see was in a different league from any she had done before. The one that showed she could be a serious artist, not just a competent one. It was possible that Tessa might consider that was worth the sacrifice.

'She's an artist,' he said thoughtfully.

'Would she want to do a child's drawing all her life?'

'No. No, she wouldn't.' For a moment a ray of hope shone through his darkness, before with practised skill he extinguished it. 'But it doesn't mean she'll be able to forgive me for what happened.'

'Has she said she can't?'

'No. But there's little enough reason why she should. I dropped her in it. Even leaving aside all that went wrong, I should have known this wasn't the right place for her. There are some very nasty people in Llanfeddin, but it was almost worse in Stetford. It would have stifled her, slowly but just as surely as if Agnes Winthrop had managed to put a cushion over her face. Death by a thousand coffee mornings.'

'And if I've screwed up this marriage, like I did the first one –'

'You screwed up your marriage? Or you and your first wife both did?'

'Well, both, I suppose. But to coin a phrase, to lose one wife might be considered a misfortune, but to lose two looks like carelessness.' He laughed bitterly.

'Have you lost Tessa?'

The gentle, persistent questioning irritated him. 'Oh, probably. Possibly. Not yet. Oh, how do I know? I only know I couldn't blame her if she told me she'd had enough. It's been my fault, the whole damn business.'

To his astonished resentment, she was smiling. 'Ah, I see. It's a guilt trip.'

'*What!*'

'You're high on guilt, that's your problem. You're getting a sort of perverse gratification from it. Look at it this way – it's actually a form of conceit.'

He gaped at her, too outraged to speak.

'Listen to me,' she said in that soft, incisive voice, 'unless you actually dragged Tessa here by her hair and paid Gavin Guest to attack her and got in the Rohypnol for Agnes Winthrop, it's not your fault. It all just happened. Things do.

'You said Tessa's an artist. That's good. Painting's excellent therapy. She's young, she's had a happy life. That's money in the bank, psychologically speaking. Respect her – she's an intelligent adult, not a child.

'You have no control over the actions of other people. No control, so no responsibility. Tell yourself that three times a day – doctor's orders. Otherwise you'll start to think you're God. Which is Agnes Winthrop's problem too.'

It took him a minute or two to digest the point she was making, rather longer to accept it as valid. Then he said wrily, 'Next stop paranoid schizophrenia?'

'Not quite, I trust.'

This time he was comfortable with the silence. As they sat on the quiet terrace, with night coming on and the seeping gold of the dying sun touching the hills with splendour, he caught the brilliant blue flash of the kingfisher, bright as a promise, skimming past them up the river.